GROW SCHOOL

An Adventure in Marijuana Growing and Weed Dealing

John Sharnetsky

Note to the reader:
The information in this story is important to me. If you liked this
book, please share it on all of your social networks.
Send them to this website:
www.growschoolbook.com
There are free downloadable chapters there.

ISBN: 9780998956503

DEDICATION

Tara Lynn Gillespie a.k.a. "Whitey"
For the folks in Brimley. Yes, that includes you, Sue
My hometown and my favorite family that lives there
Spartan Nation
Everyone from the Island of Misfit Toys
And last, but not least, the 'Two Dudes'

ACKNOWLEDGMENTS

Special thanks to:

Brandy Holton and Nicole Wildman

Ken and Carol Sharp

CONTENTS

PROLOGUE: PROBIE –
THINGS YOU OUGHT TO KNOW

Everyone was talking about it—the new hybrid strain of marijuana that had hit Capital City, Michigan, which was about an hour from Detroit. The city became the test market for Probie, (pronounced Pro-bee) and when that single word was shared across social networks, the local fans of this particular strain of weed knew instantly that a fresh batch had been grown, harvested, and cured, and was ready to be sold. Dealers were quickly summoned, and with the scorching sales rate, Probie practically disappeared overnight, turning into a big pile of cash. The high induced by this type of cannabis was considered uniquely the finest by any standards.

Probie was named in tribute to its inventor's childhood hero, who was a professional hockey brawler from Detroit. The inside joke was that this strain of marijuana packed a serious punch, but in truth it was aptly named. Even though grit was necessary as a hockey enforcer, it was the ability to maintain balance under extreme conditions that lead certain knockout artists to legendary status. Losing your balance during those fights on the ice usually resulted in a broken nose or a grill knocked in.

To the inventor, Probie the hockey hero was a master of balance under extreme conditions and the inspiration behind the new, modified recreational drug. The term *balance of extremes* was the foundation for his genetic design in this new breed of cannabis.

Marijuana connoisseurs would tell you that there's a world of difference between the two primary species, indica and sativa. The forgotten stepchild of the marijuana world, cannabis ruderalis, was rarely ever discussed. To the growers, higher values were predominately placed on indica and sativa, because they resulted in a predictable product with distinctive benefits that customers craved. Each species also came with a unique set of negative side effects.

Cannabis indica had a reputation for delivering a relaxing body high. Many indica fans found this product to be a great help as they decompressed after a hard, stressful day at work. One potential negative effect of indica was "couch lock." If too much was consumed, or if the chemical composition of this marijuana species was too potent, the user could fall into an abnormally relaxed state and would have no desire to leave the sofa. Induced by comfort, this form of paralysis could also lead to extreme laziness, a constant state of lethargy, and a reduction of one's ambition. This was one extreme the Probie creator took into consideration.

On the other hand, you have the cannabis sativa consumers, who enjoy what's referred to as a head high—a condition where sensory perceptions heighten, including stimulated thought processes with creativity and imagination. This feeling was ideal for those looking to dance and party at nightclubs, where enhanced gratification from the music, lights, and social scene was abound. The downside to sativa was that, if too strong, the consumer may go through a kind of psychosis, including memory loss, feelings of insecurity, or paranoia. Like the effects of indica strains, this extreme was contemplated by the Probie innovator during his planning phase.

Considering both of these extremes, the inventor asked himself how to acquire the desired positive qualities of both indica and sativa while avoiding the negative aspects. His solution was to replace natural selection with artificial selection: crossbreeding, cloning, and genetic engineering. Then, he had an epiphany. Probie's designer knew the majority of the current marijuana growing community was shortsighted and off balance with their approach.

All marijuana strains contain approximately 483 chemical compounds, including at least 113 cannabinoids, which are the active agents that react with the neurotransmitters in the human brain and body. Many people who enjoy cannabis recreationally operate under the misconception that it's all about one cannabinoid, delta-9-tetrahydrocannabinol, more commonly known as THC. This is the primary psychoactive component that creates the pot smoker's high. As time went on, the marijuana community demanded higher and higher levels of THC, and growers were more than happy to deliver—at a premium dollar, of course. This was truly an American concept—excess is best. If a little of something was good, than a lot was always better.

Probie's creator, however, knew that this was a fallacy. To him, the manipulation of the chemical composition threw off the balance of the plant and skewed the desired effect for users. Elevated THC counts came at the expense of unnaturally low amounts of other cannabinoids—particularly cannabidiol, otherwise known as CBD. This chemical was not psychoactive, so a high would not be produced during consumption, but it served to counter balance THC by warding off negative side effects. In a sense, CBD was the yin to THC's yang inside the cannabis plant.

When typical marijuana growers engineered their highest THC level plants, these plants had a lower CBD concentration. Although left artificially unbalanced, the plant induced a stronger high, which meant it was exceptionally valuable on the street. The high that came from these orchestrated plants was radical; a stronger sense of euphoria was partnered with intense negative symptoms, like overwhelming 'couch lock' or an even deeper sense of paranoia.

Probie was created differently. The plant's genetic designer manipulated the THC concentration, but there was something unique about the crop. In the past, THC and CBD were offsetting elements of their ratio. One was raised by lowering the other. What the Probie strain did was something new. THC and CBD levels were increased simultaneously, to extremely high levels. Probie consumers found that they enjoyed the benefits of heightened relaxation and enhanced sensory perception without many negative side effects. There was no lazy 'couch lock', paranoia, or memory loss, and in a sense, Probie reached its objective of becoming a *balance of extremes*, the perfect high.

1

RONNIE HARDING AND HIS FAMILY

The State of Michigan rarely comes to mind as the finest place to grow marijuana. People usually consider the Pacific Northwest, California, and the Rocky Mountain states, which are more naturally conducive for the plant due their natural climate and higher elevations. Interestingly enough, Midwestern public universities house some of the world's most elite agricultural colleges. Inside those institutions are several brilliant minds conducting research in the field of plant biology.

Through their research process those academic programs have bred the highest caliber of plant geneticists in the world. Those scientists would create magnificent innovations in the food and agriculture sectors, such as the Honeycrisp Apple from the University of Minnesota, a drought resistant strain of corn from Iowa State University, and the highest yielding barley from the University of Wisconsin. Another elite agricultural college on that list was Michigan Agricultural and Military University— otherwise known as Michigan A&M— located in a suburban town called East Meridian, just outside of Capital City, Michigan.

On a late spring day, the flowers were still in bloom and a fresh floral fragrance surrounded those on the beautiful sprawling and well-manicured campus of Michigan A&M University, as families from all over the United States gathered on the banks of the Red Cypress

River for the spring semester graduation ceremony. Graduates sat proudly on the outdoor stage dressed in their traditional green caps and gowns with yellow tassels.

Ronnie Lee Harding, inventor of Probie, sat nonchalantly with other graduating students. He was set to receive his Master's Degree in Plant Biology from the Plant Breeding, Genetics, and Biotechnology program. The 26-year-old was graduating with high honors after taking botany and plant genetics—a subject that he was naturally drawn to in life.

This graduate's fascination with genetics stemmed from being born into a family where the men were large in stature, at least six feet tall, but he stood at only five feet nine and a half inches. His father and brother could have been described as rugged or tough looking; where Ronnie's facial appearance could have been characterized as boyishly cute, maybe handsome, depending on the observer. He was different from the other men in his family. Many of his physical traits were inherited from the men on his mother's side, which made him a target for his older brother's abuse. The mental and physical torment never broke him and instead strengthened his resolve with overcompensation. Ronnie would never back down from any physical confrontation or intellectual debate. That type of tenacity led him to conquering lessons in the classroom and laboratory. His brother would never get the best of him, and he would be damned to let these college books beat him either.

As the graduate sat on the stage, he appeared uninterested in the ceremony— this was a facade. Not only was the recipient proud of the academic honors he had earned, he was excited for the research he had been recruited to work on while at the university. He was researching ground breaking possibilities that would end up helping thousands of people. His coffee brown eyes had witnessed the outstanding positive results of the research.

Sitting on the stage, Ronnie's brown hair hung below his shiny green graduation cap. It was mostly straight and stopped at the middle of his neck, except for the strands that curled around his ears. He looked down at his white hands tapping on his knee. The speaker at the podium, the current U.S. Secretary of Interior, James McPartlin, was boring his audience to tears with a lengthy speech about his vision for the United States. McPartlin went on to talk about the important role that these graduates were going to play in his view of the country's imminent future, but the audience was slowly growing weary.

Some spectators, watching the government official's sermon, were members of the Harding family, there to watch Ronnie receive his diploma. Ken Harding Sr., Ronnie's father, had spent 38 of his 57 years working for a machine tool company that serviced the Detroit automotive industry. Ken—a tool and die expert—never complained about waking up early every morning, walking in to his machine shop, and breathing in that industrial air. The thick and burly man believed in an American concept—that parents have to endure tough jobs so their children can enjoy a better life. Money was invested in his children's education with the promise that they would never have to experience the hard factory life.

Even though this was a proud day for the graying, nearly bald father, he was losing patience with the long, drawn-out speech. Continuously fidgeting, Ken Senior pulled on the blue tie hanging from his white dress shirt collar as he leaned over to his wife, Sue Harding, and whispered, "How long is this dumb ass going to keep speaking for?"

Ronnie's mother was a thin, 55-year-old brown haired woman, who was wearing a yellow and white floral patterned sundress. As the matriarch, Sue was the glue that held her rambunctious family together. Enjoying this proud moment, her eyes darted left towards her complaining husband. Her silent glare quieted the man and she turned back to the speech.

Ken Sr., unfazed by his wife's reaction, leaned forward to look past his wife to check on his seven year old granddaughter, Kimber. The blonde girl was adorable in her pink dress as she sat on her father's lap. Ken Harding Jr., the 31-year-old eldest son of the Harding family was the spitting image of Ken Sr., down to his receding hairline. However, their distinctly different styles set them apart. Ken Sr. was an industrial blue-collar man who looked awkward in a dress suit while, Ken Jr. asserted his distinguished appearance, because he always wore the finest clothes to formal affairs—a habit acquired from a successful career as an attorney.

The grandfather looked over and his heart went out to his granddaughter. Everyone in the family knew that enduring an ongoing, bland, drawn out speech was a lot to ask from a seven year old, but she did her best as she played with her father's red silk Charvet tie. Seeing this, Ken Senior's frustrations grew even more and he whispered to Mrs. Harding, "This guy has been talking for over 45 minutes and he's not slowing down. Even the professors and students on the stage are falling asleep. He needs to get a goddamn clue."

An older man, sitting in front of the Hardings, heard the whispered complaint and turned to give Ken Sr. an approving nod. Senior, in a non-evident manner, lifted his finger to point at the man and returned the gesture of solidarity. "See," he murmured.

As if a switch had flipped, Sue's pleasant expression morphed into a stone cold face, and with a piercing stare, she said, "Don't you dare ruin this for me." Her words were calm but sharp.

Over 34 years of marriage had taught Ken Sr. that he had just crossed the line. The rest of the ceremony would be tolerated on his best behavior or he would suffer his wife's wrath when they were alone. With widened eyes, he returned an approving nod. Her husband understood her clearly. Sue's face snapped back to its original, jovial expression, and she resumed her enjoyment of the formal proceedings. Mr. Harding didn't have much longer to wait. Secretary McPartlin's speech concluded within five minutes to an enthusiastic applause from the audience, giving thanks that it was finally over.

The President of Michigan A&M University, Dr. Desiree' Quinney, took over the proceeding at the podium. After thanking the speakers, she declared that the students seated on the stage had now officially graduated, cueing more applause from the audience.

The University President continued the traditional ceremony by reading off graduates' names while handing out diplomas, followed by congratulatory handshakes. When the President read the name Ronnie Lee Harding, the Harding family members lost control of any semblance of proper manners or etiquette as they yelled and hollered in support of their new graduate. The family beamed with pride.

As the ceremony concluded and all the graduates reunited with their attending family members, there were hugs, handshakes, and photo taking abound. The Harding family was no different and they made sure to commemorate their mother's proud moment by taking numerous family photos at every scenic spot on campus. A drawn out process, but everyone knew the matriarch had to be satisfied—lest there be complaining in the future.

When Sue Harding felt satisfied with the photos they had taken, she suggested that the family make their way to their SUV and head out for a celebratory dinner. The family, as a whole, continued their walk along the Red Cypress River. The well-trimmed hedges and freshly cut lawns were complemented by the numerous colorful flowers planted by the sidewalk that ran along the riverbank. Little Kimber held on to Uncle Ronnie's hand as the family made their way to the parking lot.

Ronnie's older brother, Ken Jr., who was looking around the beautiful campus during their stroll, couldn't resist taking a jab at the new graduate. "I can't believe you received an agricultural degree from this cow college." It was the first shot across the bow, in hope of antagonizing a fight.

The two brothers attended separate schools that were bitter rivals in all things. Ronnie, of course, took the bait. "You better shut your dirty whore mouth, because I value my degree and my work a whole lot more than I respect your law degree from Ann Arbor University. I know farmers are more valuable than lawyers."

The smugness was obvious as Ken Jr. retorted, "Oh, and that's why we make so much more money than farmers do."

The graduate enjoyed lively debates with his brother. "Just because this country has misplaced priorities on how it values lawyers and farmers, doesn't make you right on this issue."

Ken Jr. scuffed his foot on the gravel. "No, that's what it precisely means. Lawyers make more money, because we're worth more. Without the law, you have no civilization."

Ronnie could feel his blood pressure rising. "Yeah, but without food you have no life. There are over 7 billion people on this planet who are sustained on a daily basis by the collective work that farmers do on their land. Your law degree doesn't mean anything when you're starving."

The sibling rivalry between the two brothers was an ongoing affair, which had led to numerous childhood fistfights and adult kitchen table debates on all kinds of issues. This conversation was just another example. This disagreement led to unfiltered profanity from both brothers until they reached their father's Ford Expedition—in the nearly empty parking lot—and Ken Sr. took it upon himself to end the squabble. "Okay, that's enough! You two are giving me a headache."

The two sons obeyed their father as they stared at each other, each dismissing the other's point of view and silently declaring himself the winner. As the family stood together at the SUV tailgate section, Ken Sr. asked his youngest son, "On that note, have you made a decision about accepting any of those job offers?"

Still holding on little Kimber's hand, Ronnie looked at his father, "Yeah, I've made a decision. I going to turn down those job offers and stay in school. I was accepted into the doctorate program here. I'm also been asked to stay on Professor Rittenburg's research team. He has enough funding to take care of my tuition and can pay me a $1,600 monthly stipend."

The father's face contorted. "$1,600 a month. That's less than $20,000 a year. When we invested in your education, we had a plan that you would get a good paying job and go on to have a growing family."

Ronnie shrugged; his father's reaction was predictable. His brother rolled his eyes, head shaking.

Air blew past Ken Senior's graying burly mustache as he attempted to keep his anger in check. "Some of those job offers were great opportunities. You had one with that St. Louis Company that was nearly $80,000 in starting salary. What the hell's wrong with that?"

"They're fine offers, but I don't want to spend my days developing genetically modified corn and soy. Right now I have another option and even though it's a delayed gratification, I think I have a better opportunity by staying in school. It won't cost you a single penny. I'll cover it on my own." Ronnie's words were steady.

Again Ronnie's father struggled to steady his blood pressure as he clutched the car keys in his hand. "Yeah, but you're not going to get ahead in the job market by doing that. I just think you're avoiding responsibilities, and trying to stay in school for the rest of your life. You just don't want to get a real job."

The graduate shook his head. "That's not true. I just have window of opportunity to invest in myself, here, and earn this doctorate degree. Once I complete this, the world will open up with other prospects, including teaching at the university level, jobs in the corporate world or maybe a position with the government. Who knows? You will never have to worry about me being able to provide for myself. Money will never be a problem." Ronnie was steadfast with confidence and brought his free hand up to point as his own face. "Look at me, Dad. Look at my sincerity. Every day, since we were kids, as you walked out the door to go to work in that same machine shop, you preached to us about how important it was for us to follow our passions. I want you to know that this is my passion." He brought the hand down and stared directly at his father with validity.

Ronnie's mother and brother were just spectators during this mini-standoff. They watched as the two stared at each other, neither one backing down. Narrowed to slits, the father's eyes remain focused while his lips compressed and stiffened.

At that moment, little Kimber tugged on Ronnie's hand. He looked down at his young niece as the seven-year-old looked up with endearing green eyes and asked, "Uncle Ronnie, can I say a bad word?" Her facial expression was sincere.

Without thinking too much he replied, "Sure."

The little girl faced all the adults standing at the tailgate of the SUV and immediately said in a confident tone, "Fuck!" Her voice was clear and manner business-like as she remained still with no giggling or apprehension.

Surprisingly, none of the adults reacted overzealously. They were a little stunned about the quick turn of events and their eyes widened as each adult looked at one another for verification of their disbelief. The young girl stood stoically.

Silence was broken as Kimber's father, Ken Jr., tilted his head at his younger brother. "I oughta knock your goddamn teeth in!" His eyes were piercing and words were restraining anger.

A crooked grin broke out on Ronnie's face, stemmed from embarrassment, as he muttered, "I thought she was going to say poop or something like that." He lifted a hand in a calming gesture. Ken Jr. seemed calm but was holding back anger as he offered a simple nod.

Ronnie took his cue and knelt down to in front of his niece, so they were looking at each other eye level as he asked, "Hey, how'd that make you feel?"

"Pretty good." Her smile was glowing.

Ronnie could feel the heat from his family's stares on the back on his neck as he continued the conversation with the youngster, "It is pretty liberating saying things like that, isn't it?"

The young girl's smile restricted to a tight lipped grin as she nodded in agreement.

Her uncle murmured, "You know you got me in a lot of trouble here."

Kimber bit down on her lip, maintaining a grin as she again nodded.

"Let me tell ya," Ronnie explained in a clear friendly tone, "you're free to think and say anything you want in your own mind, and that's the beauty of it, but you have to use really good judgment when the words come from your mouth like that, especially in public. You got that?"

Still calm, Kimber said, "Yeah. I'm sorry about that."

"I feel ya, but do you promise?" He asked.

The young niece gave a reassuring nod.

Ronnie offered a comforting smile as he requested, "Can I get a hug to seal the deal?"

Her grin reverted back into a smile as Kimber leaned forward and hugged her uncle, who squeezed her back. *She's definitely a Harding,* Ronnie thought.

The proud uncle stood up and faced his family, while his niece grabbed his hand.

Kimber's father, Ken Jr., looked at Ronnie and declared in a strong tone, "If Kristy were here, I don't think I could hold her back from killing you."

Ronnie offered a devilish grin in return.

At that moment, the mother, Sue Harding took control with a demanding voice, "We're reaping what we sow here. We swear and fight way too much in front of this kid and this is the result. We're going start changing our behavior, as of right now. None of you will ruin this proud moment for me. I swear to God, I will beat each and everyone one of you!" She gave her family a steely glance to emphasize that she meant it.

Each member returned an approving nod and offered his or her own unique, "Yes Ma'am."

Satisfied with their responses, the mother's disposition shifted with a pleasant smile. "Fine, let's go to Casa Nova's and have a good time like we always do. Remember this is a proud moment for us. If there is one thing that we know how to do as a family, it's celebrating. So, are you ready?"

The Harding family members all nodded at each other with smiles. They walked over, opened the doors to the SUV, and climbed in. As Ronnie was about to scoot in the backseat with his niece and brother, he thought, *God, I love my family.*

2

THE NEW BIG FOUR

"Captain, I need a little more time to get myself in the proper position," said a voice through the police radio. Sitting in the covert police tactical van, Captain Robert Williams held his wire microphone in front of his lips. "Okay Rico, just let us know when you're set, then its go-time. Over."

The voice over the radio replied with a quick, "Roger that, Captain."

Reviewing tactical and surveillance reports in the back of the van, Captain Robert Williams contemplated his life. Some people know what they want to be from the get-go. Since childhood, the only thing Robert Williams had wanted to be was a federal agent. As a youngster, he had viewed himself as the hero-type.

Back in the day, he was consumed with daydreams of carrying a gun and chasing criminals with the financial resources and power to do so without jurisdictional laws getting in his way. The desire was ingrained into his soul. It became his career objective, growing up in Baltimore, throughout his teens, and all the way through college, until he earned a degree with high honors in forensic science from George Washington University. During his formative years, his daily routine consisted of his studies and an intense workout regimen. The fair skinned, blue-eyed man completed a rigorous cardio workout every morning and pumped iron every evening. Looking at him, it showed. His face and body looked like they were carved from hardwood.

Robert joined the U.S. Army Military Police Corp immediately after college graduation, and received considerable training in site tactics, weapon usage, and investigative procedures at Fort Leonard Wood, Missouri. In his mind, this was the final requirement to qualify for his dream job as a Federal Agent. After his honorable discharge from the army four years later, he applied to work with every Federal Agency that was hiring at the time, including the FBI, DEA, ATF, and the U.S. Marshalls Office. Unbeknownst to Robert, a series of personal characteristics flagged him during the interview and psychological profiling process.

It was never revealed to Robert that the Federal Government's thorough screening method discovered that he had an extreme Narcissistic Personality Disorder with strong sociopathic tendencies. The reports suggested he was strong candidate to abuse his authority. There were other negative characteristics that popped up during this review process. Each agency declined to offer him a job, because despite his overachieving resume, he was considered to be too much of a liability. As he received each rejection letter one after another, Robert could only react with bewilderment. *How could this be?* He thought. *I did everything right. I followed the rules.*

As he was rejected by each job opportunity everything good in him faded away and was replaced with feelings of bitterness, hatred, and a desire for vengeance so strong he doubted it could ever be satisfied. Someone was going to pay for destroying his dreams and he couldn't wait to find out whom it would be. Unfortunately, each negative quality listed in the pages of his Government Personality Profile turned out to be true. One question remained; who would give this man the chance to do what he believed was his purpose in life?

Robert's opportunity arrived when Maurice Chamberlain, a long-time friend of Robert Williams's father, was elected Mayor of Capital City, Michigan. Maurice was known by the cheesy nickname of "Big Moe". Some enemies of the newly elected Mayor were within the

Capital City Police Department. Current leaders within the P.D., including the Chief and the Union leaders, despised the way that the Mayor had been elected – he had run an anti-government employee campaign. Once elected, Mayor Chamberlain had to reseed the Police Department with a new breed of police officer that was completely loyal to him, and that's when he opened the door for Robert Williams.

Robert was hired to lead a special unit in the Capital City Police Department called the Mayor's Anti-Crime Task Force, unofficially known as The Big Four. This new team was modeled after a similar unit from the Detroit Police Department that had existed during the 1960s and 70s, whose sole purpose had been shutting down crime by any means necessary. The major difference between this modern tactical squad and Detroit's version from the past was the application of Asset Forfeiture Laws; the alleged ill-gotten criminal money was confiscated by the city and used as an aid to prevent crime. This was the sales pitch fed to the public, but the truth was that the Mayor was making a play for the all the illegal street money within his city's borders. Big Moe became the hunter, and the Big Four were his hounds.

The Big Four was a diverse team. Williams recruited three additional tactical officers, solely based on their skin color and ethnic insight. Jason Ridgeway, an African American, was the first to join the team. Rico Galaviz, the next recruit, was of Mexican American decent. Last to join was Michael Finch, who would describe himself as McKraut—a watered down version of someone of Irish and German heritage.

When this unit rolled up strong on a suspect, that day was likely to be the worst day of that person's life. Today, the Big Four was after a man named Gerald Duffy, who made his living as a handyman but supplemented his income selling pot in the REO Town section of the city. Gerald was a 48-year old red head, known as "Smashy" on the streets. Years ago, a car accident had left the bridge of his nose pushed in towards his face. He was a small time dealer, which usually allowed him to evade the police radar, but, by chance, he had secured a large amount of Probie. Smashy was now the sole Probie supplier for all of REO Town, which generated quick money for the handyman. Even at a premium price, high demand led to fast and steady sales.

Unbeknownst to Gerald Duffy, his good fortune had ended two and half weeks ago, when a client by the name of Jamie Castle had been arrested for a DUI. During the time of his arrest, Jamie was in possession of a half ounce of Probie that he had bought from Duffy a few days prior. Probie was known as a "loud" form of marijuana due its high chemical concentrations, which gave off a strong stench. Plastic bags were inadequate when it came to containing the smell, so if a person were to walk around the streets carrying Probie in a zippered plastic sandwich bag, the smell would practically yell out to any passerby, "Hey! I got weed!" To remedy this problem, most consumers carried Probie around in airtight, screw top canning jars.

When Jamie Castle was arrested, his sealed 4-ounce glass jar of Probie was found in his car's glove box. A quick whiff of the jar by the arresting officer meant Jamie was in for a lot more trouble than a DUI. While he sat in jail, the investigation was turned over to the Big Four, who were on the lookout for Probie. The four officers used fear and intimidation, including threats of harsh legal consequences and physical violence to convince Jamie to snitch and give up his friend and supplier, Gerald.

That's how the process always started. The Big Four would nab a small fish and twist the perpetrator's arm until they gave up a name of a bigger fish. They worked the system up and up, arresting criminals and seizing money until they landed the ultimate score: the primary source. The primary source consisted of the biggest criminals with the largest pile of money. That's what brought the Big Four to South Street in REO Town, near the new power plant, just outside Gerald Duffy's house, with a warrant. They were on their way to finding the primary source of Probie.

A new white Chevrolet Express Cargo Van that displayed 'Capital City Carpet Company' on the side was parked down the street from the suspect's house. Inside the back of the van, the Big Four team leader, Captain Robert Williams, was waiting with two other detectives, Jason Ridgeway and Michael Finch. Seated in the back of the van, they had just completed the pre-raid briefing, analyzed the house layout, and prepared for a possible weapons situation and several potential occupant scenarios. They were waiting for the fourth member, Rico Galaviz, to secure his position at the back of the house.

While waiting in the van, Robert Williams, who, at 46-years-old, was approximately 10 years older than his team members, loved listening classic rock on the radio.

Jason Ridgeway criticized, "Why do we have to listen to this ancient classic rock and roll shit?"

The squad commander answered in a grave voice, "Because, unlike your generation's music, the lyrics actually mean something. This song has a passage about how in every cop there could be a criminal, and inside every perpetrator could be a saint. It takes me back to a time in my youth when I believed that the difference between right and wrong was black and white; now my life has become one big fucking shade of gray. I understand what it means now to have sympathy for the devil."

Ridgeway fully understood his sentiment, and he responded with a somber, "That's deep."

"That's why I like listening to this kind of music." The leader's tone was clear.

At that instant, Rico Galaviz's voice came through the earpiece of the tactical communication radio, "Captain, I'm in position."

Robert Williams grabbed the rigid microphone wire positioned in front of his lips and said, "Rico, sit tight. Wait for my mark. Over."

"Understood, sir," Rico's voice answered over the radio.

As the three police officers inside the van finished securing their black body armor and tactical gear, their squad commander looked at his team and said, "Okay, let's do this."

Inside the house, Gerald Duffy was relaxing on the sofa in his living room, wearing green shorts and same colored t-shirt with

'Michigan A&M' printed in yellow across his chest. He appreciated the Michigan weather this time of the year. In his mind, it was perfect. There was no need to run the heat or air-conditioner; cheap living at its finest. It was 10 a.m. and he had just flipped the channel on his 60-inch flat screen to watch his secret guilty pleasure: *The Perspective.* It was a daily television show where a four-woman panel discussed issues in a witty and charming manner. Insecurities forced him to keep this television hobby secret from his friends. His dog, Pee Wee, a 155-pound 7-year-old male Rottweiler was lying on his side, asleep in the middle of the living room floor.

The Perspective was going through its warm up routine, which consisted of audience of mostly women, clapping, cheering, and celebrating the start of the show, followed by the opening comedic conversations from the ladies of the panel. As the show began, the main host, Amanda Langford, was about to start off the first serious discussion of the day, but Gerald didn't hear it because a loud crashing sound blasted through his living room as the police battering ram burst through Gerald Duffy's front door. Broken pieces of wooded trim and splinters flew everywhere as the door fell lopsided off of its frame.

Gerald looked to his left and saw the first police officer step through the door in black SWAT gear. He had a Sig Sauer Pistol drawn, took aim, and fired a single shot. The bang from the 40-caliber slug resounded, and was immediately followed by the Rottweiler's yelp of pain. Shocked, Gerald looked forward to see Pee Wee's repetitive yipping as he had a spasm and convulsed for a few seconds, then went silent and laid still. His blood splatter contrasted with the stark white of the far wall.

Without thinking, Gerald stood up and moved to help his dog. At that moment, the first officer yelled something at Gerald, who heard nothing over the ringing in his ears. He was freshly shocked and emotionally traumatized by what he had just witnessed. The first police officer slammed Gerald's face down on the hardwood floor as he restrained him with handcuffs. Unable to move, Gerald lay on the floor, facing his lifeless dog, and began bawling, apologizing repeatedly to his deceased pet, "I'm so sorry Pee Wee! I'm so sorry! I'm so sorry!"

As the single officer subdued Gerald, his repetitious apologies continued. The three other police officers swept the remaining portions of the house to insure no one else was inside and the situation was secure. After a few minutes, all three officers returned to the living room and reported back to their leader with a single word, "Clear."

At that moment, the squad leader, Robert Williams, removed his helmet and said to two of his team members, "Help him up." The two officers helped Gerald to his feet and sat him down on his sofa.

Robert spoke to the suspect in a direct and calm voice, "Listen Jerry, we can do this the easy way or we can certainly do this the fucked up way. You decide, but you're going to tell me where the drugs, money, and guns are at in this house."

Gerald snapped out of his trance and defiance kicked in, accompanied by anger, "I'm not telling you shit and you can fuck yourself!"

The squad leader calmly closed his eyes for a moment, opened them slowly, and shook his head. "Jerry, when the devil comes to your house; he doesn't knock on your door. He just walks right in."

Gerald was about to fire off another profanity ridden reply, but Robert lifted his hand to interrupt him. The officer pointed a finger directly at Gerald's face and said, "This is the part where you're supposed to say, 'Oh my God, I'm completely screwed. I'll tell you whatever you need to know.'"

Gerald looked down at his dead dog. He then returned the officer's stare, looking directly into Robert's eyes as he said, with the calmest tone possible, "I'm going to fucking kill you."

The Captain exhaled, drastically, with frustration, as he nodded to the officers on either side of Gerald. Officer Ridgeway and Finch grabbed the detainee by his arms and stood him up. They both kicked the back of his knees, forcing him kneel. In unison, they nudged Gerald forward, and with his hands cuffed behind his back there was nothing to break the fall. His face bounced on the hard-wood floor.

Stunned from the blow, with his forehead throbbing from the impact, Gerald found himself being dragged across the floor and he was laid face down next to Pee Wee's carcass. Then, he felt a pair of gloved hands turn his head to the left so he was looking directly into the face of his dead pet. After looking into Pee Wee's face, he squeezed his eyes shut. Gerald felt the imprint of the hard rubber tread from a tactical boot against the side of his face, as one of the officers stepped on his head and immobilized it. He also felt boots on the backs of his legs as the other cops stepped on him, holding down his entire body.   He was completely under physical control of the Big Four.

Robert Williams was squatting down behind Pee Wee's carcass as he grabbed the scruff of the dead dog's neck with both hands. Robert ordered his victim in a calm tone, "Jerry, open your eyes."

The detainee lifted his eyelids to look directly into the face of his beloved pet. Memories of bringing home up the 8-week old puppy popped into his mind. Remembrances of the numerous times they had played tug-of-war with a sock filled his mind as tears welled up in his eyes. Gerald's lip began to quiver as he cried.

The squad commander picked up the dog's head by the nape of the neck, with both hands, as he used a taunting baby voice, "Daddy, it's your fault that I'm dead. You were such a bad man. It's all your fault."

Gerald yelled out, "Stop it!" He felt more downward pressure by the boot on his face to keep him from moving. He also felt the pressure of other the officers as they stepped harder on his body.

Robert enjoyed this part as he pushed the dog so the former pet's wet nose bumped Gerald's face over and over as he continued, "Daddy, I miss you so much. Can we go outside and play?"

Gerald began to bawl as he screamed, "Stop it! I'll tell you whatever you want!"

The team leader smiled as he lifted the dog's head over the detainee's face, so the dog's tongue dragged repeatedly across his face.

"I wuv you, Daddy. I wuv you very much. You're the best Daddy in the world," Robert said as he dropped the dog back on the hard floor.

Gerald went silent as he closed his eyes and continued to cry. He was broken. Robert nodded at his team members as they lifted Gerald off the ground and sat him back on the couch.

"Okay, let's start again from the beginning. You were going to tell me where the drugs, guns, and money are at in this house. Weren't you, Jerry?" Robert's voice was calm and commanding.

An exhausted Gerald looked that the television, where his favorite show was still playing. What just happened to him seemed like it took place over several hours, but less than 15 minutes had passed.

He exhaled and said, "Inside the walk-in closet in my bedroom, there's an access hatch to the attic. My stash is above the ceiling, through that hatchway. There's a step ladder right there. Under my bed there's a 12-gauge and inside the nightstand drawer, next to the bed there's a handgun." He took a deep breath and let it go as he continued, "Lastly, by the kitchen you'll walk down stairs to the basement and under the stairwell. If you move the cardboard boxes, there's a floor safe."

"The combination?" asked Robert.

Gerald explained, "The combination dial has letters, not numbers. The combination is M. A. M. Like Michigan A&M. There's about $40,000 in cash in the safe. That's it. That's all I have for you."

Upon hearing that, without saying a word, three of officers walked out of the living room and through the house to verify what Gerald had told them.

"One more thing," added Robert, "before I can end this nightmare for you. You're going to have to tell me who provided you with the marijuana."

Gerald exhaled. "I don't know his real name but he goes by the street name, the Indian. He contacts me with disposable phones. I have no idea how to get a hold of him. That's the truth."

"Do you mean like the dot in the forehead type of Indian?" Robert asked.

"No," Gerald explained, "He's like Sitting Bull type of Indian."

The squad leader stared deeply in his detainee's face. His instincts told him that Gerald was telling him the truth.

The three other members of the Big Four reentered the living room and each one offered a simple nod verifying that what Gerald had explained to them was true; it was all there.

Robert looked at his criminal suspect and said in a calm tone, "Jerry we're going to arrest you now and charge you with the crime of drug trafficking."

Gerald responded, "Fine, take me to jail. Just get me the hell away from you psychos."

The squad leader looked at Officers Finch and Ridgeway and instructed, "Go ahead and read him his rights and let's book him." The two police officers escorted the handcuffed perpetrator out of his own house to the van parked on the street.

Still standing in the living room, Robert Williams watched his suspect being led away. He looked at Officer Rico Galaviz standing next to him and asked, "Who the hell is the Indian?"

3

ST. BILLY AND PROFESSOR RITTENBURG

Almost a decade ago, when Maxwell was born, he was the toast of the City of Toledo. It's not every day that a zoo successfully births a male baby chimpanzee in captivity. He was exactly what the Lucas County Zookeepers needed as they mourned the passing of their beloved Henry. At 56 years old, Henry had been the oldest chimpanzee to ever live in an American zoo and his death had been hard on the people who worked for the well-respected Lucas County Zoo. For decades, the gentle spirited primate touched the lives of animal lovers from this Ohio city.

Maxwell had been named after Scottish mathematician and physicist, James Clerk Maxwell. The Staff at the Lucas County Zoo had felt that too much notoriety was given to talentless reality television celebrities, so they started a trend of naming their animals after great scientists and artists. The birth of Maxwell, also known as Baby Max, brought a renewed vigor to the zoo's staff as they were reminded of the circle of life. The baby chimp was a gentle and joyous soul; as he grew, he warmed the hearts of everyone who encountered him. However, once Max was a little over one and a half years old, things started to go very wrong. The lovable chimpanzee started having repetitive seizures and losing consciousness up to twenty times each day. The frequency of the biological attacks increased over time. The numerous fits took an emotional toll on Maxwell and the once bright, friendly animal became depressed and withdrawn, and avoided other chimpanzees in favor of hiding in the corner of his sanctuary.

An extensive medical examination of Maxwell revealed that he had been born with a gene that causes a rare form of epilepsy. The veterinarians, zoologists, and administrators of Lucas County Zoological Society met in a boardroom at headquarters to discuss how they were going to treat the beloved chimpanzee. As the members sat around the large, darkly stained oak conference table, they discussed their options. They decided against any of the medical procedures available to them, including experimental brain surgery, the use of Thorazine, and electro shock therapy. In the collective opinion of the zoo's staff, each treatment would cause more pain and had little chance of treating Max's affliction. During the discussion, they realized that euthanasia was a real option.

That's when the Zoo's Senior Veterinarian, Dr. Brandy Holton, suggested they should look at Professor William Rittenburg's work at Michigan A&M University. The strong-willed animal physician spoke with authority when she said, "The professor's research is making strong positive steps in treating symptoms similar to Maxwell's, and he's currently working, with the approval of the FDA, to conduct animal testing for his treatment of epileptic seizures."

The lead veterinarian also shared videos, and the board members gathered around her iPad to watch. She showed them the treatment process. Before treatment, each test animal had a preexisting condition and suffered from brutal seizures. With a dab of marijuana-derived liquid, CBD, under the tongue, each test subject became fully functional with normal behavior and no observable side effects. After a long debate, the board issued a notice to proceed

Dr. Brandy Holton was never the kind to hold back when given the green light. The veterinarian initiated contact to Professor William Rittenburg and explained the situation. Over the next few days, an immediate rapport was built as the two shared Maxwell's medical information. Dr. Holton presented findings from the chimpanzee's medical records. This, with additional results from Maxwell's blood work, demonstrated that he was a great candidate for the professor's treatment.

For Dr. Rittenburg, this was a rare circumstance where situational need met an ideal opportunity. Maxwell was in need of treatment, and the doctor's research needed more data on a larger hominidae classification in order to progress toward future human testing. He offered his immediate help to the Lucas County Zoo.

As the medical procedure moved forward and CBD marijuana-based medication was administered to the chimpanzee, the immediate change in Maxwell's physical condition astounded the zoo's staff. His seizures stopped almost immediately. After some minor adjustments, the animal was showing little to no signs of convulsions.

Over the next 16 months, Professor Rittenburg's team developed a preliminary report stating that Maxwell's natural genetic condition would cause certain neurons of his brain's frontal cortex to have excessive electrical discharge, which led his body to seize. A section of the chimpanzee's brain was firing too hard.

When the CBD chemicals were introduced to Maxwell's body, they traveled through the blood stream searching for natural cannabinoids receptors in his brain, like floating keys searching for matching locks. When those keys inserted themselves into the correct neurons of the frontal cortex of Maxwell's brain, the CBD would suppress the excessive flow of neurotransmitters to normal levels, which allowed proper electrical reception through the affected section of the brain and severely decreased his seizures.

Regardless of Rittenburg's findings, the majority of the Lucas County Zoo staff was simply happy to have Maxwell back and healthy again. All signs of depression and isolation disappeared and Max was active and happily socializing with the other chimpanzees in the zoo sanctuary. During the treatment process, Maxwell's sleep pattern and appetite returned to normal, and his biological test results showed a reduction in toxic brain protein levels. With proper neuron function and normalized sleep patterns, the chimp was flushing out the toxic waste that had built up inside his brain. Max was on the road to recovery in terms of physical and mental health.

Maxwell's case was documented and the data was combined with the professor's previous animal testing results. All of William Rittenburg's observations and findings were published in the Journal of Medical Proxy Research, including all qualitative observations and quantitative results of biological examinations on each test subject within the last decade. When the professor's findings were released, the response was energetic. The researcher was credited with strict adherence to proper objective scientific methodology even when other academic teams challenged the data. As Rittenburg's work was scrutinized, it withstood the criticism.

Many of the voices that objected to the published report didn't come from the scientific community, but from the political world. Several conservatives felt that the motive behind the findings was simply to promote marijuana legalization under the guise of medical research. There were skeptics abound. In spite of the dissenters, significant evidence prompted the U.S. Food and Drug Administration to issue a rare approval, allowing Professor Rittenburg to proceed with testing his cannabis-based CBD medicine on human beings. He also received permission from the U.S. Drug Enforcement Administration to move forward with cannabis plant cultivation, as long as the final product did not exceed a THC concentration of 1 percent.

With the FDA and DEA approval, the professor received numerous offers from large pharmaceutical corporations from all over the world to fund his research, but Dr. Rittenburg turned them all down. He put together research funding proposals and submitted them to the National Science Foundation, the National Institutes of Health, and the National Academy of Sciences. He received ample long-term financial resources to conduct his work. The objective panels at these institutions wanted to know the immediate and long-term scientific effects of this promising medication on humans.

After the funding was in place, the professor needed to build a solid team of researchers to help him complete his testing at Michigan

A&M. One of the most important parts of his research was finding someone to develop a marijuana strain that was high in CBD concentration with little to no presence of THC. Everything had to be patented, including the developed cannabis plant's genetics, the CBD extraction process, and chemical refinement method, and the medication development procedures. Every step had to be protected as intellectual property or his research could be stolen by a competing research team.

Even with ample funding, the professor was turned down by nearly every graduate student and associate professor he invited to work with him. Most were afraid to jeopardize their potential careers or the risk of a criminal investigation by working on a project that was associated with growing marijuana, regardless of the support the project had received. Professor Rittenburg's frustrations were mounting until one day he received a recommendation from Dr. Melissa Black, a professor from the Michigan A&M's Turfgrass Science Department. Professor Black recommended an honor student and first year master's candidate in plant biology and genetics: Ronnie Lee Harding. The graduate student was working for Professor Black as a lab technician, developing lawn grass seeds that would grow in dense shade. The graduate student was a great help, but Professor Black did not have the funding to pay for his services. That is why she made the recommendation; it was financially best for the student.

When Professor Rittenburg approached Ronnie Harding to see if he had any interest in working together, the personal chemistry between the two men was almost instantaneous. After a brief interview process, the professor disclosed that he was looking for someone who could engineer and grow a very specific cannabis plant for his medical research. Dr. Rittenburg offered full tuition funding and $1,000 a month as a fellowship stipend, if the young man would work for him. Ronnie answered with an immediate yes. The professor gave Ronnie second chance to back out, stressing that there may be a possible career stigma from working on research with marijuana, but the graduate student wasn't concerned. Ronnie was on board.

During the next year and half at an off-campus, indoor grow laboratory, Ronnie Harding cultivated by crossbreeding certain hemp plants with strains of the sativa variety to yield a new strain of cannabis that resulted in delivering 13-16% CBD concentrations while delivering only .03% THC content. The CBD-enriched seedlings were identified after breaking through the soil's surface and before reaching the matured flowering stage. Next, they were cloned to create a series of engineered harvests. Ronnie kept a detailed log of his step-by-step procedure with specific details about every aspect of plant cultivation, including the grow room set up, lighting cycles, nutrients formulas, watering patterns, and atmospheric carbon dioxide/oxygen ratios. The plants responded to his care with near record levels of CBD concentrations.

However, the current CBD yields were not good enough for Ronnie. He wanted to cross the 20% concentration threshold. In a series of harvests, he tweaked his procedure and cultivated with due care, hoping to surpass his goal. Samples were sent the University of Mississippi's Marijuana Research Project for official results. Unbeknownst to the majority of the public, it was Ole Miss, who, for nearly 50-years, had assumed the role of the leading laboratory for cannabis research for the country, and their review made everything official.

Today was May 20th, and the day had arrived when Rittenburg's research team was going to get official results on their latest harvest. That's what brought Ronnie to the basement level of the 60-year-old Ingersoll Hall on Michigan A&M's campus at 10 o'clock in the morning.

Ronnie continued down the hall to Room B-50, the office suite of Dr. Rittenburg. The beige suite was divided into four, sparsely decorated rooms. The walls were covered in paper charts and dry marker boards with schedules and objectives drawn on them in red and black erasable ink. The larger room served as main reception area of the suite and the work area for the secretarial portion of Rittenburg's team. The other rooms were work areas for administrators in the pharmaceutical chemistry and medical implementation portion of the research team. The last room was Dr. William Rittenburg's office.

As the graduate student walked in, the team's main office administrator, 34-year-old Emily Sadler, greeted him. "Hey Ronnie, congratulations on your Master's Degree."

The researcher replied, "Thanks," while looking around at the nearly empty suite, "Hey, it looks like everyone took off for the summer."

"Yeah, everyone is taking a little break before the Medical Proxy Research Conference in Chicago next month, but Doc is waiting for you in his office," Emily replied. Everyone on William Rittenburg's research team called the professor, 'Doc'. It was this kind of informal leadership style that created the relaxed work environment and allowed all of the team members to enjoy their jobs. Life was too short not to enjoy the people you worked with each day.

Ronnie pointed at the office administrator and said, "Thanks, Emily." He continued to walk across the reception area to the open door that led to Professor Rittenburg's office. The researcher knocked on the open door.

"Hey!" Responded 56-year-old gray haired William Rittenburg, "How was the graduation ceremony?"

Standing in the doorway, Ronnie smiled. He had always kept secret that he loved that Doc was 5 foot 6 and shorter than he was. The student had spent his whole life being the smallest man in his home. Now at school, his height felt normal. His little secret put an impish grin of his face. "It was pretty good, but I have an idiot older brother, who is always out to one-up me. He could never let me have any of the spotlight without photo bombing me with his bare ass."

The professor laughed and rubbed his graying goatee that stood out against his pale skin. "I have one of those too. I go to NYU for undergraduate and he goes to Columbia. I get a Doctorate in Pharmacology from UC San Francisco and he goes to John Hopkins Medical. I performed medical marijuana research at a university and he's a surgeon at Ba'al Haness General. I worked my butt off my whole life and somehow even in my late 50s, I always felt like a failure in my parents' eyes in comparison to my brother." The professor tried to relate. Their similar backgrounds strengthened the bonds of friendship between the two men.

Rittenburg began to search through the papers on his desk and lifted up a white, 9X12 envelope. "I guess you're here for this."

The student nodded, stepped in to the office, and took a seat in front of the professor's desk. Rittenburg opened the envelope's clasp. "There's no suspense here. I already looked at it. Congratulations, your latest harvest sample cleared 23.4% CBD concentration while only yielding .02% THC. According to Ole Miss, that's highest confirmed analytical test results that they have ever seen for CBD concentrations within any cannabis strain. I guess it's safe to say you're the reigning world champion in this category."

The sense of accomplishment washed over the young man's face. "Why thank you. I just want you to know I officially named this particular strain of marijuana."

"Yeah, what's that?"

A grin overtook Ronnie's face. "I'm naming it Saint Billy, after you."

"After me, why?" William Rittenburg chuckled.

Ronnie's chair squeaked as he leaned back, "Because of all the work you do trying to help people. You're like this plant. You both are saints. That's why I'm calling it, Saint Billy."

The professor's cheeks tinged pink for a moment. "Well, I'm flattered by the gesture, but I think this is one of those times when my parents will never understand the honor."

Both men laughed at the statement as Ronnie leaned forward and picked up a 4x8 picture frame from Rittenburg's desk. It was a photo of a female veterinarian standing in her white lab coat holding hands with a chimpanzee. The young man stared at the photo for a moment before he stated, "Doc, I love this picture by the way."

A wave of warm nostalgia washed over Rittenburg's face and he leaned back in his office chair. "Yeah, Dr. Holton was great, and the chimpanzee, Max, was just a trooper." The professor's expression changed as he added, "To tell you the truth, animals kind of scare me a little. I was raised in Manhattan and we didn't have any pets. I really had to depend on the zoo's staff to help out in that regard."

"How are they doing now?"

"I just got an email from Dr. Holton yesterday," Rittenburg added, "They're expecting a couple new additions this month, including a baby giraffe and a couple of otters. As for Maxwell, he's been seizure free and he has had very few side effects from the medication. What makes me the happiest is that Maxwell has been socially interacting in a positive manner with the other chimpanzee in his community and he shows no signs of depression."

The student placed the framed photo back on the professor's desk. "Well Doc, you did well on that."

"Wait until you see what we're doing with humans." Rittenburg added, "The preliminary results have been excellent." He interrupted himself, "Oh, on that note. Are you still coming to Chicago for the Medical Proxy Research Conference? I've made all the arrangements."

"Yeah, you can count me in 100%. I wouldn't miss it for the world."

A devilish smile popped up on the professor's face. "Wait until you see what I got planned for my conference presentation."

4

THE INDIAN

In Capital City, there was only one source to get the best strain of marijuana: from Ronnie Harding and Paul Mollett. Their collaboration gave them everything they needed for a successful business. Ronnie, the grad student, grew and cultivated Probie for harvest in a secluded grow-facility, while street savvy Paul became the 'D-boy', as he developed a sales and distribution system on the streets. They split the profits 50/50.

Their business model worked. The product spoke for itself and Probie could not be imitated because of its distinctive smell and unique high. Everyone wanted it, so prices rose in accordance with demand. Not only did the word spread on the streets, it traveled across social networks. Ronnie and Paul's illegal business grew substantially over two years in terms of both volume and profit. With their success, the two became like brothers.

During their years as partners, it became a custom to eat together twice a week at their favorite restaurants around the Capital City. Ronnie was now 26 and had just earned his master's degree. For this occasion, he wore a navy blue long sleeve t-shirt as he sat with a cup of coffee in his favorite booth next to the front window of Casa Nova's Restaurant. It was 3:30 in the afternoon - between the lunch and dinner rush. Ronnie's phone pinged and he read the text, "Almost there, bro." Paul was never on time.

We're so alike and yet so different, Ronnie smiled at the thought. *The only real difference between us is that I had a good family that supported me and kept me out of trouble. Paul didn't. He was just dealt a bad hand. That's what set us apart. Regardless, he's been my counterbalance.* Ronnie stirred his coffee, took another sip, and pondered their friendship while gazing out the front window.

As he waited for his business partner, Ronnie thought about the horrible chain of events that made up Paul's life. Before Paul was out of his teens, he had watched each of his parents die.

Paul's parents were Gary Mollett and Shoni Diabo. In their youth, Gary and Shoni were very much in love. Although love can be a beautiful thing, it has the power to bring out the worst in people. These two were stuck in the bad habits of youth. They were passionate for one another, which led to the best sex of their lives. This fed their addiction to one another, which enhanced their insecurities, jealousies, and possessiveness.

Individually, they were attractive people and flirting with friends and strangers was not uncommon. Unfortunately, they were also immature, and that meant that every text or phone call raised paranoid suspicions. They routinely accused one another of cheating, which led to defensive overreactions followed by heated arguments. The arguments became dramatic fights and typically ended in domestic violence. Both were guilty of physically striking the other and their uncontrolled alcohol habits only made it worse.

Paul's father, Gary, was a tough guy and a Marine with a sculpted face and chiseled body. It was his bad boy appeal that made him so alluring to Shoni. All of Gary's life skills were built by Marine Corps discipline, and his self-control came crashing down the day he met Paul's mother, Shoni. In a sense, her power was stronger than the Marines Corp.

Shoni was of French Canadian and Mohican decent, supermodel beautiful in her face and figure. Her flawless natural tan skin was soft, smooth, and unblemished, but it was her face with her ice crystal blue eyes and her full lips that captivated Gary, even though Shoni was a consistent hot mess. He never stood a chance; Gary had found his Aphrodite.

When Shoni gave birth to their son, Paul, the couple hoped that having a child would push them out of their selfish universe. No matter how hard they tried, even with Paul in their lives, they reverted back to the same cycle of drama. They decided that for Paul's sake, the best solution was separation.

Before he reached adulthood, Paul witnessed each of his parents die. First was his mother, who initially had sole custody of Paul following their break up. Shoni, the once exotic beauty, stopped drinking and got a job as a check-out-girl at the local grocery store. She was doing her best to raise her son on her own with all the love she had left.

Their routine carried on until one day when the nurturing mother took her eight-year-old son grocery shopping in the very store where she worked. Early in the evening, Shoni felt a chest pain when the aortic valve in her heart inverted and refused to open and close. Numbness was followed by intense shooting pain down her left arm as she called out to her child.

The startled boy ran back to his mother, who fainted on the floor. When the boy cried out for help, other patrons whipped out their mobile phones and called 911 immediately. The local paramedic team arrived soon after. The EMT did his best to revive Shoni but to no avail. Eight-year-old Paul watched his mother die from heart failure at the grocery store. Shoni died from a broken heart.

Paul's father, Gary, now sober as well, was devastated by the news of Shoni's passing. Even though his relationship with her had been crazed and often resulted in domestic violence, she had been the love of his life. Without her, Gary, who was now out of the Marine Corp, resigned to living a hollowed out existence. His daily routine began with rising from bed in the morning to go work as a safety inspector for an automotive brake plant. His days ended at home, where he ate a small dinner, to only relax and go to bed alone.

The news of his former lover's death caused Gary's heart to tear like paper, but his Marine training taught him that in time of crisis it is necessary to set aside one's emotions and do what is required. His son needed him; Gary was brought back to life again with a sense of responsibility. He took custody of Paul and raised his boy through his teenage years to the best of his ability.

Gary did an excellent job in nurturing and teaching Paul all the way up until the week of his high school graduation ceremony. It was just before Paul's 18th birthday. Father and son sat at the breakfast table and Gary complained about an intense headache and pain behind his eyes. When Gary spoke, his words came out like gibberish; his speech was unrecognizable. Confused, Paul cried out as he watched his father faint to the floor. Blood gushed from his nose and flowed from his eyes like tears. Gary died at that moment from a massive stroke and brain aneurysms.

Paul had witnessed both of his parents' passing. By the time his father was laid to rest, Paul had just turned 18 and graduated from high school. The now orphaned young man would have to make his way in this world on his own.

Almost fully matured, Paul had inherited the best physical characteristics of both of his parents. He had his father's finely sculpted face and carved body and his mother ice-blue eyes, but it was his long, silky, and straight black hair that became his most distinctive feature. Paul's black mane was a genetic connection to his Native American ancestry and he loved to show it off.

Over the next couple of years, without any parental guidance or support, Paul stumbled his way through life in more than ways than one. Everything became about the present; there was no concept of tomorrow for this young adult. With women, there was no love, just sex. When it came to employment, there were no careers, just temporary, low wage jobs. Having little training and minimal education, employment opportunities were rare. He turned to selling marijuana just to make ends meet. Even slinging dope was difficult because he was on the bottom of the drug dealing hierarchy, working the hardest for the least amount of money while taking the majority of the risk. He was learning the game from the bottom up and it wasn't easy. To climb the drug dealing ladder he tried to grow marijuana in his own house, but failed to produce anything of quality.

By chance, Paul's fortunes changed while working on the campus of Michigan A&M University. The 22-year-old, now 6 feet tall and just over 195 pounds, took a job as a temporary construction laborer during the renovation of Old Calhoun Hall, which stood next to the Cypress River. During his lunch break one afternoon, Paul stood in the middle of a concrete pedestrian bridge over the river, tearing the crust from his sandwich to feed the ducks swimming below. Watching the mallards swim towards the floating pieces of bread put a smile on the struggling worker's face until he noticed some floating popcorn that had been thrown toward the same ducks.

Looking down the bridge, Paul turned and introduced himself to then 24-year-old graduate student, Ronnie Lee Harding. Lunchtime conversations about the ducks and other aspects of life became a daily habit, and the two young men became friends. Over time, Ronnie grew comfortable and disclosed to Paul that he was growing marijuana for university medical research. Ecstatic and astounded, the younger man was sure that this grad student must be a godsend; he pleaded and begged Ronnie to help fix his own crop. Although somewhat reluctant, Ronnie agreed to lend a hand to the obviously struggling young construction worker.

After the first week, Ronnie decided it was best to start from scratch, and he threw out Paul's old, worthless crops. The grad student contacted a highly skilled marijuana grower from Grand Rapids, Michigan and secured some seeds for a high THC strain of indica, called Hilda Green. The conservative Republican bastion of Grand Rapids had a dirty little secret: The West Michigan community was settled by the Dutch and many folks there maintain relationships with those in Amsterdam, where some of the best cannabis seeds in the world originate. Hilda Green came to Paul's grow room from Amsterdam via this trade route. Once the seeds were in hand,

Ronnie used his scientific method to grow the new harvest. The difference was unbelievable: the quality of Paul's crop improved exponentially. Now, he had something worthwhile to sell to his clients.

Helping Paul inspired Ronnie to try something new. He crossbred the high THC indica strain of Hilda Green with his medical research strain of sativa, called Saint Billy, which had a high CBD concentration. The result of the genetic engineering was a new indica/sativa hybrid with predominately sativa characteristics. According to Ronnie's laboratory testing, the new type of marijuana had extreme elevation of both cannabinoids, THC and CBD. The unique combination carried approximately 26% THC and just under 21% CBD. This was when the Probie cannabis species was born and named.

When the two sampled Ronnie's new creation with a smoke test, they were both blown away with their experience. Simply, it was the best high either man had ever felt. After coming down, their excitement remained and the two agreed to establish a business partnership. They decided that Ronnie would engineer and grow the product and Paul would sell it.

When Paul recruited dealers on the street for his sales force, Paul Mollett ceased to exist, and instead, he became known as The Indian. None of his business associates ever knew his real name. When The Indian was running the show, everyone followed a strict set of rules. He dictated the terms of communications, distribution, and payment. Paul had a kind nature, but when he played the role of The Indian he was cold and harsh, and he spread a fear of violence to keep everyone in line. This was the way things were done on the streets to keep order among the chaos.

The balance between the two partners was the key to their success. Paul was yin to Ronnie's yang.

Currently, sitting alone and still staring out the restaurant window, Ronnie was lost in thought when a brown-haired 20-something waitress in a powder blue sleeveless button down shirt walked up to the table and introduced herself, "Hi, I'm Jess, and I'll be your server for today. Are you by yourself?"

Shaking his head, Ronnie answered, "No. My friend is on his way. He's running a little late, but I would like to order some appetizers."

The server took order in a friendly manner and left.

It wasn't much longer before the now 24-year-old Paul walked up and sat down in the booth opposite Ronnie. He donned a worn denim jacket over a bare chest, showing off his well-defined collarbone. Reaching behind his head, Paul swept his long, straight black hair back before he asked, "Did you order?"

"Yeah," Ronnie answered, "But just appetizers. I got us chicken tenders and onion rings."

Smiling, Paul pressed him, "Did you remember my Mountain Dew?"

"Of course, I did." Ronnie was slightly self assured.

With a happy smirk, Paul threw in, "Because you know me so well."

Ronnie offered a simple nod, while the waitress returned and set down the beverages in front of the two men. As Jess set a glass of ice and Pepsi in front of Ronnie, the two made eye contact.

With a pleasant smile, Jess brought out her small pad of paper and asked, "Alright you two. Are you ready to order?" Her stare lingered on Ronnie.

The two men placed their entrée orders and this time Paul noticed how the waitress and Ronnie's eye met again.

When the waitress was out of sight, Paul declared, "You are such a pussy chaser."

"No, I'm not," Ronnie said defensively, with a slight laugh, "I'm just looking for the-one-girl." He thought a moment before he added, "I guess until I find her, they're all candidates then."

Smugness spread across Paul's face. "Who the hell is the-one-girl?"

With a slight head tilt and grin, Ronnie exhaled deeply before he explained, "My father used to say that it's all about the last hour of the day. When the kids are put to bed and the dishes are done, all that is left to do is to spend the last hour of the day with your favorite girl. That's the-one-girl. It's the person I'll meet that I can't live without. I'll know her when I see and get to know her. My gut will tell me when I find her. Until then..." Ronnie offered a shoulder shrug and then he interrupted himself with a little distain in tone, "Well, look at you! Who the hell is talking right now? You go through women like tissue paper and now you're on your soapbox with me. Please."

The arrogance was no longer subtle on Paul's face, when he declared in his full egotistical fashion, "First of all, she doesn't exist. There's no one-person. There's only Miss Right Now. And the last hour of the day after my nut is usually filled with awkwardness or sleepiness."

Closing his eyes and shaking his head, Ronnie silently disagreed.

Looking over, Paul lifted a single finger to pause the conversation as Jess returned and set the appetizers on the table. The waitress instructed, "Be careful, these are very hot. Your dinners will be up shortly." She offered another friendly gaze and walked away.

Reaching behind his head and stroking his long black hair, Paul's facial expression lit up and he said, "On that note, I can't wait to tell you what happened to me last night."

After the last couple years of running with Paul, Ronnie was sure nothing else could surprise him, and he added, "I can't wait for you to tell me." A smirk spread across his face.

After looking over both shoulders, Paul began his story, "Okay, I was hanging at Alibaba's, the strip club downtown. You know, Tony Johnson's place. I'm chilling at my table by myself and enjoying the show. The girls are doing their thing. Well, after a while, this portly middle aged white guy and his wife asked if they could join me at my table. Both of them were in their mid-40s."

Closing his eyes and letting out breath, Ronnie shook his head. This is part of the story where he know it was about to get weird. He returned his full attention as Paul carried on, "So, out of politeness I said, 'Sure.' They seemed like nice people. They were buying me drinks and generously tipping the girls. There was a lot of friendly small talk. He was the owner of some heating and cooling company, just outside the city in the burbs somewhere. The wife, she didn't say that much, but kept whispering in her husband's ear."

"Well, what did she look like?" Ronnie's curiosity bested him.

Paul leaned back in the booth before he explained, "She looked like him, in her mid-40s. She was short and chubby with dishwater-blonde hair. It was cut really short, professional-like, and she wore these glasses that made her look like a librarian."

A librarian, this is going to be trouble, thought Ronnie, rolling his eyes.

Now leaning over the table, Paul added to the story, "While she was whispering in her husband's ear, he just kept nodding his head. Then all of a sudden, the guy makes me an offer."

Intrigued, Ronnie's eyes widen while he leaned forward. "What did he say?"

"He offered me $1,000 if I would bang his ole lady and let him watch. They wanted to pick up a nice suite at the Madaris Hotel, downtown for us. They explained that this wife is a big-time reader, has been since she was a kid, and she loves reading those trashy paperback romance novels. She was pretty fond of the stories about pioneer women who would were captured by tribes of Indian Warriors and forced into passionate sex while settling in the new world. She was caught up in a fantasy and I looked like her favorite book cover." A calm arrogance shone from Paul's face as he resumed stroking his long mane of black silky hair.

With a chuckle, Ronnie closed his eyes; he knew the answer before he asked the question, "Well, what did you do?"

"What do you think I did?" Paul answered, "I took the money and we went to the hotel. I went to work on her for three hours while he watched. I banged the chubby librarian as if I were the little drummer boy, rum pa pum pum. I kept flipping her on her front and then her back, over and over again, like I was making a grilled cheese sandwich. I put a sweat on us both. The weird thing was that during some of the heated moments, she would say things like, 'Fuck me, you savage!'

"Ha!" jumped from Ronnie's mouth. Then his curiosity forced him to ask, "Well, how'd that make you feel?"

A puff of air passed through his lips when Paul explained, "Dude, I'm way past all that racial shit. If you're paying me or you're fucking me in a good way, then you can call me whatever you want to. They did both."

Shaking his head with his eyes closed, a smile broke out on Ronnie's face before he inquired, "In the moral compass that's in your head somewhere, is there anything that's telling you that any of this is the wrong thing to do?"

"No, not one bit. A hard dick has no conscious," Paul answered definitively.

Ronnie gazed back at his friend. "You know you're nothing but a walking id."

Paul's face soured, before he replied, "I have no idea what an id is. Enlighten me college boy."

"Well," Ronnie sat up straight in the booth and explained, "It's a Freudian term that describes a part of anyone's personality that's rooted in their physical needs, wants, and desires. You're solely motivated by the instant gratification of your sexual impulses. You are living and breathing id."

Paul's lips puckered as he stared at the ceiling, pondering for a moment, before he replied, "You know what? I can live with that label. I think that's pretty accurate for me. My dick always overrides my brain. I accept your term."

Leaning forward and tapping his finger on the table, Ronnie pressed on, "My next question is what the hell was the husband was doing while you were fucking his wife?"

Closing his eyes and shaking his head, Paul added, "It's not what you think. He wasn't whacking off or trying to palm my ass during any part of it. He didn't participate at all. He sat there and watched, making sure his wife was safe and pleasured, I guess."

"He's a cuckold." Ronnie calmly stated.

With bewilderment all over his face, Paul said, "Again college boy, with these words. I have no idea what you're talking about."

Chuckling, Ronnie explained, "A cuckold is sexual fetish term. They're usually associated with the male half of a committed relationship. It's a person who is turned on by watching their partner receive sexual pleasure from a third person."

Paul folded his arms while he contemplated the definition. "I would have to say you're correct in your categorization of him as well. So one more time, I accept your term."

"Here's one more term you're going to have to accept." Ronnie with a caviler smile added, "And that's the word, whore. So, now when I say shut your dirty whore mouth, I'm just being accurate."

Lifting his plastic glass of Mountain Dew, Paul offered, "Again, I accept your term, brother."

Ronnie lifted his own glass. Paul mirrored his action, nodded, and they both took a drink. When he finished, Ronnie said, "Since, you made an easy $1,000, you can pick up the tab."

Biting on his bottom lip, Paul uncorked his secret, "Ronnie, that $1,000 is nothing. Wait till you see what I have in a duffle bag for you in the trunk of my car."

5

FRANCESCA AND MOLLY

Sea foam green is the ugliest color for a minivan, thought Ronnie Harding as he drove his 13-year-old Ford Windstar home from his lunch with Paul. Ronnie had bought this vehicle from a Capital City public school teacher six years ago. It had served him well as a college student, but it was a complete failure as a chick magnet. He was driving carefully with both hands on the steering wheel, trying not to attract police attention. Ronnie's mind wandered to thoughts of selling the minivan on Craigslist.

With a grin on his face, Ronnie thought about the cheap black vinyl duffle bag resting on the passenger's seat with $115,700 in cash in it. He imagined the car he could buy with that amount of money. Even though the fantasy tickled him, he shrugged it off. He was determined to keep his double life a secret, and flaunting a fancy car would definitely seem suspect. Of the two lives that he was living, one, growing and selling drugs illegally and the other, researching them in a professional laboratory, he loved the academic side more. Keeping his other life a secret was necessary. That meant not spending any of his drug money. It also meant hiding the cash as soon as possible. The effort required ego checking and self-discipline. These weren't Ronnie's strong suits, but he kept his lifestyle consistent with the standard poor graduate student. Unfortunately, that required him to keep driving this same sea foam green minivan piece of shit.

The cash in the gym bag came from the illegal sale of Ronnie's one-of-a-kind genetic cannabis breed, Probie. Not only did the marijuana strain deliver a unique smell and an excellent high, but the yield per plant was extraordinary. Most amateur indoor weed growers would be perfectly content to obtain 2 to 4 ounces of cured harvest per plant, but Ronnie was no rookie grower and Probie was a special breed. The plant's genetics and the graduate student's growing technique regularly yielded an outstanding harvest of 21 to 24 ounces per plant. As Ronnie refined his growing technique, each Probie harvest improved in terms of weight. This strain's sensimilla, the unfertilized flowering buds, grew monstrously—sometimes longer than three feet and thicker than footballs. Ronnie's cannabis seeds delivered on both quality and quantity.

Each four month harvest, Probie grew in terms of size and worth. With the last 65 plant harvests Ronnie and Paul were able to obtain nearly 77 pounds of pot, sold at the wholesale price of $3,200 per pound, which gave them $246,400 gross revenue. They would subtract $15,000 to cover utility costs, equipment upgrades and incidentals. The money left over netted the pair $231,400 profit to be split equally between Ronnie and Paul. That's why, today, Ronnie was driving his ugly minivan with a cheap duffle bag containing $115,700 in cash.

The 77 pounds of marijuana that had been grown trickled through Paul's network of dealers and onto the street. The pounds were broken down to smaller packages and sold for the premium price of $400 per ounce, which created $492,800 worth of street value. Even at these high prices, the demand was greater than the supply. The inventory disappeared off the street and turned into cash almost instantly.

It was 6:00 in evening when Ronnie pulled his minivan into the parking lot of Drummond Lake Village Apartments. When he parked and turned off his engine, the graduate student's feelings were mixed. Staring at the duffle bag sitting on the passenger seat, Ronnie thought about the contents. The cash inside the bag was the root of his emotional conflict. The money represented his pride and sense of achievement, but also embodied his fears. All that cash risked everything that was important to him. He hadn't come to college for this. He'd only started the business to help out a friend, but he had no idea that doing so would explode into a booming business endeavor. He loved it and loathed it at the same time.

Closing his eyes as he exhaled, Ronnie pulled his focus back to the present. He slung the bag of cash over his right shoulder. His book bag of school research notes went in his left hand. As Ronnie walked across the parking lot, he thought about carrying the results of a double life, one in each arm.

The mind of the troubled graduate student was filled with concern as he made his way to building 1571 of West Pond Drive, his three story brown brick apartment building. When Ronnie looked up to the third floor balcony, he saw the dark haired 20-something woman who lived across the hall, leaning against a guardrail. She wore mirrored sunglasses as she talked on her iPhone. The girl and her roommate had just moved in a month ago.

Smoking hot, Ronnie thought while he glanced at the tan young woman, noticing her long, silky dark hair that hung down her back and her white bikini top and snug jean shorts. An unobtrusive jeweled belly button ring hung from her navel and called attention to the petite, but athletic figured girl's flat stomach. The button and zipper of her faded denim shorts were left open to reveal the white bikini bottom underneath, which inspired Ronnie to shake his head slightly as the thought repeated in his mind: *Smoking hot.*

As he approached the door of his building, Ronnie was about to reach for his keys when the young lady on the balcony yelled down, "I've got you, neighbor!"

He looked up to see her wave as she put her phone in her pocket and disappeared from the balcony. It took approximately two seconds before Ronnie heard the familiar buzzing sound. He reached for the door knob and shouted, "Thank you!"

Walking up the carpeted stairs to the third floor, Ronnie stopped for a moment to stare at the door of apartment C. For a moment, he thought about knocking and introducing himself. Inhibition and doubt intervened; Ronnie quickly talked himself out of it and proceeded to apartment A, across the hall.

Flipping on the lights in his one bedroom apartment, the graduate student felt at home in the drab man-cave. There was nothing decorating the plain white walls. The beige crushed velvet couch had been a garage sale purchase. A pair of green folding lawn chairs sat beside the scratched up wooden coffee and end tables, completing his living room setup. The seating faced a 38 inch flat screen that sat on a small wooden credenza on the opposite wall. The TV didn't have cable service; it was connected to a laptop. Ronnie preferred streaming television shows and movies on his own time to watching them on a cable TV schedule.

After dropping his book bag on the couch, Ronnie continued to his bedroom. He moved by his futon, stepping over the piles of clothes on the floor. The young man dropped the duffle bag of money on the closet floor, gathered up some dirty clothes and buried it in laundry. *I'll deal with that over the weekend,* he thought. Pulling off his shirt and tossing it on the pile in his closet, Ronnie grabbed a dark green hoodie from the back of his desk chair, pulled it over his head and stretched it comfortably around his torso. From the top drawer of his dresser, he took a small baby food jar and put it in his hoodie's pouch as he walked out of his bedroom.

Ronnie walked back to his living room and flipped on a light switch for the lamp sitting on an end table. He reached into his book bag, sat on the couch, and pulled out a text book called *Organic Farming* and a red fine tip pen. The graduate student took a seat and began to read a section on organic pesticides. He didn't move for an hour and a half.

Deep in concentration, Ronnie was usually strict when it came to his studies. During the last 20 minutes or so, his concentration wavered. Thoughts of the girl next door kept popping into his head.

The image of her wearing those mirrored sunglasses while her full lips moved as she talked on her iPhone threw off his focus. Ronnie couldn't keep the thoughts of the young lady's small jeweled belly button ring out of his head. He pictured her standing in those tight jean shorts undone, and that was it. Something primal went off his brain. It was enough for Ronnie to close his book and set it down on the coffee table in front of him. At that moment, human ego took over and inhibitions were cast aside. He had made up his mind. He was determined to meet the girl next door.

Ronnie's internal debate was over. Normally, self-doubt would talk him out of acting out on impulse, but on this occasion, desire overrode fears. Ronnie stood up from the couch, walked out of his apartment, crossed the hall to apartment C, and without hesitation, he knocked on the girl's door.

The next 10 seconds seemed to last an eternity, but surprisingly Ronnie remained calm and cool. His renewed mental focus kept his heart rate under control. He didn't care about the results, but he couldn't live with himself if he didn't try.

Ronnie wasn't nervous at all when he heard footsteps walking toward the door. The knob turned and the door opened to reveal the girl next door. She was still breathtaking, standing there wearing a white shirt with a knot on the bottom right side that exposed her midriff and jeweled belly button ring. Her faded jean shorts were now buttoned and zipped and they fit snuggly around her curved, narrow hips.

Without her mirrored sunglasses, she was even more alluring. Her tan complexion and long dark hair contrasted with her pale green eyes. Ronnie was more mesmerized by the girl's beautiful face than he ever had been as she greeted him, "Hey, neighbor."

Ignoring his impulses and thinking on his feet, Ronnie responded, "Hey, I need a favor. I was getting ready to bake some muffins and I don't have enough sugar. I really don't feel like running to the store, so I was hoping I could barrow a couple cups from you."

"Oh," the neighbor girl said, "what kind of muffins?"

Thinking quickly, Ronnie improvised, "Carrot cake with cream cheese filling. It's my mom's recipe."

"Oh my God, that sounds utterly delightful. Do you think we can get some?" she asked.

With a crooked half-grin on his face, Ronnie answered, "Sure."

"Well, come on in, I'll grab it for you." The young lady opened the door and gave an inviting nod. Ronnie followed her into the apartment. At first glance, the apartment was similar to his own, mainly in layout. However, the décor could not have been more different. It was beautifully decorated with figurines on the shelves and paintings of colored birds on the walls. It smelled nice, like fresh flowers. The living room furniture was a matching set with the sage green cloth couch and loveseat. In the corner a 42-inch flat screen sat on top of a small entertainment center. A brown and beige Sultanaband area rug and a glass coffee table set completed the room. Due care was used in the placement of everything in the apartment.

On the couch sat another dark haired 20-something girl, her bare feet on the cushions, engrossed in her reading. She wore a white, sleeveless button-down shirt and a pair of pink Capri denim jeans. She looked directly at Ronnie and gave a slight wave. He returned the gesture and she returned her attention to her book— *Ham on Rye* by Charles Bukowski.

The young lady that had invited Ronnie into the apartment turned toward him. She extended her hand. "Well neighbor, I'm glad you stopped by. I think it's important to be neighborly. My name is Francesca by the way; Francesca Alexander, but my friends call me Frankie."

The young man gently shook her extended hand and introduced himself with a friendly smile. "I'm Ronnie Lee Harding. You have a beautiful place."

"Well thank you, Ronnie," returned Frankie, "but all the credit for the décor has to go to Molly, my roommate." She pointed to the girl sprawled out on the couch. Molly looked up and grinned again before returning to her book.

Still friendly, Frankie added, "Listen Ronnie. Let me get you that sugar. I'll be back in a second." She walked off to the kitchen.

When Frankie stepped out of the room, Molly placed a bookmark in the crease of her book and closed it. She looked at the man standing in her living room. "Ronnie, can I ask you something?"

With a curious expression, he answered, "Sure, go ahead?"

Still looking comfortable on her couch, Molly asked, "Are you an assassin or are you a serial killer?"

"What's that supposed to mean?" A confused Ronnie couldn't hold back a chuckle as he asked his question.

"You know," Molly explained, "only assassins and serial killers go by their full name. John Wayne Gacy, Lee Harvey Oswald, Mark David Chapman, John Wilkes Booth..."

Ronnie pointed his fingers like a gun and countered, "Sic semper tyrannis." Those were the words that John Wilkes Booth yelled after he shot President Lincoln. With a little laugh, he added, "And no, I'm neither assassin nor serial killer. I'm just not that interesting."

Molly smiled as Ronnie continued his explanation, "It started when I was a little boy. Every time I got in trouble, my mom would yell out my full name. So, since I was in a constant state of mischief, all I ever heard was God damn it, Ronnie Lee; you better stop that, Ronnie Lee; I'm going to whip that ass, Ronnie Lee. That's all I ever heard growing up and after enough repetition, it just stuck with me. Plus, I like the way it sounds when I introduce myself to people."

"Well, if you're not an assassin or serial killer, why don't you take a seat, Ronnie Lee?" Molly said with a welcoming smile and a gesture toward the loveseat.

Accepting the invitation, Ronnie walked over to the smaller sofa and sat down. He noticed the glass figurines and vases that rested on the coffee table in front of him. One larger glass piece in particular drew his attention. It had a narrow cylinder at the top that expanded into a wide base, like a laboratory beaker. There was a small bowl connected to a thin glass stem that was inserted into the wider glass base. Ronnie pondered for a moment and abruptly asked in a higher pitch, "Is that a bong?"

A pinkish hue filled Molly's pouty baby face cheeks as she explained, "Uh yeah, I was going to jump up and try to hide when you walked in, but I decided to not call attention to myself and just play it off. I was hoping you'd think it was a vase or something."

"Well, it looks well maintained, clean and very pristine," Ronnie said, impressed.

Walking into the room, Frankie extended her hand to offer Ronnie a small Tupperware container of sugar as she interjected herself into the conversation, "It ought to be. I'm the one who cleans it. Smoking through glassware is a big part of my heritage."

Accepting the container of sugar and setting it on the coffee table, Ronnie inquired, "So, you're Arabic?"

"No," Frankie explained, "I'm actually half Persian from my mother's side."

The young man hummed for a second and added, "Interesting."

"It is. Isn't it? But that's where I learned to smoke herb through glass hookahs. The Persians have been doing it for centuries." Frankie paused for a moment. "It's too bad we don't have any weed right now."

Reaching into the front pocket of his hoodie, Ronnie said, "I have some." He pulled out the capped off baby food jar full of Probie, and handed it over to Frankie. "Here."

With a naughty grin on her face, Frankie held the clear glass baby food jar with her index finger and thumb and inspected the tangled green, red, orange and purple strands inside. She brought the jar closer to her nose and unscrewed the cap. The strong, pungent aroma caused her face to instantly contort. "Oh my God!" the standing young lady exclaimed, "This is the strongest weed I've ever smelled in my life. It's overwhelmingly skunky, but it has sweet citrus smell to it. It's like orange blossoms with nutmeg and pine. I've never smelled anything like this before."

An astonished smile broke out on Frankie's face as she screwed the lid of the jar back on. She gazed at Ronnie and asked, "Do you really want to get high?" Frankie passed the jar back to him.

Setting the baby food jar on the glass coffee table, the young man shrugged and said, "I don't have anything else going on tonight, so yeah, I'm game."

Frankie turned her attention to Molly and asked, "Well, what about you?"

"The only thing I have is a 12:30 class in the afternoon tomorrow, so I'm good if you guys are." said Molly.

With a scoundrel's smile on her face, Frankie walked over to the coffee table and picked up her elegant bong. "I'll get this ready." The gleeful young woman walked to the kitchen.

Ronnie and Molly were left in the living room. He leaned forward in the loveseat and said, "You know, not to be uncool or anything, but I never smoked out of a bong before."

Molly sat up on the sofa and put her feet on the floor, while she looked at Ronnie's face. "Well, you're in for a treat, because she really does know what she's doing. This will be one of the best ways you'll ever smoke pot. We'll show you how. Don't worry, we've got you."

Upon hearing that, Ronnie appreciated her understanding and maturity. He began to notice Molly's physical beauty as well. In the background, Ronnie could hear the sounds of trickling water as it filled the bong. Curiously, he also heard the familiar sound of ice clanking against glass. While the bong was in the kitchen being pre-pared, Ronnie thought about how the two girls were like a 'Ginger and Mary Ann' metaphor. Frankie was an exotic beauty, like a movie starlet, and Molly was the adorably cute one that every boy would have a crush on. Molly was the girl next door. He felt lucky to even be where he was, sharing this experience, and proud that he had plucked up the courage to walk over and knock on the door.

Genuinely humming a happy tune, Frankie returned to the living room with the bong ready to go. There was water in the base and ice cubes in the top cylinder. While she set it on the table, Molly spoke kindly, "Hey Frankie, Ronnie has never used a bong before. Could you explain it to him?"

"Absolutely, no problem." Frankie said in a considerate fashion. She pointed at the water filled wider base beaker portion of the bong while she explained, "Okay Ronnie, there are a lot of different types of bongs out there. Mine is called a double diffuser. It has two water filters. The first one is here at the fatter base." She first pointed at bottom of the bong while she explained. Then, she pointed higher up on the vertical glass tube, "And the other one is here on the narrow cylinder." Frankie continued, "THC in marijuana is not water soluble, so it passes through the water filters, while the soot, ash, and the other non-desirables are caught in the water. You'll be taking a purer hit during your drag."

Ronnie interjected himself, "Well, what's the ice for?"

"Do you see these indentions on the glass cylinder here?" She pointed at the top tube portion sticking out from the fatter base and continued, "Just above the smaller second water filter." Ronnie nodded before she finished her explanation, "These notches are ice catchers. The filtered smoke will pass over the ice cubes, here in the tube chamber portion, which will cool the temperature of the smoke and allow you to take in a less irritable hit. You'll feel the difference as you inhale."

"Go ahead Frankie, show him how it's done," insisted Molly.

Watching intently, Ronnie observed while Frankie she knelt down near the coffee table. She moved with an elegant grace as she set down her iPhone and reached for the baby food jar of Probie. She neatly packed the marijuana into the small bowl section of the bong's clear glass downward stem that flowed into the wider glass base of the bong.

Frankie reached into her jean shorts pocket, pulled out a green translucent cigarette lighter and with a single flick of her thumb; she lit the flame to apply it to the marijuana in the bowl. With a hypnotic motion, she leaned forward and brought her lips to the open o-ring glass cylinder mouth piece and created a seal as she inhaled. Her breath drew the flame into the bowl and the marijuana embers glowed red and gold, while the water at both filter levels bubbled as smoke moved past the first diffuser. More bubbles percolated as a milky white smoke began to build up and fill the wide base of the bong's chamber.

With a smooth hand movement, Frankie removed the bowl stopper from the glass downward stem. The wispy smoke shotgun passed the second water diffuser filter on the upper cylinder while it bubbled hard as the bong was cleared. She was no beginner. The filtered marijuana smoke passed over the ice cubes within the narrow cylinder and was cooled before she inhaled it. The chemically enriched smoke entered her respiratory system, spread the deepest part of her lungs, and infiltrated the permeable tissue of her alveoli, where oxygen enters the blood stream. There, the marijuana's chemicals, the cannabinoids within the smoke, particularly THC and CBD, hitched a ride and circulated throughout her body.

After inhaling, Frankie removed her mouth from the glass cylinder opening. She closed her eyes and held her breath for a moment before she exhaled. Frankie opened her eyes and for a brief moment, stuck the tip of her tongue through her lips as smoke swirled from her mouth. The young lady then looked at Ronnie, and said, "It tastes a little like mangos and berries with a lot of cedar. But it was very smooth."

Frankie passed the glass bong over to Molly, and high took effect on Frankie's body. She had no idea she had just smoked such a unique strain of marijuana. The young woman had smoked some good pot over the years but those varieties of cannabis were typically high in THC only. Probie, on the other hand, was Ronnie's unique hybrid, and its high concentrations of CBD counteracted some of THC's negative qualities. The two chemicals entered her blood stream and worked together to create a distinct high in her system.

Within moments, the THC in Frankie's blood made its way to the base of her brain. It located the appropriate receptors of her ventral tegmental area, near her brain stem, and caused an increase in the production of dopamine, the happy hormone in her system. The increase of this body chemical caused a mental and physical sense of euphoria throughout her whole being as her body relaxed and her mind mellowed, while all her senses heightened. Her imagination was stimulated as she enjoyed increasing waves of physical, mental, and emotional pleasure.

Generally, the downside of high amounts of THC was that it negatively affected things such as motor skills, learning function, and short-term memory. This usually resulted in mental haziness, physical clumsiness, and patches of amnesia. This was why people who were stoned would often ask in the middle of a conversation, "Huh, what were we talking about?"

That's where the higher concentrations of CBD offered its benefit. The CBD moving through Frankie's circulatory system found the receptors of her hippocampus within her brain ahead of THC and protected her temporal lobe. This prevented her from suffering short-term memory loss or learning problems. Her mind was totally free to enjoy all the THC induced pleasure without any mental restrictions. The CBD in her system also shielded the receptors of her brain's cerebellum and basal ganglia from THC, which allowed complete control of her physical motor skills. She was enjoying her full body high with little to no clumsiness.

The most important benefit of the CBD floating in Frankie's system was that it prevented high concentrations of THC from overwhelming her brain's amygdala. A portion of the amygdala was known as the fear circuit. This is where the fight or flight response originates. When THC bonded with the receptors in this part of the brain, a person would experience strong paranoia, which was a negative side effect of marijuana. Probie's elevated CBD concentrations jump ahead of its THC counterpart and protect this section of the brain, so there were no excessive fears or related disorders during a Probie based high. In short, there is no wigging out on Probie.

As the high grew within Frankie's mind and body, she took her second hit from the bong and watched the other two do the same as the bong was passed around the coffee table. Feeling her full high take over, she looked at the young man sitting comfortably on the loveseat and said, "Ronnie, this is really good weed."

Feeling the elation himself, he agreed with a simple nod.

After some time, the THC that was in Frankie's system was now bonding with more receptors of her brain's hypothalamus and her body responded by revving up the production of the hormone ghrelin. As this natural chemical started to increase in her body, Frankie began to feel a little hungry. The 'munchies' were setting in as she look at Ronnie and said, "It's too bad we don't have any of those muffins now."

"What muffins?" a surprised Ronnie answered.

Frankie's eyes widened as she had an epiphany. Her attention jumped to her roommate, who was sitting on the couch, and she emphatically declared, "Molly, this guy just ran the 'can I borrow a cup of sugar' line on us. And it worked."

With shock, Molly's mouth opened and she said, "No! He didn't."

"Yes, he did." Frankie added, "There were never any carrot cake muffins with cream cheese filling. He played us." The two girls both stared at the young man sitting in their loveseat.

His face turned red as he defended himself in a high pitched voice, "No. No. No. There are muffins. They're my specialty. I'll have some over tomorrow. I promise."

"You'd better." Frankie responded and broke out in uncontrollable giggles.

Trying to restrain her own laughter, Molly added, "You know Ronnie, you're not allowed over again until you bake us those muffins, and they'd better not be store bought either."

Ronnie could feel his face warm as a mischievous grin spread across his lips. "No, I promise. I'll bring you over the muffins and I'll bake them with these very hands." He held up both palms and wiggled all of his fingers, and attempted to restrain his own snickering.

With the high of the marijuana now taking its full effect, Molly had a difficult time scolding him, as "You better," was the only thing she could get from her lips between the giggles that were now unmanageable. The room broke out in laughter and the three friends could not restrain themselves any more. The euphoria of their high was tickling them on the inside uncontrollably. Everything now was ridiculously funny. Probie was in full effect.

The laughter and merriment continued for awhile and at some point Ronnie and Molly joined Frankie on the floor by the coffee table. Now, as the laughing subsided, everyone was breathing hard between chuckles. With tears of laughter in their eyes, they began to mellow out but they were still feeling the gratification of their full body and head high. Ronnie's ribs were actually sore from laughing so much, when Frankie repeated her compliment, "Hey, this is really good weed. It may be the best I've ever tried. I haven't laughed this hard in a long time."

Nodding, Ronnie agreed when he returned his own compliment, "Yeah, and smoking this bong, with the ice in it, was the smoothest hit I've ever tried. You guys definitely know what you're doing."

"Why, thank you," returned Frankie.

At that moment, the iPhone on the coffee table began to ring; Frankie picked it up and looked at the display. She hit the accept button on the screen and bought it to her ear. "Hey you," was her greeting. She stood up off the floor and held up an index finger to her roommate and Ronnie, excusing herself. They nodded as she walked through the glass sliding doors to step on the balcony. The sliding door closed behind her, leaving Ronnie and Molly alone on the living room floor.

Leaning toward the coffee table between them, the young man looked at Molly's adorable face and restarted the conversation, "Well Molly, I told you the story behind my name. What's the story behind yours?"

"Well, my full name is Molly Jo Donnelly. And the answer to your question is Whiskey in the Jar," said the young woman with a glowing expression.

Still enjoying his full high, Ronnie stared into her soft brown eyes and asked, "You mean the Metallica song?"

"Well, my dad was more of a Thin Lizzy fan." Molly was reminiscing while she continued, "The song is actually an Irish folk song that goes back to the late 60s. Over years, when the Irish settled in Detroit, near old Tiger Stadium, they brought their music and traditions with them. When Thin Lizzy recorded their version, well that was it for my dad. When all the local bars and pubs were blaring that song over their speakers, my father thought the Molly in that song must have been the most beautiful woman in the world. So, when I was born, there was only one choice for my name and that was Molly, the Irish version of Helen of Troy."

As she told her story, Ronnie listened intently and paid special attention to her facial features. He noticed her shoulder length, dark brown hair that contrasted her soft pale skin. Her small nose with baby-like puffy cheeks and pouty lips made her absolutely adorable in his opinion. When she finished her story, Ronnie offered a simple hum, before he said, "I'm going to have to go home and download it. I'll give it a good listen this time."

Molly returned a simple appreciative glance before she asked, "Do you want to play some Yahtzee?"

"Yeah," Ronnie answered, "I don't mind if we do."

"Well boy, prepare to get your ass pencil whipped." The young lady said before she made the whip cracking sound and a matching hand gesture.

Still feeling good from Probie's effect, Ronnie offered a slight laugh when he said, "Bring it on, girl. Bring it on."

Molly's pouty lips couldn't contain her admiring smile as she got up off the floor.

While she left the room, Ronnie thought, *Wow, there's something really special about this girl. I'm so glad I came over here and knocked on the door.*

6

HEAD AND DEM CREEK BOYZ

Certain parts of Detroit are tar pits. They're traps without an escape. As economic conditions deteriorated in pockets of the city, the locals were robbed of the means to fix up their neighborhoods. There was nothing to stem the tide. As the bottom fell out of the Motor City, residents were stuck in the city because of their own financial ruin. Life savings and net worth disappeared in the shrinking equity of Detroit's homes.

Those who remained in these crippled communities witnessed their neighborhoods crumbling daily. Most felt powerless to do anything about it. It was a hard life for many residents; to prevent themselves from becoming victims of others in their own community, many chose hurting and stealing as a way of life. The Rouge Creek neighborhood, also known as The Creek, was located on the city's southwest side and considered one of those economic tar pits.

To escape the societal entrapments of Detroit, a lot of the young people in these neighborhoods developed unique plans to get out. Rap demos and sports aspirations were only pipe dreams for the majority, but for the rare, gifted individual, they were a ticket to a better life.

25-years ago, Bill Hutchinson was a senior in high school. He was one of those exceptional Detroiters. Football was his ticket out of The Creek and his escape plan from Detroit. He was a running back for John C. Kronk High School and he led the Jesters in back-to-back city and state championships during his junior and senior year. Bill had a rare combination of great size, unmatched speed, tremendous power and a fearless nature to deal out punishment every time he carried the rock. The 6-1, 225 pound running back ran a legit 4.4 in the 40 yard dash and had a great spin move backed by a brutal stiff arm that routinely threw defenders to the turf. If a tackler tried to go low and take his knees out, they were hurdled immediately. He was a wrecking ball who could easily run around you and then run you over. He had good hands too. The only thing that could bring down Bill was a gang tackle, and when that happened, he took every dirty shot without complaint because later in the game, he'd dole out his own pain as revenge.

When he was a boy, Bill's family and friends had given him a nickname. Bill had one very distinct body feature: a very large, thick, and oblong shaped skull. This is where he got the nickname Head. His momma called him Head, and the rest of his family followed. No one ever talked about his other physical characteristics, like his bronze skin or the dense freckle patches on both of his cheeks. Certainly, no one ever mentioned anything about his lazy eye. It was always about that big ole cranium, his trademark and nickname.

Football was Head's plan to get out of the hood. During his senior year, ever major college in the country was recruiting him. He was leaning to play for one of the big Los Angeles Universities, until a medical examination discovered that he had an extreme arrhythmia -- an irregular heartbeat. Once the word was out about his health issue, every college dropped his recruitment, scared of the liability. Some colleges wouldn't even take his calls. Head's dream of playing college football died.

Angry at the world, Head went through his grieving process. For the first year, he felt sorry for himself. He refocused his life with one simple phrase: "Fuck Hollywood." Giving up on his California dream, Head decided that if he was going to be stuck in the trap, then he was going to get some control. He wasn't going to be at the mercy of The Creek. The Creek was going to be at his mercy.

When his younger brother, Wayne Hutchinson, introduced him to the art of growing high quality marijuana, Head saw the potential. He saw his destiny. Head and his little brother, who was known throughout the neighborhood as Baby Hutch, along with their crew of loyal friends, were going to control the weed game, not only in their neighborhood, but in the entire Southwest corner of Detroit. They had an ambitious plan.

Over the next several years, through intimidation, violence and a willingness to do whatever was necessary, Head and his crew drove out the competition and went on to monopolize the marijuana trade in The Creek. Prohibition and violence went hand and hand. These young dealers never bothered with cocaine or heroin in any of its forms; they saw the devastation that these narcotics brought to their community and wanted no part of it. They made it a part of their mission to chase these types of drugs out of the Creek. They stuck to the only thing that they liked, which was dealing weed. It was their niche and they weren't going to be challenged in their own neighborhood. On the streets, their crew was known as Dem Creek Boyz, or the DCBz for short.

With their monopoly came tremendous monetary success. Their organization expanded, but remained efficient under the control of their fearless leader, Head. He was the boss and CEO. No one challenged him and lived to tell about it. The only two people Head trusted were the two babies. The first was his little brother Wayne Hutchinson, or Baby Hutch, and his other captain, Scott James, who was known as Baby Jay. Baby Hutch was responsible for the supply and distribution of marijuana as their primary form of cash flow, and Baby Jay was responsible for all the things that no one wanted to talk about in public.

Over the next 10 years, under Head's executive leadership, Dem Creek Boyz made an ingenuous investment. They took a big portion of the cash from dealing marijuana and bought the old abandoned manufacturing site for the Panther Steel Company on Slug Island, which just sat off the coast in the Detroit River. They bought it from the county for a small fraction of back taxes owed, because no one else wanted to clean it up. Head and his crew were going to convert this site into their own scrap and salvage yard. They called their new business enterprise Nain Rouge Recycling, after the Red Dwarf from Detroit folklore.

The Slug Island location was perfect for their operation because the site was a large industrial fenced-in lot with ample railroad spurs and a shipping dock right on the property. In the scrap game, it's about moving weight, and there is no cheaper way to move tonnage than by train and cargo ship. Scrappers were cutting any kind of metal they could find from the abandoned buildings littered across the Motor City, and they would bring their scrap copper, aluminum, brass, and other salvage metals to the Nain Rouge yard to make some money.

Each haul of scrap metal was sorted and weighed before the weigh-master would offer the scrappers their options on receiving their payment, "How would you like to be paid? Would you like that in check or cash?"

All the scrappers would answer uniformly, "Cash, please."

"No problem," The Nain Rouge staffers would reply, as they paid off each scrapper with their illegal marijuana money in cash.

Head's company would then collect the sorted metal by the ton and sell to a commodities broker or the foundries, directly, for re-smelting. Nain Rouge Recycling would always be paid with a check. They would deposit checks into a bank where they had their business checking account. Proper accounting books were kept and, most importantly, taxes were filed. Head never had a problem paying taxes, because he knew that's what they got Al Capone for when he ran the streets of Chicago.

The two business operations were symbiotic. Their illegal weed business kept them flush with cash and the scrap business enterprise laundered the money. Both ventures grew and profited, but it was the salvage business that allowed Dem Creek Boyz to transition into legitimate businessmen. We're talking multi-millions here. With legitimate money, they made political contributions to the Mayor and County Commissioner's Offices. They also contributed to the Police Chief's Widows and Orphan fund as a charitable deduction. This helped them stay off law enforcement radar.

In recent years, Head and the DCBz also made the daring investments back into their own neighborhood, buying up old abandoned buildings for next to nothing and either fixing them up or tearing them down. They wanted to improve housing quality while making money cleaning up The Creek, and create legitimate jobs for the locals in the process. They paid generously, cleaning up parks and ball fields throughout The Creek. This allowed Dem Creek Boyz to develop reputations as the Robin Hoods of Detroit's Southwest Side. No local would cooperate with law enforcement against Dem Creek Boyz out of loyalty and admiration for the good they did. Head and his crew were loved in The Creek. In many ways, they were no longer drug dealers and gangsters; they were genuine leaders of the community.

Today, Head was 43 years old and 25 pounds heavier than in his football glory days, but he kept himself up well. Wearing a form fitting dark green polo shirt and a pair of blue Carhartt worker dungarees, Head sat in a conference room in his office main building at the salvage yard. It was sparsely decorated, but neatly organized. A large oak table sat in the middle of the room surrounded by chairs. File cabinets lined the back wall. His little brother, Baby Hutch, 39, was seated to his left. Baby Hutch was a smaller and stockier version of his brother. He was shorter at 5-10, darker in complexion, and both of his eyes were straight. The other man at the table was Baby Jay, 40, and unlike the other men in the room, was very thin at 185 pounds. He considered himself to be a younger version of Billy D. Williams. He was a smooth talking black Casanova who never became visibly excited, no matter the circumstances. The three men sat on one side of the conference table with Head in the center.

Another man sat on the opposite side of the table. Otis Hall Jr., a 28-year-old African American and a long-time resident of The Creek was just looking for a job, either with the Nain Rouge salvage yard or elsewhere on their construction crews. This was his job interview with the three men in charge, and he needed the work desperately. Sitting upright in his chair, Otis felt he did well answering the interview questions. With his hand resting on his knees, the conference table concealed the job seeker's fingers, which were nervously tapping away as Head reviewed his employment application and checked his qualifications.

Flipping through the application and attached résumé, Head said in his deep rich tone, "Well Otis, we would like to offer you a job as a construction laborer. It pays $18 an hour."

In a wave of relief, an uncontrollable smile sprung on Otis's lips. "Oh my, thank you, sir. You won't regret this."

Reaching, Head grabbed the yellow legal pad that was on the tabletop. He took his pen and began to scribble some notes. Head tore off the top sheet from the pad and handed it to Otis as he instructed, "Next Monday, I want you to go over to this address on Harrington Street at 9 a.m. It's a four story brick apartment building. I want you to go the manager's office and ask to speak to Crazy White Man."

"Crazy White Man?" Otis's bewilderment was obvious.

With a smirk on face, Head explained, "Don't worry, he's the building owner. I want you to tell him that we're paying you and that you're going to be helping him out for a month. I want you to work hard for the man; he needs help fixing his apartments units. He needs a good carpenter and laborer. Can you handle that?"

Otis nodded his understanding. "Yes, sir."

Head stood up and walked around his two other seated associates to Otis's side of the table. Head extended hand to the new employee and the two men shook hands to seal the deal. The business owner patted Otis on his back before he instructed, "Now, I want you to go talk my office manager, Francis. She'll help fill out all the paperwork to get you on our payroll. You're going to need your driver's license and your social security card."

"Yes, sir." Otis folded the yellow sheet of paper and stuck in his front jeans pocket, before he said, "Sir, I just wanted to say I truly appreciate this opportunity. You won't regret this."

Escorting him out of the room, Head said, "I know. Go ahead and talk to Francis. If you have any problems, make sure you let her know. Okay?"

Nodding his understanding, Otis let himself out of the room.

Head closed the door before he turned and faced his two executives still seated at the conference table. He took a seat facing his two associates. It was Head's little brother, Baby Hutch, who spoke first, "Why do you have such a soft spot for Crazy White Man?"

"Just hear me out." Head smiled, but explained, "When we decided to go into real estate as a business venture, resetting our own neighborhood, we knew it was going to be a big pain in our ass. All the rich billionaire corporate guys are buying up all the large buildings downtown in a skyscraper fire sale, but they're ignoring the neighborhoods where the people live in the city."

Baby Jay sat still at the table and Baby Hutch nodded his understanding as Head continued, "We're some of the few people trying to fix up The Creek. When you fix up one building on a blighted block, what happens?"

"You'll lose your ass." His little brother answered, "No matter how much money you put into a single building, you'll lose equity instantly if it's on a neighborhood block that's hit. There will be nothing gained and plenty lost. It becomes a money pit."

With a leer on his lips, Head said, "Right. You have to fix every building on the block in order to get a bump on appraisals across the board. That's how you make money in the hood. We're acquiring these buildings for next to nothing because no one else wants them. We've been paying the locals to work on them fixing them up, so we're providing legitimate jobs. Now that the buildings are freshly renovated, we've been having no problems renting them out. So, we're also creating quality housing. With our buildings full of paying renters, what's happening to our property appraisals?"

Widening his eyes, Baby Hutch answered, "They've been going through the roof across the board."

Head pounded his fist lightly a couple times on the table top before he pointed his finger at his brother. "With elevated appraisals, now when we go to the banks to refinance the properties, they have no problem saying yes. Then they pay us out with a check. We're making a profit and the money is laundered. You got that?"

Baby Hutch nodded his agreement to his older brother.

With both of his muscular arms resting on the table, Head interlocked his fingers. "It's a daunting tasking fixing up this fucked neighborhood one block at a time. To tell you the truth, we can't really do it alone. We're not getting much help out there. One of the few people that are helping us fix up these buildings is who?"

Folding his arms across his chest and offering a conceding expression, Baby Hutch responded, "Crazy White Man."

"That's right," Head's leadership was coming through as he carried on, "This man inherited 12 Section-8 HUD buildings in our neighborhood. He fixes them up and runs them like the buildings were somewhere in the suburbs. He's not a slum lord. It's probably driving him crazy in the process and I'd bet he's barely making it financially, but the buildings he's restoring are on same blocks that we're working at."

Pausing a moment, Head brought his hand to his chin. "I actually talked to the guy for a bit on the street. His name is John something something. I asked him, 'why are you putting yourself through all this?' You know what he said?"

Raising his eyebrows, Head's little brother asked, "What?"

Head immediately answered, "It was his father who left him the buildings when he passed away. He said his dad would have done it the exact same way. He's doing it to honor his father." The boss cleared his throat, before he continued, "That's why I have a soft spot for the guy. Plus, we need him to succeed. The job that he's doing is helping our property valuations. We actually need more people like him, because we can't carry this weight on our own. Do you see the big picture now?"

Closing his eyes for a brief moment, Baby Hutch's lips curled into a grin. "Yeah, I see the big picture," The little brother relented.

The third man in the room, Baby Jay, sat patiently while two brothers hashed out their issues. Baby Jay never spoke a word during these conversations because he had known the Hutchinson brothers for nearly 30 years and had learned it was pointless to get involved until they settled down. He sat quietly during the exchange.

With all three men sitting at the conference table, it was Head's little brother who restarted the conversation, "Hey, I want to talk about something important."

"Go ahead." Head acknowledged.

"Well," Baby Hutch spoke, "Some of our dealers are telling us that there's a new weed strain coming out of the Capital area. The reviews have been outstanding. It's fetching top dollar and inventories are disappearing overnight. There's not much supply out there, but from what I'm hearing, it seems to be steadily growing. I'm thinking it's a small time grower or two."

The boss looked at his little brother and said, "So what?"

His office chair squeaked as Baby Hutch leaned back before he folded his arm across his chest. "I scored some. I was able to try it out. It's good, really good. And as much as I hate saying this, it's better than anything I've ever grown. They're calling it Probie, after the hockey player. I would say if you blindfolded me and put me up to the taster's challenge. I would pick theirs, 9 out 10 times. That's a potential problem."

With his eyes narrowing, Head commented, "Probie, I remember that cat skating on the ice. That guy could brawl. We should watch some of his old fights on YouTube." He paused to refocus himself on his little brother's concerns. "I just don't see the problem about these small-timers."

"I want you to know, it's that good. This Probie is a game changer." Baby Hutch explained, "Small time growers have a way of blowing up in the weed game. You have to think back to 20 years ago when we started off. We were small-timers too. We were able to lock down and hold this market because we grew the best. Right now, I'm telling you as your expert this is something to be concerned about if they expand their production or worse yet, if a rival gets control of it. They can use it to devalue our prices or force their way back into The Creek. We'd have to compete for our territory again."

Head's eyes widen before he answered, "Now, I see the problem. We have too many things up in the air and we need every dollar from all of our operations. We can't have anyone throw a wrench in our machine. We've been too successful for too long and we can't get complacent."

Nodding, Baby Hutch said, "Now, you see the big picture."

"Yep." Head replied. He immediately turned his attention to the quiet man at the table. "Baby Jay!"

The quiet man answered, "Yeah, Boss."

"You want to ride up to the Capital?" Head said to his most trusted friend. "We'll put you up in a nice hotel and you can beat the streets looking for the source of Probie. I bet you it's them college kids up there at Michigan A&M."

"What do you want me to do when I find it?" asked Baby Jay.

Cracking his knuckles on his hands, Head simply said, "We'll cross that bridge when we come to it."

Now, on a mission, Baby Jay nodded and started walking toward the door. He spoke clearly when he said, "Yo, man. I got this. I'll take care of this really quick for you, boss."

Head calmly replied, "I know you will."

7

GROW SCHOOL

S tanding in his narrow apartment kitchen, Ronnie picked up his iPod and synced it with the portable Bluetooth speaker that sat on his countertop. With a swipe of his thumb, he scrolled through the list of artists and stopped the screen on his 'metal' playlist. A light tap opened the group's song list and with another tap the Bluetooth speaker roared to life with loud waves of electrical guitar chords as the song *"Whiskey in the Jar"* began to play.

The oven was set to 375 degrees, and the fourth tin of carrot cake muffins was baking. The previous batch of muffins had turned out perfectly; they sat on the counter and cooled on a wire rack, almost ready to be pumped full of cream cheese filling. Ronnie waited for his last tin to finish in his comfortable clothes: dark blue cotton shorts and a gray baseball shirt with dark blue sleeves. He leaned against the kitchen sink with his eyes closed and moved his head to the beat. With his eyes still closed, Ronnie allowed every part of the song to fill up his soul as he took in every lyric.

With both hands tapping out the drummer's beat on his thighs, Ronnie thought about the girl in the song, Molly. *She had to be a hell of a girl,* thought the young man. He knew he was in a hazy state of infatuation with the girl who lived across the hall, also named Molly. Like the inspirational Molly in the song, the girl across the hall was the reason he was baking these muffins. Since they had met a few days ago, she hadn't left his thoughts.

With his eyes closed and head bobbing to the rhythm, Ronnie started to sing out loud, completely immersed in the song. He was smiling as he thought about the two Mollies. As the song was nearing its end, Ronnie heard his door buzzing repeatedly. Slightly startled, he walked over to the intercom on the wall and pressed the button. "Yeah?"

Paul's voice came yelling through the speaker, "Dude! I've been standing here ringing this button for over two minutes now. I know you're up there. I can hear your music blasting throughout the whole courtyard."

Laughing, Ronnie pressed the intercom button again and said, "Sorry man, come on up." He pressed another button on the intercom panel and unlocked the door.

A few moments later, Paul walked into Ronnie's apartment wearing a black V-neck tee shirt and relaxed cut blue jeans with a pair of black work boots. He walked in as the song, "*Whiskey in the Jar*" ended. While Paul was standing in the living room, the sound of a heavy church bell bonging came from the speaker, followed by a series of heavy metal guitar riffs. It was the intro to the next metal song, *For Whom the Bell Tolls.*

Paul heard the first heavy electric guitar chord and immediately spread his legs and strummed his best air guitar. His long black mane of silky hair flipped and flowed in the air as Paul bobbed his head with the beat, heavy metal style.

Ronnie laughed as he watched his friend's mock performance but then thought, *He does look like a rock star.* Smiling, Ronnie walked over to join his friend and jammed out on his own air guitar. Shifting his weight from his back foot to the front one and back again while dropping his head on every mock guitar's down stroke, Ronnie was getting into the music. For a few moments, they were lost in their rock and roll fantasy. It was a case of two 20-something-year-old men having some gregarious fun.

In the middle of the song, Ronnie snapped out of it. He reached into his shorts pocket, pulled out his iPod, and immediately pressed pause. The speaker went silent and Ronnie heard the oven's buzzer going off. "Damn! You almost made me burn my muffins." He hustled back over to the kitchen.

"Man," Paul hollered out, "I didn't know you could bake. Is that what smells so good?"

Grabbing an oven mitt from the counter, Ronnie opened the oven, pulled out the muffin tin, and set it on a kitchen towel. He closed the oven door and reached for a toothpick to poke his muffin tops. "Ah, they're perfect." Turning off the oven, Ronnie felt relieved as he flipped the last batch of muffins on the wire cooling rack on the remaining counter top.

Sticking his head through the kitchen doorway, Paul asked, "Hey, can I get one of those?"

"Grab one from that rack over there." Ronnie pointed and instructed, "Those are already cooled and filled."

Paul grabbed a carrot cake muffin and smelled it before taking a bite. His face showed pleasant surprise while he said, "Damn man, this is good. Like seriously, I didn't know you could bake."

Placing the empty baking tin into the sink, Ronnie smirked at his friend. "I can follow a recipe."

"Let me guess. This whole baking thing is about a girl. Isn't it?" Paul asked before he took another bite. Ronnie turned his palms up and shrugged his shoulders.

"Your silence says everything." A devilish grin spread across Paul's face, as he continued, "You keep thinking there's the one, the-one-girl who is going to be the last hour of the day for you for the rest of your life. I keep telling you that fate doesn't work that way. People only come into your life for period and then they go on to something else. You have to use what fate throws in front of you at the moment."

Repeating his gesture, Ronnie closed his eyes and shrugged his shoulders. As he shook his head, he was determined not to engage his friend in a debate about women.

Paul understood that it was futile to press the conversation, so he turned walked back toward the living room and stared at Ronnie's sparsely decorated apartment. "Man, what the hell you do with your money?" Staring at Ronnie's furniture, Paul continued with a tinge of disgust in voice, "In the last year or so, you made over a quarter of a million in cash and you still drive that shitty minivan. You have one of the worst looking student apartments I've ever seen, so I'm so confused about what you do with your money."

Walking out from the kitchen into his living room, Ronnie simply answered, "I hide it."

"What do you mean, you hide it?" asked Paul abruptly in a higher pitch, "Do you like stuff all that cash in your mattress?"

Ronnie walked over to his old crushed velvet couch, plopped down, and put his bare feet on the cheap wooden coffee table, before he responded, "I just go see The Cutter."

Taking a seat in one of Ronnie's folding tailgate chairs, Paul asked, "Who the fuck is The Cutter?"

"It's this guy in Bloomington, Indiana." Ronnie explained, "He was born and raised there. Down in Bloomington, back in the day, the Hoosier college students use to refer to the locals as Cutters. It was supposed to be a disparaging put-down, as it traced back to local limestone industry there. Most of the locals worked in the quarries cutting away large slabs of rock. That's where the term came from and that's why my man calls himself that."

Paul nodded his head. "Go on."

Clearing his throat, Ronnie continued, "The Cutter actually graduated with his masters from the university down there in geology. He specialized in rare metal and minerals including..." Ronnie paused for dramatic effect and then said, "Gemstones."

Taking his work boots off the coffee table, Paul leaned forward, curious about what his friend had to say, "Go on."

"Gemstones are a concentrated kind of wealth." Ronnie explained, "It's really difficult walk around with $100,000 in cash in your pocket, but if you bought that amount in diamonds, rubies or sapphires, you could pull it off, and no one would know. It's the way to move large cash sums across international borders."

Paul's eyes narrowed and his forehead crinkled while he encouraged his friend with a keep-it-coming hand gesture.

Taking his cue, Ronnie continued, "Let's say you want to move large sum of money into a Swiss Bank account. The problem is getting the cash past airport security or customs. That's where the gemstones come in. It's easier to smuggle them into Europe than a duffle bag full of cash. Once there, you head off to a gem broker in let's say, Antwerp or Amsterdam, and then you convert the stones back into a brief case full of Euros or U.S. Dollars. Your next step is to take a ski trip to Switzerland and do your banking. According Swiss law, bankers are forbidden from disclosing even the existence of the account without permission, so your money would be safe and hidden. Gems -- it's the way things have been done since Marco Polo."

"Wow," Paul asked, "you mean to tell me that you have a couple hundred thousand in diamonds lying around here in this apartment?"

Smirk came across Ronnie's face as shook his head. "First of all, I never hide anything here. Secondly, this time it wasn't diamonds. It was five emeralds out of Zambia for $110,000 cash in the last duffle bag you gave me. The Cutter was in Africa doing exploratory core samples for the copper industry there and he was able to smuggle in some high quality emeralds in the rough out back into the United States. He cut and polished the rough stones into high quality facet gems and I bought them off of him at the friend price. Anytime I want, I just give back the stones and he gives me my cash back, dollar for dollar, with no interest."

Paul's eyes and forehead relaxed while he said, "It sounds risky."

"A lot of it is based on trust," Ronnie explained, "In this gem dealing world, there are not a lot of contracts and there are a lot of cash deals, so you have to trust the people you're dealing with. I trust him. I have never told anyone else about this and I want you to know I trust you explicitly."

A smile showed Paul's gratitude and he said, "Thanks bro. That means the world to me. I guess that brings me to the reason why I came over to see you in the first place."

"What's that?" Ronnie was slightly confused.

Paul sat up in his chair and shifted his facial expression to more of a serious one. "One of our dealers, Gerald Duffy, was busted last week."

The look of pain was apparent on Ronnie's face as he exclaimed, "Shut your whore mouth! Really?" His voice winced.

"Yeah," Paul was somber as he explained, "it was a pretty bad bust. They busted down his front door and shot his dog."

With disbelief, Ronnie said in a whisper tone, "Man, they always shoot the dog. I hate that."

The room was silent for a moment and Ronnie brought both palms up to his face while he processed this new information. When he uncovered his face, Ronnie exclaimed, "I want out! I didn't come to college for this."

"I know bro. You did this to help me out because I was in a bad way when I met you. This whole thing just took a life of its own. I understand this life wasn't meant for you and if you want out, then I want you out too. You come first in this whole thing." Paul consoled his friend.

Ronnie was a bundle of nerves as he brought both palms back to his face and groaned into them. The balance of his double life between medical researcher and illegal drug dealing was completely overturned. He had known a pattern of bad decisions would eventually bring him to a situation like this.

When Ronnie brought his hands down, Paul looked directly into his face and asked, "What do you want to do with this last harvest?"

"Just junk it. We're done!" Ronnie was emphatic.

Paul closed his eyes for a brief moment and exhaled through his nostrils before he explained, "Listen Ronnie, you need to take the emotions out of the game here. This harvest is going to be the largest ever. It's going to be over 150, maybe 160 pounds. Simply abandoning it in our grow room, with our fingerprints everywhere, doesn't seem like a smart move. Taking it and throwing it a dumpster or burning it in a bonfire seems like a dumber move. This is when people panic and get sloppy. When criminals get sloppy, they go to prison. What we need here is a smart exit strategy."

Taking in a deep breath and exhaling slowly, Ronnie agreed, "Yeah. So, what do you think?" He was regaining his composure.

Combing his fingers through his long black hair, Paul calmly explained, "We need to sell off the whole inventory properly, but I think we need more growers to cultivate this strain for the future. Right now, we have a monopoly because no one is growing Probie but us, and that means our plant's chemical fingerprint will always work its way back to us. Right now, it's just me and you. If other people are growing it, then we can fade away and stay off the radar; it'll become a commodity. That is an exit plan to me."

"Well, how do we do pull that off? Do we just give it away to the other growers?" asked Ronnie.

"No," Paul declared, "we open up a grow school so they can learn to do it right."

Ronnie reacted with shock and disbelief, and said, "Have you lost your goddamn mind?"

Leaning forward in his folding chair, Paul explained calmly, "Listen. Remember last March when I attended the LegalNow Conference in Denver? I was able to hang out with well known growers from all over. I brought a lot of Probie and I partied with some folks there. Trust me, we got rave reviews by some of the biggest names in the growing world. Besides the Colorado growers, we got some big props from all the Humboldt County guys, along with people from Eugene and Vancouver. They were more than impressed."

Pride spread across Ronnie's face as he nodded, while Paul continued, "I tried to explain that THC/CBD thing, but I don't really understand it. They did though. When I showed them your lab print outs, they were more than impressed with the ratios. All the growers knew it was something new and unique. They kept pressing to get seeds and clones as well as real sellable merchandise."

"Yeah?" Ronnie was interested in some more information as he brought his bare feet off the coffee table and sat up on the couch.

Paul placed both hands on his knees and said, "I've maintained a close relationship with those guys online and if we opened up a school to teach your growing method while allowing them access to our seeds, clones, and inventory, then they would be more than happy to pay. They would pay big money too. It's a pot growers' university, where some of the best growers around the world meet and share ideas. It's renaissance-like."

Ronnie's eyes widened as he asked, "Do you think we can pull it off?"

Paul was trying to take the lead on this as he instructed his friend, "If you can devise step by step lesson plans on your techniques and procedures, then yes. It's like what you said about following a recipe. We do that, along with some good marketing, we can get rid of our current inventory, all of our seeds and future plants all by the end of summer, before the start of the next school year. Then, you can choose whatever boring life you want to live."

"How do we get started?" Ronnie pressed.

Paul brought his hand to his chin, before he asked, "When is your Chicago conference?"

Ronnie answered, "In a week and a half."

"If you can finish the lesson plan on paper, then I will have a classroom set up for students as soon as you get back. I promise. Just let me handle the rest. Know this though -- you're going to be working your ass off teaching." Paul reassured his friend.

Excited, Ronnie stood up. "Well, I'll have my end covered."

Paul stood up and with his arm bent, held up a hand. "We got this."

Ronnie slapped his friend's hand as two locked their grip. He looked at Paul's face and said, "I just want to say thanks for being understanding."

"Listen Ronnie," Paul explained, "When I first met you, I was in a really bad way. My life could have turned out very differently without your help. I appreciate everything you've done for me and I'll do anything to watch out for you."

Still hanging on to their grip, Ronnie said. "I just want to say thanks for that."

When they broke off their handshake, a crooked smile broke across Paul's lips as he added, "No problem, bro, but wait until you see what we're going to pull off. Just like your medical research conference in Chicago that brings together some of the finest minds in your field, we're going to bring together the best weed growers on the planet. They'll be in our facility, sharing ideas and concepts and paying a premium to buy our inventory, seeds and equipment. We'll be out and paid! But the most important thing is that Probie will go on living and spreading throughout the country. That will be our legacy."

"Dude, I'm in 100 percent." Relief broke out on Ronnie's face as the feelings of doubt passed.

Paul offered an arrogant smirk, "Alright, now let me get to work. Watch what I'm going to do for you. I'm going to blow your mind."

8

TELL ME A SECRET

Opening up his kitchen cupboard door, Ronnie reached for the long narrow box of plastic wrap. Using his fingernail, he peeled from the seam and stretched the clear plastic sheet carefully over the stack of 13 muffins sitting on his white china serving plate. Presentation was important to Ronnie; he turned the plate 360 degrees for one final inspection. He wanted this to be impressive.

Wearing a snug pair of blue jeans and a dark green, long sleeve t-shirt, Ronnie picked up the serving plate with a proud smile on his face and walked out of his apartment to the neighbor's door across the hall. The young man paused for a moment before he shook his head to replace his over exuberant grin with a calmer and confident expression. Ronnie wanted to play it cool.

Ronnie took a deep breath and knocked on the dark wooden door. He heard footsteps and looked down to see the two shadows under the door. Someone was staring at him through the peephole. He heard the door knob jiggle and the door was opened by Francesca's roommate, Molly. She wore pink jean shorts, a white, sleeveless button-down shirt and her dark framed glasses. Around her left ankle was a woven purple anklet with a heart charm. Molly greeted him with a welcoming smile, "Hey Ronnie. Frankie isn't here right now."

"That's okay. I baked these for both of you." A friendly grin spread across his face as he held out the plate of muffins.

"Oh, then come on in." Staring at the plate, Molly swung her in hand behind her and stepped to the side.

Walking into her apartment, Ronnie marveled at how neat and orderly the girls were.

Molly pointed at their small dinner table. "You can set them there." She went to the kitchen as she instructed, "Take a seat, let's try 'em out. We'll see if you're any good."

Ronnie sat down at the table and unwrapped the serving plate. Molly returned from the kitchen and handed him a paper plate and a napkin. She laid hers on her placemat and returned to the kitchen. From the other room, Molly yelled, "Did you actually bake these or did you buy them from the store?"

Placing an oversized muffin on each of their paper plates, Ronnie responded, "Come on now, I baked these with my own hands. My kitchen sink is full of dishes."

Molly returned with two glasses of milk and set one in front of Ronnie. She took her seat and set her own glass down. Smirking at Ronnie, she picked up her muffin and broke it in half to reveal the whipped cream cheese filling. Molly leaned over her plate and bit one of the halves. With a mild curiosity, she closed her eyes and chewed delicately.

Waiting patiently, Ronnie observed at the details of her face; he was becoming more enamored with her with each passing moment. With a delightfully surprised expression, Molly opened her eyes wide. She tilted her head as her eyes narrowed and her lips puckered before she said, "Boy, you've got some skills. I can taste sweetness and spice at the same time. It's perfectly moist without being like a cake, and the cream cheese filling, mmm, you nailed it."

The young man could not control his grin -- he beamed with pride. It was the reaction he had hoped for. He responded with a formal, "Why thank you. I'm glad you like them." He picked up his own muffin and took his first bite.

Between bites of baked goods and sips of milk, Ronnie asked, "What were you up to before I knocked?"

"I was reading on the Better Green Building Initiative." Molly answered, "I'm applying to architectural school a year from now and I want to specialize in the energy efficient building designs. You know? The next generation green stuff. I think there's so much room for improvement."

Ronnie raised his eyebrows and said, "Molly, sometime later, please remind me to show you my off-campus laboratory. I have some things there that will blow your mind if you're interested in eco-friendly building design. There is a lot of other highly sensitive stuff there, but our energy system is awesome. We built it ourselves."

"Wow! That's sounds great. I would love to see it," Molly responded. She was becoming smitten with him with every passing moment. Molly stared at his face and she thought, *Fuck! He is charming, but is he here for me or is he just like the rest, trying to hook up with Francesca?*

With a slight head shake, she adjusted her glasses, but on the inside her emotional guard went up. Ronnie had a natural habit of being comfortable with strangers. He always put new people at ease with him and right now, his mojo was working. Molly wanted to know him better, but part of her was afraid to find out what was actually there. She was emotionally conflicted about the young man from across the hall, but her courage and fascination with him won out. Molly folded her hands in her lap and took control of the conversation with a bold step, saying, "Ronnie, will you tell me a secret about yourself?"

"Well, what do you want know? I mean are you asking if I drink out of the milk jug or not?" Ronnie laughed a little.

Blushing slightly, Molly explained, "I know I'm being forward, but I want to know something about you. Over our last few conversations we've had a lot of small talk, so I don't want to know about your schoolwork or anything like that. I want to know something about you about that you haven't shared with anyone else."

"Let me think about that," asked Ronnie accepting her challenge. *Man, I don't want to tell her that I'm a newly successful drug dealer who recently decided to get out of the business.* Ronnie thought about it some more before he said, "Okay, I have something for you."

With a simple nod, Molly couldn't control her grin as she waited eagerly.

Ronnie cleared his throat. "I'm a different kind of screw up. Well, I have this pattern in my life that I'm working on fixing. It's a self-sabotaging mechanism. Since I was little, things like school came easily for me, so I usually got what I aimed for with a minimal effort. I always had a part-time job, so between the doing well in school and being gainfully employed, I had a get out of jail free card when it came to mischief with my parents. It worked well when I was a kid, but now that I'm older the stakes have gone up. I realize I have to rethink some things."

A devilish grin broke out on Molly's face while Ronnie moved in his chair. He continued, "Like everyone, I run into situations where I need to internally debate the situation and consequences before making a decision. You know? That little angel and devil sitting on each shoulder. Let's just say, I'm smart enough to know the difference, but I've always been scared to death of living a mundane life, so the little devil usually wins. I've never played it safe. I'm a creature of instinct."

Shaking her head, Molly asked, "What do you mean?"

Resting both of his hands on his knees, Ronnie leaned forward. "I was also one of those kids that had a hard time saying no to dares or any challenges. I was a thrill seeking junkie. My mom would ask me, 'If all your friends jumped off a bridge, would you?' To her surprise, I would say, 'hell yeah, I'm not missing out on that experience. My ass is jumping.' I'm a smart guy and I consistently lack good judgment skills. I've gotten away with everything so far, but I'm reaching a point in my life where I want to start growing up."

"Well, well Peter Pan hits his mid-life crisis," replied Molly with a smirk.

Reaching out, Ronnie picked up his glass of milk and took a drink. "Well, you wanted to know something about me. That's my flaw. Don't judge me, I'm a work in progress."

"At least you understand you have a flaw. Most people go through their lives thinking that they're perfect and the world is completely messed up." Molly appreciated his effort. She stared at him, studying the details of his face in silence. Then she asked, "Would you like to know my secret?"

"Absolutely." He answered kindly.

A grin spread across her lips, but it disappeared quickly. She paused for a moment. "I absolutely hate my brother and sister."

Ronnie's forehead crinkled while his eyes narrowed. "Seriously?"

Closing her eyes for a long moment, Molly reached down deep inside herself. "Ronnie, I'm older than your typical college senior. I had to take a couple of years off."

Molly paused for a second and saw the encouraging expression of the young man's face. She felt relieved and appreciated the opportunity to express herself.

"I got a call from my older sister telling me to come home. I'm the youngest of three; my sister is the oldest and my brother is in the middle. Our father raised us on his own because our mother bailed on us. My mom and dad were high school sweethearts and married early. They were probably too young to start a family, but they had three kids together. When I was a little, my mom met this rich guy at work. She ended up divorcing my father for Daddy Big-bucks, and because she didn't want us kids messing up things in her new life, she basically divorced her children in the process. My mom called it a do-over."

"Are you okay with that?" asked Ronnie with concern.

With a calm expression on her face, Molly nodded and answered, "Yeah. Today I'm fine with it, but back then, it hurt a lot. It was crushing. The feeling of abandonment was intolerable, but over time our father loved us all so much that we grew up not missing her too badly. He made up the difference on his own and never complained once. My father dated occasionally, but nothing serious developed and he never remarried. Raising his children was his top priority. That man is the rock of my life, so when my sister called, telling me to come home as soon as possible, I knew it was about my father's health." Her voice began to tremble toward the end of her explanation.

Reaching for her napkin on the table, Molly remained stoic as her eyes welled up. She dabbed the folded napkin under her eyes before she continued, "When I got home, my dad explained to me that he had an aggressive form of pancreatic cancer. It was stage three and spreading quickly. The doctors had told him it was untreatable. He was terminal." Molly's face betrayed her sadness as she remembered her father.

Ronnie instinctively reached his arm out and rested it on the table with his palm up. He moved his fingers in a come-hither motion. Without thinking, Molly placed her hand in his. She felt the warmth of his hand and was comforted while she took in a deep troubled breath. Molly carried on with her story, "We were devastated by the news. It was an emotionally crippling time. There were a lot of tears."

With her free hand, Molly wiped her tears. "After we calmed down, my father had a lot to say. First, he wanted to die at home. He didn't want to pass away in a nursing home or a hospital bed. I told him I'd leave school and stay home to care for him. Both of my siblings promised they would help out too."

Molly could feel Ronnie's thumb and finger gently squeeze her hand. She felt relieved as he asked, "Are you doing alright?" She nodded.

"Please continue," insisted Ronnie.

Following his lead, Molly explained, "I have to say, in the beginning, taking care of my father was greatest time of my life. With his health still holding out, my dad was living his life to the fullest. He wasn't holding back, he laughed and celebrated everything he did. It was great to see him smile. Then his health slid, quickly, and my heart broke. He had constant nausea and pains. The roughest part was his rapid weight loss. I could see him physically deteriorate in front of my eyes. He was the strongest man in my world and he was being reduced to nothing by this disease."

More tears rolled down Molly's face and she used the wadded up paper napkin to dry them. When she stared at Ronnie's face, she was looking to see if he was in escape mode, but the only thing she saw in his eyes were concern and sympathy. He asked her, "Well, why do you hate your brother and sister?"

"I'm getting to that." Molly said, "I was the one caring for my father during that time and I never complained about it. I did everything. I cleaned up the vomit. I took care of him when he used the bathroom. I clipped his fingernails and toenails, and I gave him sponge baths."

Suddenly, Molly's expression turned to anger. "I didn't have a problem that my brother and sister barely showed up to help out care for my father. What pissed me off was when my father really started to slide near the end. My brother and sister actually stood in my dad's house and argued about who was inheriting what. While my dad was on his death bed, they were arguing about the worth of the house and who would get the car. They fought over the power tools and the dishes. They argued over the fucking dishes!" She let go of Ronnie's hand and folded her arms across her chest, her face full of pain and anger.

Ronnie could see Molly's scowl as her eyes narrowed. She gritted her teeth and added, "I loved my whole family growing up, but my siblings turned into vultures picking at my dad's body before he was dead. I know they broke his heart before he passed and I can't forgive them for that. That's why I hate them. After the funeral, I came back to Michigan A&M to restart my life and I vowed to never go home again."

With a kind and supportive expression, Ronnie appreciated Molly's effort of baring her soul to him. He stared at her, studying the details of her face, not saying a word. During her story, she had run the gambit of emotions: fear, pride, love, and disgust. The mental exhaustion was obvious as she finished purging her feelings to the young man. Molly picked up her glass of milk and took a drink.

When she set down her glass, Ronnie said, "I come from a rowdy and rambunctious family. We're very close, we're also a lot of fun, and it's my mother that holds it all together. She makes us all live by one simple creed, and that's 'family above all.' You seem to be cut from the same cloth as my mom."

When Molly heard that statement it put a look of gratitude on her face, before she said, "Well, I just put all of my ingredients on my label for you to see. I'll understand if want to run for door." She added a small giggle.

The sharing of their stories was one of the most intimate things Ronnie had ever done. His feelings for Molly were growing from more than just infatuation or physical attraction. He was starting to fall for her. Ronnie gazed at her pretty face and told her, "Do you want to go grocery shopping with me right now?"

"Where?" Molly grinned.

Ronnie answered, "Herrick's, the farmer's market on the west side."

"Oh," said Molly, "I've heard great things about that place." It was the opposite of what she had expected.

Placing both of his hands on his knees again, Ronnie added, "It's the best farmer's market in the country. And any place that gives away free flavored gourmet coffee while you shop is awesome."

"They give away free gourmet coffee?" Molly was astonished.

"Every day," Ronnie said, "They have this self-service station in the middle of the store. You can help yourself to six different varieties along with cream and sugar. It's a great sales ploy. I was never a coffee drinker until I tried their toasted coconut and the Traverse City cherry flavor. After that, I bought my own coffee maker and grinder. I'm hooked."

Molly adjusted her glasses. "It's a smart move to get customers hopped up on caffeine while they're shopping."

"They also sell glasses of wine and beer to their customers while they shop, and their new popcorn stand serving freshly popped flavored popcorn. It's the bomb." commented Ronnie.

"No way!" She laughed a little and added, "Alright then, let me get changed and we'll go." With feelings of relief, she stood up and walked to her bedroom.

When she left, Ronnie watched her walk out of the room. He thought for a moment and whispered to himself, "Could she be the one?"

9

CHINESE HERBAL MEDICINE

S taring out his 4th floor office window in the Capital City Police Department Headquarters at the white State Capitol Dome across the street, Ming Zhāng was thinking about how grateful he was that over the last decade, the Capital City Mayor's Office had invested in the infrastructure of his police department's forensic laboratory. The new office space and technical equipment, along with the addition of new personnel, were greatly appreciated. The Chief Chemist for the Capital City Police Department credited his upgraded scientific facility and staff with the 38 percent increase in the crime conviction rate over the last two years, but he was also proud of the 23 people whose convictions had been overturned by his forensic work. Those people, exonerated by his laboratory's effort, represented the values of truth and justice over political ambitions of others. To Ming, protecting the rights of the innocent was just as important as convicting the guilty. It was his personal creed.

It was about 8:15 in morning, and Ming was starting his day by adding a little powered dairy creamer to his cup of coffee before settling in his office. The money that was allocated for his laboratory upgrade hadn't been spent on office furnishings. Everything in Ming's office, including his workstation desk and chairs, were near the bottom in terms of quality. Gray metal file cabinets piled high with stacks of boxes lined the room's perimeter. The office was a highly organized mess. While he glanced over the daily laboratory docket on his clipboard, Ming took a drink from his coffee cup and started reviewing the day's workload. He heard a knock on his open door and looked up as two plain-clothed police officers walked in.

Ming addressed the two men. "Well, well, well, Captain Robert Williams and Detective Rico Galaviz. What can I do for the famous Big Four?" The forensic scientist was professionally courteous, but these particular police officers' reputation of harshly treating citizens had left a bad taste in his mouth. He kept this a secret as the two detectives stepped closer to his desk.

"Well Ming, I heard you completed the laboratory test on the marijuana samples from the Gerald Duffy bust and you found something interesting," Captain Williams said with polite authority.

The Laboratory Chief nodded and turned in his office chair to face his computer keyboard. He shook his mouse to snap the desktop out of screen saver mode. With a few clicks, Ming brought up a PDF of his chemistry report. With a few more clicks, the laser printer to his left began to whir and spit out a series of printed pages. Ming picked up the stapler from his desk and stapled the sheets together to create two mini reports. He looked at the two detectives standing in his office and calmly requested, "Why don't you two have a seat?"

Captain Williams and Detective Galaviz sat down in the two open chairs in front of the desk before Ming handed over the stapled reports.

"Flip to page two," instructed the Laboratory Chief.

Holding the stapled sheets of paper, the two officers turned past the first page.

Ming took another sip of his coffee before he said, "Other than the obvious physical characteristics, like the colors and smell of this particular cannabis sample, there's something very distinct about it. It has a unique signature. In section two of the report, you will find the chemical composition of the marijuana seized during the arrest of the perpetrator, Gerald Duffy. From the notes of the arrest, I take it they're calling this particular strain of cannabis Probie on the streets."

Robert Williams nodded in agreement.

The forensic scientist continued, "We ran several tests to verify our findings, but something unusual occurred when we looked at the chemical composition, and the results were consistent."

"What was that?" asked the police captain.

Ming adjusted his metal framed glasses. "The THC count of this particular strain of cannabis was just under 25 percent, which is very good by street standards. We've found higher concentrations in evidence seized by our department during other arrests – we've had samples here over 26 percent. What's unusual about this particular breed of cannabis is that it's at nearly 20 percent in CBD as well. We've never had a specimen that yielded this particular combination before. We typically find that high street quality cannabis has elevated THC concentrations for the high, but usually there are just traces of CBD. This sample has a high THC count and the CBD level is off the charts."

Rico Galaviz interjected, "So, you're saying we've got some sort of super-weed?"

"Nah, I wouldn't say that. The CBD is non-psychoactive so it shouldn't increase the high." Ming explained, "The CBD element of marijuana is usually cultivated for medicinal purposes. It demonstrates capabilities like reducing nausea, especially with people going through chemotherapy. It also serves as an anticonvulsant. I would estimate that this particular strain you have here, this Probie, is medical marijuana with a super kick of THC bred into it. That's where the street value lies; some of these people are getting medicinal benefits on top of getting an extreme high."

A sour expression appeared on Rico Galaviz's face. "Ming, all that medical marijuana stuff is bullshit. It's a head fake for the folks who just want to legalize their favorite recreational drug. There's no real medical benefit to marijuana." Galaviz closed his eyes and shook his head, before focusing on the conversation again.

Turning his chair again, Ming Zhāng grabbed his mouse and pulled up a web browser. He typed, "Shennong" into his Google search bar. With his left hand, Ming turned the monitor to face the two officers, which displayed an ancient Chinese drawing of an older, kind looking man with obvious reverence, before he explained, "My family comes from Hong Kong. Although I've was westernized being raised in this country, my parents emphasized the importance of my Chinese heritage. Like this man here. This is Shennong. In Chinese folklore, he becomes the mythical father of eastern herbal medicine. He's held in high reverence throughout the Far East."

Both men grinned at Ming in embarrassed disbelief. Captain Williams and Detective Galaviz sat up in their chairs as Ming Zhāng carried on with his history lesson, "According to Chinese mythology, this man was the ruler of China about 5,000 years ago. He's credited with leading the way for the Chinese people to develop their agricultural system, including the use of plants and herbs for medicinal purposes. Even though he's a mythical character, this man is credited for writing one of the first medical textbooks in human history, the *Shénnóng Běn Cǎo Jīng*. The written version of this book dates back to around 300 BC, and it's the one of the first textbooks on plant medicine. It covers the medical use of cannabis. The book called it, 'ma'. It described marijuana as a balancing medicine between the masculine and feminine. To the Chinese, the concept of balance is a very important part of culture and medicine. Medical use of marijuana has been documented for thousands of years in many other ancient cultures, including the Persians and Egyptians."

Rico's forehead crinkled as his eyes narrowed, before he implored, "Come on, Ming. I understand that the Chinese are going to be players on the global stage in this century, but you're telling me that your medicine is based off of a fictional leader from mythology who wrote some made up book. That sounds off to me. It's like believing mumbo jumbo witch doctor stuff over science and that's no way to develop a medical system."

"Don't be so ethnocentric, Rico." Ming went on, "Your western medicine is based on some folklore as well."

Detective Galaviz challenged him dismissively, "Like how?"

With a grin on his face, Ming responded, "Rico, what's the name of the tendon that connects your calf muscle to your heel?"

"The Achilles," answered Rico.

Raising his eyebrows, Ming said, "Named after the Greek hero slain by a poison arrow during the Trojan War. It's a generally accepted medical term by any western doctor, but the person, Achilles, never existed. He was invented by Homer as a part of Greek mythology and the story was passed down verbally until someone wrote it down. Now, it is taught to college students all over the world. Every culture has some part of their hokey past that resonates in the modern world."

With a smirk, Rico rolled his eyes before he responded, "Touché."

Sitting patiently while his frustrations were building up, Captain Robert Williams interjected into the conversation, "Can you two carry on with this discussion during your lunch break? I'd like to get back to talking about the evidence of Duffy bust."

"I'm sorry, Captain." A contrite Ming redirected the conversation, "I just wanted to point out that the sample seized during that arrest demonstrated unusual test results in our lab. You're looking at a form of cannabis that is uniquely developed; I've never seen a strain with this high of a THC and CBD ratio in the history of this department."

With a focused stare, Captain Williams' contemplated this as Ming added, "I even cross referenced our results with the database at the University of Mississippi's Marijuana Research Project. They have nothing comparable to it in their 45 plus years of collecting data. Ole Miss had recorded strains of cannabis high in THC concentrations and others high in CBD, but they have never seen any concentrations this high, simultaneously, in both chemical compounds of a single species. There's never been anything like this across the country in recorded history. What you have growing here in Capital City is truly unique. It's a unicorn." Silence fell in the room as Ming finished his statement.

Rico Galaviz sat and stared into his captain's face. Robert Williams' eyes moved to the nine by nine inch gray tiles on the floor. He fell into a momentary state of deep concentration until he suddenly snapped out of it. With his left hand, the captain reached out and tapped Rico on his shoulder. "Come on, we have work to do." A degree of seriousness appeared on Captain Williams' face.

The two seasoned police officers stood up from their chairs. With a slight head nod, Captain Williams said politely, "Thank you, Ming. I appreciate you taking the time to share this information with us."

Returning the respectful head gesture, the Laboratory Chief simply replied, "No problem, Captain. If you have any questions, please stop by anytime."

When the two detectives left his office, Ming noticed the look of focus and determination on Captain Williams's face. *Jesus, I wouldn't want to be the guy growing that Probie marijuana.* Ming thought, *Captain Williams is going to bring out the hounds to hunt that man down. There's a storm of trouble brewing and it's heading in that dude's direction.* He took another sip of coffee.

As the two detectives walked out, Rico noticed that his captain seemed determined as they marched passed the forensic laboratory down the hallway to the elevator lobby. Captain Williams pressed the button on the wall firmly before he turned to Rico. "I want you to round up officers Ridgeway and Finch. Give them a briefing on what's going down. I want to step up the full court press on this Probie. I'm not having a new kind of drug developed in my backyard, so twist whatever arm you want until they snap, but we're going to find that source. I want that unicorn's head hanging on my wall."

Rico Galaviz had seen this behavior in his captain before and he knew there was only one appropriate calm response: "Yes, sir."

10

PROBIE'S WEED LAB

A few years back, a single event had set off a chain reaction of opportunities. The incident had occurred in a doctor's office. "You got to be fucking kidding me!" flew out of Jim Finley's mouth when his doctor, Salman Kapoor, revealed his medical diagnosis: a rare form of cancer called Mesothelioma. It turned out the complaints about his chest cavity were more serious than the suspected common cold.

Jim had started his working life at 19 in the steel mills of Gary, Indiana. At the age of 41, he opened his own metal fabrication and welding shop in the industrial section of the north end of Capital City, Michigan. Fourteen years later, at 55, he had inhaled enough asbestos fibers to activate cancer cells in his respiratory system. The malignancy spread with aggression across the exterior lining of his lungs.

Doctor Kapoor informed Mr. Finley that the cancer was inoperable and untreatable. His diagnosis was terminal and he probably had about 18 to 20 months left. The medical specialist directed his patient to a specialized law firm, which filed a claim against the established asbestos victims' trust fund on Jim Finley's behalf. Within a month, he received a $330,000 settlement check that was only lessened by his lawyer's commission. With the settlement in hand, along with his savings of $180,000, Jim thought it was pointless to continue his business operations at J. Finley Welding and Fabrication. His plan was to live out his last days to the fullest on the beaches of Mexico along the Baja California peninsula, just north of Cabo San Lucas, in a surfing village near Todos Santos.

Regretfully, Jim Finley let his remaining four welders go as he closed the doors of his 3,500 square foot industrial building for good. The building was paid off and the owner didn't want to go through the hassle of selling it. He simply didn't have the time to decommission the equipment and clean up the property. That's when Jim was approached by his late friend's son: Paul Mollett. Paul requested to use Jim's former welding shop for his marijuana growing business. He was upfront and honest about his intentions because the young man was shameless about his plans. Paul wanted to use the building to grow his new marijuana strain, Probie, with his partner, Ronnie Lee Harding.

The former welding shop owner had a soft spot for Paul; the young man was the only child of his best friend, Gary Mollett, who had passed away a few years ago. Jim Finley didn't have any children of his own, so he tossed Paul the keys to the building, said to use it any way Paul wanted, and shook his hand. Jim also gave him $10,000 in cash and wished his friend's son well in his new business venture. The cancer victim was leaving the country and he would be dead in the foreseeable future, so any legal ramifications were no longer his concern.

The industrial building of Jim Finley's welding business was the perfect location for an indoor marijuana growing facility. The former metal fabrication shop sat on a large fenced in lot on the North side of Capital City, in the town's manufacturing section, away from any residences. It was a secured property, far from any prying eyes. Paul and Ronnie were only responsible for paying the utilities and property taxes.

Fortunately, the building's utility accounts were left in the business name of J. Finley Welding and Fabrication, Ltd. What usually led to many indoor marijuana growers' arrest were their elevated electric and water bills. Growing cannabis indoors required high amounts of energy for light and water use. Law enforcement investigators would regularly review utility consumption records for suspected grow houses. When a house or dwelling in a residential subdivision has electrical and water bills five to ten times higher than its neighbors, they're typically flagged, giving law enforcement probable cause to begin a criminal investigation. With the utility bills in the business's name, Paul and Ronnie's marijuana growing operations remained off of law enforcement's radar. Their power and water usage were consistent with typical industrial and commercial operations in the area.

When Paul acquired the building for their marijuana business, his partner, Ronnie, secured the growing equipment. As the chief agricultural graduate assistant for Professor Rittenburg's medical marijuana research team, Ronnie was allowed to replace the indoor cultivating equipment in his university greenhouse, within budgetary constraints, as he saw fit. When the researcher decommissioned his old university equipment, such as 1000-watt high pressure sodium grow lamps, power ballasts, industrial air conditioning units, and heavy duty carbon filters, the graduate student transported the equipment to the Michigan A&M University salvage yard to be sold off to the public. Once the old equipment hit the University Salvage Yard sales floor, Paul would immediately buy it all at a fraction of the normal price. He paid in cash, of course. This allowed the new business partners to secure the equipment needed to start their grow business on a shoestring budget.

The most important item that Ronnie obtained for their illegal business was the control systems software that he copied from his university research operations. Professor Rittenburg had the funding to commission the Michigan A&M computer department to create a program that allowed a single computer tablet, using Bluetooth technology, to digitally control all the cultivation equipment, including timing for plant irrigation, drainage, light levels, and temperature control. The computer app also monitored the nutrients and pH level in the irrigation solution and the grow room's sensors, which tracked the lighting power. These environmental controls allowed for optimum growing conditions. Ronnie and Paul's illegal growing operation closely resembled the Michigan A&M's state of the art indoor horticulture facility, where Professor Rittenburg's medical marijuana strain, St. Billy, was cultivated.

Over the next two years, the basement of the former welding shop became a marijuana grow factory, filled with plants in various development stages. Since Probie was a sativa dominate hybrid, many mature plant stalks were approaching seven feet or more in height and buds were blooming everywhere. In a different part of the building, there were new seedlings and clones in small cup-sized containers growing under lights as they began their journey toward maturity. Plants were grouped by various development levels in-between the two extremes of seedling and full maturity. Each of Ronnie and Paul's harvests progressively grew in number of mature crop producing plants and consumable marijuana inventory. The quality of the product was unbeatable.

On a typical Friday, around 9:27 p.m., Ronnie Harding was wearing his traditional green Michigan A&M long sleeve t-shirt and blue jeans, working by himself in the main section of Probie's basement level grow room. He was tending to a group of adolescent plants. The light sound of classical string instruments could be heard from the Bluetooth speaker system as Vivaldi's Four Seasons played through Ronnie's iPad. There was no scientific merit to his theory, but the graduate student theorized that playing music brought out the best quality in his harvests.

Working diligently, Ronnie continued taking his meter readings and caring for his plants when he heard the familiar sound of someone turning the basement level's entrance door lock. There was no suspense. It was his friend and business partner, Paul. They were the only two people who had entered the building for two years.

Turning down the music, Ronnie listened to the repetitive thudding of Paul's footsteps faintly echoing against the basement concrete ceiling. Ronnie looked around the rows of plants and watched

Paul walk down the aisle where he was working. Paul wore a faded denim jacket over a black V-neck. Paul's normally flowing mane of silky black hair was neatly braided down each side and fell symmetrically in front of both shoulders. Ronnie couldn't help but notice the fitted turquoise beaded necklace around his friend's neck.

Paul was proud of his Native American heritage and often made little accessory choices that paid tribute to his cultural traditions, but Ronnie always thought it was done for vanity, in an attempt to attract the attention of a girl. With that idea in his head, Ronnie laughed to himself as he greeted his business partner with a simple, "Hey."

Making an arm gesture, like an orchestra conductor, Paul pointed toward all the healthy plants growing around him and said, "Can you believe what we've accomplished in a little over two years? I mean look at this. Look what we've done. Have you ever seen a more beautiful sight than this? This will be our biggest harvest ever!" A sense of worth was expressed on the young man's face.

"They are looking really healthy, aren't they?" Pride was also apparent on Ronnie's face as he gazed across the grow room at his healthy and budding marijuana plants.

A mild look of contempt appeared on Paul's face. "Well, duh!" The young man's usual devilish expression returned before he continued, "Dude, you're like a mad scientist here and you're churning out the best smoke that this town has ever sampled. I mean just look at these plants! Everyone is waiting with money in hand for this next batch." The compliment was flattering and the sentiment was sincere.

As his eyes moved toward the concrete floor, Ronnie's face couldn't hide his internal conflict. "I can't explain it, but I really do enjoy growing this plant. It's a labor of love. I also take pride in people really enjoying Probie and the money we make validates that, but..." Ronnie paused to carefully word his next sentence.

"Here comes the big hairy butt," Paul interjected with a touch of cynicism.

Ronnie was holding back his concern as his restrained grin turned into a momentary smirk, before the truth came out, "Aren't you a little pissed at me since this will be our last harvest?" He was purging guilt; he was genuinely concerned about their relationship.

Paul took a moment and looked directly into his best friend's face. "Ronnie, if you want out, then our friendship will always come first. So, if you're asking if I'm ticked at you because we're shutting down our fledgling business enterprise, my only response to that is all good things..." Paul paused and smiled with a shrug. His silence nonverbally communicated that their friendship was solidly intact.

"Must come to an end." Ronnie's words were a relief. His brown eyes broke away to the side and his gaze slowly went to the floor. He took in a deep breath, gently nodded his head, and all blame was let go with his exhale. "Thanks, man," Ronnie replied.

His hand moved up to his collarbone and Paul adjusted his light blue beaded necklace, before interrupting the silence. "On top of that, Ronnie, when we started this business, the only thing I was hoping for was to make a little extra money, so I wouldn't get evicted or have my power turned off. I had no idea that our business would take off like this. I have more money than I ever thought possible, thanks to this business. And I never had to punch a clock to earn it."

Paul looked around at all the healthy growing plants, as he proudly reminisced about how far they'd come. He added, "In the drug dealing game, it's always better for small timers like us to get in and get out with our money and lives intact. The only problem in succeeding in this field is you grow too quickly and attract the attention of the wrong people, whether its law enforcement or real heavy hitters who would be more than eager to turn us into their farming slaves. Neither option sounds appealing to me, so I agree it's time to get out with our skin still on our back. Plus, I want to get on with what I really want to do with my life."

With anticipation, Ronnie took the bait. "And what do you really want to do with your life?"

Raising his right hand to stroke the braid dangling on his right shoulder, Paul declared with obvious vanity, "I want to be a model and an actor or maybe a porn star."

Ronnie made a light rippling sound, concealing his small laugh.

Paul reacted with higher tone, "You doubting me, bro?"

"No. No. No. You've definitely got that glamour-boy thing down, and the arrogance and vanity to go with it."

Taking that as a compliment, Paul replied, "Why, thank you."

With a smirk, Ronnie added, "But you're going to need some classes and training. You're also going to need to meet the right people." Pausing a moment to think, Ronnie added, "The money we're going to make on this last harvest should be a big help with that."

Paul always appreciated Ronnie's honest advice. He said, "Yeah, I have to agree."

With a serious look on his face, Ronnie asked, "On that note, how are we coming with the other growers? Are they coming in just like you said they were?"

A high degree of confidence was in Paul's answer, "Oh yeah, they're all coming in and they're bringing a truck load of cash. They want to buy it all. They want the seeds, the saplings, and any clones and plants that we have for sale. They also want any and all equipment. Our going out of business sale should be a huge success. We'll be out of the game, free and clear, with plenty of cash to move on with our lives. Just go to your medical conference and I'll handle everything by the time you get back."

A sense of relief took ahold of Ronnie as he said, "Man, that sounds great."

Paul silently thought for a few moments, before he asked sheepishly, "Ronnie, those guys that are coming in are really smart and they know a lot about growing, like you do. You know, they're book smart with experience. Also several are pretty arrogant, and hate being told what to do." Paul paused for a moment.

"Yeah?" Ronnie was trying to prod his friend to continue.

"Well," Paul added, "I was hoping you could teach me a little bit about what you do here, so I don't look so stupid when the other growers show up."

Ronnie nodded his head; he understood the crowd that would attend the grow school. Good marijuana growers could be strong willed to the point of arrogance. With this understanding, the graduate student began his explanation in the simplest language he could muster, "Okay Paul, first of all, every plant you see here is female. We cultivate these from seed and as soon as we're able to identify the males, we eliminate them from the crop."

Paul interrupted, "How do we identify them?"

With a little head tilt, Ronnie explained, "We spot them by their sex organs."

"You mean our weed plants have dicks!" blurted out Paul.

A chuckle escaped from Ronnie's mouth before he said, "Well, they're more like balls than dicks. They're called pollen sacks." A smirk appeared as he continued, "Our plants also have lady parts, called pistils, and sometimes, on a rare occasions, we'll run into hermaphrodites."

Cutting in again, Paul said, "You mean we can have both dicks and va-jay-jays on the same plant at the same time?"

"Yeah, in a sense," Ronnie said, "once we identify male sex organs, we eliminate those plants from our crop. One male plant in this room can pollinate, or knock up, virtually every female here and ruin our whole harvest."

Paul's forehead crinkled when he asked, "How's that?"

Pointing at the top of a nearby mature marijuana plant to the dew covered bud, Ronnie explained, "You see that bud right there? That's what you're after. That's an unfertilized budding cannabis plant flower, otherwise known as sensimilla. Once our gal here gets knocked up, she'll stop producing buds and focus here energy on reproducing. If not pollinated, the female plant will direct its energy toward flowering and growing bigger buds, which means we get a larger harvest."

Pulling one of the stems closer, Ronnie pointed out, "See those little droplets on the curled leaves, here, on this bud? As the marijuana flowers mature, they form these little sticky liquid bubbles, called trichomes, and that's where a plant produces the chemical cannabinoids, like THC and CBD. Your curing process can also influence the chemical concentration. Our plants here are doing something revolutionary in chemical production, that's why these professional growers are flying in from all over to get our new strain and further cultivate it. Maybe improve upon it."

Paul pressed his friend for more information, "What about the growing process?"

Surprised that his business partner knew so little about growing marijuana, Ronnie pointed at a black growing pot's base. "Our growing process doesn't use dirt. The stuff in the pots is inert. It's just growing media. All it does is physically support the plant and root structure. We feed our plants hydroponically with an ebb and flow system. It's a little risky, because we dissolve all the food and nutrients in the water. If you screw up your solution mix, you can kill your an entire crop."

An impressed 'humph' came out of Paul's mouth as he listened intently.

Ronnie picked up his tablet and continued his lecture, "We use an automated system controlled by my iPad. The tablet controls the timers that control the pumps for the irrigations and drain system. As we flood our crops, in addition to delivering the right amount of nutrients to our plants, it drives out the oxygen-depleted air from their root system. When we drain the solution out, it draws in fresh oxygenated air, revving up metabolic rates and promoting healthy root growth. That's one of the biggest reasons our crops are doing so well."

With confidence, Ronnie elaborated more about light photons that were delivered by the specialized bulbs. He also explained the importance of maintaining the right room temperature and carbon dioxide air concentrations. Paul understood that growing high quality marijuana was a test of patience and skills in precise nurturing. It was an art and a science.

An hour passed while the two young men walked around their grow room, until Paul's mobile phone rang. It was his disposable phone and only members of his Probie wholesaler network called the pay-per-minute number.

Paul's eyes narrowed as he looked at the display on the phone with concern. It was 11:19 pm. He looked at Ronnie and said, "It's the drag queen, Cocoa Lavender." Paul pressed the accept button and answered the phone, "What up, Girl?"

Trying to eavesdrop, Ronnie couldn't hear much except when Paul would let out an occasional "Uh-uh." Paul concluded the phone conversation with, "Okay, I'll be there in a half hour." He then hung up the call.

A crinkle developed on his forehead, when Paul explained, "Cocoa told me she's got a drop of cash for us, but something seemed a little off." A bit of bewilderment was in his voice.

Ronnie watched as Paul's eyes turned to the floor. Ronnie listened as Paul seemed to be talking to himself out loud, "I never had a beef with her and her money is always right. She been our number one merchandise pusher and basically outsells the rest of our dealers combined."

Shaking his head, Ronnie said, "I just never understand how you keep referring to a drag queen as she, her, or hey girl. I just get so gender confused talking about Cocoa. I never know what to say, him or her."

"Dude," Paul exclaimed, "the first thing you have to learn is that it's all Cocoa's world and we just live in it. Next, if he wants to be referred as a she, I really don't give two shits, especially when she's putting money in our pockets. So, I don't even play the pronoun game with her. Got that?"

"Okay, shut your dirty whore mouth and go take care of business." Ronnie relented as the muscles tightened with trepidation around the back of his neck.

Reaching up with his right hand, stroking his left braid, Paul said, "Ronnie, just as you're good at your job, I'm good at mine. I appreciate your concern, but I've got this. Just like before. Now, let me go to work."

Watching his partner, Ronnie noticed Paul's persona changing quickly as if he were getting into character to play a role on stage. His usually jovial personality was replaced with a more hardened street character. This was a job requirement. Ronnie's exterior mimicked his partner's confidence, while he offered Paul an understanding nod.

Taking his cue, Paul turned and strutted out of the basement with attitude. As the heavy steel door closed, Ronnie was left alone with the largest illegal marijuana harvest he'd ever created. Letting out a troubled breath, he dropped the façade. The tightness around the back of his neck worsened, as Paul's worries about Cocoa seeming 'a little off' stayed with him. Ronnie could feel his teeth clench as he squeezed his eyes shut. Taking in another deep breath with a long drawn out exhale, he opened his eyes before saying, "I just can't wait to get out of this business."

Even though he consistently worked alone, for first time in a long time, Ronnie felt lonely. Craving a break from the solitude, he reached for his phone and scrolled through his contact list. He stopped and stared at the name: Molly.

Working around his routine of internally debating whether to call her or not, Ronnie pressed the dial button. He was now committed to the call. It rang three times.

"Hey you." Molly's sweet voice came through the phone.

"Hey." Ronnie inquired, "What do you have going on tomorrow morning?"

After a slight hum, she said, "Nothing really. Why, what are you up to?"

Feeling better just talking to someone, Ronnie asked, "What would you say if I treated you to the best breakfast you've ever had?"

He could sense her smile when she answered, "I'd say I'm very interested."

"You'd have to get up early, and we'll have to leave around 7:30. It's important to get an early start." Ronnie threw out the contingency.

"That won't be a problem," Molly added, "but I think you're way out on a limb claiming the best breakfast ever."

"I'm confident I can deliver." Ronnie was slightly brash.

Molly said, "Alrighty then. I guess I'll see you tomorrow at 7:30."

Excitement filled his chest and Ronnie said, "Okay, I'll pick you up then."

"Sounds good, I'll be ready." added Molly before she said, "See you then. Bye."

"Bye." Ronnie pressed the end call button.

Thinking about the girl across the hall, Ronnie felt his loneliness fade away and went back attending his plants. As time went by he felt his stomach grow uneasy, because his intuition was telling him something was wrong with the situation with Paul. Never feeling this way before about his friend, he whispered to no one in particular, "I hope he's going to be okay."

11

COCOA LAVENDER

That same Friday night, inside the Quiche Lorraine, currently the hottest gay bar and rave spot in the Capital City, the last live drag queen show of the night was in full swing. The elevated runway divided the dance floor. All eyes were on the performers, whose wigs and makeup had been perfected to enhance their feminine beauty. Combined with their false lashes and form-fitting sequined gowns, their elegant transformation from everyday men to fashionable stage goddesses, known as the C.C. Divas, was complete.

The queens took turns performing on the catwalk as they pranced and lip synced to many of the crowd's favorite dance songs. The music was thumping through the state of the art sound system and the floor lights enhanced the show as the crowd gathered around the runway. The eclectic group was made up of men and women of various sexualities. There were the shy virgins and the curious voyeuristic ones among the spectators, but they were all party people having a great time, offering single dollar bills to their favorite performers.

At the end of the show, all the stage performers had earned tips, but tonight's big winner was a fabulous redheaded Diva called Romy Michele, who brought down the house with a club mix rendition of Tove Lo's "Talking Body." The tall and thin Romy made over $600 in tips for her performance.

The performers gathered on the stage to salute the audience with their final curtain call and the night club owner and master of ceremony, Cocoa Lavender, took the microphone. Cocoa was a thin, 5-10, light-skinned black drag queen dressed in a skintight black Catwoman jumpsuit with a white faux fur collar. Large white gold shackles adorned her wrists and six-inch platform boots completed the costume. Her glossy black thigh-high stilettos made the club owner much taller onstage. Her clothing was stylish, but it was Cocoa's hair that always stole the show. Tonight's wig was big haired with loose albino corkscrew curls; it accentuated her perfect makeup.

All the queens posed behind the MC. Microphone in hand, Cocoa addressed the audience, "Ladies and gentlemen, the C.C. Divas." The crowd erupted into boisterous cheers and applause, while the performers conducted the time-honored tradition of the graceful curtain call bow to the gathering of admirers.

The MC addressed the audience again, "We would like to thank all of you homos and heteros and everybody in-between, for coming out and enjoying our show. I understand that many of you work jobs that you absolutely hate. Believe me, I've been there. Here at Quiche Lorraine, we understand this. If coming to our club makes your life a little bit better, then I want you to know that we will work hard to make sure the time spent with us is absolutely memorable. We accept you for who you are!" The audience broke out into another loud ovation.

With a clearing of her throat in the microphone, Cocoa drew the spectators' attention. The club owner declared in a clear, strong voice, "I want to say something loud enough, so all those so-called social conservatives that work under the Capitol Dome can hear me. I also want to say something to those crazy fundamentalists that are protesting, just because they hate people like me. I want you to know that your judgment of our lifestyle means nothing! I want to tell you that your personal beliefs do not give you ownership of this country. This is our home too! This is America, land of the free and home of the brave, honey. In this club, we are free, liberated enough to choose our own lives, and brave enough not to back down from the likes of you!" The crowd again broke out in joyous screams of pride.

Feeling charged and feeding off the energy of the room, Cocoa giggled into the microphone before speaking again, "Let me tell you a little secret." The admirers in the crowd listened intently. The club owner pointed at all the spectators then declared, "Secretly, they want to be you! Because you are free! You are emancipated from the judgments of the outside world. They are so consumed by fear of judgment; it paralyzes them. They're frozen by their own gossip mills and opinion polls. They have to keep pouring themselves glasses and glasses of bourbon, just to numb themselves from their self-imposed prison. They're not free, not at all. There's no fun in their world and they know it!" Cocoa paused to further draw the audience's attention, before bellowing out, "That's why they secretly wish they were you!"

The audience erupted in bedlam-like roars again as Cocoa instructed the frenzied group, "Now, go have some fun. Be kind to one another and try to find a little oral stimulation tonight. We all could use a little more oral stimulation in one form or another," Cocoa grinned as people laughed. "So, have a great conversation, kiss another person, and yes, by all means, go ahead lick somebody tonight. It makes the world a better place." The drag queen giggled again.

The multitude of party people in the club laughed before Cocoa ordered, "DJ Pheromone, play some music!"

In that instant, a remixed version of the song "Beng Boom" from the Acid Crew blasted through the speaker system with its techno beats, while the standing divas gracefully exited the stage, leaving Cocoa alone. With their hands in the air, the dance mob went off with yells and cheers. The club owner smiled and stared out at the hundreds of ravers on the crowded dance floor, shaking, bumping, and grinding as they broke out into sexually charged dances. The flashing disco lights boosted the energy level in the room.

After a few moments of people watching, Cocoa turned, walked off stage, and went down the brick hallway to her dressing room, where a boxer-turned-security guard, Niles Hawthorne, opened the door and said in rich tone, "Great show, Cocoa."

With a smile, the club owner replied, "Why thank you, Niles."

As Cocoa walked into the dressing room, the security guard closed the door behind her and remained in the hallway. Standing alone, the head diva glanced over the 250 square foot brick walled dressing room with its luxuriously lit vanity and walk-in closet filled with elaborate costumes. Cocoa walked to the far wall where artistically sculpted wooden heads served as stands for an assortment of wigs.

Staring into the mirror hanging on the brick wall, the club owner picked up a white towel off the nearby table and poured a bit of rubbing alcohol in it. With the damp cloth, Cocoa's fingers ran across the wig's seam and the alcohol broke up the glue. After a few minutes, the large curly wig was carefully removed from Cocoa's completely bald head. Carefully, the wig was placed on its stand, before she opened the walk-in closet to remove her boots and stage costume.

Donning a powder blue silk robe, Cocoa took a seat at the dressing room's ornate vanity. Once her dangling white gold earrings were removed, the person staring in the mirror was no longer the Stage Diva, Cocoa Lavender. He was now his true persona, Bryan Tatum, a light-skinned African-American man with an adoring smile and the most perfect eyebrows ever seen.

Beginning his makeup removal routine, Bryan Tatum stared at the one photo taped to his mirror. It was the one person who meant the world to him: his mother, Lorraine, for whom he named his successful club. His mother was the only person who loved him unconditionally. Feelings of nostalgia flooded his mind as he thought about how far he'd come, despite the obstacles that had stood in his way.

Bryan thought about his hometown. He had grown up in The Rouge Creek Neighborhood of Detroit's southwest side, which he despised. Bryan always felt it was tough enough being a black man, but being a black man with feminine mannerisms made him an outcast with many of the folks from The Creek. This part of Detroit had a tough reputation; many residents thought that there was no room for sissies and faggots. Bryan was often beaten down for being himself.

Staring in the vanity's mirror as he removed his eye makeup, Bryan reminisced about his childhood. During his time in the public school system, there had been a looming misconception about him. Many thought he hated girls. Nothing could have been further from the truth. Bryan envied them. He felt that he was a female spirit, that Mother Nature had simply given him a male body by mistake. On the playground, when the majority of the boys were picking teams for a game, he preferred to gossip with a group of girls by the marry-go-round.

By the time he enrolled at John C. Kronk High School, Bryan was the constant target for a group of tormenting, thug-like boys, lead by Ricky Darnell. The feminine teenager was constantly harassed and taunted, but it wasn't in Bryan to back down. His only weapons were a clever mind and a smart mouth - useless in a fist fight. Talking shit usually led to a weekly beat down by Ricky, the schoolyard bully, and his crew.

Bryan's mother, Lorraine Tatum, knew her son was in hell at school. She took it upon herself to find him an exit strategy from the Creek. Lorraine passed the state civil servants exam and took employment with the State of Michigan. During the middle of Bryan's senior year, she moved them both to the Capital City, leaving the Creek behind forever.

In his dressing room, Bryan sat his vanity, staring into the mirror, removing eyeliner residue with a cotton swab and thinking about how the Capital City environment was a blessing. This city's environment was a multi-cultural one, with a growing middle class of all colors and races. It was near a large public university, Michigan A&M, where students from around the globe wanted to learn new things and were open to new experiences. There was a variety of food, art, and entertainment. People were free to be themselves. That open-mindedness allowed Bryan to flourish as he took up employment in the city's night club scene.

Bryan started tending bar, and over the years, moved into special event planning and club promotions. However, the real money came from dealing drugs, mostly weed, ecstasy, and some cocaine. The party scene was a nightly habit for Bryan, and he always had access to plenty of people looking for recreational drugs. Suppliers sought him out because he could move a product with little effort and he always kept the money right. Bryan also knew the right people to bribe to keep law enforcement away. With this business infrastructure in place, it didn't take long for him to amass quite a bit of cash in a short time.

Bryan made enough money to acquire his own cabaret liquor license. He bought an old brick building, formerly a meat packing warehouse in the Old Town district, and converted it into his dream establishment: a rave dance bar with a stage to perform his own drag shows.

With his contacts and club promotion skills, Bryan opened the doors to Quiche Lorraine and was an immediate success. The party people simply called the establishment, "The Q." As the club grew, Bryan felt more emancipated than ever before. That's when he embraced the idea of becoming a drag queen. Dressing up for the first time in elaborate women's clothing was the very moment Bryan became his alter ego, Cocoa Lavender. In costume, Cocoa became what Bryan always wanted to be: she was brave, strong and flamboyant, and most importantly Cocoa was a rich and powerful woman, liberated in every possible way.

With a long exhale, Bryan, who was still staring at himself in mirror, let go of all the nostalgic feelings he had built up inside. Sometimes, he just wanted to cry about all the bullshit he went through to get to where he was. He looked in the mirror and said, "You have to remember your inner Nietzsche. What doesn't kill you..." He nodded to himself, finishing the cliché in his mind, *makes you stronger.*

A knock on the door startled him back to the present and Bryan answered, "Come in."

The door opened and Niles the security guard entered. "Cocoa, there's a gentleman here to see you. His name is Scott James. He says he's from your old neighborhood."

Brian recognized the name immediately. They had grown up on the same block in The Creek. In high school, it was Scott who had put a stop to numerous beat downs that Bryan had endured. Scott did it out of a sense of duty, like preventing someone from abusing a dog. The two never became friends, but Scott treated Bryan just like anyone else, which was really all Bryan had ever wanted. Feeling nostalgic, he reacted, "Oh good lord, let him in!"

With a quick hand gesture, the security guard signaled for the man in the hallway to enter. A moment later, Scott James entered the dressing room, wearing a dark blue Ravazzollo business suit. Everyone from the Creek knew Scott James as Baby Jay on the streets. He was the chief enforcer for Dem Creek Boyz. The security guard closed the door, leaving the two men alone in the room. Slowly scanning the room, Scott took in the details of the dressing room before turning his attention to the man sitting at the mirrored vanity, "Bryan. What's it been, 20-some years?"

Modestly pulling together the collar of his silk robe, Bryan answered, "Well, well, well, Baby Jay paying my little establishment a visit. It can't be good news when Dem Creek Boyz come strolling through your door."

"No dawg," Scott James responded in a calm manner, "it's nothing like that. I see you've done well for yourself since leaving the Creek. I respect that. What's got our interest is that Probie weed you've been pushing on your party crowd."

His lips tightened and curled, like he tasted something sour and Bryan said, "So the fuck the what? This is my club. That Probie bud is better than any of that shit you got coming out of the Creek. I'll do whatever the hell I feel like doing without your permission. I don't need anything from anybody, especially from folks in the Creek."

Scott James took a few steps forward before he calmly explained, "Listen Bryan, you're getting all worked up over nothing. I'm not here for you; I'm here for your Probie supplier. The sooner you get him here, the sooner I stop being your problem and start being his."

Standing up from his vanity, still clutching the collar of his robe, Bryan spoke boldly, "Baby Jay, you're hearing me, but you're not listening. You got nothing. You have no authority here. I call the shots. You, Head and his little brother can go…"

Bryan was interrupted as Scott James pulled out a 38 caliber Smith and Wesson revolver from inside lapel of his suits jacket. He aimed the snub nose 38-Special at Bryan's face, inches from his forehead. The well-dressed gangster's hand didn't move a bit as he calmly instructed, "Don't finish that sentence."

Still defiant but calm, the club owner rolled his eyes. "Baby Jay, this isn't the first time I've had a gun pointed at my face."

Scott James' thumb pulled back the hammer of his pistol: click.

Snapping his tongue, Bryan came to the realization, "Wait, wait, wait! I just remembered something."

"What's that?" Baby Jay inquired in a slow, drawn out manner.

Raising his perfect eyebrows, Bryan said in higher tone, "The last time I had a gun stuck in my face, I was poor and I had nothing to live for. I'm not dying now over this bullshit. I just forgot how good it is to be wealthy in this country. That was my pride talking."

Scott James released the hammer of the handgun and brought it down slowly. "Good," Baby Jay said, "now, make the call. Let me be that guy's problem, not yours. You feel me?"

Thinking that any gunfire in his club would be bad for business; Bryan again rolled his eyes and resisted the temptation to call out for his security guard. Relenting, the club owner picked up a white bedazzled iPhone from his vanity. Shaking his head, he dialed his supplier, Paul Mollett.

As the phone rang, Bryan thought, *I just need to stay focused. I need to get this mother fucker out of my club.* The phone answered and Bryan immediately changed into his drag queen alter ego. "Hey Paulie, it's me, Cocoa. How's my little Indian boy doing?" Cocoa was the only one allowed to call Paul by his real name.

"What up, Girl?" Paul answered over the phone.

"Well, I sold out early. I'd love to give you your money now. I'm leaving here tomorrow morning for Savannah for a couple weeks and I wanted to make sure you got the moolah, dear. So, if you by stop as soon as possible, I can get you paid up." The drag queen offered the money as bait.

Paul replied, "Okay, I'll be there in a half hour." The called ended quickly.

Bryan's wrist bent back with his phone in his hand and he stared at the man standing in his dressing room. "He'll be here in a half hour or so. That boy is never on time."

Knowing that he had some time to kill, Scott James started a new conversation, "I saw one of your high school friends last week."

"Who's that?" Bryan inquired.

With a crooked smile on his face, Scott simply said, "Ricky Darnell. Or should I say Pastor Rick."

"Pastor Rick!" flew out of Bryan's mouth.

"Yeah," Scott added, "he's built up a huge congregation in the Creek. His flock loves his sermons, especially the ones on the evils of homosexuality, the fall of family values, and encroachment of Islam on Detroit."

With his eyes turned up to the white painted concrete ceiling, Bryan shook his head before he said, "Oh Jesus, please save me from your followers." He then closed his eyes and laughed to himself.

Scott James added, "Yeah, I hate that motherfucker too." Usually a stoic man, a rare smile broke out on Scott James's face as the two men continued the reminiscing.

Forty-five minutes went by while the two men carried on, until they heard a knock on the door. Bryan yelled out in his Cocoa manner, "Come in!"

The security guard, Niles, opened the door and the loud club music filled the dressing room. "Cocoa, there's a young man out here in the hall to see you. He said that you invited him."

The club owner instructed, "Thanks Niles, let him in. Once you close to door, do not come back in, no matter what you hear. Keep everyone out. Okay?"

Nodding his understanding, the security guard walked back into the hallway and escorted Paul Mollett into the dressing room. The music was muffled when the door shut behind him.

Looking around, Paul saw Cocoa without his wig and makeup, sitting at the vanity in a powder blue silk robe. Paul was a little taken aback; the young man had rarely seen the club owner out of costume. He also noticed another man in a suit staring back at him coldly. The man was tall, thin and had a neatly trimmed moustache. Feeling a little queasy, Paul greeted his perceived friend, "Hey Cocoa."

The club owner got up and walked over to Paul with his arms stretched out, "My little Indian-boy. You look so cute with your hair braided like that." Cocoa walked over and hugged him. As he leaned in he whispered into Paul's ear, "Be careful."

Not reacting to the warning, Paul simply returned the hug and gave a reluctant smile.

With a graceful hand gesture, Cocoa turned and introduced the other man in the room, "Paulie dear, this man here is from my old neighborhood. Everyone calls him Baby Jay." Cocoa turned and presented the younger man in the room, "Baby Jay, this is Paul. He's my main supplier. Everyone around here calls him The Indian." The club owner took a step back from between the two men.

Pulling out his handgun and shoving it in Paul's face, Baby Jay quickly took control of the situation. Reacting, the younger man in the room blurted out, "What the fuck, Cocoa?"

"Just talk to the man," the club owner implored, "and it will all be over quicker than you'd think."

Shutting up, as his heart pounded in his chest, Paul stared at the gun and listened to Baby Jay. "Do you know what type of man I am?"

Paul answered, "Yep." His breathing became shallow.

"Good," the gangster explained, "I want to be clear here. I'm a pure lie detector, so don't fuck up. I'm also the kind of man who doesn't care about the bigger picture. I live for the single focus of my mission and right now, that means finding this source of this so-called super-weed. I'm asking flat out, are you the source of Probie?"

The talkative young man stuck to a short answer strategy, "Yes and no."

"That's not an answer," insisted Baby Jay, agitated.

Amazed at how still the gun in his face remained, Paul clarified his answer, "Yes, we did cultivate this particular strain from scratch, and we are the only growers, but this is our last harvest. We are getting out of the business."

With a slight eye twitch, Baby Jay asked, "Why are you getting out?"

"Because my partner is a smart mother fucker, that's why." Paul elaborated, "He was smart enough to get cold feet at the right time. Right now, I'm starting to think that my boy may be a little bit psychic. That's why we are hosting our grow school. It's our going out of business sale. We're cashing out. It's our exit strategy."

Baby Jay's eyes narrowed, before he asked, "What's a grow school?"

Feeling a little bit calmer, Paul offered a few details, "We've invited some of the best growers from around the country and to attend our little school in exchange for a tuition fee. They're buying the rights to procure our seeds and our entire inventory, along with our equipment. They're also coming in for my partner's lesson on the cultivation process, so they can get the best results."

Paul's eye widened as he heard the click of Baby Jay pulling back the hammer of his revolver. Now, fearing for his life, the young man squinted. He listened to the gangster's voice, cold and calm, "I'm going to ask you a simple question and I'm going to know if you're lying to me. Is anyone coming to your school from Detroit?"

"No." Paul explained, "There's no one coming from anywhere in Michigan or in the Midwest at all. We wanted to move production as far away from us as possible."

Pausing a moment to think, Baby Jay's thumb gently released the hammer as he brought down his handgun for first time during this conversation. "We're sending our representative now to your little school. You got that!"

Feeling emboldened, Paul answered, "I can add you to our list. There is a $10,000 buy-in, plus you have pay for all the seeds, clones, and inventory you want. Cash, of course."

"That won't be a problem." An irritated Baby Jay replied, "Just because we're black doesn't mean we need affirmative action to attend your school. We can pay just fine, just like everyone else."

Paul's lips formed a crooked grin, before he said, "Of course. We're not out to mess with anybody. We're just a couple of guys who created something new and want to get out of the game."

Putting his gun back in its shoulder holster, Baby Jay affirmed, "Alright, this should take care of my mission. We'll bring the cash and you'll have another student at your little grow school."

Exhaling, Paul was relieved. "We'll take good care of you. I think you're going to like what you're about to learn from us. The best of the best growers from all over are coming in for this class session and everyone is going to be eager to share information. " Paul's grin turned into an outright smile, before he added in a cheery tone, "Class starts the next Saturday after next at 9 a.m."

Baby Jay buttoned the lapel of his Italian suit as he walked out the door, "We'll bring donuts."

As his anxieties drained, Paul instructed the man, "Get a hold of Cocoa for our contact info."

Baby Jay offered a simple nod and walked out of the dressing room. When the door closed, Paul turned and looked at Cocoa, "What the fuck?! I thought we were friends. That motherfucker was about to kill me, wasn't he?"

The club owner rolled his eyes. "He probably would have killed me too. You knew this was part of the life when we got into this game. You handled yourself beautifully, my little Indian-boy."

Cocoa walked into the closet and returned with a small duffle bag. "Here's 20-grand. I put an extra five large in there for you for the trouble I caused you, today." Cocoa handed over the money and instructed, "Paulie, please take care of these people. Otherwise, these boys can create a lot of problems for both of us."

Taking the bag and slinging it over his shoulder, Paul nodded his understanding before he said, "Don't worry I'm going to take care of everyone. We're going to shine."

Again, pulling together the collar of his silk robe, the club owner replied, "Paulie, I know you will." Exhaling, Cocoa stared at her wigs and decided that she needed some shopping therapy. Tomorrow, she would buy something beautiful, shiny and encrusted with diamonds. Cocoa was now in the market for a designer handgun.

12

THE MORNING HARVEST RESTAURANT

It's an assault on all your senses, thought Molly Jo Donnelly as she stared at the one story brick building, painted pastel aqua and gold. It could only be described an eclectic swirl of chaos. Every exterior wall of the building was decorated with graffiti and an assortment of road signs and memorabilia, which gave off a nostalgic playhouse vibe. Aghast, the young woman gawked at the Morning Harvest Restaurant. More shocking than the building's decoration was the line of people waiting to get inside.

When Urban Finger Magazine released its list of *The Top 25 American Diners to Die For,* The Morning Harvest Restaurant in Capital City's Old Town District came in at number 12. It was the only diner from Michigan to make the list; it was a no-brainer as to why. Typically, when a person has a favorite restaurant, they'll have a favorite dish on the menu. This was not the standard case at Morning Harvest. Although the classic menu was well respected, a white board hanging on the south wall was the reason why locals loved it. The board listed the daily specials, which were imaginative menu items that drew crowds.

One of the co-owners, Lane Cooper, was the head chef and main grill man. Lane was originally from Oregon and out there they know a thing or two about gourmet breakfast food. He brought the concept to the industrial Midwest and started the Morning Harvest

Restaurant. The little diner became a gold mine. Lane was a mad scientist of the culinary arts and the local community loved him for it, which is why they lined up outside his restaurant every day, even in Michigan's freezing winter temperatures, to try the specials of the day.

Saturday morning around 8:28, Molly stood in line outside the Morning Harvest restaurant for the first time. Even though it was a little early for her on a Saturday, she appreciated the midsummer weather. It was a beautiful day with only a few clouds in the morning sky.

Feeling good, Molly looked at the man standing beside her. It was her neighbor, Ronnie Harding. He had invited her to breakfast at his favorite diner. Standing against the painted graffiti on the east brick wall, the pair had been waiting in line for over 40 minutes before they made it to the front door.

Molly was able to read the entire stencil print on the glass entryway, which said "Welcome to the Morning Harvest. Rule #1: Don't be a dick. It will ruin your dining experience. Rule #2: The line starts here on this side of the door. Please wait here until we are able to seat you. NO EXCEPTIONS! Rule #3: If you are racist, sexist, homophobic, or an asshole...don't come in. Rule #4: Most importantly – Be kind to one another."

Molly laughed.

Ronnie concealed his smile with tightened lips and shook his head. He added, "The only thing they don't tolerate around here is intolerance."

At that moment the restaurant's second owner, Veronica Cooper, opened the door. The beat of techno music came through the doorway as she stuck her head of plum colored hair outside. She offered a pleasant greeting to one of her favorite customers, "Hey Ronnie. How many are in your party today?"

The young man held up two fingers.

The restaurant owner smiled and said, "Good, we have a small table that just opened up."

Ronnie led Molly through the door into the dining room.

With the sights, the sounds, and the smells, the assault on Molly's senses spiked as she walked through the door. She immediately thought, *this is how Alice must have felt stepping through the looking glass.* When Molly gazed at the interior for the first time, the designer inside her was amazed how small the dining room actually was. It efficiently held over 30 people, who were all enjoying their meals. In this busy space was a quick moving open kitchen, a counter with 10 stools and a seating area with tables. The service staff also had room to maneuver. She thought it was great use of space.

Looking around, Molly turned her head to the right, the left, and back again, taking in the explosion of art and memorabilia hanging on the pastel gold painted walls. A look of astonishment broke out on her face as she saw at the random assortment of bumper stickers that were stuck on every vertical surface. The haphazard collection consisted of nostalgic black and white photos from past roller derby queens and classic celebrities of Hollywood's heyday, and paintings done by various local artists. The ever present symbol of the Jolly Roger could be found throughout the dining area, reminding folks that this little business was fighting the good fight against the corporate restaurant take over. Molly had never seen such a collection of in-your-face artwork at a place of business and it tickled her.

Snapping out of her wonder, Molly looked at Ronnie, who was holding a chair out for her at their table, set against the north wall. Feeling her face warm with a tinge of embarrassment, she walked to him with an uncontrollable grin and took her seat. Ronnie joined her, and Molly could tell he was in a great mood. The young man was moving his head to the smooth beat of techno coming through the restaurant's speaker system. Ronnie reached into the pocket of his jeans and pulled out his smartphone. He said, "I apologize for this, but I love the music here; I'm always looking for good suggestions to add to my playlists. This would be a great one."

Using his index finger Ronnie activated Shazam app on his phone and held it up to the wall mounted speaker. The phone listened to the mystery song's electronic rhythm. The bluesy bass guitar riff blended in as the song's hook and the vocals were low, deep, and distorted. The lyrics were unrecognizable, which only peaked Ronnie's curiosity more as he waited for the app to tell him the name of the song.

Ronnie smiled. "I got it."

"What is it?" Molly asked.

With his bottom lip sticking out, Ronnie said, "It's Blood, Milk and Sky - The Miss September Mix. I'm definitely downloading it when I get home."

Molly gazed around the dining area and thought, *this edgy, non-mainstream music coming over the speaker system is the perfect fit for ambiance of this place. The Cracker Barrel crowd would hate it.* She laughed to herself.

Putting the phone back into his pocket, Ronnie explained, "Sorry again about that. I'm not one of these phone obsessed guys. I'm more into dealing with people face-to-face." He laughed a little before he continued, "I can't stand when I catch guys on dates and they're paying more attention to their phones than the girl sitting across the table from them."

"Girls do it too," added Molly as she looked around at some of the couples who were seated in the dining room doing exactly that. She stared at some of the folks who had no attention span for each other; they were desperately looking at their phones for the latest social media postings. Molly sighed and said, "Our whole generation is addicted to electronic media. I think we're losing interpersonal skills. The virtual world seems to be more intriguing than the actual world."

Raising his eyebrows and offering a little devilish grin, Ronnie slightly shook his head. "Not me. I'm not making that rookie mistake; I'm totally into what you have to say." Leaning across the table, he tilted his head and made direct eye contact.

"You're a cocky S.O.B., aren't you?" Molly replied before she concealed her smile.

"Maybe," Ronnie explained, "but that doesn't mean I'm not sincere about wanting to hear what you have to say. I'm just glad you're here, enjoying this morning with me."

Molly felt a little insecure because she wanted to giggle. That's when a tall, thin man with salt and pepper hair walked up to the table. The man was wearing a fitted brown sleeveless shirt that said "Coffee Pimp" in white letters. He was carrying a glass coffee pot and asked Ronnie and Molly, "Anyone here want coffee?"

The young lady turned over her cup and said, "Please, thank you."

Ronnie copied her actions and nodded his head.

The man filled both cups and said, "You're server will be here shortly."

When the coffee pimp walked away, Ronnie explained, "The avant-garde décor and the rebel attitudes around here don't mean shit if they can't deliver a good meal. It's all about the food at this place - this will be the best breakfast of your life. I promise." He pointed at the white dry marker board hanging up on the south wall. "Those are today's specials. So, never mind the menu on the table, just pick something on the board and let the cooks work their magic. It's all about trust and I'm quite confident they're not going to let you down."

Molly stared at the white board hanging high on the south wall, reading over each item. Her cheeks took on a pinkish hue while she said, "I think that Pompeii Wake-Up Call sounds utterly delightful, but isn't that a slang term for waking someone up with oral sex."

Ronnie offered a simple grin and nodded his head affirmatively. "I can't think of a better way to start someone's morning."

Rolling her eyes, Molly simply added, "Regardless, I want to order that. It has sweet spicy sausage, diced and sautéed Honeycrisp apples, arugula, Vidalia jam, crispy parsnips, sharp cheddar and maple chevré." Pausing a moment, Molly asked, "Chevré. That's French goat cheese, right?"

The young man answered with another nod, "Yep."

Enjoying the atmosphere of the diner, Molly asked, "Well, what about you? What are you getting?"

Mulling over the menu, Ronnie said, "Well, this morning I woke up wanting something spicy, so I was considering El Red Mendoza, but after reading The Gorillaz's French Toast, I have to say I'm a little intrigued. Now, I want something sweet. Buttered sautéed bananas with a caramel and sweet cream glazing on my French Toast sounds like the ticket for me. I've never had it, so I think I'm going with that."

Molly offered an approving nod as a tall, thin waitress approached their table. The waitress had tied her brownish-blonde hair up in a bun. She greeted the couple and took their order with a friendly grin.

As server walked away, Ronnie asked Molly, "Hey, remember when we played that game in your apartment? You know, tell me a secret."

"Yeah," she smiled, "the day you brought over the muffins."

His eyes lit up up and Ronnie proposed, "How about we play my game now?"

With a little apprehension in her voice, Molly answered, "Alright, but what's your game?"

"Ask me anything." The young man explained, "We'll take turns asking each other questions until our food arrives and the other person has to answer honestly. No holds barred. Can you handle that?"

Her eyes narrowed as Molly accepted the challenge, "Okay, that's sounds good, but you go first.

Ronnie offered a quiet whistle before he started, "Do you ever think about me?"

Molly's cheeks flushed bit as she closed her eyes for a moment, before she relented, "Yes, I do think about you. I've reached for my phone a few times and been too nervous to text you. I'll type you a nice text, stare at it and then delete it."

"Why wouldn't you send me a text?" Ronnie asked immediately.

Taking a few moments, Molly adjusted her glassed and thought about a reply before she spoke, "I didn't want to seem desperate or clingy. I'm also a little guarded about getting rejected." Her cheeks took on deep shade of pink as she continued, "It's an insecurity I've been dealing with since my father passed. My grieving process and the fallout with my siblings had really left me feeling isolated. I feel like don't have any family anymore, and its messed with me a lot. I just don't feel as strong as before, and I feel like any rejection could make me crumble. That's why I'm a little guarded right now."

Molly picked up her cup and took a sip of coffee, before she added, "But I'm grateful that you texted me first and invited me out for breakfast today. It means a lot." Gratitude and relief could be seen in Molly's face and heard in her voice. She concluded with a question, "So, how did I do?"

"Wow! That was awesome." Ronnie answered, "That was vulnerable, authentic and bare-knuckle honest. I liked it. I liked it a lot." The young man offered an approving smile, while he said, "Alright, now you go. Ask me anything you want."

Mischievousness was all over her expression when she looked in Ronnie's eyes and said, "Okay, who would you rather see naked, me or my roommate, Francesca? Remember, you promised you'd be honest."

"Wow!" Ronnie was a little taken back, "You really are good at this game."

Proud of her candor, Molly returned a simple grin as she waited for his response.

Ronnie puckered his lips, gazing at the ceiling. He thought it about it for a brief instant and then answered, "Francesca is definitely a beauty. She's exotic and gives off that stereotypical sexual vibe, but I find her a little bit shallow. In comparison, I like talking to you and I appreciate the things you say. I enjoy that you like reading books and you have a charming frankness. I find it all very attractive. Your personality is nice and I find your physical form really alluring. You've got it going on, girl."

Molly's happy expression was uncontrollable as Ronnie continued, "I love that smile. When you're not paying attention I'm checking that body of yours, especially that cute butt when you're walking around in those jeans. So, if you're asking me who I would like to see naked, you or your roommate. I would have to answer hands down; it would have to be you."

Whether she believed it or not, it was nice for Molly to hear. Her ego and self-esteem were boosted by Ronnie's flirtatious comments, and Molly felt relieved. She'd often had feelings of inadequacy as Francesca's best friend and roommate. Francesca was the girl that all the boys would stumble over trying to get her attention. Molly always felt second best in this regard. It was something she had accepted. Ronnie's declaration made her feel that she was first.

Looking at Molly's grin, Ronnie couldn't resist the opportunity to tease her a little bit. He brought up both of hands and pressed two fingers on each of his temple. "Speaking of that, I'm going to use the power of my imagination right now. I'm picturing you in your underwear."

Molly's mouth opened in shock while Ronnie continued, "I'm seeing you in these cute comfortable white cotton panties with some pink stripes. Yeah, that's looking good."

Ronnie thrived on joking to get a rise out of his friends.

They both started laughing when Molly said jokingly, "Okay, knock it off."

Of course, seizing the opportunity to mess with her some more, Ronnie defiantly pushed it, "And your bra. It's white, comfortable, with little strawberries…"

Bringing down his fingers, Ronnie was interrupted by the coffee pimp, who asked, "Would anyone here like a coffee refill?"

"Yes, please." Molly was trying to regain her composure as she responded, while Ronnie just sat with a silent smirk and shook his head no.

The tall thin man with the neatly trimmed, graying hair filled her coffee cup and said, "Your orders are coming up next. They'll be here shortly."

Molly offered a warm smile. "Thank you." The host nodded and walked away.

Ronnie paused for a moment and asked, "Do you want to keep playing?"

"No, I'm good," Molly answered with a slight giggle, "but that was fun." She added some cream and sugar to her fresh coffee and gave it a little stir. Watching the swirl of coffee in her cup, Molly raised her eyes to look at the young man across the table, "Ronnie, thanks for asking me out."

"No problem, girl. I'm glad you came with me," returned Ronnie with a nod.

At that moment, the thin blonde waitress placed an omelet in front of Molly and a plate of French toast in front of Ronnie, and asked, "Do you need anything else?"

"I'm fine." Molly declared as she looked over the beautifully presented omelet.

Ronnie looked up to the server and requested, "Can I have a glass of milk?"

With a smile, the waitress said, "No problem, be back in a second." She nodded, turned and walked away.

The presentation of Molly's omelet was masterful. Closing her eyes, she brought her face down, closer to her plate, and took in the aroma. The omelet's braised sausage, its melted cheddar and goat cheese and the sautéed apples offered an incredible sensation as the young woman nodded in approval. She picked up a fork and knife. "Thanks again Ronnie for bringing me here. I'm having a great time."

"I'm just glad you came and shared this experience with me. This place is a whole lot better when you're with someone." Ronnie added.

Taking the first bite of her breakfast, Molly tasted the sautéed Honeycrisp apples. The cooking process brought out even more flavors as the sweetness from the apples mixed with the slight spices of the sausage meat. The taste sensations blended with melted cheeses and fresh crispy greens along with eggs that were cooked to fluffy perfection. She reacted, "Oh my God, you're right. This is amazing."

"And now you know why people are still lined up out the door," informed Ronnie.

The couple enjoyed their meal together, and Molly added, "Hey Ronnie, remember asking me to remind you about showing me some stuff at your university research facility? You said there was some green building technology there that would be an interest to me."

He reacted with an inquisitive tone, "Yeah."

"This is me reminding you." Molly said, "I would still very much like to see it."

The waitress returned and set down a glass of milk. Ronnie said, "Thank you." The server smiled and walked away.

Looking at his milk, Ronnie contemplated her request. He seemed to be weighing some things out for a couple moments. "Okay, how about we do it after breakfast? But you have to promise me, you will keep this a secret. There are some things there the university would like to keep on the down low."

With an expression of excitement, Molly vowed, "Oh yeah, absolutely. I can keep a secret."

"Cool." Ronnie explained, "Because there is a lot of stuff there that will blow your mind."

Taking another sip of her coffee, Molly's eyes lit up with anticipation as she said, "I can't wait to see it."

13

THE NEW JERSEY DUDE

"Oh my God, you were right. That was the best breakfast I've ever had," declared Molly, sitting in the passenger seat of Ronnie's worn out, sea foam green Ford Winstar minivan. Ronnie had bought the minivan years ago; it had been his hangout before he had his own place. When his dad was driving him crazy and his mom was nagging him to a breaking point, he would call his friends and they would sit, chill, and smoke a bowl. This was where he realized the medicinal benefits of marijuana: when he'd started to have stress migraines during freshman year. Between classes, he would sometimes lie in the back of the car and let the smoke take away his pain.

Molly was excited that Ronnie was going to show her his research facility. The curiosity of what he was going to reveal to her was only part of the reason for her enthusiasm. She liked that he was taking an interest in her and that he was kind and funny. She stared at Ronnie while he offered an approving nod as he drove off. Daydreams took over as they drove; various movies that featured research facilities came to Molly's mind. She wondered if Ronnie was working on something that could cure a disease or recreate dinosaurs, which she had secretly wished for since she had first seen *Jurassic Park*. She smirked and decided to keep her secret to herself.

Their 30-minute drive ran the gambit of living demographics. It started off completely urban from their downtown Capital City location and progressed through 'the hood', then through upscale suburban neighborhoods until they reached the beautiful campus of Michigan A&M University. Ronnie had no problems going into the city, but there was a distinct line between downtown and the safety of the campus. On the other hand, Molly could feel her blood pressure go down when she crossed onto the university's property. Television news reports of shootings had been on the rise for years in the city and the media always overdramatized reports of stories about thug-like behavior.

Once they drove out to the agricultural research part of the campus, everything was rural. Michigan A&M's agricultural research area included over 6,000 acres of dedicated farmland. The majority of the students majored in something other than agriculture and never knew much about this section of campus, except that when the wind was right the smell of cow manure would float to main campus. Since Ronnie had received both his bachelor's and master's degree in plant biology, he knew this part of campus well. Ronnie felt like he could walk the grounds backwards while giving Molly a tour. He pointed out the window while he drove down the country roads. "Over there, we have alfalfa research and over here we have soy, and over there we have turf grass. That building over there, that's our livestock judging pavilion."

The two took turns grinning at each other, blushing, and making stupid jokes until they reached Sandhill Road. The surroundings changed from agricultural farmlands to more of dense forest woodlands. Nothing could be seen except for the thick leaves and trees that Michigan was known for. They drove for another 10 minutes until Ronnie turned left down an unnamed dirt road that was tucked away into the thick forest. Down that stone road, they reached a section where two concrete posts stood with a steel chain stretched between them. There was a sign hanging on the chain that read, "Private Property – No Trespassing."

Ronnie stopped his van just before the chain. He looked at Molly and said, "Remember you promised to keep this a secret. I've never shared this with anyone; not even my family knows. The President of the University personally wants to keep this facility hush-hush. What's inside is controversial, and as a public school, which gets a lot of tax payer support, this could be a political firestorm if the wrong people found out. Professors and researchers at other publicly funded schools have lost their jobs over things like this."

Molly blinked as she tried to think of another person who had trusted her with something so important; no one she knew required that much faith. She knew that, since Ronnie trusted her that much, he must really like her. "I can't tell you what it means to me that you have so much confidence in me with this. Ronnie, I promise I will not betray your trust."

Nodding his gratitude, Ronnie got out of his minivan. He unlocked the chain and dropped it to the stone road. He returned to the driver's seat and drove over the chain. Ronnie glanced at Molly and wiggled his eyebrows, he looked so mischievously adorable. She flashed him a grin.

Ronnie drove down the dirt and stone road until the dense forest cleared into an opening. There stood a relatively new white steel agricultural building, a 7,500 square foot pole barn. He stopped the minivan; turned off the engine, and they got out. Molly noticed that the building was totally secluded in the forest. There were no neighbors for miles. It was almost like taking a step into the past, when farming was what most people did for a living and the closest thing to social was the town banquet.

What caught Molly's attention next were solar panels that completely covered the south side of the building's gable roof. "Wow, that's a lot of solar panels," she said.

"That's over 25 kilowatts of energy production." Ronnie explained, "That's only part of the system I want to show you. I thought that you'd appreciate this because of your interest in studying green building in architectural school. The big secret is my work inside."

With her mind filled with excitement, Molly declared, "I want to see it all!"

"Well, come on in. Let me show you." Ronnie motioned his hand, inviting her in.

The couple walked to the side door of the building. There was a key pad next to the door where Ronnie punched in his security code, 4408, and the door buzzed. He pulled on the handle and motioned his hand, saying, "Ladies first." Ronnie held the door open for Molly as she walked in. He followed her and turned on the lights.

At first glance, Molly saw the plainest, most unimpressive office space ever. Inside the 300 square foot room, there were two desks with personal computers on them. Behind the desks were bookshelves filled with unimpressive three inch binders in bland colors and with worn binding. There was a high end laser printer on a counter next to a collection of charts and schedules that hung on the wall. In the corner was small white dorm refrigerator with a microwave oven sitting on top. There was another closed door on the far end of the room. Ronnie said, "What I want to show you is on the other side of that door." Molly's heart sank as her hopes of dinosaurs crashed and burned.

Ronnie walked over and turned the knob. He entered first and Molly followed him. When she stepped into the room, astonishment permeated her body. Molly was staring at a 7,000 square foot warehouse nearly filled with the largest, bushiest marijuana plants she'd ever seen. Her mind flashed back to all the stoner movies she had ever watched, and the first time she had smoked weed with her roommate during sophomore year. The plants were extraordinarily tall, more than twice Molly's height. The scale of the plants that filled the room was mindboggling and made Molly feel even shorter than usual.

With her mouth open, Molly moved down the aisle between the large potted plants and her mind raced. The air was thick with a heavy smell. It was at the point where the young lady could almost taste the fragrance and feel it on her skin. With the size and scope of the operations in front of her, several thoughts reveled through her mind, and her heart sunk so low that she was surprised it wasn't resting at her feet. She turned on Ronnie and asked, cautiously, "Ronnie, are you a drug kingpin?"

A small laugh was Ronnie's reaction before he explained, "You could smoke every single plant in this room and you'll never get high. Each plant here was cultivated to have almost no THC content, so they have zero street value. It's like smoking a bag of lawn clippings. Most importantly, everything we do here is with the blessing of the Federal Government. DEA and FDA are both involved. This particular crop is for harvesting cannabidiol, or CBD. The chemical compound is being used for medical purposes. Come on, I'll show you." He offered a comforting smile and turned to walk back into the office area.

Molly could feel her pulse in her fingertips. Nervousness and apprehension filled her as her blood pressure spiked. Remaining calm on the outside, she followed him through the doorway and back into the office area.

In the office, she watched as Ronnie, who was standing, bent over slightly, grabbed his computer mouse and shook it to snap his computer out of sleep mode. He entered his password and gestured his hand. "Molly, please take a seat." She couldn't understand how he could be so calm, how he could expect her to be so calm. She was too shocked to be angry, but she knew that rage would soon win out without a damn good explanation. Now, she knew why he had refused to tell her what he was researching: he'd feared she wouldn't come.

Without saying a word, she sat down in the office chair in front of him and watched as he maneuvered the cursor on the screen. Ronnie opened his hard drive and opened a file folder labeled "Saint Billy." He scanned folder for a file and double clicked on the icon. The media player immediately opened and began to play the video. An older and distinguished gentleman with neatly trimmed salt and pepper hair appeared on the media player's screen as Ronnie pressed pause to explain, "This is Professor William Rittenberg. He's the head of this research project and what you're about to see is his work. I'm just here as a part of the team. This video was taken last year." Molly still sat, silently, attempting to wait for his explanation before allowing herself to say anything.

Ronnie pressed play and the video resumed as the professor was making a video log entry. "Today is March 22nd and I would to introduce you to Lindsey Pendleton. She's a little over two years old and was diagnosed with Dravet syndrome just before her second birthday. Dravet is rare form of Myoclonic Epilepsy that usually begins in infancy. The cause of Lindsey's affliction is a genetic condition that causes interference of certain channels of her brain, which leads to severe physical seizures. Our observations show that Lindsey suffers from 20 to 30 physical convulsions per day. Each seizure's lasts approximately two to 30 minutes and they are randomly scattered throughout the day."

Molly's eyes narrowed as she focused on the video showing the infant girl struggling painfully with her near constant seizures. It was hard for her to watch.

Professor Rittenberg continued with his narration, "All forms of typical and approved seizure medications have proven ineffective for Lindsey. The U.S Food and Drug Administration and the Department of Justice have approved clinical human trials for our new medication, which was developed from cannabidiol extract, also known as CBD, a chemical compound from the cannabis plant. Lindsey was approved as a clinical candidate by all involved parties."

Immediately Molly turned her head and looked directly into Ronnie's face, as he stood directly over her right shoulder. She returned her attention to the video on the monitor just as the oral medication was administered to the infant. There was no immediate reaction and there were no visible signs of seizures. Professor Ritternberg's voice continued as the video of the toddler played on, "Our qualitative observations over three days of administering medication to Lindsey revealed that there is no sign of any seizures. Our subject has been readjusting to normal sleep patterns and her appetite has normalized. Her overall condition appears to be improving without convulsions."

Molly was mesmerized by the image of the little girl, who previously appeared to be enduring excruciating pain, with a smile on her face. She seemed to be enjoying an average human existence. Ronnie pressed pause on the media player. Suddenly, the shock disappeared and the standby anger took its leave.

Molly stared at the face of smiling little girl on the computer screen. "Is that kid high?" she exclaimed.

"No." Ronnie answered, "THC is the only part of marijuana that can get you high. Through the growing and refining process, we've removed all forms of THC from the medicine. The only active chemical is CBD and it doesn't induce a high, not one single bit. It works with the body's natural system, and it appears to decrease the electrochemical activity in the nerves and brain, which is ending her seizures with no apparent negative side effects."

Shaking her head in disbelief, Molly asked Ronnie, "This is what you do here?"

Nodding, he answered, "Yep. Every marijuana plant you see back in the warehouse is for the sole purpose of developing medicine for children like Lindsey. We know our medication works, but right now, we're gathering biological and physiological evidence to prove why it works. Once we prove that, we can apply for FDA approval and become a legitimate medicine."

Trying to process the information, Molly's winced before she asked, "Then why all the top-secret stuff? You're doing legit research here trying to help people." Part of her wanted to kick Ronnie for almost making her go off, but she kind of wanted to kiss him at the same time.

"I know," Ronnie tried to explain, "But you have to understand you're talking about something controversial here. The university administration recognizes the merit of the work, but it's a publicly funded institution that's under the scrutiny of politicians at the Capitol Building, who also have their own agendas. You're talking about giving marijuana extract to infants and toddlers. Even if it has medical benefits, that statement alone can cause a PR disaster for the school. There are a lot people out there who would have a heart attack over this, and that's what this university wants to avoid. That's why getting all these government agencies to sign off on this research was the hardest part."

Butterflies fluttered in Molly's stomach; she felt a mixture of excitement and relief that her new interest wasn't marijuana cartel kingpin.

Reading the expression on her face, Ronnie asked, "Pretty cool, huh?" A naughty grin followed. He felt bad for the conflicting emotions that showed on Molly's face, but he had been afraid that if told her what he had planned to show her that she wouldn't have come. How badly he had wanted to bring her here made him more nervous than the possibility of being turned over to the university. He had never brought a woman here, ever. Attempting to play it cool, he flashed another grin.

Returning the smile, Molly answered, "Yeah. That was very cool. Thanks for sharing it with me. I love the phenomenal things we do at universities."

Shaking his head, Ronnie said, "It is pretty awesome, but the stuff here on the inside is only part of the reason that I brought you here. You told me before you want to study green building technology as an architect. I want to show you something really fantastic in building science. It's outside. Come on, let's go see it."

Standing up, Molly followed Ronnie to the exterior of the building. They walked around to the southern face and Ronnie pointed at the roof as he said, "See those solar panels?"

"Yeah," answered Molly, looking up.

"Well," Ronnie explained, "it takes a lot of energy to grow these plants indoors. The power bill is our biggest cost. Those solar panels generate more electrical power than what we use at this facility during most of the year. In the past, if we had surplus power we just sold it back to the grid as clean energy. Also in the past, especially during the winter months, those panels may not generate enough power to run our operation, so we had to take additional electricity from the grid, which in our case is coal sourced and not very clean."

The young lady inquired, "So, what do you do now?"

Gesturing for Molly to follow him, Ronnie added, "Come, let me show you." He walked to the opposite end of the building to another door. He punched in his four-digit code on the keypad next to the door to open it.

Molly looked inside the room and saw more electrical building equipment.

Pointing at the first piece of equipment, which was encased in a metal box, Ronnie explained, "This is our mechanical room. Now, when we have surplus energy from the solar panels, instead of selling it back to the grid, we run it through this apparatus. It called an electrolysis device and we use it to separate hydrogen and oxygen from water by forcing an electrical current through it. We release the oxygen to the atmosphere, but we collect and compress the hydrogen gas for storage. We use those storage tanks on the outside of the building." He moved his hand and pointed to the large storage tanks in the yard.

Molly's eyes followed his fingers while Ronnie continued, "Those are 1,000-gallon storage tanks. There are 10 of them. They normally would have stored propane for heating a house, but now they're being used to store our hydrogen gas."

"So, what do you do with the hydrogen gas?" Molly raised her eyebrows, before she asked. Ronnie's voice was deep; he wasn't naturally soft spoken like she was. He kept her attention, although she could barely process what he said as he stood there. She only knew that she could spend hours listening and she'd remember this day for a lifetime.

"That's the next step." Ronnie couldn't wait to explain, "As I said before, during the winter months, we get less sunlight, and those solar panels may or may not have covered our electrical needs. Before we would tap the grid for supplemental power, now we just run our stored hydrogen gas through this device here." He pointed at another larger metal box in the mechanical room.

The young woman listened intently while he explained, hanging on the words like she wanted to hang onto his hand. "That's our fuel cell. When the hydrogen gas enters the fuel cell, it combines with the oxygen found in the atmosphere to form two products: water and electricity. We use that electricity and the power from the solar panels to meet all this facility's power needs during the shorter days of the winter. We are 100 percent off the grid and carbon free."

"That's amazing!" Molly's face beamed with astonishment, before she immediately asked, "Did you come up with this design?"

Shaking his head, Ronnie said, "It's the New Jersey Dude's concept. We just copied it."

A small laugh burst from Molly's lips and she asked, "Who's the New Jersey Dude?"

Ronnie explained, "He's this guy on YouTube. If you search things like 'hydrogen solar home New Jersey', his video usually comes up near the top. We based our system on his prototype." Ronnie's face soured and he changed the direction of the conversation, "That guy just wanted to show a new way of looking at things, maybe a better way, but I've heard the powers that be have been making things really tough for him. It's like if you come up with a better idea, you'll be punished for not toeing the line or promoting the status quo." Frustration was apparent on the researcher's face. "With powerful people, it seems like every step forward is like a step back, even in a country where there is supposed to be freedom. If you don't have the money to pay off our politicians then you're at the mercy of the ones who do."

"Why would someone go out of their way to smear someone for coming up with a green housing innovation like this?" asked Molly.

Running his fingers through his hair, Ronnie answered, "I think it has to do more with the gas pump than making houses more energy efficient."

Molly's eyes narrowed. "How so?"

Ronnie began to explain, "What makes America a great social experiment is the fact that we've combined democracy and market-based capitalism. Both of those concepts are rooted in the notion that people are allow to choose. We weigh decisions with the information on hand at any particular time and then we make a choice. It's freedom. From those fundamental ideas, we built our society and now we have an incredible selection to choose from. Look at the variety on grocery store shelves or the channels on cable. With over 300 million people living in this country, we have something for just about everyone. Variety, it's the American way."

"So, what does this green building technology has to do with the gas pump?" pressed the young woman.

A slight smirk broke through when Ronnie reacted, "We have nearly every choice in every facet of life, except in one important area: our transportation fuel. At the pump you can only get gasoline, diesel, or an ethanol blend, and all three are based on petroleum. It's what makes us go, but if we put this green building technology on every roof of every home, then it would change everything - even how we fuel our cars."

A skeptical expression appeared on Molly's face. "And why's that?"

With confidence Ronnie clarified, "If you Google 'fuel cell GM,' 'fuel cell Ford,' 'fuel cell Toyota,' or something similar, you'll see that nearly every American, Japanese, European and Korean automotive manufacturer already has working prototypes of fuel cell engine cars ready for mass production. There's one problem that keeps these cars from hitting the market: there is no fueling infrastructure. This building system could eliminate a big part of that problem."

Pulling her iPhone out of her pocket, Molly opened up a browser and Googled it. She tapped her phone screen several times verifying what her friend had told her. "Wow, those are good looking cars." Molly added, "But I'm not connecting the dots here."

Ronnie contained his enthusiasm, "Those cars are fueled with compressed hydrogen gas. This green technology system for this building is designed for that purpose. With this building system and those cars, you could fuel up your vehicle at your own house for free." He tilted his head and offered a devilish grin. "And the only thing that comes out of your tailpipe is drinkable water."

As her eyes widened, the epiphany struck Molly while she said, "So, we can power our homes and gas our car for free. It's zero carbon emissions and totally green." Molly thought about it and asked, "Then how come we're not doing this?"

"Just ask the New Jersey Dude." Ronnie responded, "You'll get run over in the process if you take on the largest monopoly in the history of civilization. All the guy wanted to do is give us another choice and the ability to choose ends the oil monopoly on transportation fuel. There goes their ability to make record profits. They'll have to work for their money like everyone else. Our ability to choose scares the hell out of them. That's where the politicians come in."

Molly stood there in silence and the latent anger from earlier slowly came to surface as she calculated how much money she spent on all that bullshit gasoline prices.

He added, "That's why it's important for young people, like us, to go on to architectural and engineering school and develop this new technology. Get it out there to the public, change things for the better by giving society better and better choices." His idealism was apparent.

His words were like liquid inspiration pouring into her soul. Molly broke silence, "I just can't wait to get architectural school and start working on this stuff. I see a working prototype right here in front of me and there is so much potential for the future. I'm so inspired right now!" She let out a deep exhale. "Thanks Ronnie. Thank you for bringing me here."

The two stepped out of the mechanical room as the door closed and locked. As they walked toward Ronnie's minivan, Molly could feel her infatuation for him grow with every step. Ever since her father had passed away from cancer, she had walled herself off with her grief and feelings of abandonment. With a slight turn of her head, she looked at Ronnie out of the corner of her eye. The young man was doing and saying everything right. This allowed her to slowly take down her emotional wall brick by brick. Molly could feel the healing process starting, and she was nothing but grateful to her new neighbor.

When the couple reached the vehicle, Ronnie stopped and looked her. "Molly, I have to go to Chicago next week, Thursday to Friday, for a Medical Proxy Conference. The school is picking up the tab and they have me down for a plus one. I know its short notice, but would you go with me?" His voice was initially sweet and kind, but before she could answer, Ronnie continued his invitation with a more nervous inflection, "It a nice hotel right downtown on Wacker Drive. They have me down for a suite, so you can have the bed and I'll take the fold out couch..."

Her eyes lit up as she interrupted him with her answer, "Ronnie, I would love to go with you."

Feeling relieved, a smile spread across his lips. "Oh, I wanted someone I could share the town with. I've only been there once, and I was a kid, so I thought this would be a great experience."

She returned, "Let me clear my schedule, but I would be happy to go with you."

"We're going to have a great time," Ronnie tried not to look too shocked or grin too stupidly as chest expanded with happiness. "The professor is going to make a presentation at the conference and he promised to blow all the attendees away. I can't wait to see what he brings to the podium." Although he attempted to return his voice to its previously casual and nonchalant inflection, his brain was singing. *She said yes! She said yes!*

Molly watched the sunshine reflect in Ronnie's eyes as she replied, "Neither can I."

14

THE PROFESSOR'S PRESENTATION

It terms of publicity, it had been one of the worst grand openings for a luxury hotel, ever. The original 35-story Kilgore Hotel was located on Lower Wacker Drive along the south bank of the Chicago River. The Downtown Chicago location was perfect for a luxury hotel, and the design lived up to Chi-town's standards for lavish accommodations. The amenities were not the problem during the hotel's grand opening; rather, the date was an issue. The ribbon cutting ceremony was held on October 30th, the day after the Great Stock Market Crash of 1929, otherwise known as Black Tuesday. The economic calamity kicked off the Great Depression that paralyzed the American economy. It also trumped the newspaper coverage, pushing the hotel's grand opening ceremony out of the limelight.

The failed promotional event was the start of series of unfortunate circumstances that led to decades of financial struggle for the luxury hotel. Throughout the years, the original hotel structure fell into a state of disrepair as the Downtown Chicago property on which it stood dramatically increased in value. Eventually, the land was worth more than the hotel, and the old building had to go.

In 1995, the 66-year-old hotel was torn down and three years later the new Kilgore Hotel was constructed on the same site. The 70-story skyscraper was made of steel, concrete and glass, and added to the famous Chicago skyline. The ribbon cutting ceremony for the new building took place on October 30, 1999, and this time, everything went almost perfectly. The sentiment around the new hotel's grand opening ceremony was second chances. The new building lived up to its creed, as it had all the modern accommodations, including high end restaurants and bars, and a luxurious convention center, which hosted numerous professional gatherings.

Today, the new Kilgore Hotel was fully booked while it hosted the annual convention for the National Association of Medical Proxy Researchers. The lobby was packed with medical professionals, most of whom worked in pharmaceutical sales. Since the hotel was filled to capacity, the elevators were constantly in motion. If your room was on the upper floors, you may spend 20 minutes or more waiting for an elevator to take you to your room. However, Ronnie Harding and Molly Jo Donnelly had a suite on the second floor, so they skipped the wait and took the stairs.

Exiting the stairwell, Ronnie and Molly entered the busy lobby. Even though they were dressed for the occasion, it was obvious in comparison to the other attendees that the couple was a pair of poor college students. Ronnie wore dark gray slacks and a white dress shirt with a striped black and silver satin tie. He looked at Molly, who donned a black and red floral patterned skater dress with a hemline well above her knees. She carried a small black leather clutch. They both sported laminated conference identification passes on lanyards around their necks.

"You look nice by the way," Ronnie said as he snuck glances at Molly. He had been peeking at her, discreetly, since they started their early morning train ride from Michigan to Chicago. Nothing they had seen in the city so far had kept his attention as much as Molly's smile.

Feeling good about getting dressed up and being at a professional event, Molly's face turned a slight pinkish color before she said, "Why thank you. You don't look so bad yourself." Molly had never known how to take compliments and his words made her feel warm.

The two made their way through the crowed lobby. Some of the attendees greeted each other in small social circles; others were walking with a purpose, like they were late for something. The people around them seemed to move so fast that they were no more than a blur of cell phone conversations and touch screens.

Ronnie returned a friendly expression and wondered if Molly knew she was beautiful.

The room became more congested. Molly followed Ronnie through the crowds of people as they left the lobby and made their way into a large hallway. The young man reached down and instinctively took a hold of her hand as he led her through the crowd. When his hand made contact with hers, Molly felt secure and safe, amazed at how close to him this simple gesture made her feel. The two walked quickly down a long lavish concourse, passing by the other full conference halls packed with observers watching presentations of the latest medical findings.

When they found Conference Hall H, Ronnie let go of Molly's hand. He had never been much for public displays of affection and this place was full of potential business connections. Business had to come first during this conference. Molly stretched her hand, suddenly unsure of what to do with it. She felt awkward letting it hang at her side. There were two attendees, an elderly man and a middle-aged woman, sitting at the table in near the entrance. The man addressed the young couple. "Welcome to Hall H, can I see your identification please?"

Leaning forward, Ronnie held out his laminated conference ID hanging from the lanyard around his neck. Molly repeated his actions.

The elderly man reached into a file box and pulled out two over stuffed 9x13 envelopes. He handed one to each of them. "Mr. Harding, you are in seat 199 and Ms. Donnelly, you are in seat 200. You are both in the back row. Please hurry; the presentation is about to start."

"Thank you," returned Ronnie. He then nodded to Molly, signaling for her to follow him.

When Molly stepped through the doorway into the conference hall, she gazed at the large, extravagant, rectangular room. There were rows of tables covered in white cloths and over 200 chairs filled with attendees. At the front of the room was an elevated platform and a podium, and behind the stage a large white movie screen hung from the wall. This was the fanciest set up she had seen for an event in her life.

With another head nod, Ronnie led Molly to the back of the conference hall. As she walked, Molly felt the lush burgundy and gold carpet under her feet. They carried their envelopes to their seats at the back of the room and Molly noticed the large theater speakers hanging from the side walls. *This could almost pass for a concert venue,* she thought, *even if the greatest pop divas were singing.*

The two went to the back row of tables and took their seats, numbers 199 and 200 respectively. Each pulled out their phones and turned the ringer to vibrate before sitting down.

Ronnie picked up glass pitcher of ice water that was on the table and offered, "Molly, you want some?"

"Yes, please," she answered.

He filled their glasses. They had been so busy; Ronnie was not surprised they were thirsty.

Molly said, "Thanks", before she asked, "Ronnie, do you have any idea what the professor is going to say during his presentation?"

He answered, "No, I have no idea, but he loves doing these appearances." Ronnie had always enjoyed his professor's lectures; he was the most brilliant man Ronnie had ever met. That brilliance was something Ronnie hoped to learn from the professor.

At that moment, an older, heavyset gentleman with a white beard and mustache walked across the stage and stood at the podium. "My name is Dr. Jeremy Edmondson and I'm the Vice Chairman of the National Association of Medical Proxy Researchers," he said. "I would like to thank you for attending today's presentation on the history and future of medical marijuana research." He was wearing a dark brown business suit that looked like it was from one of the expensive Chicago shops.

The audience applauded politely, before the man, who vaguely resembled Santa Claus, continued, "Today, one of our oldest tenured members, Professor William Rittenburg from Michigan A&M University, will try to cut through the political dogmatic misinformation propagated by the government. The purpose of this presentation is to examine the intertwining of science and politics as it has developed the policies we live under today. With this seminar, we will the look at the positives and negatives with an attempt to get to the truth of the matter."

Another round of robust applause filled the room until Dr. Edmondson proceeded, "Now, with no further adieu, I would like to introduce my friend and distinguished colleague, Doctor William Rittenburg."

The room filled with an enthusiastic ovation when Professor Rittenburg stepped on the platform dressed in a soft gray tweed sport coat and comfortable beige slacks. He adjusted the wireless microphone on his lapel before testing it. "Can you hear me okay?"

Various members of the audience nodded or hollered out, "Yes!"

"Well good," the professor grinned and said, "let's get this started."

The room lights dimmed slightly as a black and white image from the 1930's appeared on the projector screen. Pointing at the white man with dark hair in the image, Rittenburg explained, "This is Jimmy Lane." The image on the screen changed to another black and white photo of different man with lighter hair. "And this is Ralph Wiley." Both men on the screen had crazed and sinister looks about them. Some of the audience members recognized the men in the photos and snickered.

The professor offered a smirk as he said, "These two men are fictional characters from the 1936 cult classic film, 'Tell Your Children', which was later re-titled, 'Reefer Madness'. This movie was directed by Louis Gasnier and financed by a moral reformist group in the middle of prohibition and the Great Depression with the sole purpose of warning parents about the evils of marijuana. The movie was designed/produced to show that cannabis use could lead to homicide, rape, violence, hallucinations, or an incurable state of insanity."

The room was filled with levity as Rittenburg walked to the opposite end of the stage. He re-engaged the audience as he gazed around at a new generation, the generation he hoped would make a difference. "Now, the problem with this movie was timing, because the drug policies that were established during this era have greatly influenced today's legal standards and ramifications. Think about it. In the 1930's, the Moral Reform and Prohibition Movements were gaining momentum throughout the country. During the Great Depression, many viewed the excesses of the Roaring 20s as the cause of America's downfall. For many out there, it was time for moral reform. This movie, along with so-called yellow journalism, fed exaggerated misinformation to the general public, claiming that marijuana would cause societal violence and individual lunacy. That type of national climate set the stage for this man."

Some moans and groans came from spectators when another black and white photo of strong looking, heavy-set, bald man in a business suit appeared on the movie screen. Dr. Rittenburg could hear his voice echoing through the crowd.

The professor remembered when, years ago, as a young man, he had given his first lecture. Hearing his own voice through the microphone had made him more nervous than any of the strangers listening to his stuttering and rushed words.

He smiled at the memory as he spoke, "This is Harry Jacob Anslinger. In 1930, he became the first commissioner of the United States Federal Bureau of Narcotics. In a sense, he became our nation's first Drug Czar. This man drafted the first federal law placing marijuana under the complete control of the Federal Government with the Marijuana Tax Act of 1937. Also during his reign at the Federal Bureau of Narcotics, the Commissioner initiated an anti-marijuana campaign with the support of many industrialists, who likely viewed hemp fiber as a commercial threat to other forms of established industrial materials that were used at the time."

Adjusting his metal rimmed glasses for moment, the professor continued, "Mr. Anslinger told the country that marijuana was a pathway to violence and a gateway to harder drugs, like cocaine and heroin, which would lead to the ruin of individual lives. It could have been considered that Federal Bureau of Narcotics had racial undertones in their policies directed against Latin and African Americans of that era, because it was viewed that these groups were the primary marijuana consumers of this time period. The Commissioner was unwavering in his stance during his 32 years on the job. Under his leadership, from 1930-1962, the Federal Government solidified its position against marijuana, even in the face of contradictory science. "

The eyes of the audience followed the professor while he walked to the center of the stage as another black and white photo of a robust white man with dark hair and a kind round face. A little grin appeared Rittenburg's lips before he clarified, "To many New Yorkers, like me, it's hard not to recognize Fiorello La Guardia. He was the Mayor of New York City from 1934 to 1945, and also a moral reformer himself, but in the middle of his tenure of office in 1939, the Mayor assembled the La Guardia Committee with researchers from the New York Academy of Medicine. This was recognized as one of the first legitimate scientific studies on the human consumption of marijuana. The committee's findings were the complete opposite of the stance of Harry Anslinger and the Federal government."

The digital picture that now appeared on the projector screen revealed bullet point text as Rittenburg moved to the podium. The professor was not like many from his generation; he appreciated and understood modern technology. The speaker pointed at the screen. "After the five-year study, The La Guardia Committee found that smoking marijuana does not lead to addiction in the medical sense of the word. The committee also stated that smoking marijuana does not lead to morphine, heroin or cocaine addiction, and is not necessarily a gateway drug. The findings additionally declared that smoking marijuana was not a determining factor in criminal activity, including juvenile delinquency. The report summarized that all the fears of catastrophic effects on society were unfounded in New York City. And what do you think was Harry Anslinger's response to the study?"

Reaching inside the podium, Rittenburg took out a plastic bottle of water and took a sip before he continued. The Professor was used to giving lectures. He had taught at a university for years. However, teaching college students and changing the general public's mind about marijuana legality were two very different tasks. "Anslinger basically called it unscientific hogwash. The Federal Commissioner slammed Mayor La Guardia and his committee, and then he instructed them to never conduct any future scientific research or study on marijuana consumption without with his personal permission. Anslinger began to establish total control of the marijuana issue until the early 1960s, when he stepped down from his position."

A yellow peace sign on a green background now appeared on the overhead screen when the professor stepped out from behind the podium and walked toward the front of the stage. "Now, we enter the post-Anslinger years. As the 1960's progressed in America, the Hippie and Counterculture movement was in full swing and marijuana was no longer reserved for Latin and African American use. It crossed all racial barriers and demographic lines. Marijuana became the leading illegal recreational drug in the nation. As the 60s turned into the 70s, there was a growing legalization movement until this..."

The room laughed and snickered as a retro cover of People Magazine appeared on the projector screen. There was a smiling young woman on the cover. Rittenburg explained, "For some of you who don't recognize this young woman, this is Emmy and Oscar award winning actress, Cloris Leachman." For years, Rittenburg had a crush on Leachman and he could not help but smile at the photo. "She's not what I was referring to. There is an article inside this issue of People Magazine dated December 09, 1974, which cites the findings Dr. Robert Heath's Marijuana study at Tulane University. The article was an attempt to take Dr. Heath's research to the mainstream public."

Rittenburg had spent too much time talking before this lecture. Between prepping and meet and greets, his throat was dry. Clearing it, Rittenburg carried on, "For those who are unfamiliar with Dr. Heath's work, it sometimes referred to the Marijuana Monkey Study. It was said that Dr. Heath gave his test monkeys extremely high doses of cannabis smoke through a gas mask contraption. During the experiment, some monkeys died. When their brains were examined, scientists found dead brain cells and Dr. Heath declared, in this People Magazine article, that 'Marijuana damages the brain.' The Heath study became the scientific basis and standard reference for the political push back against marijuana legalization."

When the digital projector changed the image on the screen to a photo of Presidents Nixon, Regan, Bush Sr. and Clinton, the eyes of the audience again followed the presenter as he walked back to the opposite end of the stage. While he was walking, Rittenburg continued his speech. "This report was cited by President Nixon as the basis of his decision to place cannabis on the Schedule I Narcotics list, making it an illegal drug with no medical purpose and declaring it as one of the most dangerous drugs on the planet. Then President Regan also used the Heath study for not only his 'Just say no' public campaign, it became one of his scientific sources in declaring his 'War on Drugs'. President George Herbert Walker Bush escalated this war further and installed his 'get-tough' policies, including minimal sentence legislation that forced judges to hand out longer prison sentences for people selling pot than for violent crimes, like murder. These minimum sentence policies were further enhanced under the Clinton Administration with his 'three-strikes' legislation. Today, there are more people in prison for marijuana-related offenses than any other drug crime."

"The problem here," the professor said as he folded his arms across his chest, "is that these policies were based on bad science. The Heath study is commonly discredited by other scientific professionals as they look at the methodology. The monkeys that were used in the study were given such large doses of marijuana smoke through their gas masks that they suffered long periods of suffocation. It was the oxygen deprivation that caused the monkey's brain damage and their ultimate demise, not the chemical compounds found in marijuana."

The room was filled silent disbelief and eyes widened in shock as Rittenburg continued, "The Heath study has been discredited by two other controlled research programs. Both of these reviewed studies were designed to avoid asphyxiating the test monkeys with smoke, and to examine the effects of marijuana's chemical composition on their test subject's brains. Both of these studies concluded that the chemicals found in marijuana smoke did not cause any physiological brain damage. None. Human studies that were conducted later verify these findings."

With a look of determination, Rittenburg implored the audience, "We have based our marijuana policies on bad science and on the personal agendas of powerful men." The speaker paused again while he looked down and adjusted the metal rimmed glasses that he had bought years ago, but refused to replace. "The basis of our policies was a lie."

Smiling to the observers, he continued, "The lie is basing a war on pot, costing the taxpayers billions, while sentencing people to near life in prison for selling something that science is now saying is not harmful to the brain. According to the ACLU, over half of people arrested for drugs in the United States have marijuana related convictions. I say the new revolution should be based on good science that's looking for the truth, not just telling powerful men what they want to hear for their self-serving agendas. So I ask you, what is the good science?" It was hard for Rittenburg to keep the frustration out of his voice.

The image on the screen changed to a photo of an older man with white hair and a receding hairline. The speaker on the stage explained, "This is Israeli researcher, Raphael Mechoulam. With his fellow scientists, he studied the effects of cannabis on humans and discovered something revolutionary about the human body. They found the endocannabinoid system. It exists inside every human being. This same system is also found in every bird, fish and mammal." Mechoulam was an interesting man and a hero to Rittenburg. A rebellious scientist of his time, just like Rittenburg, he had begun a movement that would change history.

Walking back to the podium, Professor Rittenburg placed both of his hands on the platform before asking, "So what is the endocannabinoid system?" The image on the screen changed to an instructional drawing of a human body. Rittenburg continued, "Inside every human is a brain and nervous system, which is the body's information superhighway. This system conveys thoughts, feelings, and sensory input, and motor skills. Every time you move an arm, or smell freshly baked bread, that's your central nervous system at work. It also activates every time you feel boredom, when you're hungry or when inspiration strikes."

The professor brought up both fists to eye level. He extended both of his index fingers pointing straight up, before he curled them in, so they were pointing at each other with a little space in between. Rittenburg then jiggled his right finger. "Inside this system there are synaptic nerves with a conductors and receptors. Between the nerve's synaptic gap, information and function instructions are conveyed by an electro-chemical process with the use of neurotransmitters."

Bringing his hands down, the presenter carried on, "With the endocannabinoid system there are numerous nerves found in the brain and body that have cannabinoids receptors. When these receptors bond with certain chemical compounds, called cannabinoids, it like two matching pieces of a puzzle in your body connecting. When the two connect they adjust the flow of neurotransmitter activity in the synapses, or gaps between the nerves. It scales back or enhances the electro chemical movement in the nervous system, adjusting the information flow within the mind and body, just like the volume buttons on your television remote control."

With a couple steps, Rittenburg moved just to the right of the podium. He continued. "Here is the significant part; cannabinoids are naturally produced within the human body. They are also naturally produced within every mammal and fish and in various other biological life forms. Numerous cannabinoids are also uniquely produced in the marijuana plant. The most well known is THC or delta-9-tetrahydrocannabinol. THC mimics one of your own body's natural neurotransmitters: anandamide. THC also uses the endocannabinoid system in parts of the brain to stimulate production of certain hormones in your body, namely dopamine and norepinephrine, which create senses of euphoria, pain relief, and relaxation. These are some of the desired feelings for many who consume marijuana."

The audience watched intently as the large screen displayed an image of the human brain. Clearing his throat, Rittenburg continued with his presentation. "THC also has some negative side effects. It uses the receptors of the endocannabinoid system to bond with the hippocampus in the brain to cause short term memory loss. This is why it can be difficult to have a conversation with someone who is high on marijuana and they're having trouble recalling what was just said." There was some laughter; many audience members had marijuana related memories.

"Another negative side effect," the speaker persisted, "occurs when THC connects with the cerebellum and the basal ganglia in the brain to impair physical motor skills. This is why people under the influence of cannabis appear to be moving slowly and are often clumsy." Again, there was some knowledgeable laughter.

Rittenburg walked to the front of the stage and felt the heat from the lights. Stage lights were something he could never adjust to even after he'd become a skilled public speaker. They made him sweat more than actual nerves, and he was never nervous while give public lectures. "There are some other negative side effects, like fear-based paranoia, but every single negative symptom has been documented as short term. During periods of abstinence from cannabis, THC naturally breaks down within the body and the brain reverts to its baseline setting without physical damage. There is zero brain damage caused by marijuana, because THC uses your own body and brain's natural receptor system already in place to create all of its effects, and then it dissipates on its own, leaving the brain unharmed."

The professor continued with his lecture, "Here is where I want to draw a distinction. The difference between drinking alcohol and smoking pot is that your body does not produce alcohol. It's a foreign substance. When you consume alcohol, it makes you tipsy and changes the dynamic of social gatherings, but if too much alcohol is imbibed and if your brain detects toxic levels, it will begin a self defense mechanism. You begin to vomit to purge your system. Long term alcohol abuse leads liver and brain damage, and cases of extreme binge drinking could lead to death. Studies have proven that this is not the case for marijuana. If you consume too much, you'll most likely take a pretty good nap. That's why scientific opinion states that it's impossible to overdose on marijuana. There's never been a documented case. Not one."

Looking over his audience, Professor Rittenburg noticed a lot of people were acknowledging his information; he had hope for this generation. There were, of course, the classic stoners in the crowd who just loved to use marijuana as a recreational drug, but he also knew there were more advanced minds. There were those who knew the benefits and supported them. There were those who wanted to change the world. "Where do we go from here?" The presenter paused a moment and said, "The discovery of the endocannabinoid system flies in the face of the Federal Government's stance on marijuana and its decision to place it on the Schedule I Narcotics list. This list officially makes cannabis one of the most dangerous drugs on the planet, and denies any medical benefit. I wanted to prove to you that history and science say that this is not the case. The understanding of the endocannabinoid system within the human body has opened the doors to numerous opportunities for research and the development of medicines derived from the marijuana plant. There are many more cannabinoids in cannabis than the psychoactive one,

THC. There are at least 66 other compounds, like CBN, CBG, and CBD that can be extracted from the marijuana plant. Each of these chemical compounds would utilize your body's endocannabinoid system and could lead to a significant pathway for medicine development. Pot is more than a recreational drug."

Rittenburg adjusted his glasses again, before he declared, "At the risk of their careers, many researchers across the country have made tremendous strides in cannabis studies with the development of medicines and treatments for various afflictions, including multiple sclerosis, epilepsy, autism, and cancer. My own research has made tremendous progress with our work, even though the Schedule I listing made it nearly impossible, bureaucratically. It's been difficult, but our research team has finally been approved for human testing."

With his lips curling into a grin, the professor gazed out at the attendees in the room. "I would like to take this opportunity to invite you back when I present my team's research findings. I guarantee you that it will blow you away." Exhaling, the Rittenburg concluded, "With that said, I would like to thank you for attending my presentation. I hope to see you again next year." He closed his eyes and gently bowed his head.

The audience immediately reacted with an enthusiastic ovation. During the clapping, Dr. Jeremy Edmondson took the stage carrying a traditional microphone in his hand. He walked up to Rittenburg and gave him a nod and a pat on the back. Dr. Edmondson spoke into his microphone, "Thank you, Professor William Rittenburg." The crowd offered another round of applause.

Speaking into his hand held microphone, Dr. Edmondson said, "That's our last presentation of the day for this hall. I encourage each of you to stop by the main convention area and see the display booths that we have up. There are a lot of revolutionary new ideas and products out there that people want to share. So, please feel free to stop by. Thank you for coming." With that said, the attendees stood up and stretched.

Sitting in the back of the room, Ronnie gazed at Molly sitting next to him. Her presence had distracted him throughout the professor's lecture and they hadn't spoken a word. He knew more about the color of her eyes than any topic the professor had discussed. He asked her, "So what do you think?"

With a smile, Molly answered, "I can't believe that the marijuana policies that we've living under today were rooted in the ignorance powerful old men." Thinking about it, Molly had to admit to herself that she did know hardly anything about a drug that she had tried numerous times.

Offering a nod, Ronnie instructed, "Come on. Let's check on the professor."

Molly agreed as the two got up and walked across the crowed room. Near the stage there was small gathering of distinguished looking men standing around Dr. Rittenburg. The professor noticed Ronnie and Molly walking toward him and he immediately acknowledged the graduate student, "Hey, how did I do?"

"Great, of course. I really enjoyed it," answered Ronnie. Just then the young man remembered to introduce to his friend, "Professor, this is Molly Jo Donnelly. She joined me for the trip."

Ronnie watched as the Professor brought out his warm smile and greeted Molly in almost a flirtatious manner, "Why, hello young lady. It's a pleasure to meet you. Are you enjoying yourself here in the Windy City?"

"Yes. I am having a great time." Molly smiled, "I thought your presentation was very informative and entertaining."

Rittenburg was obviously proud of himself as he accepted the compliment. "Thank you." The professor immediately turned to his research assistant, "Hey Ronnie, I'm meeting up with some old friends from New York for dinner, so why don't you two go out and enjoy the town. Maybe we'll meet up for breakfast tomorrow."

Feeling relieved that his responsibilities for the day are over; the young man smiled and said, "Thanks professor." Molly smiled and waved goodbye.

Rittenburg returned an approving nod; while he watched the couple walk off. Ronnie looked over to his friend and explained, "Hey, we're free for the day. We can do whatever you want."

Excited, Molly asked, "Can we go see some buildings?" There were Christmas lights in her eyes.

"With that look on your face, how can I say no? Is there anything else you want to do?" returned Ronnie as thought of the many things he would do to keep the light in her eyes.

"Yeah," Molly's face lit up even more when she said, "Can we go see the big shiny jelly bean?"

Ronnie's forehead crinkled when he answered her with bewilderment, "Sure. I have no idea what you're talking about, but yeah, we can find your big shiny jelly bean."

With obvious excitement, Molly couldn't control her grin.

The couple stepped out into the concourse hall when Ronnie stopped and reached into his pocket to pull out his phone. "Oh, I forgot about my ringer."

The young man stared at the screen and saw he had a text from Paul. It said, "Hey bro, when ur free...hit me back."

With his eyes narrowing and his lips tightening, he couldn't hide his concern. A text like that from Paul meant something; he would not have contacted Ronnie during his weekend with Molly unless something was wrong. He had an ominous feeling in the pit of his stomach.

"Is everything alright?" asked Molly. She hadn't seen that look on Ronnie's face before, but she didn't like it. She knew that, no matter his response, something was up.

"Yeah," Ronnie explained, "I got some things to deal with later, but right now, it's our time. Let's go have some fun." His expression returned to normal and he offered a simple smile.

Feeling slightly relieved, Molly's excitement resumed. "Great, I can't wait to explore the town." They looked at each other and felt their hearts skip a beat.

15

THE BIG SHINY JELLY BEAN

Under the night sky, Ronnie stared into his distorted reflection in the 33-foot tall stainless steel public art sculpture, like a giant drop of mercury at Millennium Park in the heart of downtown Chicago. He noticed the lights from the tall buildings behind him reflecting in the warped image, like a funhouse mirror. The young man reached up and touched the sculpture's cold metal skin and whispered, "There aren't any seams. How does he do that? "

Staring at his own bended reflection, Ronnie could feel his emotions changing. He thought about how fortunate he was to be where he was, enjoying everything around him. He was grateful to be alive, to be here in this moment, experiencing the lights and sounds of the city, and the art he was not able to see back home. That's when he felt Molly arm's embrace him as she whispered into his ear, "How does it make you feel?"

Living a secret double life as both a graduate student and an illegal weed dealer was taking its toll on the Ronnie. At that moment, all of his concerns drained from the bottom of his feet and Ronnie's face appeared innocent and renewed when he answered, "It makes me feel appreciative that I'm riding on this huge ball floating in the universe, just to experience this moment right here, right now. Being here with you has me awestruck." It was the only way to describe how he felt, because he had never experienced an emotion like this before. Rarely in his life did he have moments like these. Molly was beautiful; he had known that from the moment he met her. Standing in the midst of all these buildings that had stood the test of time, the extent of Molly's beauty finally registered with him. She surpassed any beauty in this city and he would rather look at her through the night than at anything else.

"Awestruck?" Molly replied playfully, "Good word choice there, Ronnie Lee." The young lady offered a teasing grin when she let him go and turned toward the large skyscrapers behind them. Molly had wanted to see this place for years - since she had seen a picture in her dad's travel magazine as a teenager. Seeing it was more wonderful than she had imagined. Staring at the buildings around her, she felt insignificant and important all at once.

Still facing the mirrored structure in front of him, Ronnie asked, "So, this is your big shiny jelly bean?"

Looking 180 degrees in the opposite direction, Molly stated, "You know, the artist hates any use of the word 'bean' in describing his work. It's called Cloud Gate."

"Cloud Gate?" Ronnie pondered that before he said, "Yeah, I can see that. In the middle of the afternoon with the blue sky and white wispy clouds above the Chicago skyline that would be a hell of view. I have to say though, calling it the big shiny jelly bean makes me want to sink me teeth into it." His mouth moved as if he were taking a bite of air.

At that moment, a joyous squeal came from Molly. "Ronnie, look!"

He turned and saw the floor of the pavilion around the public artwork light up like disco dance floor as wind chime music began to play. Ronnie turned his gaze back to the mirrored sculpture and saw the light show dance on the distorted and reflective surface, playing tricks on his eyes. Staring for a long moment, he took in the sights and sounds; the new age music playing only enhanced the experience. "Awesome," he whispered.

Turning, Ronnie drew his attention to Molly, who was clapping uncontrollably as people of all ages joyously moved toward the illuminated floor. She turned and faced her friend. Ronnie stared at her mesmerized smile, completely taken by her. Without thinking, he leaned in and pressed his lips against hers.

As he pulled back, Ronnie looked at Molly's eyes; they were wide and full of astonishment; he immediately apologized, "I'm sorry. I was just caught up in the moment."

"No, no, no." Molly implored, "It was just like that movie, *Hearts in Atlantis*. I just wasn't ready. Please do it again." She paused a second and then added an additional sincere, "Please." There was eagerness in her eyes as Ronnie wondered whether her heart was beating as fast as his, like a bass drum in his chest.

When Ronnie obliged and leaned in again slowly, Molly could feel the warmth of his face as he gave her the sweetest kiss he could offer. The lights and music in the park seemed to flow into their bodies, passing back and forth between them.

This time when he pulled back, Ronnie gazed at her face and saw her eyes were closed as the music and lights slowly moved back outside of her body. When Molly opened her eyes, she said, "Thanks for that." A mesmerized smile appeared on her lips.

Without thinking, Ronnie said, "You're just irresistible, aren't you?" He could still feel the bass drum in his chest, but it was the beat to his new favorite song, a song Molly had unknowingly written.

She nodded in response, so happy that she felt like lights should be shooting from her and out into the crowd.

"Well," the young man asked, "what do you want to do now?"

Molly exclaimed, "I want to see more of Millennium Park. I want to go over there and see the Crown Fountain. There's a huge urban botanical garden over there too. And if you want, we can go to the Navy Pier and look at the skyline from a distance." Her grin glowed with an innocence and excited enthusiasm.

Her happiness was priceless to him as Ronnie was caught up with infatuation. The only thing that he could say was, "Sure, we can do whatever you want."

Molly had never felt that she came first in her life. She always had to support others and do whatever they wanted to do. Tonight, Ronnie was making her a priority. The couple did exactly what she wanted to do and that was a new feeling for her.

As the night went on, they saw the large electronic digital faces displayed on Crown Fountain and walked the paths of the Lurie Garden, enjoying the Chicago skyline. Molly felt comfortable and took pleasure in every bit of their conversations.

The two decided it was time to check out Navy Pier as Ronnie hailed a cab off of Columbus Drive. When the yellow cab pulled over, Ronnie followed Molly inside. The driver's face startled him. Ronnie blurted, "Oh my God, you look just like James Earl Jones."

Accentuating every syllable, the taxi driver reacted, "Who is this James Earl Jones?" His voice was deep and rich.

Ronnie picked up from the driver's accent that he had emigrated from another country. Ronnie thought before he explained, "He's a famous American actor and you look just like him."

"Is he popular?" the cabbie asked in slow, drawn out manner, annunciating every part of every word.

"Very." Ronnie answered, "He beloved by millions of fans of every genre."

"Hmm," the taxi driver said, "This is a good thing." He offered his passengers a brilliant smile.

Molly watched with amazement as Ronnie engaged in conversation with his new acquaintance. Ronnie leaned forward and read the driver's identification card. "Your name is Amdi Obi?"

The cab driver answered, "Yes. That is a good pronunciation."

"Well Amdi," Ronnie asked, "where do you come from?"

The cabbie said, "Lagos, Nigeria. I come from the Igbo people." The driver turned his head and looked directly at his two passengers. His eyes narrowed as he offered them an intimidating scowl before he asked, "Are you from the Hausa tribe?"

Slightly laughing and going along with humorous conversation, Ronnie replied, "No. We both grew up in the suburbs of Detroit."

"Detroit. That is good. I want you to know I do not care for the Hausa people at all. I am glad you're not a part of them or I may have had to to kick out of my car." Then, with a smile, the driver asked his passengers, "Okay now, where do you want to go?"

Unsure whether the driver was joking or not, Ronnie answered, "Navy Pier, please."

"Okay, I will get you there. Hold on now." The driver instructed as he pulled away and took off down Columbus Drive. He made his way down the road with little traffic. Ahead, a red light turned green and a few pedestrians were still straggling slowly in the crosswalk, including the last person walking: a slow moving, portly-around-the-middle man in a dark blue sweat shirt with the same color baseball cap and khaki pants. The cab engine roared as the driver pressed the gas pedal to the floor. The taxi was now full throttle, racing toward the crosswalk and the directly at the straggling middle-aged man.

Looking ahead, Molly reached over and grabbed Ronnie's arm. She hollered, "Oh my God! He's going to run him over. He's going to kill him!" The driver was unfazed by Molly's yells.

The last pedestrian in the crosswalk hurried to move out of the taxi's way, just in time -- the cabbie never once stepped on the breaks. As the car ran through white painted crosswalk, Ronnie turned his head and gazed out the passenger window. He made eye contact with the lucky pedestrian, who was now safe on the curb, shaking his fist, and screaming at the cab.

Ronnie turned his attention to Molly. Her eyes were wide with astonishment. They both remained outwardly dumfounded, but on the inside they were freaked out and also a little tickled as their spiking adrenaline levels returned to normal and they shared the feeling of relief that they were not witnesses to vehicular homicide.

The cab driver, still looking forward, calmly spoke out, "I was not going to kill him, but he should have not been walking in the crosswalk during a green light. That man had be taught a lesson. This is Chicago for God sakes. Plus, he could stand to lose some weight."

The elegant foreign accent made the comment only slightly humorous while raising suspicion that the cabbie may have been certifiably nuts.

Ronnie spoke evenly, trying not to seem confrontational, "Whatever you say, man. We're good." Ronnie did not want to upset the potentially unstable person behind the wheel. Not wanting to antagonize the situation, the two passengers didn't say another word.

The rest of the cab ride was uneventful as the taxi pulled around the oval of Streeter Drive to drop the couple off at the main entrance of the Navy Pier. The driver said, "That will be $7.25, please."

Reaching into his pocket, Ronnie handed over a ten dollar bill and told him, "Keep the change."

"Thank you." The driver accepted the money.

The couple bolted from the cab and stood in the taxi staging area, just in front of Navy Pier's entrance. They watched the yellow car pull away. Molly turned and looked at Ronnie. "That driver was insane. He was going to run that man over. Maybe we should report him." Concern was all over Molly's face.

"How about we pretend it never happened and not let that guy ruin our evening?" suggested the Ronnie.

Molly thought for a moment as she tilted her head and looked up at the buildings around her, causing her to do a slight back bend. "It has been great night other than that..." Molly offered another grin before she added, "Okay, mister crazy cab driver, you're now someone else's problem."

Moving his head in a come-hither motion, Ronnie held out his elbow. Molly seized the moment and grabbed it with both hands as the two walked through the red metal gate entering Navy Pier. As they entered, she squeezed his arm and said, "Ronnie, you're definitely not a boring date."

An acknowledging glance was his only response.

The couple walked along the concourse of the pier to the Grand Staircase near the large lit up Ferris wheel. They leaned against the metal railing and stared out at the dark waters of Lake Michigan, looking at the beautiful buildings of the nighttime Chicago skyline. With all the lights, it was breathtaking.

The two were silently soaking up each other's company and enjoying the ambiance, when Molly spoke up. "Ronnie, I have to tell you something."

"Okay," he said, "go ahead."

She stared out at the water for a moment and said, "I want you to know I come from a dysfunctional family. My parents' marriage was a disaster, so I don't have a good frame of reference when it comes to relationships. I've dated guys before, and I just felt like a piece of the puzzle that never fit anywhere. They all ended up in failure, some of them bitterly."

Ronnie encouraged her to go on, "And?"

Taking in and releasing a deep breath, Molly continued, "Well, I just wanted to say that in the short time, I've known you, I'm starting to feel more like a piece of the puzzle that is starting to fit in." She moved her eyes from the water and looked him in the face. "You're making me feel that way and it scares the hell out of me, because I don't know what I'm doing here."

Looking back at her, he said, "My mom always gives me her best advice. She been married to my dad for over 30-something years -- since they finished high school. That's a long time to be with the same person. You know what she said was the secret to a successful long-term relationship?"

"What?" Molly reacted.

Ronnie's eyes widened and answered, "Bad timing."

She offered an inquisitive raised eyebrow.

He immediately explained, "My mom told me that it was bad timing that saved their relationship. Like anyone else, they had their ups and downs, and when she felt like quitting, my dad didn't. He would fight to hold it all together. Then, when my father was ready to throw in the towel, my mom wasn't ready, and she would do whatever it took to keep their marriage intact. If they would have had good timing and wanted to quit at the same time, then its likely they would have divorced. So, my mom always wished that her children would always have the same bad timing in their future relationships."

There was a curious "Hmm" while Molly absorbed the wisdom for moment, before she asked, "Okay, that's what your mom says, but what do you say?"

With a slightly smug look, Ronnie said, "Oh, that's easy. It all depends how you answer this next question."

Curiosity immediately filled her, when she asked, "And what's that?"

The young man raised his eyebrows and said, "Do girls fart or not?" His appearance remained steadfast.

Molly's face scrunched as if she just bit into something sour. "Oh my God, I can't believe you just asked me that."

"Well," Ronnie spoke out in a self-assured manner, "if you just hang with me a little during the conversation, you may come to an epiphany."

Realizing a challenge was thrown out, Molly accepted it, "Okay smarty, I can't wait to see where this goes."

"You have to answer the question first. Do girls fart or not?" His confidence was apparent as a mischievous grin appeared on his face.

Complacency was all over Molly's face when she said, "To answer your question. No, girls do not fart." A pinkish hue overtook her cheeks as she said the lie while knowing Ronnie wasn't stupid and would not believe her.

His face lit up. "I had my suspicions. You see any time when a group of guys gets together, like when I lived in the dorms as an undergrad; it's a regular fart factory. Guys will be sitting at their computers or lounging on the couch watching TV, then someone will let one rip and no one reacts. Life goes on, and no one thinks any less of anyone, because we're truly comfortable living with one another. We accept it as an everyday part of life. It's guy code. We accept each other for who and what we are."

"You mean pigs." Molly added with a flare of sarcasm.

Shaking his head no, Ronnie said, "Human beings." He brought up his hands to animate his story. Molly brought up her hand to cover her smile while he continued, "But when the guys would ask each other if we'd ever seen a girl fart before, none of us had. It's cryptozoic, like Big Foot sightings. You only hear sketchy accounts with no substantial proof, so there's some doubt out there over whether it actually happens." The young man's charm and humor was in full effect.

Molly was amazed how Ronnie maintained his earnest composure during this conversation. She prodded him to make his point, saying "And?"

Right on cue, he explained, "Well, in my opinion, hypothetically speaking of course, if a girl farts in front of you without dying from embarrassment, then you've reached a level in the relationship where she's truly comfortable with you, because she's found somebody who accepts her for who she is: the good, the bad and the flatulent. In my opinion, that level of acceptance is the key that you're going to be in a successful long term relationship, because it's as easy being with them as yourself, warts and all. Or should I say farts and all."

Molly's expression was dumfounded when she calmly said, "Ronnie, I will never ever fart in front of you. Like you said, I would die from embarrassment."

The young man held out his elbow before he said, "Okay, we'll see."

Holding back the urge to giggle, Molly took a hold of his arm. As the two started walking down the pier, she said sternly, "I mean it. I will never ever fart in front of you."

"Okay, whatever you say," Ronnie retorted, "but never is a long time to be clenched like that."

With a slight giggle, she maintained, "It's never going to happen."

He smiled and said, "Come on, let's walk this pier. Then I'll treat you to dinner. Maybe we can get some bean burritos or something."

Laughing, Molly playfully exclaimed, "Will you stop!"

Ronnie laughed as well, "Okay, okay. Let's just enjoy evening."

The couple took in the beautiful view of Chicago and spent some time people-watching along the pier before they decided to return to the Kilgore Hotel to enjoy a late dinner and some cocktails along with a little slow dancing. The evening was enjoyable and full of laughter and rich conversation.

Without knowing it, both of these two were desperately missing puzzle pieces just like Molly had explained earlier that night. Molly had never known that something was missing and always found adding pieces to her life was impossible. Ronnie was too busy to think about anything being missing at all. Tonight, they were finding in each other what they were missing and realizing what they had been missing out on all along.

The night concluded and Ronnie and Molly made their way, holding hands, down the second floor of the hotel until they reached their suite. With a gracious dance move, Ronnie gently swung Molly so her back was to the door. He stared into eyes and said, "Thank you for coming here with me. This is one of the best trips I've ever had. Every time I think about Chicago, I'm always going to think about you."

Molly couldn't express the appreciation in her heart. Her words couldn't do her feelings justice as she said, "Ronnie, thank you so much for bringing me here. I'm having a great time too." She watched as Ronnie leaned in to kiss her good night. Molly wasn't going to be taken by surprise this time -- she leaned forward to meet his lips with hers. As their lips touched and their mouths opened, their desire for one another grew. Their chemistry was working, they made a perfect puzzle in a world of jagged pieces and they could feel it more and more with each passing moment.

The kiss went on until Ronnie pulled back. Taking the high road, he exhaled deeply, knowing things could be pushed to the point of no stopping him. His feelings were a mixture of being protective and chivalrous toward Molly while at the same time, he wanted to rip off her clothes off and do the nasty with her in all sorts of carnal positions. The gentleman in him won out, as he blew air past his puckered lips, cooling himself off. "Molly, let me take the couch."

With her own internal debate going on, Molly was unsure about whether she wanted to sleep with Ronnie so early in their new relationship. Ronnie, putting the pin back in the grenade, diffused the situation. It allowed their brains to take over where their bodies would have run amuck. With her cooling off, Molly said, "Yeah, that's a good idea."

With a swipe of the room's keycard, Ronnie opened the door and the couple walked inside.

Trying to regain her composure, Molly said, "I'm going to get ready for bed. I'll be back in a bit." She walked into the bedroom and closed the door.

Ronnie made his way to the sleeper sofa and took a seat before he removed his dress shoes and socks. The young man also took off his tie and unbuttoned and removed his dress shirt. His exposed chest allowed him to cool off as he sprawled back on the couch, reminiscing about the wonderful day he had just spent with Molly. That's when his phone pinged, signaling he just received a text. He picked up his phone and looked at the time: 3:08 A.M. Central time. With a finger tap on his display, a message was revealed from his partner, Paul. "Hey bro bro, I just wanted to tell you that the other growers are in town and they brought lots of money. I'm partying right now with a bunch of them and they can't wait to see our inventory. When are U coming home?"

Ronnie tapped on his phone's keypad, "We're taking the train tomorrow and we'll be home in the evening. Plenty of time for the Grow School class on Saturday morning. I got this."

Soon as he hit send on his phone's display, the bedroom door opened and Molly appeared in the doorway. The young woman wore one of Ronnie's white dress shirts. He looked over while she asked in a shy and coy manner, "Ronnie, why don't you come and sleep with me?"

Hearing that, Ronnie powered down his phone and placed it on the coffee table. He walked over to her and asked, "Is that my dress shirt?"

Molly bit down on her bottom lip, before she said, "Yes."

"What are you wearing underneath?" Ronnie asked with devilish smirk.

The young woman looked into his eyes and said, "Why don't you come find out?"

16

BABY HUTCH GOES TO SCHOOL

"Well, what the hell's going to keep me from getting jacked?" Wayne Hutchinson asked while riding in the passenger seat of Scott James' black Denali SUV.

"Fear." The answer came simply from Scott. "Fear of our reprisal and retaliation will keep everything in check. This club owner, Brian Tatum, is from the Creek and he knows our reputation. There's going to be a complete understanding that he'd better not fuck around with this shit, otherwise things will get really ugly, really fast, when we set this mother fucker off. You know how we do things."

Closing his eyes for a moment, Wayne lightly shook his head and resumed staring out his passenger window, lost in thought.

In the gangster world, Wayne was about as far from a solider as one could be. In the beginning, out of necessity, Wayne had dabbled in violence, putting a required beat down on some folks. It was just enough for him to know that the role wasn't for him. Normally, his responsibility in the organization was consigliore: the boss's top advisor. The job was always slated for the intelligent, calculating and shrewd. That was Wayne. His older brother was the boss. When dirty deeds were required, they fell to the underboss and the soldiers. Those jobs were handed over to Scott James and his subordinates.

As the older Hutchinson brother, Bill had shielded Wayne from the ugliness of their world - until the day they formed their set, Dem

Creek Boyz. While in the gang, Wayne was responsible for growing their major cash crop: high quality marijuana. This made him an artist and an underground legend. "Baby Hutch" was Wayne's nickname, and it had been since the formation of their clique. The nickname stuck. Being a "gangster," Wayne knew it came with a stereotype. A hard thug life was portrayed in movies and rap songs, but Wayne understood the truth. The real top gangsters never got their hands dirty and they were normal people too, flaws and all, but still hustling, trying to get ahead. He was far from a thug, but that didn't mean he wasn't a gangster.

It was just two of them, Scott and Wayne, in the SUV, and they were riding an hour west from Detroit to Capital City to attend a Grow School. The gangsta hip hop song, "Choices" was playing on the radio and the two men, in unison, were saying, "Nope" and "Yup" with the singer. The two were on a mission. They were out to gain control of a new strain of marijuana, called Probie, for their home market.

Watching the rural farmland pass outside window, Wayne thought about U.S. history. He also understood that high school textbooks never told the real story - that many great American families had criminal origins. He recognized that one of our nation's founding fathers, John Hancock, was a smuggler, and the list of affluent American families who secretly made their start up money illegally during Prohibition was too long to write down. Crime had been the denied foundation of this country, as much as each brick in every government office. Each dollar floating around in America had ancestry in bootlegging, gambling, or drugs. Wayne figured that he was just keeping up with that American tradition that someone in the family line had to take a chance and walk the crooked walk so the future of the family could prosper. That tradition was as American as apple pie, and so far, the plan was working.

What enabled the plan to succeed was the quality of the marijuana product that they always produced and controlled. Wayne always tried to grow the best weed possible to supply his Detroit customers.

It was a matter of personal pride for him. The quality of their product allowed them to secure their territory and kept all their business operations flush with cash. It was that concern for product excellence that brought Wayne over an hour west from Detroit to Capital City to get control over this new strain of marijuana: Probie.

Watching the trees and farms go by, Wayne asked, "Hey Baby Jay, how's this going to work again?"

Turning down the radio, the driver kept his eyes forward while he answered in his usual monotone, "No one knows where the location of this Grow School will be, so I'm going to drop you off with Brian, who knows these growers personally. Later, he's going to get a text telling him where to go. Together, you two are going to ride in his car to the location, so you can do your thing. I was specifically asked not to come, so, you get to do this alone." Even though he was quiet, Scott had a naturally terrifying demeanor, starting with his voice. There was a somber smoothness to his tone that sounded like the murky waters of the Detroit River flowing under Ambassador Bridge.

When the rural backdrop turned into an urban setting, Scott James added, "Hey, one more thing. Brian has some sugar in the tank."

"He's gay?" Wayne's voice jumped a few octaves. While he was a proud dick owner, Wayne never understood with all that fine pussy out there, why a man would want to sleep another man.

"Yeah," the driver remained monotone, "he's gay, and a crossdresser too but he's also really good at business. Brian can also hustle on the street. Most importantly, he never fucks around with the money and everything is always right. There's some potential for the future. Can you handle that?"

Wayne sniffed, set his jaw, and answered in his normal tone, "Of course. We're here for pure business. That's it. Who he rubs his dick against is none of my business."

Still with his eyes forward staring through the windshield, Scott said, "Good, because it's all about the cash. Plus, we're almost there."

The two continued their drive until they could see the office buildings of the Capital City's downtown skyline as they worked their way to the Old Town District, where Brian's club was located. They pulled into the parking lot, where night club owner and two of his security guards were waiting for them, standing next to a new crystal white Cadillac CTS. Wayne saw at Brian standing there looking fashionable in his fitted, dark purple pant suit. He resisted the urge to cringe. Flanking the club owner were his two muscle bound security guards, who wore black on black. Wayne glanced them up and down and wondered if they mistakenly thought they were intimidating. Looking over at Scott, he knew he was thinking the same.

Parking the SUV, Scott James and Wayne got out and stretched. Wayne slung his black and red Nike Air Max duffle bag over his shoulder as the two walked over to Brian. The club owner greeted Scott, "Whaddup, Baby Jay."

"Nothin' Brian, or should I call you Cocoa?" returned Scott with his poker face. Wayne knew Scott had never beat up a fag for just being gay, he just didn't know how to act around them.

Brian offered a crooked grin; he seemed to enjoy making Scott nervous. "When I'm not performing on stage, I'm just Brian."

"Well dawg," Scott proceeded, "This is Head's younger brother, Wayne Hutchinson."

Extending his hand, Brian spoke out, "Well, well, well, I finally get to meet the famous Baby Hutch. Your reputation precedes you. You don't get enough credit for what you do."

Wayne reached out and grabbed Brian's hand, pinching down and pulling back on his finger tips. Squeezing down, they both pulled back hard and their fingers fired off a single, clear snap. It was the customary greeting for folks from the Creek. Wayne smiled and replied to Brian's comment, "That's what I keep telling everyone. I'm just so under appreciated." Everyone laughed for moment, except for Scott James, who remained silent and stoic. The compliment and hand greeting were effective in diminishing the tension of the initial meeting.

Brian spoke out, "Well Baby Hutch, I got the text just before you pulled in. Now, we've got to get you to school on time, so we better get going. My security guard is going to have to pat you down, because no guns are allowed on this campus. And Baby Jay, that's why you can't come." Brian added a sassy smile to his comment.

"Jokes aside, Brian," said Scott James, with more deep smoothness in his voice than usual, he didn't like jokes. Humor was something he saw as overused and overrated, especially in situations like this, when one of his own was on the line. "If anything bad happens to Wayne here. I'm bringing all my heavy hitters to your door and you're not going to like it."

With a tongue click, Brian rolled his eyes and dismissed the comment, saying, "Baby Jay, try to be professional here."

"I can't. I have trust issues." Scott replied with absolutely no apology in his voice.

Shaking his head, Brian instructed, "Wayne, get in the car. We have business to take care of."

Getting into the passenger side of the Cadillac, Wayne looked around at the interior of the small sporty luxury car. "Nice whip." He complimented Brian when he got in the driver's side.

Politely, Brain replied, "Thank you. The car fits my persona: clean and pretty."

The driver pushed the start button and stepped on the gas. The ride was smooth on the way to the industrial side of town. There was an awkward moment of silence before Brian looked at Wayne, who fidgeted nervously. "Am I making you nervous?" asked Brian.

"No dawg. It's not you. I always get little edgy when I go to school." Wayne added, "I never told anyone, but I always wanted to go to college. And this is what it feels like, so I'm a little mixed up emotionally. I don't know what to expect. There will be some of best growers in country there; I'm just this city kid from Detroit. I'm not sure if I belong." The doubt of worthiness was present.

Brian sympathized with that awkward feeling. He said, "Well, now you're going to grow school, trying to become the next George Washington Carver of weed."

"Yeah, that's it." Wayne answered unsurely.

Wayne's self-conscious issues were apparent to Brian. He knew the trick to solve this. Brian picked up his iPhone and held down the button. The iPhone chimed, "Bee-Beep."

Brain spoke into the mouthpiece, "Play the street anthem playlist."

The iPhone's Bluetooth was synced to Cadillac's premium sound system and the boom-boom-boom of the first song *Act Right* came through the speakers. Wayne's face lit up as the bass bumps filled the car. With his eyes wide, he looked over at Brian, who was moving his head rhythmically to the song's intro. When the lyrics broke out, the two sang out loud in unison with their lips curled and chins out, mugging. The lyrics were a street anthem, and the song permeated their beings as they lived the lyrics in real life. Brian was quickly becoming the first gay man that didn't make Wayne feel awkward.

The iPhone rolled into the next song on the playlist, *Full Time*. That's when Brian turned down the volume. Drawing inspiration from the music, the once self-doubting Wayne was now reassured as he considered that both of them hustled on the streets to build something from nothing. He was reborn with confidence. Wayne looked over at Brian and said, "Thanks man, I needed that." He surprised himself with his words.

Brian nodded. "No problem dawg, it's a good thing, now we're here."

The Cadillac pulled into the fenced off parking lot of the industrial building that used to house J. Finley Welding and Fabrication. The duo parked the Cadillac and entered the heavy metal door adjacent to the large overhead garage door. Once inside, they were greeted by Paul Mollett, "Wud up, Cocoa?" Paul wore his usual outfit of jeans, a denim jacket, and a pair of black work boots. His trademark black hair was long and flowing. As always, he looked like an Abercrombie model. Brian batted his eyelashes.

Brian immediately walked over and extended his hand to Paul, pretending to swoon. Paul shook his head and laughed. Their hands gripped as they both leaned in for hug. As they pulled back, Brian introduced Wayne, "Pauley, this here is Wayne Hutchinson. Everyone knows him as Baby Hutch. He's from the Creek in Detroit and he's looking forward to taking your class."

"You're one of Baby Jay's boys, aren't you?" asked Paul, feeling hurt from his last run in with Scott. He would keep his eye on Wayne while he was here, that was for fucking sure.

Putting down his duffle bag, Wayne said, "Yeah." He paused briefly and clarified, "Scott has a way of rubbing people wrong and plays a little rough at times." *Fuck*, Wayne thought. The little held-at-gun-point run-in between Scott and Paul had slipped his mind until that exact moment. There was already shit between the two and they had just met.

With a slight head tilt, Paul's face contorted. "Rubbing people wrong? Your man went all Tarantino on me. He tried to one-eight-seven me, right then and there. I didn't think I was going to see another sunrise." His voice winced a little, but his blood was boiling. Fire filled his eyes like a sunset stretching out to every inch of his pupils.

Wayne had heard the stories before, and circumstances like these always brought out his confidence. Finally, he felt like himself again and the thug he became into so long ago. He tried to be diplomatic, "Yeah, Scott does have that effect of people, but that could have been your ass when Baby Jay comes knocking on your door. Hey, but that's just the way it is, just consider yourself lucky you're breathing." Wayne paused a moment and then asked, "So, are we cool?"

"That depends." Paul answered, the flames in his eyes only intensified by Wayne's response, "Do you have money for me?"

Reaching into his pants pocket, Wayne pulled out an overstuffed white envelope. He handed it over. "Here's 10-large, just like we agreed. That should cover our tuition fully. Again, are we cool?" Wayne didn't like repeating questions and never was one for patience. If he had not needed to be on Paul's good side, he might have smacked him upside the head.

Taking the envelope, flipping over the fold, Paul ran his finger over the stack of $100 bills on the inside. Scanning the money, it looked good, like all $10,000 was there. With a pleasant expression, he immediately said, "Yeah, we're good. We have you set up in the front row. My partner, Ronnie, is getting ready to get his started the lecture. He's really smart and you're going to enjoy what he has to show you. We can't wait to show you guys our grow room."

With a come-hither head nod, Paul escorted Wayne and Brian to their seats in front of the room, which was set up with dozen folding tables with two chairs at each table. The tables were set up in classroom lab formation in three columns, right, center and left. The tables went four rows deep. A large movie screen hung on a tripod in the front of the room, displaying an image cast by an old fashioned overhead projector.

As Wayne and Brian sat down at the front left table, Wayne set his duffle bag at his feet and turned to the three-inch binder on the desktop. He scanned the room and saw each table seated either a couple or a single person. Every ethnicity, gender, and adult age group was represented by the gathering of professional growers. Wayne noticed the studious looking man standing in front of the room. He was looking at Paul's partner, Ronnie Harding. *He must be the instructor,* Wayne thought. *There are 12 tables paying $10,000 a pop to be here. That's $120,000. Not bad for a day's work. There must be good money in teaching.* He smiled at the thought and wondered if he could ever have the patience to teach a grow school. He looked around at the other people in attendance. *Probably not,* he thought.

After the two were seated, Paul placed a sealed sandwich bag full of seeds at each table. That's when Instructor, Ronnie, called the meeting to order. "Okay, let's get this started. What you have before is my creation. It's an Indica/Sativa hybrid cannabis seed that displays Sativa dominate physical traits. What makes this product unique? Unlike any other plant out there, this one's chemical composition has high levels of both THC and CBD. This particular strain of cannabis carries approximately 26 to 27 percent THC count, and it carries over 20 percent CBD content. I've searched all academic records and could not find any strain of marijuana with a ratio at these high levels. If you've sampled our product, then you know you have something very distinctive."

Ronnie was interrupted by a slim African American man who was seated in the front row, opposite Wayne. The man at the table stood up and looked at the room. "Yeah I tried it. I never felt anything like it. It was da lit. It's very good weed, maybe the best I've tried. And I smoked a lot, so that's saying something." The man faced Ronnie and added, "That's why I'm here. I think you have something very special and I want to bring it to my market." He resumed his seat.

"Well on that note." Ronnie instructed, "Why don't we introduce ourselves using nicknames representing the areas where we come from? How about you go first?" He pointed at the man who had just spoken.

The man stood up again and proudly said, "Hollywood," before quickly resuming his seat.

Wayne knew Southern California was represented. He watched as the two older white women behind Hollywood stood up next and said, "Redwood." Now Wayne knew that Northern California, proba-bly Humboldt County, was also participating in this mini-conference. He watched as each person gave off their pseudonym to represent their home territory. Oregon, Washington State, and Colorado intro-duced themselves. The Texans and Alaskans were also present. The international community was represented by folks from Vancouver, Amsterdam, San Quintin, Mexico, and Phuket, Thailand.

Observing each person individually, Wayne thought, *It looks like the who's who from marijuana world is here. Every major weed capital had made it in, maybe except from the Hindu Kush.* Although the round of in-troductions seemed a little odd, the information was valuable. Wayne started to respect Ronnie more and more.

It was clear to Wayne that everyone here loved to grow pot. It was their passion and their business, just like him. A little awestruck by the reputations in the room, Wayne was slightly startled when all the eyes of the room turned to him. It was the school-like environment that brought out his insecurities, but now it was his turn to stand and introduce himself.   As he stood up, his fingers were tapping away on his thighs with all of his nervous energy he had built up.   Looking back at the room, Wayne cleared his throat and simply said, "Motor City."   When he sat down, everyone knew Detroit was in the house. As one of the most dangerous cities in the country and one of the most feared in the underground world, it was also one of the most respected.

With the introductions out of the way, the instructor, Ronnie Harding, began the seminar.   "Now, in front of you are two things. Inside the clear bag is 200 seeds we cultivated here, and in the three-ring binder on each of your table tops, you'll find the specific growing instructions that we've successfully implemented.   What you have before you are seeds from my strain of marijuana, called Probie."

Wayne looked through his binder and saw that it was well organized and included sections about seed genetics and plant strains. The step-by-step instructions were easy to understand, and explained how to grow the most productive plants, including the vegetative, flowering, and harvesting stages. What drew Wayne's attention wasn't the easy reading, but meticulous instructions regarding Ronnie's hydroponic ebb and flow system that listed within the pages.   It was something he had always wanted to try. Wayne thought, *I can't believe it. I'm in a college class for growing weed.* He was jumping up and down on the inside with nerd excitement, but kept a nonchalant expression.   A reputation was an important thing to keep, especially for a drug dealer.

While Wayne scanned through the binder, Ronnie was interrupted by one of the two gray haired women from Northern California. "Young man, according to your program here, you're using a hydroponic system to grow your harvest. Is that correct?" The woman's question was asked sternly and directly. Wayne wondered what the hell she was doing here; he thought she looked like she should be baking cookies, not weed brownies.

"Yeah," Ronnie answered, "that's correct."

With a sour look on her face, the woman said, "Well, we only grow outdoors in natural dirt where we're from. We don't bother with all that artificial lighting and liquid nutrients. Mother Nature never meant for this plant to be grown like you're showing. We're purely organic and natural."

Fuckin' hippie, Wayne thought.

Ronnie knew that advanced growers were strict about the way they grew their plants. They presumed that they already knew the best way to do it, and everyone else was doing it wrong. The debate was on, and everyone took a side. Many people agreed that the all-natural way was the best way and considered all other ways an abomination. The people who held the opposite view said that indoor growing controlled the environment and engineered a predictable final product. Technology ruled. For a moment or two, the heated conversation escalated as pride and vanity trumped professional courtesy. The heated discussion broke down to the point of profanity and name calling.

That's when Ronnie took control of the room by hollering out, "Ladies and gentlemen!" The room fell silent and everyone turned to the instructor. "I think it's time we go downstairs and take a look at my grow room. Please take your seeds and binders with you. I promise you that you're going to value what you have in your hand."

With a simple hand gesture, Ronnie was able to lead everyone from the main floor of his building down the metal stairway to confines of his basement level grow room. Astonishment filled their faces one by one as they reached the bottom of the stairs. The 3,500 square foot basement was filled with thriving marijuana plants.

"Holy shit, would you look at the size of those colas! They're nearly three feet long and thicker than footballs," Hollywood blurted after seeing the tremendous size of Ronnie's mature marijuana buds. "You mean that weed we've been sampling produces that much in volume? How much are you harvesting per plant?" The industrial basement was filled from wall to wall with plants groups in different stages of development. The harvest was huge.

Ronnie tilted his head. "We're up to just under 30 ounces of dry harvest per plant."

With wide eyes, Hollywood asked, "30 zips per plant! You mean that quality weed we've been smoking produces that much in weight? Do you know how much that's worth in my market?"

"Yeah, I do," answered Ronnie.

"Why the hell would you want to get out of this business? You could be richer than your wildest dreams." The man from Southern California pressed the conversation.

The young instructor's gaze turned toward the concrete floor for a moment, before he looked back into Hollywood's eyes and said, "I want you to know I love this plant more than words can describe. It's my baby. I nurtured and cultivated it to what you see in front of you. But I want you to know I'm working on something else and that endeavor gives my life meaning. This plant jeopardizes my other work, and if I have to choose between the two, I choose my other work. That's why I'm entrusting you with my baby."

Wayne narrowed his eyes at Ronnie; he couldn't think of a single reason why a person should bail out on a business like this. Phrases like "Wow, what a fucking idiot" shot through his head.

Hollywood was flabbergasted as he pondered what was just said. Nodding his head, the only thing he could say was, "Fo sho." The man from Cali clutched his binder even tighter against his chest.

Ronnie reciprocated by nodding his head and adding his own, "Fo sho."

As the two men concluded their conversation, the two older women, presumably from Northern California, engaged Ronnie. One asked in her gentle grandmotherly manner, "Young man, sorry for the ruckus I started. You know how things are in our world. Everyone thinks they're the best at what they do and I'm no different."

Unoffended, Ronnie returned a tight lipped grin and a simple nod.

The woman continued, "Well, even though we don't agree with your methods and the use of GMO seeds, we do see the value in your results and the information you provided. We're eager to see how your plant is going to perform using our natural growing method and we're hoping we can match or improve your results. I want you to know we appreciate your information."

"I want you to know I want you to take this plant out there and make it better. I'll be happy to see what Mother Nature has in store for it. You have great DNA in those seeds. Please keep me updated." Ronnie's face was warm with gratitude.

The older woman requested, "We're going to walk around some more. If we have any questions or would like to purchase more, can do that through you?"

"Yeah," Ronnie said, "I'll be here all day. If you need anything just let me know."

As the two women walked away, Wayne stood back with Brian and watched as Ronnie addressed the attendees' needs one at a time. Just over an hour had passed, and once everyone else was busy walking around looking at the all the phases of the grow room's harvest; Wayne approached Ronnie, who stood alone. Wayne held his binder in one hand and his duffle bag slung over the opposite shoulder. He asked, "Excuse me."

Ronnie turned as said in friendly manner, "Yes."

Still feeling nervous, as if he were addressing a professor for the first time, Wayne asked, "I was looking over your manual here. You talk quite a bit about this control software you use in managing your crops from a single handheld tablet. How do I buy a copy of that software?" He held Ronnie's eyes in his own, relaxing as Ronnie's face revealed that he knew who Wayne was and he understood that he required a certain respect.

Awkwardness overtook Ronnie's face when he said, "Out of respect for my current employer, I can't give or sell you a copy of that specific control software, but I can give the contact information of James, Wisdom and Manish. They're the undergrads at Michigan A&M's Computer Department, who developed that particular software system. You'll be surprised that for a little extra beer money or some free weed, they'll develop a custom program to fit whatever you need. They're really user friendly too. I highly recommend them and you can drop my name."

Ronnie had a way of making people feel at ease. Him and Wayne hit it off as they discovered they had a lot in common - more than just growing marijuana. During their personal banter, it was revealed that they both had overbearing older brothers whom they loved and hated at the same time.

As the two enjoyed each other's conversation, they were interrupted by Ronnie's partner, Paul. "Excuse me, Bro, but I have some bad news for you."

"What?" reacted Ronnie.

"Well," Paul explained, "all the little stuff is just about sold out. You know the seeds, seedling, and young clones. It's easy to smuggle the little stuff back to their home territories, but no one wants to cross state lines with the big stuff, our ready to go inventory here. We may be stuck selling it off ourselves."

Ronnie's eyes closed as he let out a deep and frustrated breath.

At that moment, Wayne spoke up, "I'll offer you $600,000 for the whole thing, including the equipment."

As his eyes narrowed and forehead crinkled, Ronnie said, "It's not worth that much."

"I know how much it's worth." Wayne was now in professional mode that brought out confidence, his voice was wearing a silk suit and tie, as he explained, "I've been in this business probably since you were in junior high. If I buy up this inventory up, will there any more of this strain produced in Michigan?"

Shaking his head, Ronnie answered, "No. What is in this basement and in those seeds is unique. If you buy all of the inventory here, you'll have a monopoly until the other people in this room cultivate enough seeds to sell on the open market."

Wayne immediately asked, "How long until that happens?"

"At least couple years, maybe three or four," answered Ronnie.

With a self-assured poise about him, Wayne said, "For that monopoly I'm willing to pay $600,000 in cash for entire inventory."

Stunned, Ronnie asked, "Are you serious?"

As a devilish grin spread across his lips, Wayne kneeled down and put his duffle bag on the concrete floor. He unzipped it to reveal numerous gangster rolls of cash, each secured by wide, egg noodle-like rubber bands. "Here's $200,000 in cash. We'll get you two more bags just like this for a total of $600,000 for everything here." Wayne knew a profit when he saw it, and he knew that other gangs would too; he had to act now or someone else would have all that money.

Paul, who was standing next to Ronnie, interjected himself into the conversation, "Once we get the money, we'll give you the keys and walk away." Paul's mannerisms were filled with suspicion.

Quickly reacting, Ronnie said, "No, we'll give you the keys right now, because it's all about respect and trust."

"I knew there was something I liked about you," Wayne declared, "but we'll honor our word and you'll get your money. So do we have a deal?" Wayne held out his hand like an arm wrestler.

Immediately answering, Ronnie said, "Yes." He reached out with his hand and locked his grip with Wayne's. They pulled each other in close and tapped each other on the back with their other hand to close the deal. At that moment Ronnie realized, to his relief, that he was now out of the drug dealing business. The world was lifted off his shoulders.

When the two men pulled back from their ritual embrace, Wayne said, "We'll have your money over here tomorrow. We'll handle the move. There is one thing we're good at and that's moving a lot of weed, quickly. We won't have any problems with this."

"Thanks," Ronnie added, "if you need anything, we'll exchange numbers and you can call me for advice, like customer support."

"Thanks man." Wayne said kindly, "And Ronnie, I hope we can remain friends well after this deal."

Ronnie answered, "Me too." He handed over the building keys.

Upon taking them, Wayne offered simple smile and walked away. Brian, who was standing next to him, followed Wayne and said, "Hey

Baby Hutch, what about me? I want in." Excitement showed through his voice.

Ronnie and Paul could hear Wayne's answer, "Yeah, yeah, yeah, Brian. We can do some business, but you should really think about coming home to the Creek."

"Why would I want to come back to Creek?" screeched Brian's voice.

As Wayne and Bryan continued their conversation and walked up the stairs, out of the basement, Ronnie looked at Paul and said in a low restrained manner, "We did it."

"Yes, we did, bro." Paul answered back, holding out his fist.

To Ronnie's relief, he was out of the drug game. The plan had actually worked. He looked at Paul's fist hanging in the air. He pounded it, and then looked at the bag of money sitting on the floor. With a long exhale, Ronnie asked, "Well, how do you want to go celebrate?"

"Easy," Paul answered, "Let's go make it rain at the titty bar."

17

ALIBABA'S

Strip clubs weren't really Ronnie's thing. He considered them a waste of money because the only thing they offered him was sexual frustration. On the other hand, they were the only place in the world where Paul felt at home. Tonight, Paul talked Ronnie into a little 'going out of business' celebration at his favorite place in town: Alibaba's.

As the two entered the lobby of the downtown night club, they were abruptly stopped by the large doorman doubling as the club bouncer. "I need to see your ID," demanded the large, bald white man. He seemed to growl as they looked at his bulldog face.

Rolling his eyes, Paul reached into his back pocket and pulled out his wallet. "Dude, I come here every week and you keep asking for my ID."

The man at the door took Paul's driver's license, looked at it, and stared into his eyes. The bouncer's forehead crinkled, before he said, "Because I hate your goddamn face."

Only slightly fazed by the comment, Paul returned pretentiously, "Well, it's a good thing that your boss likes my goddamn face and all the money I spend here every week." His cavalier attitude was reflected in his cocky smirk.

"No." The doorman answered, "It's a good thing for you that the man that pays me seems to like you a lot or I would have sent you to emergency room a month ago with a crushed windpipe."

Paul's grin slowly faded as he tried to remember this bulldog and why he would have cause to kick his ass. Sometimes it was hard to keep track of the people he had pissed off - the list was constantly growing. In a higher tone, Paul reacted, "What the hell did I ever do to you?"

Grinding his teeth, the bouncer handed back Paul's identification card. "You don't know, do you?"

Paul was stumped. "Dude, I barely know you."

Astonished, Ronnie couldn't believe his ears as the doorman continued, "Does the name Charity ring a bell?"

With the realization, Paul's face lit up and with a long, drawn out, "Oh!" he answered, "You're the revenge-fuck dude." There was a slight glee in his voice. Paul wasn't always so great at talking his way out of a fight. In fact, as he grew older, he got better at talking other people into them.

Ronnie noticed the throbbing blood vessel near the bouncer's right temple as the large bald man spoke in his gravelly voice, "Yeah, that's me."

"You got caught cheating on her." Paul carried on with astonishment, "When she found out, she went rogue on you, looking for someone fuck around with to hurt you back. And that's when she found me. She told me all about it." There was amusement in Paul's voice. "She kept taking pictures of us with her phone while we were doing all sorts of nasty things. We had to stop every ten minutes because she actually typed out more texts, describing, in detail, we were doing in real time. Didn't she?"

The bouncer snarled as he balled his fist.

Ronnie knew it was on. The doorman had hit his tipping point.

Suddenly, Paul looked directly in the large man's eyes and said the magic words. "You know you hurt her, don't you?" Paul was gleaming, sensing the big man's guilty conscious. He wasn't going to be punched in the face without making this guy feel like a dick first. When he met Charity, he had thought he was doing something honorable by sleeping with her, like he was helping her somehow. It had made sense to both of them at the time. This guy was the only tool who didn't understand his own hypocrisy.

With those words, the bouncer's evil scowl was replaced with a painful wince. Noticing, Paul carried on, "Charity was your best friend and she trusted you completely. I want you to know, she cried during the whole thing, but she was determined. Hell has no fury. Those photos you got that night were nothing like the real thing. It was a mess. She was out of her mind from the pain and grief of your betrayal. All she wanted to do was make you feel her heartache. And dude, you ripped her heart out."

The doorman's attitude deflated. He looked like Paul's dog when he yelled at him for pissing on the floor.

With his own sense of purpose, Paul preached on, "If you want to blame someone, you'd better look in the mirror." Letting his words sink in, Paul added, "You should have appreciated what you had there, big boy." Paul had no idea what Charity had seen in this mutt, but he couldn't believe there was a guy dumb enough to cheat on her. Charity was a beautiful, fun woman. This guy looked like an inbred sock puppet.

With that last statement, Paul witnessed the bouncer's eyes begin to water. His realization of truth had put an end to the potential fight. Paul had kicked his ass without throwing a punch, as his head gestured, signaling to Ronnie, "Come on, let's go." Passing the door-man dismissively; Paul strutted into the night club.

Unable to believe what he had just witnessed, Ronnie reached into his wallet and handed over a $20 bill. "This is for our cover charge." The man just took the money as Ronnie hurried past him into the bar.

When Ronnie stepped inside, he was hit by the sounds of the hip hop rhythm from TrillionCTN's song, "I Can't and I Won't." The empowering girl anthem was becoming one of his new favorite songs that streamed on his phone's independent artist channel. The bouncing bass was playing across the high end sound system as he looked across the dimly lit room that was awash in pink and green neon lighting. In the opposite corner of the bar on the brightly lit stage, a single woman wearing nothing but a black sparkly G-string performed for the room full of men. The guys in the room relaxed joyously as they watched the show.

The young, pale skinned, yellow haired dancer knew her craft well. She swayed slowly and gestured seductively, keeping time with the beat of the music. Each move by the short, curvaceous, quarter stick of dynamite performer was designed to captivate the attention of her male audience, and it worked, even on Ronnie. The young man stood, entranced by the blending of the lights, the music, and the single dancer on stage.

The spell was broken when Paul yelled out, "Hey Ronnie! Come here. I want to introduce you to somebody."

With a slight headshake to readjust his mindset, Ronnie snapped out of it and walked to the bar where Paul was standing. When he got there, Paul introduced the man behind the counter.

"Ronnie, this is my good friend, Tony Johnson. He's the owner of this lovely establishment."

Ronnie looked at the sturdy man with the high and tight haircut and professionally extended his hand. "It's a pleasure meeting you." Tony looked misplaced in the strip club with his two-piece suit, what looked like a black satin tie, and…was that an effing handkerchief?

Shaking his hand, Tony clarified, "Well, I'm actually not the owner. My father, Larry, is. He's not in good health right now, so I've been running it for him full time." Tony's boyish face made him look out of place even more behind the bar.

Glancing around the room, Ronnie felt the energy of moving commerce around him as the sexual energy and debauchery led to the free flow of money for overpriced drinks and private table dances. Ronnie complimented him. "Regardless, your family business is kicking ass." The room was filled with male egos running amuck.

With a simple grin, Tony accepted the praise before grabbing a purple bottle of Casa Noble Anejo from under the counter. He set up three shots of tequila on the bar. Tony smiled and said, "Yeah business is good, but I would go broke if I had more customers like this jerk off here." The bartender laughed and gestured toward the man sitting on the barstool next to Ronnie. Addressing the seated man, Tony said, "Hey Bubba, tell them what you do for a living."

The thin, bearded stranger wearing a red flannel shirt turned to face Ronnie and said, "I sell pee."

Ronnie's face contorted as he reacted. "Like, as in urine?"

Shrugging his shoulders, the man answered, "Yeah." He went on and explained, "Half this town is on probation for an alcohol or drug related offense. Part of the terms of their probation is abstaining from drugs and alcohol, and they have to turn in urine samples when called in to do so to see if they're in violation. You know, convicted party people never really stop partying, but when they're caught with alcohol or drugs in their system as a probation violation, it's back to jail for them. When they're called in by their probation officer for a random test, they need a source of clean pee in hurry – so they call me. I sell it for $40 a sample cup and I have more customers than I know what do with." Ronnie wondered if he also sold vomit, because he could feel some rising up his throat.

Shaking his head in disbelief, Ronnie added, "And you make more every day."

"Every day," the stranger concurred.

Looking down at the man's glass on the bar, Ronnie inquired, "So what are you drinking now?"

The man sitting on the bar stool tilted his head. "Pepsi."

Tony interjected himself, "That's why I would go broke if I had more customers like Woody here." He let out a jovial laugh.

Upon hearing the laughter, Ronnie understood that Tony was a kind soul.

The song came to an end and the DJ's raspy voice came over the speakers. "Gentleman, put your hands together for Arianna!" The audience applauded enthusiastically, as the dancer collected her tip money from the stage before she exited.

The DJ's voice then said, "Next up is Cleo."

In a moment, Ronnie watched as another young, beautiful woman emerged from the dressing room in a white string bikini. The platinum haired dancer sported a pixie-cut and walked calmly in her white platform heels. As the tall woman passed by the bar, she waved at Tony and hollered, "Hey, tell your dad thanks for letting me stay the night with him!"

"No problem, Cleo." Tony said, "Break a leg."

The fine-looking woman gave the barkeep a confident wink before making her way to the stage.

Paul immediately asked, "Your dad is sleeping with her?"

With a chuckle, Tony answered, "Oh no, with my dad's heart condition, having sex with a woman like that could actually kill him." The barkeep paused a second and said, "Last night Cleo had some drama with her boyfriend, who got so pissed off, he changed the locks on her. She had nowhere to go at 2:00 in the morning, so my dad told her that she could stay at his house. Cleo tried to offer him money, but my father refused."

A little redness appeared on Tony's cheek before an impish grin spread across his face. "My dad suggested she could make it up to him by cleaning his house, naked." Letting out a little snicker, Tony added, "Well, this morning, he got up early to come in here to take inventory and count cash receipts, and left Cleo to sleep in. When he got home later in the afternoon, he found his house completely spotless."

Laughing, Tony carried on, "Seeing that, my dad yelled out, 'Hey, I thought you were going to clean naked?'" Tony put his fingers around one of the shot glasses. "You know what Cleo said to him?"

Ronnie listened as Paul asked, "What?"

Tony's lips curled into a smile. "She said, 'I did, but you weren't here to see it,'"

All three men broke out in laughter as Tony lifted his shot glass from bar. He offered a toast, "To my father, Larry Johnson – he's one of a kind."

Ronnie and Paul picked up the other two shot glasses from the bar. All three men lifted their drinks and downed the tequila.

Placing their empty glasses on the counter, Paul said, "Thanks for the stories, Tony. We're going to grab a table and watch the show."

"No problem guys, enjoy yourselves," Tony replied, "and make sure you spend lots of money. I need a new turbo charger for my Mustang."

Paul reached into his front pocket and pulled out a thick roll of 100 dollar bills, secured with a large rubber band. "Don't worry I have plenty of rags to toss around."

"Good man, now go have some fun. It was a pleasure meeting you, Ronnie." Tony waved.

Nodding, Ronnie returned, "Likewise."

Ronnie and Paul walked to other end of the bar and took seats at a table in the back on the opposite side of the stage. During Cleo's performance to J Skee's song, "Whole City Jumpin", a waitress walked approached them and asked, "Can I get you two gentlemen anything?"

Paul asked, "What kind of champagne do you have here?"

"We have Krug," responded the server.

"How much?" Paul followed up.

The beautiful server answered, "$200 a bottle."

"We'll start off with two bottles, but check with us little later." Placing his order, Paul asked, "And can we get six glasses with that?"

As she left, the waitress replied, "Sure."

Ronnie looked at Paul and asked, "What are the other glasses for?"

"You'll see," answered Paul.

It didn't take long for Ronnie to understand what the extra glasses were for. Nothing attracts a stripper's attention more than free champagne and the smell of cash. One by one, dancers came over, introduced themselves and took a seat at their table. The girls helped themselves to the champagne and Paul kept ordering more bottles. Their table was full of women, overpriced champagne, and laughter as more dancers joined in. It only attracted more girls until the two men were surrounded by pretty smiles and minimally clothed bodies.

Watching a few more dancers perform their two-song dances, Ronnie thought it was odd that Paul never got a private dance at the table or in the VIP room. Both men declined every invitation, but Paul kept making it rain as their party's momentum picked up steam.

As their celebration carried on, Paul leaned over to Ronnie and asked, "How are you feeling?"

"My ego is out of control." Ronnie answered, "I feel like a sultan king with a harem."

Laughing, Paul looked at each beautiful girl sitting their table, before asking Ronnie, "How come you're not getting any table dances?"

Ronnie slightly shook his head. "Bumping, grinding and dry humping – that's just not my thing. Plus, I have someone else on my mind right now." He paused. "Well, what about you, Mr. DTF? How come you're not swimming in the deep end of the stripper pool?"

Lifting his eyebrows, Paul said, "I wanted to talk to you about that."

"What?" asked Ronnie.

Paul looked over both shoulders. "You know. Remember when you were telling me that you're always looking for the-one-girl, that one person you want to spend the last hour of day of the day with for the rest of your life?"

"Yeah," answered Ronnie. This was definitely the deepest relationship conversation they had ever had, and Paul had only just begun speaking.

"Well," Paul explained, "I think I found her, the-one-girl for me.

Ronnie's bullshit alarm went off as he narrowed his eyes. Paul had always dogged on Ronnie for wanting relationships as he screwed his way through the 20-somethings in their city. After narrowing his eyes until they were practically closed he asked, "Oh. Reallyyy?" As he thought, '*bullshit*'.

Nodding, Paul said, "Yeah, I can't stop thinking about her. We've gone out several time and we seem to have hit it off. I think she likes me too, or at least my dick, because the sex has been phenomenal. We've been doing the deed all over town. And I have to tell you, I would give up the lifestyle for her. I would change everything. That's how much of a hold she has over me." Ronnie tried to immediately forget part of what Paul had just said, while he fixed his eyes on the new Paul.

"Sounds serious," Ronnie said flatly, still not buying it.

Paul's eyes widened. "It is, but there's a problem. She always keeps me at arm's length. There's always some mystery about her."

"What do you mean?" Ronnie asked. He couldn't help his curiosity, even though he was waiting for Paul to say he was just fucking with him.

"Well, she comes over to my house whenever she wants and we hang out together. Later, we fuck, it's amazing, and then she gets up leaves with no explanation. She's never stays the night. I feel like a cheap whore." Paul let out a chuckle before he said, "I think she's just using me as a booty call. The problem is I actually know nothing about her. I don't know where she lives. I don't know if she's in a relationship or if she's married. I just want to know her better. The more I press her for information, the more secretive she becomes. For the first time in my life, I don't know what to do with myself."

"You caught up on the rules of obsession?" asked Ronnie.

Paul's mouth opened, before he said, "What the hell are those?"

"Easy," Ronnie offered details, "Rule #1. You always want what you can't have."

"Check." Paul agreed.

Ronnie continued, "Rule #2. If you want someone to love you, you love them back. If you want someone obsessed with you, you push them away. That's what she's doing to you."

Shocked, Paul opened his mouth again. "I am obsessed. She's got me hooked." The realization set in.

Ronnie's skepticism slowly faded. He had never seen his friend talk or act like this before. "Where the hell did you meet her?"

"She works here." Paul confessed, "And that's why I'm not interested in a table dance from anyone else. I'm living in a cliché. I fell in love with a stripper." Ronnie almost snorted, but managed to maintain an empathetic look.

The song ended and the dancer on the stage finished her routine. The DJ's rough voice came over the speaker. "Gentlemen, put your hands together for Glitter. Next up, is Frankie." There was a round of enthusiastic applause.

Ronnie felt a nudge from Paul's elbow as he whispered, "This is her, man."

Oh my God, that's my neighbor, thought Ronnie when he saw Francesca, Molly's roommate walk out of the dressing room door and toward the stage. The young woman wore a form-fitting gray and white plaid mini-skirt with a snug white button down shirt. She donned a gray blazer and a matching plaid necktie, so her outfit resembled a private schoolgirl uniform. Gracefully walking towards the stage, she stopped and reached down to remove her black stilettos. Stepping onto the platform, the stage lights dimmed and Francesca stood in the spotlight in her black knee high stockings. The private schoolgirl uniform cosplay was complete.

Ronnie noticed her thick, plastic framed eyeglasses with a strip of masking tape wrapped around the bridge to give the illusion that Frankie was a nerdish bookworm type. The theatrics worked. She remained perfectly still in silence for about a minute, drawing in the attention of her audience as they quieted down for the performance. Then, the elegant piano played the introduction to Acey Baby's R&B song, "One and Only". The melody echoed through the house speaker system. With her jet black hair pulled back into a silky ponytail, the dancer remained perfectly still as the music filled the room.

As the lyrics of first verse began, the dancer moved with the music. Her movements were the opposite of sexual, rather, they radiated an innocence that matched the song. Francesca's performance was stylishly done as she elegantly swayed and maneuvered across the stage. She treated the audience to the art of dance as she innocently removed articles of clothing one by one until she stood in only a black string bikini bottom. The song finished and the audience roared with applause as Francesca posed elegantly, standing perfectly still.

The second song, "Wet-Wet" by Acey Baby, began, and the bumping of the techno/hip hop beats dominated the speaker system as Francesca resumed her performance. Her moves blended perfectly with Acey's sexy raspy voice. This time, innocence was thrown out the window and the dancer's movements were designed to seduce the entire room. Her eyeglasses were whipped off and Francesca, with one move, let her hair down. With every grind, gyration, and turn around the pole, her sexual prowess became fierce and confident; it was the opposite of the demure dance she had just done. The two-song routine showed an uninhabited sexual butterfly emerging from its innocent cocoon, and the spectators loved it. She captivated her audience, and when she finished, they clapped and cheered louder than they had all evening.

Ronnie noticed Paul was completely drawn in by the performance. He knew that Paul's narcissism had him thinking that the last song was secretly dedicated to him. Ronnie understood that in Paul's world, it's all about Paul. Not sure what to do with himself, Ronnie just watched Francesca gather up her clothes and tip money from the stage and walk back to the dressing room.

Paul immediately blurted, "Isn't she awesome!"

Paul dating Francesca wasn't a problem for Ronnie. His predicament was that it made it impossible for him to keep his worlds separate. The two lives that he was living and had worked so hard to keep apart were now starting to rub together. Ronnie's living space, his new love life, his academic career and his drug dealing world were about to converge at this very night club table.

Listening to Paul's question, Ronnie could only nod in response. Growing indecisive, his mind began to swim. Unsure of what to do, he remained still. Even though his exterior was calm, on the inside his thoughts were racing. Ronnie was tempted to run for the door, but elected to play it cool.

Inside Ronnie's head, everything was out of sync. After 15 minutes, the fated event occurred as Frankie emerged from the dressing room fully clothed and made her way to Ronnie and Paul's table.

Paul jumped up and walked over to greet her with a kiss on the cheek, "Hey babe. Great job."

Leading her back to the table, Paul added, "I want to introduce you to someone."

Frankie looked up and said, "Hey Ronnie."

"You guys know each other?" Paul was befuddled.

Looking at his next door neighbor, Ronnie offered a long, drawn out, "Yeah." Before he added, "She my..."

Taking a seat next to Paul, the beautiful Frankie interrupted him, "One of my friends has a big time crush on Ronnie." She steered the answer.

"Really?" asked Paul, pleasantly surprised, "Maybe we could go on a double date sometime?"

Watching the mild reaction of surprise on Frankie's face, Ronnie answered, "Man, I see you too much in my normal life. Having you in my romantic world would be excessive."

Paul laughed as he added, "You may be right, bro."

Even though she was calm on the exterior, Ronnie could tell by Francesca's body language that she wanted to keep her worlds apart as well.

Paul was ogling Frankie's every action. Ronnie waited for his opportunity to leave when Paul asked Frankie, "Hey you want to go to work in the VIP room?"

"Sure." The dancer answered.

At that moment, Ronnie addressed Paul, "Hey man, I had a great time, but I'm going to get going. I'll grab an Uber home."

"Are you sure?" asked Paul, "Why don't you stay a little longer and hang out?"

"Na, you two enjoy the rest of the evening," added Ronnie as he stood up from the table.

With a calm and confident expression on her face, Francesca said, "You know Ronnie, it is true. Molly has definitely fallen for you."

Ronnie could tell she was being sincere. "Yeah, I've fallen for her too."

"I want you to know," Francesca informed, "She's really a tender hearted girl, so you'd better not hurt her."

Ronnie gave a reassuring look, and said, "I won't Frankie. She's important to me too."

Accepting his reply, Francesca gave him an approving nod. Ronnie could tell that Frankie cared for Molly very much.

Preparing to leave, Ronnie offered his friends a humorous fare-well, "You two have a great time, but if you need bail, give me a call."

Obviously still enchanted by Frankie, Paul said, "Don't worry man, if I need bail, you'll be the first person I call."

Ronnie chuckled, but something in the pit of his stomach didn't sit right as he walked away.

18

THE CLEANING LADY

I can't believe how much I hate my job right now, thought Tonya Vento as she proceeded to clean up her scheduled office suites on the fourth floor of the 10-story Copeland Office Tower in downtown Capital City. This particular building was the home of the Michigan Department of Management and Budget. Tonya had loved her job when she worked as a government employee, before they had downsized and she'd been laid off. She had once enjoyed a decent wage of $16.50 an hour, plus full benefits, to clean these offices. Under those working conditions, she had been perfectly content, and it had been obvious based on her job performance. Everything had been spotless. Now, she was getting $11.75 an hour with her fringe benefits stripped away for doing the same job through a private cleaning company. Every incentive for her to do her best work had gone out the window. Unfortunately, privatization was the new trend in government. Instead of taking pride in her work, Tonya just went through the motions in her daily routine.

On Saturdays, just before midnight, these office buildings were typically empty, except for the cleaning crews. Feeling disgruntled, she did her job in the late evenings and searched for other employment during the day. With each toilet she scrubbed, floor she vacuumed, and trash can she emptied, her level of cynicism grew. It was amazing how the reduction of one's wage and benefits could make such a difference.

Walking over to the large glass window of the fourth floor, Tonya's bitterness was reaching the disgust level. As she stood, staring out at the top level of the neighboring parking structure, Tonya couldn't believe her eyes. Ten feet in front of her, she saw a couple, fucking, on a 1970 Olds Cutlass convertible. The convertible's top was down; the naked woman straddled the nearly undressed man as he laid back across the trunk with his feet dangling toward the back seat. The exhibitionists were fierce in their display of sexual fury, with powerful grinds and thrusts during their throws of passion under the clear night, with the stars, the moon and Tonya as their witnesses. They were performing at the base of these nearly empty office towers as the crisp night air surrounded their bodies.

Unbeknownst to Tonya, she was watching Paul Mollett and Francesca Alexander. The lovers decided to engage in their lewd act after Francesca had finished working at Alibaba's. Watching, the bitter cleaning lady was aghast with moral outrage, so she reached into her pocket for her smartphone. Tonya pressed the Google app button and the phone beeped. She spoke into the phone's mouthpiece, and said, "Call the Capital City Police Department."

The phone beeped again and dialed the main police station. It rang once and a female dispatch officer, Lynn Conklin, answered. "Capital City Police Department, may I help you?"

"I would like to report an act of public lewdness," answered the cleaning lady.

Officer Conklin asked, "What's the nature of the act?"

Tonya answered, "There are two people having sex on the top level of the parking garage on the corner of Allegan and Capitol."

"Are you sure?" The dispatch then asked in higher pitch. Her skepticism was obvious.

Squeezing her phone tighter, Tonya Vento answered in a commanding manner, "I know what it looks like when two people are having sex."

"Okay, okay," Officer Conklin said, "Can you describe what they look like?"

The cleaning lady said, "Yes. They are both white and they both have long dark hair. They're either partially dressed or completely naked, having sex on an older model convertible. Do you want me to be more graphic?"

Sexual deviancy was the secret thread woven into the fabric of any legislative capital from D.C. on down. Capital City, Michigan was a covert deviant playground for certain egomaniacal politicians and their influential staffers who were exchanging political favors for sexual ones. Underground sex clubs, escort services, and prostitution had run rampant in the city until Mayor Maurice Chamberlain was elected. Big Moe cracked down on the illicit behavior.

Officer Conklin understood there was a zero tolerance policy against prostitution and public indecency, so she answered the caller, "No, no. That's fine. We're sending a patrol car; it should arrive shortly."

Tonya hung up her phone and stood at the window. She knew she should get back to work, but she didn't care anymore about her stupid cleaning job. This was going to be way more interesting.

It took less than five minutes before she noticed the police patrol car with its headlights turned off, creeping slowly up the parking ramp to the nearly abandoned top level, unnoticed by the lovers. The cleaning lady was engrossed in the turn of events as the dark blue police car stepped on the gas, speeding towards the convertible. The couple was taken by surprise as the blue and red patrol lights flipped on and the sirens blared loudly for a second. The police car's spotlight was blinding as it revealed Paul and Francesca, who hurried to clothe themselves. The two, caught in the middle of their act, were immediately arrested.

Feeling devilish, Tonya Vento was enjoying the scene as the couple was handcuffed. She watched as the exhibitionists were placed into the back seat of the squad car and a tow truck was called to impound the convertible.

Unbeknownst to the cleaning lady, Capital City followed the lead of other cities around the country and had a policy allowing them to seize automobiles used during the suspected solicitation of prostitution. It was a tool that elevated the threshold of financial pain for the so-called 'Johns' looking to buy sex off the streets of the city. The impounded cars served as brutal monetary consequence for these types of acts, but it also generated a lot of revenue for the city's coffers.

As the classic car was hauled away, Tonya considered regretting her call to the police. She pondered her past, and recalled how she and her ex-husband had done stupid things in their youth. As feelings of guilt built up inside her, she whispered, "Fuck them. My life sucks; welcome to the party." She chuckled to herself and went back to her duties.

At the police station, Captain Robert Williams was a little perturbed. As he strolled into his office, he asked, "why am I here at 10 in the morning on a Sunday?" He had been summoned to the downtown police station by a fellow detective, Rico Galaviz, who was sitting in an office chair waiting for his arrival. Galaviz looked more smug that usual.

Rico answered, "Well, you wanted me to find your unicorn, that Probie source. I have a lead." He was like a proud puppy, showing his owner a big bone.

"What do you have?" Robert lit up. Excitement and eagerness were apparent on his prematurely aged face.

A roguish expression emerged on Rico's face. "Last night, we busted this couple having sex on top of the Downtown Capitol Parking Ramp."

"Right across the street from the Capitol Building, how romantic," said the Captain, wondering why Rico thought this was important enough to share.

Closing his eyes, Rico just nodded. "Yeah."

While standing, Robert folded his arms, and said, "Just down the street from here. What balls! But what's your point about the Probie weed?"

"Well," Rico explained, "After we arrested them, we impounded their vehicle. They've been sitting in jail all night. It's our standard procedure to bring out the sniffing dogs and walk them around the cars in impound yard, and of course dogs went nuts on homeboy's car. That gave us probable cause to search it. That's when we found the jar in the trunk."

"How much?" asked Captain Williams as soon as Rico finished his sentence.

Rico looked directly into the Captain's generally intimidating stare. "We only found a QP doll, a quarter-pounder. The forensic chemist came in this morning and it's a chemical match for Probie."

Robert Williams grumbled agitatedly, "Four ounces is not the end of the world."

"Yeah," Rico carried on, "but we also found almost four grand in cash with it. The most important part is that he appears to be Native American."

"The Indian," whispered the Captain, astounded.

With a satisfied grin, Rico said, "You remember from the Duffy bust. The main wholesale guy for Probie was someone called The Indian and he was supposed to be Native American. Well, I think I have him in one of our interrogation rooms downstairs."

Captain Williams' face lit up. "Well, let's go talk to my man."

Picking up the case folder off the desk, Rico got up out of his chair and the two made their way to the basement where the city jail and interrogation rooms were located. The interrogation room was like a cell without the toilet. Each wall was made with the same concrete as the jail cells. It was like criminals were shown where they would be spending their time if they didn't cooperate with the police. Rico stopped at room I-2. "Here he is."

The Captain stood, staring through the one-way mirror, studying Paul Mollet as he sat inside the white room at the lone white table, staring at an empty chair. Rico watched as the Captain stood in silence for nearly two minutes. Captain Williams snapped out of his trance and instructed his team member, "Rico, go in there and question him, but say nothing about what we found in his car. Do not talk about marijuana or cash. Just talk about the public sex thing. Rattle his cage a little bit, let's see what type of guy he is."

"No problem, Captain." Rico responded, "I've got this."

Captain Robert Williams watched Rico when he walked into the room, carrying the case folder, and took a seat opposite of Paul, who sat there patiently, playing it cool. Captain Williams listened through the speaker box as Rico introduced himself, "My name is Detective Galaviz and I'm from Vice. I'm here to ask you some questions."

Paul did not respond. He just stared at the detective as he glanced over the manila file folder in his hand.

Rico initiated the conversation, "I just talked to Ms. Francesca Alexander and she said you raped her."

Again Paul did not respond. He knew his Miranda rights, which allowed him the right to remain silent. Paul understood if you're talking to the cop, they have nothing on you. If you're talking to the judge, you're in trouble. He obeyed these street rules.

Changing his tactics, Rico said, "Man, I was just playing with you to see if you take a joke. Everyone can tell that she was just a whore taking care of her trick." The insult was designed to provoke a response to get Paul talking. This wasn't a tactic Rico had learned in the academy, but instead from the captain. Once they started talking, nerves would take over and they would start rambling, spilling the beans in the process.

Refusing to take the bait, Paul sat numbly, staring blankly at the police officer.

Officer Galaviz evoked another strategy as he closed his folder and leaned in towards the table. "Come on, man. Just tell me why you were having sex with her in public."

Rico was astonished as Paul broke his silence, "Look at her!" With a look of disgust on his face, he immediately added, "I would have jumped off the top of that parking structure, hit the pavement, dusted myself off, run back up those stairs and done it again, just for a chance to sleep with her. You got that?" Paul's voice was commanding. He added the word, "Miranda!" Paul then took a deep breath, puffed his cheeks and puckered his lips, signaling he would remain mute.

Just then, Captain Williams' voice came through the speaker near the ceiling. "Officer Galaviz, can I speak to you a second?"

Paul sat, staring, as Rico stood up and left the room. He remained still, knowing they were watching.

While the detective stepped outside the room and closed the door, Captain Williams just stared at Paul through the one-way mirror, studying him. After a few moments, he broke his silence to his team member. "That man is a step away from what we're after. Hold him until Judge Miller gives us our anticipatory warrant. We'll put the Probie and the cash back in his trunk, just like it was. We'll put GPS tracker on his car and put him under surveillance. We'll charge him and his girlfriend with indecent exposure and public lewdness. Let him feel safe, like he got away with it. Allow them to make bail at a $1,000 each and give him his phone call. We'll see where it goes from there. We'll turn that mouse loose and let him lead us to the cheese."

Pausing a moment, Captain Williams added, "Can you handle that?"

"Yes, sir," answered Rico.

Sunday morning quickly turned into Sunday afternoon, and Ronnie Harding was sleeping in on his futon, safe and comfortable in his own apartment. His ambition and guilt kept nudging him to get up, but his exhaustion won out. Getting out of the drug dealing game was a tremendous relief for the graduate student. Now, he could focus on his academic life, and hopefully,

Molly. Not a lot of people understood that living a double life was draining. But, not many people had experienced it. Ronnie understood that living a secret life is the same as living a lie, and lies get heavy to carry over time. Putting this one behind him, Ronnie felt relief as he slept in.

Waking in and out of his dream state, Ronnie woke up for good to his smartphone buzzing. He looked at the caller ID, which said, "Restricted." It was 12:30 in the afternoon, so Ronnie accepted the call.

Urgently, Paul's voice came through the earpiece. "Ronnie, I need your help!"

Ronnie realized that Paul hadn't called him bro, he'd said 'Ronnie'. It must be serious. "What's up, man?" asked Ronnie, his voice scratchy from sleep.

"Remember last night when you said I could call you if I needed bail?"

With a quick cough, Ronnie cleared his throat. He calmly stated, "You need bail."

"Yeah," Paul added, "Frankie too."

Paul was about to ramble on with an explanation, breaking his own street rules, but Ronnie cut him off. "How much and where are you?" Ronnie was sensing that Paul was out of character. Normally, Paul would 'jail-good', sitting patiently, waiting for circumstances to work themselves out. Now, Ronnie could tell Paul was near panic with the motivation of getting Francesca out of jail.

"We're going to need a $1,000 each and we're at the Downtown Police Station. Just walk in and talk to the front desk and they'll tell you what to do. Please hurry, dawg!" Paul's voice cracked and Ronnie knew his concern was all for the girl.

Ronnie simply replied, "Gotcha." He hung up the phone.

With a sense of purpose, Ronnie got up and dressed. As he pulled up his jeans and threw a green hoodie over his head, Ronnie thought about Molly. With his double life over, he understood the burden of secrets and living in lies. Ronnie was no longer interested in his old lifestyle. He had to be tactful on how to handle this transition, but everything had to start anew, right now.

Walking out to the hallway, Ronnie stopped and knocked on Molly's door. It took a couple moments, but Molly answered with her endearing soft brown eyes. "Hey you."

"Hey," Ronnie brought his hand up and scratched the side of his head, "I have something to tell you about last night."

With a single "Yeah," Molly's eyebrows slightly raised.

Ronnie noticed Molly's yearning eyes looking up at him in concern. Knowing he had to be delicate and sincere at the same time, Ronnie said, "Listen, last night I was out with the guys last and we went to this strip club downtown."

"Alibaba's." Molly interjected.

As his cheeks reddened, Ronnie sheepishly replied, "Yeah." He was always amazed by a woman's network. If one guy made a mistake, some woman somewhere would inform her within a day and the man would pay dearly.

Her emotional bricks were slowly starting to stack up as Molly said, "So, you know where Francesca works?"

"Yeah, but I want you to know it was really weird for me when Francesca hit the stage, and at my first opportunity I left," explained Ronnie.

With her swirl of insecurities and vulnerabilities, Ronnie could see her emotional guard starting to go up as Molly said, "Well, I don't have a problem if you want to ask her…"

Ronnie cut her off, "Listen, I'm only interested in one person, and that's you. The time we spent in Chicago together was the best time of my life. I'm not interested in your roommate or anyone else. Life is about choices, and I'm making mine, right now. I choose you. You don't know how much I appreciate the moment you came into my life." He tried to reassure her by taking her hand and leaning in to kiss her.

Without thinking, Molly let go of his hand and reached up with both arms, grabbing on the back of his neck and head, holding him while their lips met. She whispered, "I'm not letting you go."

As their kiss continued, Ronnie embraced her, pulling her in tight. "I'm going nowhere. Here with you is the only place I want to be." His voice was soft.

The embrace comforted her. Ronnie passed a big test in Molly's mind; men own up to things, while boys run and hide. It would take a man to give her the emotional security that she needed. Molly exhaled and all her nervousness and vulnerability left her body. Her arms wrapped around him, she squeezed and held on.

Holding her tightly, Ronnie knew that this was vital to their relationship. He also understood if you're going to love someone, you had to accept them for what they are, with all their strengths and weaknesses.

Minutes passed as the two stood in her doorway, holding each other. Ronnie broke the silence, "There something else I have to tell you."

Looking up and almost laughing, Molly pleaded, "Now what?"

"After I left the club last night," explained Ronnie, "Francesca hooked up with one of my friends. I just got a call from him this morning; they both need to be bailed out of jail."

Molly reacted quickly. "Jail!" Ronnie knew Molly was thinking he had just stopped by to explain his night at the strip club. He felt bad for the unidentifiable look on her face.

Ronnie nodded his head, knowing the rest of the story would grow more and more overwhelming, even though he didn't know it yet. He had never heard Paul sound the way he had on the phone; the urgency in his voice had been new and unsettling.

"What did they do?" asked Molly as her arms flopped to her sides.

Shrugging his shoulders, Ronnie said, "I don't know, but their bond is only $1,000 each, so it can't be that bad."

"A thousand! I don't have that kind of money," exclaimed Molly.

Trying to calm the situation, Ronnie explained, "Don't worry, I just got my stipend and fellowship money in. I can cover it for both of them." A white lie; $2,000 was nothing in comparison to what Ronnie had made this weekend hosting the Grow School, but he was determined to keep his drug dealing life forever a secret.

Molly face's radiated gratitude. "Oh Ronnie, that's wonderful of you."

Awkwardly, Ronnie shrugged his shoulders. "Let's just focus on getting them out of jail."

"Do you want me to go with you?" asked Molly

"Na," Ronnie answered, "I don't like the idea of you hanging out in a city jail. I've got this."

Molly agreed, "Okay." She didn't really like heading into the city. There were too many people, too many cars, and too much noise.

"Don't worry I'll get your roommate home safely, promise," assured Ronnie.

Stepping forward, Molly looked up him. "Can I get a kiss?"

"Sure." Their lips met. It was that same electric feeling, better than any high than Ronnie had ever known.

Leaving the drug business was going to be easy with his new addiction. As their kiss ended, Molly requested, "One more."

Smiling, Ronnie was more than happy to oblige as he kissed her again, before he went down the stairs and headed out the door. The young man felt on top of the world. He had successfully cashed out, exited the drug game, and found the 'one-girl' he had been looking for. All was right with the universe.

Ronnie drove into the city until he reached the downtown Capital City Police Department headquarters. Avoiding a record while he had been a dealer and grower was something Ronnie took pride in; he felt confident that this would be his first and last time walking into a jail. Entering the front door and walking up to the on-duty police officer sitting at desk behind a thick pane of glass, Ronnie asked, "Excuse me, where do I go to bail someone out of jail?"

"You can do it right her," the officer said as he typed on the keyboard in front of him. "Who are you here for?"

Ronnie answered, "Paul Mollett and Francesca Alexander."

The police officer stared at the computer monitor, searching. "Okay. That will be $2,000 to get them both out. How would you like to pay that, cash or card?"

"Cash, please," answered Ronnie as pulled out his wallet and counted out ten $100 bills, twice, and placed them through the teller tray under the glass.

The officer raised his eyebrows, but produced a receipt for security and instructed Ronnie to wait for both Paul and Francesca to come out through the white door at the other end of the room when they finished processing. Ronnie waited patiently, but it took half an hour before Paul emerged from the door, alone. Looking exhausted but grateful, Paul walked toward Ronnie. His usually smooth pony tail was untidy in a slightly hilarious way that Ronnie would have pointed out under different circumstances. His clothes were ruffled and he had noticeable bags under his eyes. "Hey, bro. Thanks for coming."

"No problem, dawg. I told you, I've got you," reassured Ronnie as the two men hugged it out.

Paul's expression immediately changed to one of concern as asked, "Has Frankie been released yet?"

"No, not yet." Ronnie answered, watching his friend as he began to pace, unsure of what to do with himself. Ronnie had never witnessed Paul worry about anyone but himself before, but his concern now was obvious. Ronnie watched as the white door opened and Francesca emerged, wearing her black micro-mini skirt and top from the night before and carrying her black Coach bag. Her mascara was smeared and her hair was disheveled, but she had a very distinct I-don't-give-a-fuck look on her face.

Seeing her, Paul, with a look of relief, walked toward her immediately to comfort her. He was greeted by a stiff arm and a flat hand stopping at his face. Ronnie watched as Francesca halted Paul in his tracks. She never broke her stride. Without a word, she left through the front door. Ronnie continued to watch as his friend was emotionally run over.

Paul looked at Ronnie and said, "I think she's pissed that we both may now end up now as registered sex offenders." Looking staggered, Paul shrugged his shoulders.

Feeling for his friend, Ronnie's eyes turned to the ceiling and he noticed the smoke glass dome that likely concealed a security camera. He stared at it for a moment.

Unbeknownst to Ronnie, the security camera was feeding an HD signal to a monitor in an observation room on the next floor up. That video monitor was being watched by two members of the Big Four: Captain Robert Williams and Detective Rico Galaviz. Captain Williams stared at Ronnie's face on the screen, studying it. The Captain pressed a key on his keyboard and an image of Ronnie's face froze on the display. Captain Williams looked into Ronnie's eyes, before he turned his attention to Rico. "Your guy, The Indian, is not smart enough to pull this Probie thing off. We need to turn the Indian into our mouse and set it free. As the mouse scampers back, he'll lead us to the cheese."

Looking at Ronnie's face on the screen, Captain Williams' intuition kicked in as he pointed his finger. "Right there," he said, "That man is the cheese."

19

THE MOUSE AND THE CHEESE

A clear digital photo of a young white man's face was displayed on Captain William's monitor. The Big Four detectives were able to run it through the latest version of their automated facial recognition software. With this computer program, law enforcement had a new weapon against crime. The application used a series of unique algorithms to process the image against the photo databases for state identification and driver's licenses until it found a match. It did so with accuracy, and found Ronnie Lee Harding.

The original digital image was obtained by an HD security camera when Ronnie had bailed Paul Mollett out of jail. Paul was a person of interest in the Probie marijuana case and when Ronnie bailed him out, it drew the officers' attention toward him. With Ronnie's ID, The Big Four detectives looked into his public record and found out that Ronnie had no criminal convictions, but was an interesting man, especially in relation to the Probie case.

Ronnie was an honors graduate student in plant biology at Michigan A&M, which piqued the interest of the detectives. However, what set off all the alarm bells against him was when the detectives cross referenced the chemical composition of Probie to the database of the National Center for Natural Products Research at the University of Mississippi, School of Pharmacy. Ole Miss was the nation's standard institution for cannabis research and Michigan A&M's

Medical Marijuana Program participated in their registration. All Professor Rittenburg's work including Ronnie Harding's new stain of medical cannabis, St. Billy, was documented under the University of Mississippi's database.

The strain of marijuana, Probie, had a unique chemical signature that included an extremely high THC count of nearly 27%, while simultaneously having CBD concentration just under 21%. The unique combination made this particular strain exclusive.

When the Big Four compared Probie's chemical signature, it failed to match any entry in cannabis research database at Ole Miss. There were plenty of entries with THC concentrations of 26 to 28%. Those strains were developed as high quality illegal drugs to be sold on the streets with little to no CBD content. The University of Mississippi disclosed that there was only one particular strain that cleared the 20% CBD threshold and it was developed by Michigan A&M University for medical research. That unique breed of cannabis was called St. Billy, and it had virtually no THC. Ole Miss also revealed that the researcher, Professor William Rittenburg was the developer of this strain of marijuana and co-credit was issued to a graduate student, Ronnie Lee Harding, as the actual cultivator.

The Big Four detectives theorized that the street drug, Probie, had to be a crossbreed of medicinal St. Billy strain with another high THC one. They also hypothesized that Ronnie Harding was the developer of Probie and Paul Mollett was the main street dealer. The two were now connected. Writing up their investigation, The Big Four detectives had enough preliminary evidence to convince Judge Charlie Miller to issue out a county-wide investigative warrant.

With the warrant in hand, Ronnie's privacy went up in flames while the Big Four dug up every scrap of information on the graduate student. His credentials and expertise in plant biology helped him fit the profile of the Probie source perfectly.

The Big Four were putting together the pieces of the case. They had two suspects to target: Ronnie Harding and Paul Mollett. Ronnie was now labeled by the detectives as 'The Cheese' while Paul was codenamed, 'The Mouse'. The plan was to place these two under surveillance until one or both would lead the Big Four to source of Probie.

The investigation continued for days as Detective Jason Ridgeway, an African American, and Officer Michael Finch, a Caucasian, followed Ronnie wherever he went on the hunt for Probie.

Sitting in their new silver Ford Fusion, just outside Ronnie's apartment at 7:00 in the evening, the two let out their frustrations with the investigation. "I think the Captain is completely wrong on this. This dumb ass is the most boring suspect that we've ever tailed," declared Officer Ridgeway, with a little laugh. *Gandhi would have made a more interesting drug dealer,* he thought. "I mean this guy gets up. He goes to class, heads to the coffee shop, and talks to the girl across the hall. He's a normal college kid. There's nothing thug-life about this guy."

"I understand what you're saying," returned Michael Finch, "but the Captain has incredible instincts and is rarely wrong on these things. You've seen it work time and time again. He's deserves the benefit of the doubt."

With a single groan, Ridgeway nodded, acknowledging the sentiment. "I understand what you're saying, but no one is perfect, and I think our leader has it wrong on this one." Ridgeway was countless cups of coffees in, and hungry, which only added to his grumpiness and doubt of their captain.

At that moment, Ronnie Harding walked out of his apartment building in jeans and a gray short sleeve T-shirt with an English 'D' on the front. He made his way to his minivan. Ronnie started it up and took off down the road.

Ridgeway started his car. "Here we go." The two police officers tailed Ronnie throughout the campus town of East Meridian.

Driving for 10 minutes, Michael Finch warned his partner, "Man, be careful. You're following him too close."

"I've got this!" Ridgeway reacted defensively. The last straw today would be another officer telling him how to do his job. "I know how to tail a guy. Just make sure that GPS tracker we put on his minivan is working."

Looking at his tablet, Finch said, "Yeah, its working fine."

Keeping his eye on Ronnie's vehicle, Ridgeway said, "And other thing. What type of drug dealer rides around in a 10-year-old minivan?"

Michael Finch just offered a chuckle as a response. No matter what Ridgeway said, he had an unfailing belief in his captain and he would live out of his car for weeks in order to prove that Ronnie was the Probie source.

The two officers followed Ronnie through Michigan A&M's main campus, past the agricultural research area to Lumbermill Road. The suspect turned down an unnamed dirt road through a dense forest as two officers kept driving the down the main road. They pulled over and stopped.

Raising his eyebrows, Officer Finch look at his tablet and the GPS tracker stopped moving. A grin sprang across his lips. "See! Trust the Captain's instincts."

Ridgeway smirked, "Call it in. We may take this mother fucker today."

Taking out his Android phone, Finch dialed, "Captain, I think we have something here. I think we've found Probie's weed lab. How quick can we get an anticipatory search warrant? We'll use the smell coming from the building as probable cause."

Ridgeway listened as Finch agreed with the Captain a few times before hanging up the phone.

Officer Finch looked at his partner and said, "The Captain told me that he's having the warrant typed up immediately and a runner will drive it over to Judge Miller's house for his signature. We're to sit tight and monitor the suspect until the runner drops the warrant to us personally."

With a smile, Ridgeway asked, "When that warrant gets here, can we take this mother fucker?"

Finch nodded. "Yep. If the weed is inside."

At that moment, Ronnie Harding walked into his off-campus medical marijuana research facility. The warehouse was filled, jungle like, with the St. Billy strain, and they were healthiest cannabis plants he'd ever seen. He had really outdone himself. The mature, CBD enriched marijuana plants grew over 12 feet in height with strong, thick stalks and large flowering buds. Lions could hide behind these plants; an Amazon forest could exist without anyone knowing it until they walked through every path in the lab.

Pulling out his iPod Touch, Ronnie scrolled through his list of musical artists and stopped on 80s classic rock genre playlist. With a single tap, the melodic chords of electric guitar played through the warehouse's Bluetooth speaker system as the song; "You Can't Kill Rock and Roll" filled the large room. Ronnie closed his eyes and took in the harmony. When vocals sang, the meaning of the words was heartfelt to Ronnie. The song was a younger generation's sacred hymn, calling out for change from the older generation's regime. The song's meaning was as true today as it had been when it was first written. Ronnie thought about the illegality of marijuana was an old and overplayed song. So many people benefited from the medical attributes of products like St. Billy that the government was now preaching to an empty room. Even politicians were done listening. Soon enough, marijuana would be legal and there was nothing anyone would be able to do to stop it.

As Ronnie attended to his plants, the iPod played on shuffle, rotating through songs from metal to hip hop, and more. The graduate student was relieved that his illegal drug dealing days were behind him and that he could focus on what he loved to do most: his research. He wouldn't miss the slight fear of being caught selling Probie. He was ready to move on with his life and leave the march to marijuana legalization to someone whose feet weren't tired.

Ronnie knew he had one major personality defect - he was scared to live an ordinary life. Ronnie was smart enough to know the difference between right and wrong, but the allure of doing the opposite of what he should was often too strong for him to resist. Ronnie would, on occasion, intentionally walk off the righteous path just to test the boundaries of life. To his credit, his intellect always seems to save him at the right time.

His fascination with the illegal drug market seemed to take a life of its own. In the end, the lifestyle had been too fast for Ronnie, and he wasn't willing to jeopardize everything else that was important to him. Ronnie thought, *when you're riding on a speeding train that's about wreck, it's all about the dismount.* An arrogant grin appeared on his lips. He had planned his jump off the illegal weed train for weeks and he'd just stuck the landing for a perfect 10.

Kneeling down to attend his potted adolescent plants, Ronnie's iPod began to play modern metal version of *"Whiskey in the Jar"*. He thought of Molly. Now, with a smile on his face, Ronnie pondered the ways in which Molly had changed him. Caring for another person makes risk taking so much less appealing. When you screw up all by yourself, you take your own bullet. When someone else relies on you, they share in the consequences of your bad decisions, even if they don't take part in them. Ronnie felt protective of Molly and that feeling played into his decision to get out of the drug game now. He could only imagine what it would be like to have children. Having kids could hold a person hostage to good behavior, because no one wants their children to suffer over their own dumb decision making. He wondered if Molly wanted to have children one day. Maybe he was maturing.

Standing up, Ronnie started walking back toward his office as the song finished. He reached in to his pants pocket, pulled out his iPod and paused the music. The warehouse fell silent. When he made his way down the aisle, Ronnie could see the door that led to office. With his eyes wide, he was startled as two plainly dressed men, one white and one black, both wearing bulletproof vests, came through the door and pointed their black tactical 12-gauge shotguns directly at him. Both Officer Finch and Ridgeway yelled, "Freeze!"

Ronnie froze like a statue.

Finch ordered, "Get your hands up! Get 'em where I can see 'em!"

He obeyed.

With dire focus, Officer Finch stepped toward Ronnie, pointing his shotgun directly at his face. "Get on the fucking ground! Face down!"

Slowly, Ronnie knelt down. Bringing his hands down to the concrete floor to support himself, he laid face down. Ronnie felt a knee press hard against his back while each of his wrists were brought behind him. A zip of pain shot through Ronnie's body, as he felt the pinch of the handcuff as it was clicked one size too small. The officer had cuffed him hard.

Still face down, Ronnie felt a few sheets of folded paper whack the side of his head. One of the police officers said in a deep tone, "There's your warrant my man, consider yourself served."

Ronnie turned his head and listened to the two men. One spoke out, "Holy fuck, it's a fucking jungle in here. Let's sweep this place."

"I got you. Let's do this," the Officer Ridgeway answered his partner.

Ridgeway walked over to Ronnie and pointed his shotgun directly at his face. "If you move, I swear to Jesus, my man. I will kill you, so be smart." The officer's tone was chilling.

Looking up at the barrel of the gun, Ronnie closed his eyes and nodded, acknowledging the officer's instructions. Police brutality was something Ronnie had heard about on the news, never thinking it would be something he would deal with in life. The most offensive thing an officer had ever said to him was "license and registration please." He had heard about the captain and his crew of drug hunters. They had been compared to the fucking Gestapo. In his mind, he saw his life plan crumbling into tiny bits of dust to be sprinkled onto the plants he had spent years growing.

Lying there, Ronnie listened to the two men walking through his warehouse, tactically sweeping the place. One of the men yelled out, "Would you look at these plants? Have you ever seen anything like this?"

"Naw man, this is fucking crazy," answered his partner, " I've never seen anything like this. My man here is a serious weed farmer."

Even though he was sick to his stomach, Ronnie appreciated the compliment. It seemed like it took forever, but just a few moments went by before the two officers returned to him. The two men helped Ronnie sit up on the floor, Indian style, leaving his hands cuffed behind him.

Officer Finch knelt down and looked Ronnie directly in his eyes. "Is there anyone else here?"

Ronnie didn't say a word. He just shook his head no. Miranda rights; he wasn't as stupid as they hoped.

The officer continued, "So, you're the only one here."

Without a word, Ronnie nodded his head.

Finch asked, "You have anything you want to add?"

Immediately, Ronnie said, "Miranda."

Standing up, Officer Finch looked at his partner, Ridgeway, who walked over to one of the largest mature plants. Ridgeway pulled on one of the stems and leaned his face in next to a monstrous bud. "Hey man, get a photo of me with this. People aren't going to believe it. Look at this thing. It's almost a yard long and thicker than a two-liter bottle." Ronnie, very discreetly, rolled his eyes. These cops were just as stupid as he expected.

Taking out his smartphone, Officer Finch snapped off of a photo of his partner, smiling next to the large marijuana bud. Finch showed Ridgeway the image on his phone display.

Ridgeway responded, "That's great. Text that to me."

Both men were joyous with a sense of accomplishment. They had bagged their man.

Ridgeway instructed his partner, "Hey man, call it in. Tell the Captain we got Probie's weed lab and we arrested the cheese."

Surprised, Ronnie knew that the Officers had it all wrong. They think they found the source of Probie, but what they got was nothing but medical research marijuana grown for the university. Ronnie just sat there and pondered. His worst nightmare was manifesting before his eyes. Still, there was hope that his professor and the university would be able to stop all this bullshit before it began. Ronnie's phone buzzed in his pocket, but there was nothing he could do to answer it.

Officer Finch dialed his captain. "Captain, we've got him. We got the cheese. And you aren't going to believe the size of this grow lab. This Probie case is going to get closed out."

Eavesdropping on the phone conversation, Ronnie sat and listened as he could hear yelling come from the end. He couldn't understand the words, but he could tell the voice on the other end was angry.

"Yes, sir," was the response, before Officer Finch hung up.

Putting his phone back into to his pocket, Finch looked at Ridgeway. "Man, you aren't going to believe what just happened to the Captain."

Captain Robert Williams and Detective Rico Galaviz made it personal when they placed Paul Mollett under surveillance. With unbridled ADHD, Paul couldn't sit still for a moment. He never slept in same place or with the same person and kept rotating his phone and phone numbers. The only thing that was consistent was his car, a black 1970 Olds Cutlass convertible, which the Big Four tagged with a GPS tracking system. While Ronnie Harding was considered extremely easy to investigate due to his boring routine, Paul was the exact opposite - a pain in the ass.

The detectives had planned to shadow Ronnie Harding and Paul Mollett until one of them led them to the source of Probie. They were hoping for a grow facility. When one of them led the investigators to the physical evidence, it could trigger the trap to snare them both. Today, when Ronnie Harding left his apartment building, Captain

Williams and Detective Galaviz were following Paul Mollett in his car all over town.

"Man, this guy is all over the place," commented Rico Galaviz as he drove the black unmarked Chevy Impala.

Sitting next to him, Captain Williams stared at his tablet, his eyes following the GPS tracker. "I know this guy is a big pain in the ass, but just stay with it." The Captain was calm, just like he had been for the last year, looking for the source of the drug that had taken over his city. Those dumb ass hippies he had grown up with were wrong; marijuana should never be legal and he was going to make sure that it never happened. He was starting by making an example of these two assholes. He had seen too many people start with drugs like this, only to fall so far down, they couldn't get up, living and dying by their addiction. The Captain believed marijuana was a gateway drug.

The pair of detectives followed Paul to the South Side of Capital City to White Tiger Tattoos, where Paul walked in and hung out with his friends. The investigative team parked their car across the street at a liquor store and check cashing business. The tattoo parlor had a glass window store front, which made it easy to keep an eye on Paul. The area was a popular hangout spot, especially for kids so tattooed, their original skin color was no longer obvious. Tattoos disgusted the captain and he cringed as he looked at the people in the shop.

The officers took turns watching their suspect until the Captain received a phone call from Detective Finch, informing them that Ronnie Harding had led them to the grow house. That was all the Captain needed to hear. "Let's bust this mother fucker."

The detectives pulled their car across the street and parked it. They walked hurriedly into the tattoo parlor with their badges out. They were greeted by the parlor's manager, Lynnie McCormack, who had more tattoos and piercings than most of the people in her shop. "Whoa, whoa, whoa! Gentlemen, can I help you?" Her arms were open, blocking their way, but she offered a flirtatious smile.

She would bat her eyes at these known crooked cops if it would help Paul.

Rico Galaviz answered, "We're the police, and we have an arrest warrant for Paul Mollett! Where is he?"

Lowering her arms, Lynnie pointed and said, "He's in the bathroom. The door is right there."

Officer Galaviz ran to the door and grabbed the knob. Locked. With a strong front bicycle kick, he blew the door open and hurried inside with his handgun drawn. There was no one in the bathroom, but the narrow window above of the sink was open. Galaviz rushed toward it and looked outside, down an empty alley. He hurried out and yelled out to his Captain, "He's gone. Out the window."

Immediately, Captain Williams instructed, "You take the front and I'll take the back!"

Lynnie and other spectators in the parlor watched as both police officers ran to their respective doors and around the building. Curiously, Lynnie and the gang walked to the front glass storefront, watching as a few minutes passed. Numerous black and white patrol cars zoomed by with sirens blaring and lights flashing. They we're setting up a dragnet. Everyone in the tattoo parlor was engrossed in the drama that was unfolding; the customers stood up from their chairs and the artists put down their ink guns. With a smirk on her face, Lynnie turned to the tattoo artist standing next to her. "Paul has always been an outlaw, but now it's official."

About a dozen police cars swept the nearby neighborhoods, but they couldn't find any trace of Paul. Captain Robert Williams' instincts told him that Paul had pulled off a Houdini. That's when the Captain's phone rang. He answered with a distracted, "Yeah?"

Officer Finch was on the other end. "Captain, we got him. We got the cheese. And you aren't going to believe the size of this weed lab. This Probie case is going to get closed out."

With heat in his voice, Captain Williams informed him, "Well, I missed the mouse! That motherfucker got away!" He hung up the phone.

The Captain walked over Rico Galaviz, who was standing next to their car. With a scowl on his face, Captain Robert Williams said, "If it's the last thing that I'd ever do, I will catch Paul Mollett. And I'm going to tell you right now, he's not going to make it to jail." The captain was done being calm; this was war on the drug, Probie. Paul Mollett was going to be a casualty.

20

THE ONLY LAWYER IN THE FAMILY

After giving two sets of fingerprints and posing for a series of mug shots, Ronnie Harding completed the arrest and booking process. The Big Four took him into the interrogation room, where he remained mute throughout the process. For six hours, one by one, each detective ran every trick in the book, including the threat of ultra harsh punishments and the reward of light sentencing, if Ronnie would just confess in manufacturing Probie. He refused.

Ronnie understood the 1966 Supreme Court decision, Miranda v. Arizona. He was too smart for these investigators. Patiently, he waited them out, hoping for his phone call.

When Ronnie was allowed to make his one call, he called the only lawyer in the family: his brother, Ken Harding Jr. Kenny assured his younger brother he that was on the job and he instructed Ronnie to sit tight and refrain from opening his mouth. Ken assured him he was on his way to establish bail, and said that until he did, Ronnie had to sit in his cell. Laughing at his brother, Kenny said, "Don't drop the soap, brother." Ronnie's brother had always mistaken himself for funny.

Stepping inside the jail cell, Ronnie looked at the nine other men sitting in the cell. *I can't believe what just happened to me*, thought Ronnie when the clang of the jail bars closed behind him. The now arrested graduate student could only do one thing as he walked over to the open spot on the far bench and took a seat. Cells like this had been described to him by friends who been arrested for driving drunk, but they had been in no condition to remember the details of the inside. Ronnie knew he would remember every chink in the metal, every wrinkle of his fellow cellmates' faces, and every detail of his time here. As he shook his head, he wished he were drunk.

When Ronnie sat down, he noticed the old scruffy white man sitting next to him. The white haired, worn out geezer moved his hand toward his neck, and with his fingers, covered a gaping hole in the base of his throat. With a voice like a buzzer, the old man asked, "What are you in for?"

Barely hiding his initial disgust at the sight of the gaping hole in the old man's neck, Ronnie closed his eyes and thought, *Oh my God, why me?* After a moment, he reminded himself about being understanding and courteous to others. Opening his eyes, he looked at the man and said, "Being stupid."

The old man covered his hole in his throat again and laughed with his annoying buzzer voice, reminding Ronnie of a robot, "Ah ha ha ha. Aren't we all?"

Feeling uncomfortable, Ronnie returned a slight laugh, but really he wanted to build a massive brick wall between himself and the old man. *A hole like that must have come from smoking, right? Like the lady in those gross anti-tobacco ads you see on TV.* As he looked at the white haired man, Ronnie wondered if he still smoked. To distract himself, Ronnie gazed around the jail cell. Staring at the one open toilet in the back of room, he wasn't looking forward to taking a dump and wiping his ass in front of this crowd.

Shaking the thought, Ronnie contemplated his speeding train of a life. He thought of his illegal drug dealing life as the runaway train, and his recent grow school exit from the business as the most spectacular dismount of all time. With some arrogance, he thought, *I jumped safely from a speeding train that was about to crash and landed perfectly in a beautiful lake.* As the realization set in, he thought, *I didn't know those calm, serene waters were filled with hungry crocodiles.* That's why he was sitting in jail, jeopardizing everything he valued in life: Molly, Professor Rittenburg's research, his future career, and his family. He also thought about his reputation - there was no place to buy that back. Life is about choices, and Ronnie was the master of messing up a good thing. How could he have been so stupid?

Sitting in a jail cell, there was only one really appealing option: napping. It was the best way to pass the time. Sitting awake, Ronnie was really missing his smartphone. Until now, he never truly appreciated it. It was his connection to the world. Discreetly, he used his thumb to press imaginary buttons on an imaginary phone, addicted to its games. With his phone gone and nothing to do but wait, Ronnie was stuck in his own mind. Self intimacy was not his strong suit; he to be busy. Boredom had led him to illegal drug dealing.

Stuck in a cycle of unproductive thought, Ronnie tried everything he could to keep his mind from worry. Worry led to panic, and panic is the first step toward letting all the wheels come off. At first he wanted nothing to do with the other men with the in the jail cell, but after a while, he realized he needed the distraction. He turned to the scruffy old man with the open hole in his throat and asked, "What are you in for?"

The look of gratitude on the old man's face at a conversation was apparent. Ronnie figured that he wasn't the only one looking for a distraction to pass the time while sitting behind bars.

Still a little uncomfortable watching the old man's routine of covering the gaping hole in his throat, Ronnie's eyes widened as he listened to his buzzer-like voice explain his story.

"Well, I lost my driver's license a couple years back after my fourth DUI. I had a bad habit of combining two of my loves: drinking lots of alcohol and driving cars. So, three weeks back, around 11 at night, I was drinking alone at home and I ran out liquor. You know what I'm saying. Shit, I didn't feel like walkin' to the store, so I hopped on my Ford tractor and drove it there. Hell, I didn't have any problems. I drove on the shoulder the whole way there and back. I was 20-feet from my own driveway when the deputy pulled me over."

Noticing a few men in the jail cell walking closer to listen the old man's story, Ronnie asked, "So, they charged you with your fifth DUI while driving a tractor?"

"Yeah," continued the old man, "but that's not what I'm really in trouble for. When the deputy was testing my sobriety on the side of the road in front of my house, my wife came outside to scream at me. I thought she was going to hit me, so I pushed her back and said, 'Get away from me woman!' She fell back on her ass, and that's when they arrested me. Now they're charging me with domestic assault and battery on my 83-year-old wife."

Ronnie stared for a moment with disbelief as the old man carried on. "When I got in front of the judge, he said the bail for domestic assault on an 83-year-old woman is $10,000. I said to the judge, 'Are you shitting me? I ain't got no $10,000.' So, I called all my friends and family to take up a collection. They gathered up $126 bucks for my cause. That's it, $126 bucks. Can you imagine that? All your friends are taking a collection to help you out and all they're able to raise is $126 dollars? Ah ha ha ha. Without bail I have to sit in jail until my trial."

The story was both sad and funny. Ronnie would have given the man $10,000 dollars if he could. He didn't understand why someone his age would be given such a harsh arraignment; he highly doubted he could have actually assaulted his wife. Looking up, Ronnie noticed five men in the cell were now obviously listening to the end of the old man's story. That's when an obese dark skinned man with a bald head spoke up. "That's nothing. Wait until you hear what happened to me."

Hours went by as Ronnie shifted his attention to each of the men as they shared their accounts of the events that had landed them in jail. The round of jailhouse confessions continued until a Masonic County Deputy yelled through the jail bars, "Ronnie Harding, your lawyer is here!"

As Ronnie stood up, the old man with a hole in his throat said, "Tell your lawyer to give me his card."

"Sure, my man," replied Ronnie, before he stood up and walked toward the jail door. The deputy signaled and the door buzzed as it opened.

Ronnie was let out of his cell and escorted down the hall by the corrections officer. They walked to a beige meeting room where Ronnie's older brother, Kenny Harding Jr., was waiting for him. Kenny, who was obviously concerned, was dressed casually in jeans, a dark blue hoodie and a pair of white sneakers. The concern surprised Ronnie; he had expected his brother to act superior. Rivalry had always existed between the two brothers and even though he was a lawyer, Ronnie knew Kenny had never felt equal to him. He greeted Ronnie kindly, saying, "Hey, you alright brother?"

"Yeah man, but this whole thing is twisted around," answered Ronnie cautiously.

Kenny's eyes narrowed. "I'll say. They think you're the Pablo Escobar of marijuana in the Capital City. They're charging you with drug manufacturing and trafficking. Dawg, this is serious. They set your bail at a half million."

"Half million!" Ronnie reacted with a high pitch, "Can you get me out?"

Relieved, Ronnie could see the arrogance that return to his brother's face. With a steely a glance, Kenny said, "Who the fuck is your attorney?"

Ronnie understood that Kenny had waited his whole life for this moment - the very moment in their sibling rivalry where Ronnie had to admit he needed his brother. Closing his eyes, Ronnie nodded before he relented, "You are my attorney." He opened his eyes and looked at his brother's face, "You are smarter than me. You're harder working than I am. You're the better athlete. You don't screw things up like I do. And you do everything better than me." Ronnie's platitudes were necessary to ingratiate himself to his brother's ego.

Enjoying the moment, Kenny pointed a finger at his brother's face and said, "And don't forget I'm better looking too."

Closing his eyes again and breathing heavily through his nostrils, Ronnie conceded, "You are definitely better looking." When Ronnie opened his eyes, he saw the smugness on his brother's face. That last statement was just enough rolling over to please his brother's ego.

Kenny removed the smirk from his face as he explained. "I'm already on the job. I have Gary Bond's Bonding on his way over here. My law firm has sent a lot of business his way over the years and he's more than happy to get you out. You'll have to sit tight for the next couple of days until your arraignment, where you are going to plead, 'not guilty' in front of the judge, and then we'll get you bonded out. Got that?"

Ronnie nodded his understanding, gritting his jaw against the irritation he felt for his brother that was combined with appreciation.

Kenny's eyes narrowed and his forehead wrinkled. "Ronnie, there are a couple of things you need to remember. One, they're to never to question you without me present, so don't say a single word until I get there. Two, you're going to have to tell me the truth in private. You're going to have to tell me what the hell is going on."

Ronnie again nodded, "Get me out and take me home to mom and dad. I'll explain it, all at once, when we get there."

Kenny agreed and the two brothers hugged. "I've got you, brother," added Kenny.

Seeing the sincerity, Ronnie said, "I know you do."

Ronnie had to return to his cell for two more days until he was called in for his arraignment. The days passed slowly, filled with the smell of stale piss and the stories of various troubled men. He couldn't see outside the building, so he pretended the clock was the sun and the moon and the cheap beam lights were oversized stars. Finally, he was arraigned. There, Ronnie followed his brother's instructions to the letter and pleaded, 'Not guilty' with a poker face.

Obtaining the bond from the agency, Ronnie was now free from jail. When he stepped outside, the sun had never looked quite so bright.

$$\mathcal{Q}$$

When Ronnie got into Kenny's SUV, he texted Molly, "I'm sorry for not being able to get a hold of you over the last few days. They arrested me at my research facility. I'm okay. I'm out now. I will explain everything to you, but I really need your understanding. I want you to know I am in love with you." Ronnie sent the text and waited. There was no reply.

I can't deal with this now, thought Ronnie. Frustrated, he turned down the phone's ringer.

The two brothers returned to the City of Wayne, Michigan, just outside of Detroit, to their parents' home. It was the same working class home that they had both grown up in. Their parents, Ken Sr. and Sue Harding, joined the boys at the dining room table for one of the most important family meeting of their lives.

Their burly father, Ken Senior, sitting at the head of the table, kicked off the meeting. "Well, what the hell is this all about?" His paternal instincts were signaling alarm bells in his head. Graduate school had seemed unnecessary and all this research Ronnie had been doing was always mysterious. Ronnie had never let his family see his lab and he hadn't invited them to any of his presentations. Yet, when he found out that his education addicted son was in jail, Ken Senior had suffered a dizzy spell that almost made his knees go out.

Ronnie's older brother, Ken Jr., was about to explain, but was interrupted when Ronnie lifted up his hand. "I've got this." Ronnie stood and addressed the table. "The University hired me out to grow a particular marijuana strain that we're researching as a form of medicine for children." His hands were moving slowly back and forth as his body turned to address both ends of the oblong table, so he looked each parent in the eye. "I crossbred and engineered a particular strain of cannabis that was enriched with a chemical called CBD, and we've harvested it strictly for medicinal use. We did so with the blessing of the Federal government. Every law enforcement agency was informed and everything was under strict control."

"Wait a minute. Wait a minute. Wait a minute," his father interrupted, "You mean, you've been growing weed as a homework assignment? What kind of school is this?" Both of his sons had done their fair share of stupid things. Ronnie had accidentally backed his car into a tree; Ken had fractured his wrist trying to punch his hand through a door. This, however, was the most idiotic of all their idiocy put together.

Ronnie could see the redness building on his father's face. That look was something he still feared. "Dad please, let me get through this, before you start firing off here." Turning to his mother, Ronnie asked, "Mom, can I borrow your iPad for a moment?"

"Sure honey." Sue Harding's face was filled with concern as she started to worry about the tone of this meeting. She got up and walked over to the kitchen counter to retrieve her tablet for her son.

Tapping the screen, Ronnie opened the App Store and downloaded Dropbox. He could feel his pulse in his finger tips with each tap as his nervous energy built up inside him. The next few minutes, while the iPad downloaded and installed the app, seemed to last an eternity, but once it was ready, Ronnie opened Dropbox and logged in. It revealed his backup computer files that were stored on the internet.

Ronnie scrolled through the list of files and stopped at an MPEG video named, "Virginia Frey". With his fingertip, he double tapped on the icon and QuickTime media player began to play the video. Ronnie pressed the pause button and instructed his family, "Will everyone gather around and look over my shoulder while I show this."

Each family member got up, walked around the dining room table, and stood behind Ronnie. He felt the warmth of each parent's touch as his mother and father placed a hand on each of his shoulders to lean in. His father's grip was less friendly and much tighter than his mother's. Ronnie held up the tablet and pressed play.

The video on the screen showed a young mother holding her strawberry blonde18-month-old baby girl on her chest. In her mother's arms, her mouth fell open and repeatedly twitched as her eyes glazed over and began to roll back into her head. The girl's little arms jerked slightly back and forth repeatedly during her seizure. The mother held her child and patted gently on her back, offering encouraging words, "Come on, Virginia. It's okay baby. Just breathe."

Ronnie could feel his mother's fingernails dig into his shoulder as she yelled, "Oh my God! That kid's lips are turning blue. She can't breathe!"

Pressing pause on the video player, Ronnie froze the screen. "This is Virginia Frey. She's part of our research project here at the University. She suffers from a condition called SMEI, which stands for severe myoclonic epilepsy in infancy, and is also called Dravet syndrome."

Ken Harding Sr. asked, "So those are epileptic seizures."

"Yeah." Ronnie answered, "She has 20 to 25 of those a day."

Sue Harding's face winced with pain. "Oh, that poor mother. That has to be so awful to watch your child suffer like that every day."

Placing his finger on the tablet's touchscreen, Ronnie slid his finger along the bottom, fast forwarding the video. He pressed play and the video resumed as Ronnie narrated.

"Here is our research team administering the CBD-based medication to Virginia. We obtained the CBD chemical from the special breed of marijuana plant that I cultivated specifically for this project." Everyone watched as a drop of dark liquid was placed under Virginia's tongue.

"Is that kid getting high right now?" asked Ronnie's father.

Shaking his head, Ronnie was tired of answering this same question, but he said to father, "No. The only thing that gets you high in pot is the chemical THC. There's no THC in our medication. It's refined, purified CBD, which is non-psychoactive, so there will never be a high generated from our medication."

Blowing a curious 'humph' past his gray mustache, Ken Sr., acknowledged what was just said.

Ronnie took his finger and slid it across the surface of the iPad's display to fast forward the video. "Here's how Virginia's doing today," added Ronnie.

Watching the video, Ronnie's mother awed, "Oh my God, look at her! She's walking around and she looks so happy. Look at the smile on her face."

As his nerves calmed down, Ronnie pressed pause again and explained, "Since administering our medication to Virginia, she's had zero seizures. We went from 20 or 25 a day down to none." He looked up at his mother, whose mouth gaped slightly. Ronnie turned to look up at his father, who was equally dumbfounded. He felt his mother rub on his shoulders, non-verbally letting him know she was proud of him.

Setting the iPad on table, Ronnie instructed, "I need everyone to take their seat, because now I have to give you the bad news."

Each family member took their seat. Ken Sr. broke the silence, "I still can't wrap my head around the idea that you're growing marijuana as a homework project." The levity worked for a moment. Ken Sr. was beginning to think Ronnie was less stupid.

Seizing the opportunity, Ronnie immediately told his parents, "I was arrested two days ago and they're charging me with drug trafficking of marijuana."

"What?!" His mother reacted, "What the hell is going on?"

His voice slightly cracked as Ronnie said, "To tell you the truth, I really don't know. I was doing my work at my lab and before I knew it, I had two 12-gauge barrels in my face and the officer told me to freeze."

Again, picking up the iPad, Ronnie reopened his Dropbox folder and tapped on the screen. A sense of urgency spread over him as he defended himself, "See for yourself. This is a letter from US

Department of Justice-DEA approving what we're doing. We've been following through with everything that they've requested. They have us under their supervision. Here's another letter from the Michigan State Police, and another one from the Masonic County Sherriff. The University notified and received approval from every law enforcement agency within our jurisdiction about our ongoing operations, including the City of East Meridian and Michigan A&M's campus police. They know! We're not hiding anything."

Hearing that, Ronnie's brother, Kenny stuck out his hand to interject himself into the conversation. "Well, there were some wires crossed here. While I was bailing you out, I picked up some information about what went down."

Ronnie listened intently as Kenny explained, "Capital City P.D. arrested you"

"Capital City! What the fuck do they have to do with Michigan A&M's campus?" asked Ronnie.

"Well," elaborated Kenny, "Capital City P.D. was leading a multi-jurisdictional anti-crime task force that stretched over the tri-county area, including the campus of Michigan A&M. That letter you have from the Masonic Country Sherriff is over two years old. That was from the outgoing Sherriff. Now, there's a new one and he may not even know about your facility. Cause I'm telling you, they are convinced that you are the kingpin on this new strain of marijuana that's been blowing up on the streets of Capital City. They're calling it Probie."

The father, Ken Sr. asked, "After the hockey player?"

The older brother simply nodded to his father and turned back to Ronnie. "What they think they have your research facility is a whole bunch of Probie. With the amount you've grown, they're throwing a minimum 10-year sentence at you."

Fuck! Ronnie thought as his mind swirled with fear and trepidation. *They busted the wrong grow room. I will take this secret to my grave.* He wasn't big on lying, but making his family an accessory after the fact was clearly off the agenda. Sometimes secrets are best kept secret.

Ronnie's mother, Sue spoke out, "Well, they clearly got it wrong! My baby's work is trying to help people like that poor child." The mother reassumed her role as matriarch when she yelled out to her oldest son, "Kenny! You are going to defend Ronnie, aren't you?"

"Of course, Mom," answered Kenny. "No one is going to mess with Ronnie except for me."

Thanks brother, thought Ronnie sarcastically.

The protective mother bear came out in Sue Harding. "Good, because we all live by this creed...Family above all." Her tone was gravely serious.

Feeling relieved, Ronnie looked at each of his family members' faces. There was a steely eyed look of determination on every one. A warm feeling of comfort filled his being as his family rallied around him. Ronnie watched his mother lecture Kenny about doing his best to exonerate him.

Looking down in his lap, Ronnie checked his phone and saw three texts waiting for him from Molly. With his finger, Ronnie tapped on the first message. "OMG, I was taking a nap. I didn't see your text. Please call me." He tapped on the next one, "They did what? Please call me. I'm freaking out here." Ronnie felt the urgency as he tapped again on his phone's display and read Molly's last text message, which said, "Ronnie, I love you."

Ronnie sent Molly a reply text back, "I love you too. I'll call you in a bit."

While Ronnie had been locked up in jail, he'd feared that he was about to be abandoned by the people who he loved the most. Those fears were unfounded. The people who loved him were behind him 100%. More warm emotions filled his body as he watched his mother lecture his brother that there was no choice in the matter of exonerating Ronnie. According to her, it would be done.

After getting brow beaten by his mother, Kenny looked at Ronnie and asked, "What do you think the University is going to do about this?"

Ronnie returned the glare. "To tell you the truth, I really don't know."

21

THE TUPELO FIVE

As the first black female President of Michigan A&M University, Dr. Desiree' Quinney had her dream job. However, she felt it was a mixed blessing at times. She understood the significance of her position as a professional pioneer, but she thought it was a little demeaning that her gender and ethnicity were brought up in every conversation.

She was often asked, "So, how does it feel to be the first African American Female President of Michigan A&M?" The President would rather talk about the success of the school's football and basketball programs or any of its numerous ongoing research projects, but she accepted the repetitive question with a grain of salt. Rosa Parks' skin color had been significant during her brave act of defiance, but Desiree' was a modern woman who wanted to be seen for her intelligence, not her pigment. She had worked hard to become the university president and the color of her skin had nothing to do with it.

Generally, Dr. Quinney preferred to professionally downplay these items. However, when she walked across her office to her deep stain cherry wood book shelf, she would see the black and white framed high school graduation photograph of her mother, Reida Jackson. The President's mother had been a member of the Tupelo Five, a group of African American students, who, in 1963, were escorted into

Tupelo Central High School by Federal Troops to end segregation in that part of Mississippi. *What courage it must have taken for those five students to walk those hallways. Think about it. In one generation of African American women, we went from living in the segregated south to sitting in the President's office of a major university.* Dr. Desiree' Quinney then thought, *what am I complaining about?*

Desiree' had taken one step forward in history for black women and she tried to remember to be proud of what her skin color meant to the black and white communities now that she was the president of a university, and especially what this accomplishment meant to her ecstatic mother.

Keeping her inspiration in mind, Dr. Quinney smiled as she walked back to her mahogany desk and took a seat to look at her daily agenda. She was ready to take on the world. Throughout the summer, the University President had been dealing with an overwhelming load of public relation problems, mostly stemming from an incident involving the Capital City Police raid of one of her research facilities. They had arrested one of her students for growing marijuana for medical research. The Capital City P.D. had wasted no time in calling a press conference and showing the world that Michigan A&M was cultivating a Schedule I narcotic with taxpayer dollars. Newspaper articles and videos made it to the social networks and the postings went viral. The press had a field day at the University's expense, even going so far as labeling Michigan A&M, "The Grow School". The sensationalism got hits.

Now, as the summer ended, the entire student body had begun to move back for the fall semester and 'Michigan A&M' started trending again on search engines and social media webpages. People wanted to know more about the happenings at the school. The problem was that the public now saw Michigan A&M as less of an academic institution and more of a party school. Regardless, the university had already seen a huge jump in admission applications for next year's class.

Sitting at her desk, Dr. Quinney was dealing with a swirl of problems when the telecom on her desktop beeped and a female voice came through the speaker, "Dr. Quinney, Mr. Maurice Chamberlain is here to see you."

Pressing down on the telecom button, The University President answered, "Thank you, Ms. Allen. Tell him to give me a minute and then he can come in."

The voice through the speaker box returned, "Yes Ma'am."

Looking at the oak door near the corner of her office, Dr. Quinney thought, *Maurice Chamberlain, the Mayor of Capital City, Big Moe stopping by to pay me a visit. I wonder what he wants?* She smiled at her own sarcasm. The University President knew the Mayor well. Their careers had risen simultaneously. They had known each other for years, and there was now a professional respect required from both of them. People can go from being friends to being acquaintances when it comes to the professional world.

A moment later, Dr. Quinney watched as the door opened and Mayor Chamberlain walked in. The handsome dark skinned man was dressed professionally in his dark gray business suit. He could have passed for anything from a banker to an engineer, but his position was much more powerful than most in the city. The Mayor was in his mid-50s and had a reputation of being a former ladies' man that now appeared to be happily married. The bald gentleman stood confidently, adjusting his cufflinks, as he surveyed The President's office décor, before turning his attention the executive woman who stood to greet him.

The University President extended her hand, "Mayor Chamberlain, what a surprise to see you."

"Thank you, Dr. Quinney." The Mayor shook her hand and said, "First, I have to compliment you on your office. I love the rich stained wood and the earth tone colors. You have created such a warm environment."

President Quinney calls this part of the conversation The Dance of the Vipers, where two adversaries start their banter with courtesy and politeness before things turn confrontational. She knew this dance well as she accepted the compliment, "Why thank you Maurice.

That was kind of you. Now, why don't you have seat so we can talk about why you're really here." She offered a gentle smile.

Offering his own charming smile in return, Mayor Chamberlain said, "Very well, lead the way."

The University President and the Mayor walked toward the executive desk and the two took their appropriate seats. Desiree' had no problem directing the mayor to the guest chair. She had earned her presidential chair and she was not going to offer anyone her seat, even the mayor. Dr. Quinney started the conversation. "Well, Mr. Mayor, since you made the trip to see me, why don't you tell me what's on your mind?"

Getting comfortable in this leather guest chair in front of the President's desk, Mayor Chamberlain said, "You know as much as I do that things are changing in this state. There's a large constituency of voters who are fed up with old ways of union corruption and failed liberalism. Look at me. I'm a proud African American conservative who unapologetically won the Mayor's office in Capital City, ground zero for State Government workers. I won that election based on a campaign that promised tax cuts and slashes to government services. The people bought it. What does that tell you?"

Dr. Quinney offered her congratulatory sentiment, "Maurice, there's no doubt you've done well for yourself." On the inside, she couldn't stand the man. He was snobby and conniving, only referring to racial pride when it suited him and ignoring his fellow black community when it did not. Desiree' hadn't voted for him and she didn't know anyone else who had either.

"Thank you, Dr. Quinney," Mayor Chamberlain replied, "but this is only the beginning. I have my eye set on the governor's chair next. The Citizens United Supreme Court ruling is a beautiful thing. With that in place, I don't have to care anymore what the voters want. All I have to cater to is the billionaires and their Super PACs. With those connections, I'll secure more money than I'll ever need to crush my opponent, whoever he or she may be. All I have to do is take meetings with the wealthy men. I'll offer them what they want from the great State of Michigan."

The University President kept a poker face as he spoke and then asked, "And what do the rich men want from our great state?"

A smug grin appeared on Mayor Chamberlain's face before he said, "They want someone like me to bust up the unions and end the labor movement here. I would end the prevailing wage laws and enhance Michigan's right-to-work legislation, stripping the financial resources from the unions causing them to crumble through their own attrition. If I can break the unions in the State of Michigan, which will be a giant step in breaking the back of the nationwide labor movement. Without unions, there will never be a worker talking back to an employer ever again. That's what the rich men want. With their money, I'll be able to use the all-powerful media to manipulate voters to engineer the election re-sults. That's the way it's done now. In our so-called democracy, money has become more valuable than votes. Thank you, U.S. Supreme Court."

With a pleasant grin, the University President tilted her head and said, "So, you came all this way to talk a little politics with me." The distain was mounting inside.

"Well no." Mayor Chamberlain offered a rebuttal, "I'm here to talk about the difference between perception and reality."

Trying to hold back a small laugh, Dr. Quinney encouraged him. "Hmmm, this ought to be good."

The Mayor, seizing the opportunity, elaborated. "If you think about the possibilities for such a political future becoming reality, then you would have to take in consideration the idea that I could potentially be, as the next governor, a great friend to Michigan A&M, or an obstacle in terms of state funding."

Maintaining a calm exterior, the University President was grow-ing tired of the Mayor's braggadocios nature and insisted, "Maurice, please get to the point. What do you want from me?"

"Simple." The Mayor demanded, "My constituency would demand that you end all your medical marijuana research immediately. It's offensive to my backers that you would have the audacity to take tax-payer money and use it to cultivate drugs. I think a press conference with a public apology is in order."

"Maurice..." Dr. Quinney started.

The Mayor lifted his hand and cut her off, continuing, "One more thing. The public is outraged by the recent turn of events and there's a demand for justice. I think it would be best for the University for you to issue a statement and for your institution back away from this ordeal altogether. The student who was arrested broke the law and should stand trial alone. He will be the sacrifice on the altar of justice in the court of public opinion."

Hearing that, Dr. Quinney asked, "Are you finished?" Her expression was deadpan.

"I said what I came to say," answered the Mayor.

Maintaining her composure, Dr. Quinney's anger was boiling underneath. "Now, I want you to listen to me carefully, so there's no misunderstanding. I will stand up for every single student, faculty, and staff member on this campus. If you're looking to avoid a legal fight, rest assured - you're now in one. You like to pretend like you are higher up than other people, but we all know you grew up here in the city. The streets were your home and now you try to cover that up with those expensive suits. I tried to be civil with you, Maurice. But then you come into my office and threaten me? You may have forgotten where you're from, but I still remember how to settle things like we used to. So, I suggest you go prepare for your day in court."

Her eyes narrowed.

The Mayor grinned as he stood up. "I guess that's my cue to leave, but Desiree' - I want you to know I look forward to our next meeting."

There was a twinkle in the University President's eye as she said, "So, do I. Now, get out of my office."

Mayor Chamberlain pulled down on his lapel and adjusted his cufflinks again, before he turned and walked out the door.

Waiting a moment before pressing the telecom button, Dr. Quinney spoke into the speaker, "Ms. Allen, could you have our legal department, our public relations department, Jim Doyle, the Dean of the College of Pharmacology and Professor Rittenburg meet me in my conference room at one o'clock?" Today was going to be a long day. Her words had been fuel to the mayor's fire, but she did not regret what she'd said. Someone had to stop shining his shoes.

The telecom beeped and Ms. Allen's voice came through, "Yes, Dr. Quinney. That won't be a problem."

Desiree' Quinney pressed the button again, "Thank you Ms. Allen. I hope you know I appreciate all of your help."

"That's very kind of you to say." Ms. Allen's voice beamed through the speaker.

The University President stood up from her desk and walked back to the large bookcase across the room. She picked up the picture of her mother and said, "How did I do, mom?"

At the conclusion of his family meeting, Ronnie Harding called Molly immediately and he briefly explained what had happened. Fearing that his phone may have been tapped, he told Molly that he was on his way to see her. Borrowing his father's Ford Expedition, Ronnie returned to the City of East Meridian and to his apartment building. As he walked up the steps, Ronnie saw the yellow police tape stretched across his apartment door that read, "Police Line – Crime Scene – Do Not Cross". At the moment, Ronnie could have sworn he heard a train whistle off in the distance as he closed his eyes and exhaled. It felt like a hole had just opened in the bottom of his stomach and everything was draining out of him, as Ronnie realized that all of his possessions were now confiscated, categorized, and booked as evidence against him. His life and apartment had been turned upside down so quickly, it made his head spin.

Ronnie shook it off and knocked on Molly's door. He heard hastened footsteps before the door opened. Molly lunged out, grabbed him, and squeezed, resting her face on his chest. Needing the comfort of her touch, Ronnie held tight to Molly. They both stood in their embrace for several moments. Ronnie had been worried that she wouldn't want to see him again after his arrest. Many women would have walked away for less.

Molly lifted her face off of his chest and broke the silence, "Will you goddamn kiss me already."

Without hesitation, Ronnie pressed his lips against hers. Again, it was what they both needed. The moment kicked any worry and fear out of his brain, while all his energy moved to his heart. When their kissed ended, they continued their embrace.

Ronnie's mind flashed back to a memory from a few years ago. Ronnie had been treading water in a lake after he had drunkenly attempted to swim a mile across at twilight. Calling out for his friends, who were too drunk to hear, he slowly realized that there was a good chance he'd drown. He could feel his legs cramping and his arms giving out; his head was starting to bob. Suddenly, he saw a row boat approach and an old man threw him a life vest, saving Ronnie from the water. In the present moment, he held Molly like he had held that life vest in a moment where he was barely keeping his head afloat.

Holding Ronnie, Molly asked, "Are you okay?" Her voice was shaking slightly.

"Yeah," he answered as calmly as possible, "it was a little dramatic during the arrest, and jail most definitely sucks, but I'm glad I'm alive and out right now."

Molly looked up at him. "Do you remember when I asked you if you were assassin or serial killer? And you answered, 'no, I'm just not that interesting.' "

With a long drawn out, "Yeah," Ronnie was anticipating Molly's next words, hoping that he hadn't been wrong about her not leaving.

"Well," Molly said, "It's safe to say you're most interesting person on campus now."

Ronnie asked in an uneasy manner, "Why? What do you mean?"

With a hand gesture, Molly said, "Come in. I'll show you."

Ronnie followed her into the apartment. Molly walked over to her coffee table, where numerous newspapers were spread out. She picked up the latest copy of The A&M News, the local campus newspaper, and held it out for him.

Staring at his mug shot on the front page, Ronnie's eyes closed as the feeling of dread overtook his body. He read the article. It was all about this new strain of street weed, called Probie, and it included nothing about his medical research. "It's all twisted. They're missing all the facts," blurted Ronnie as he sat down on the couch. Anger, fear, and frustration permeated his body.

Molly sat down next to him. Ronnie could feel her weight as she leaned hard and wrapped her arms around him. She whispered in his ear, "You're going to be alright."

"I feel horrible that I've dragged you into this," confessed Ronnie.

"I have to admit," Molly, still holding on to him, explained, "When I got the news about your arrest, it felt like all at once my fairy tale just died. But that's the way my whole life has been. When things seem to be going right, something always trips me up. This is just par for the course." Ronnie didn't think that sounded like a good thing and his worry over being dumped returned. Her hand gently turned his face, so she could look him in his eyes. "I want you to know I will ride this out to the very end with you. I'm your down-bitch." It was her attempt to cheer him up.

Upon hearing that, Ronnie felt like there was sunshine in his gaze. "Look at you with the street talk," he said as he thought, '*Look at how quickly I've fallen for you.*'

"Google is a wonderful thing," Molly added with a proud smile. The humor worked and the mood in the room lightened up. With that said, she let go of Ronnie to give him back his personal space as she moved, positioning her back against the armrest of the couch. Molly placed her ankle sock covered feet on Ronnie's lap. As if on cue, he began to rub her toes.

Molly stated, "I guess you were right that people were going to be in an uproar over your medical marijuana research."

"Yeah," Ronnie explained, "but it's a little more complicated than that."

Raising her eyebrows, she asked, "How?"

Still gently rubbing her feet, Ronnie said, "Molly, not to be a dick or anything, but right now this is the last thing I want to talk about. I would rather spend this time curled up with you."

Trying to be understanding, a small smile sprang across her face. "You know Ronnie, that's the best answer that you could have given. There's plenty of time to talk about this later, I'm just glad you're here with me." Molly stood up. "Give me a sec so I can straighten up my bedroom a little and let's go to bed." She walked out of room.

A couple moments went by as Ronnie sat alone in the living room. His phone pinged with a text. He looked at the display. It was an unknown phone number. Ronnie tapped on the screen and read the text message, "Hey bro, u there?"

Ronnie knew the text was from Paul. His feelings began to swirl again with relief, apprehension, curiosity and fear. He typed in his response on the phone, "Yeah, I'm out."

A moment later another text came through, "Meet me at the place where we first met at 6:30 tomorrow."

Ronnie replied, "100%."

After that, Ronnie powered down his phone. All he wanted to do was spend his now valuable time focusing his attention on his girlfriend.

Molly returned to living room and said, "Are you ready for me?"

Ronnie stared at her for moment, admiring her adorable face, before he answered, "Yes, 100 percent."

22

THE PEDESTRIAN BRIDGE

After spending the night and most of the following day with Molly, Ronnie knew he had to take care of business with Paul. Last night, after receiving a text from his partner about meeting him today at the spot where they had first met, Ronnie knew he'd meant the concrete pedestrian bridge that crossed the Red Cypress River on Michigan A&M's campus between the football stadium and the library. The 6:30 p.m. meeting time was perfect. Most of the classes on campus were over and the majority of the students were in their dorm cafeterias eating dinner.

Ronnie pulled his father's SUV into a metered parking spot just in front of the Walter Adams Administration Building. Looking around the beautiful campus, he thought back about his wonderful experiences during his college years and what he wouldn't give to be a stupid freshman again. Ronnie enjoyed his reflections before he looked at his phone to check the time. It was 6:19. Just then, his phone pinged and he received a text from Paul, which read, "r u here bro?"

Immediately, Ronnie finger pecked a reply, "Yeah, just parked."

A few moments later, another text came in on Ronnie's phone, "me 2. turn off ur phone. leave it in the car. meet me at the spot."

Ronnie responded, "Done." He powered down his phone and took out the battery before placing it inside the center console.

Getting out of his vehicle, Ronnie made his way slowly to the pedestrian bridge. His emotions started to swirl. He wasn't sure who was on his side anymore and he definitely didn't know whom he could trust. Ronnie could feel his fingers tingle and his nervous energy increase with every step. He felt unsure whether he was walking towards someone he could trust with his life or someone who was ready to sell him out.

When Ronnie finally reached the bridge, he didn't see Paul anywhere. He proceeded to the center of the span and leaned against the guardrail, watching a few ducks swimming in the picturesque river below. Staring at the mallards, Ronnie thought again about the beauty of the campus and knew that his time here was coming to an end. For years, he had learned, studied, and researched amidst these brick buildings and trekked through snow and rain across this serene campus, working toward his goal with each step, believing he would change the world one day. Now, he couldn't see the light at the end of the tunnel. He heard the shrill cry of a dark, abandoned train coming for him. His feet were stuck in the track rails and he was too tired to scream as the wheels rushed forward. The sad sentiment started to take hold and Ronnie became aware of the hollowed out feeling in the pit of his stomach. The gloomy feeling was actually calming, as it allowed him to focus on his sadness. The bigger legal picture was overwhelming.

Lost in his thoughts, Ronnie snapped out of it when he heard Paul's voice, "You alright, bro?"

Aghast, Ronnie turned his head and saw his friend, whose formerly long dark hair had been cut short, bleached blonde, and spiked like a punk rocker. Ronnie was about to blurt something out, but he stopped when Paul brought a single finger to his lips, silently shushing him. Paul immediately unbuttoned his worn denim jacket and took it off to reveal his shirtless torso. Holding his jacket up, he lifted his hands and slowly spun 360 degrees, proving he wasn't wearing a wire or button camera. A couple female students walking by thought something weird was going on, but there were a lot of unusual happening on campus, so girl just kept going on their way. Paul put his jean jacket back on.

Ignoring any other pedestrians, Ronnie nodded, acknowledging the gesture. He copied it by removing his own long sleeve t-shirt and doing the same spin before redressing himself, offering Paul the same peace of mind. Ronnie wasn't the only one feeling paranoid and he knew they both felt stupid for not trusting each other.

Once Ronnie got his shirt back on, Paul restarted the conversation, "You alright, bro?"

"No." Ronnie answered, "Far from it. It's like a nightmare. But before we go into that, what's with your fucking hair?" He held back a snicker. Under different circumstances, he would be on the ground laughing and unable to speak.

Running his fingers through his short, spiky, bleached hair, Paul sheepishly answered, "Yeah, I know. I think the day you got busted, they were following me too. I was at the tattoo shop and I don't know why, but my sixth sense kicked in while I was taking a piss. I knew I had to run. I heard a little ruckus in the lobby, and I was out the window. Bam! I just kept running."

Ronnie watched his friend's eyes widen as Paul continued his story, "I hopped over fences. I hid behind cars, but I kept running for my life. My fight or flight reflexes shifted into flight gear. I just kept moving. I must have run for about five or six miles before I slowed down."

"Then what did you do?" Ronnie asked. The story sounded like a Vin Diesel movie.

"I called one of my girls, Laurie." Paul explained, "She's this girl I went out with in high school. Even though I treated her like shit, she's always been there for me." His eyes moved down to the concrete. "It must be a real pain in the ass to love someone like me." There was some remorse in Paul's words. Ronnie prevented his jaw from dropping in shock. Paul was a good friend - in fact, he was a great friend - but that had never transferred into his dating life. Ronnie stayed out of the fights he witnessed, as he had heard Paul call his girlfriends things he would have been afraid to call anyone, but he never called Paul out on treating the women he dated like shit. Ronnie knew Paul was an asshole when it came to women; he was glad that Paul had realized it.

Moving his hand in a circular motion, Ronnie encouraged, "Okay, get to the hair."

The regretful sentiment was temporary as Paul returned to his animated storytelling mode. "Laurie picked me up in her SUV and I threw my phone in the river, right then. I was so paranoid. She took me back to her place. She owns this hair and nail salon just outside of town in the burbs."

Paul's ADHD kicked in, and he interrupted himself. "I can't believe how much money women spend on hair, nails and feet. It's like with women, the salon-man gets the money first, before the rent-man does. Isn't that something?" His voice was filled with inquisitiveness. "I guess it's important how women feel about themselves."

"Dude, stay on point: your hair." Ronnie refocused Paul.

"Okay, okay." Paul resumed, "When I get to Laurie's shop, I asked her to change my appearance, because you know my look sticks out like a broken thumb. At first, I was thinking, 'Oh shit! Maybe this woman shouldn't have a pair of scissors near my head.' I thought for a moment she was going to Chucky me, like that demonic possessed doll. She reassured me she would take care of me. This is what she did." Paul's face contorted as he pointed at his hair.

Ronnie laughed and said, "It looks good. You look like a blonde Chris Cornell." He broke down and laughed some more.

Reaching into his inside jacket pocket, Paul said, "Oh yeah, look at these." He put on a black plastic pair of reading glasses and smiled.

Closing his eyes, Ronnie bit down on his bottom lip, trying not to laugh, shaking his head. "I would have never recognized you with those on."

"I know," Paul carried on, "I'm like Superman. I can change my appearance with just a pair a glasses." Taking them off and placing back into his pocket, he added, "These are just reading glasses.

I didn't know my eyes were that bad, but everything is a whole lot clearer with them on." A grin spread across his lips.

Suddenly, they were back to just a few days ago, before all the shit had happened. Standing there, talking, they both realized that their friendship wasn't going to be ruined by this. Paul reengaged the conversation. "Okay, enough about me. What happened to you? How are you out?" His manner was a little more business-like.

Ronnie understood the importance of the new direction of the conversation. The icebreaker was over. He answered, "I'm out a half-million dollar bond."

"A half million!" Paul exclaimed.

Ronnie nodded. "Yeah."

"Well," Paul pressed him, "how the hell did you make that?"

Looking directly into his friend's eyes, Ronnie explained, "My brother is a successful attorney and he's tied in with a few bonding agencies. He fronted the down payment and his friends at the agency covered it, so I'm out on bail."

Air blew past Paul's puckered lips. "Half a million. I take it they're charging you with trafficking. Aren't they?"

"Yep. They know that I do university research, but they're fully convinced that I'm the Probie source. They're playing hard ball now. They're throwing 10 years at me with no chance of parole, using mandatory sentencing guidelines against me so the judge can't use his discretion if I'm convicted. He has to throw 10 at me no matter what, even if he understands my point of view. That's the law." Ronnie eyes narrowed.

Paul immediately asked, "Did they offer you a deal?"

"Yep." Ronnie answered, "They would reduce my sentence to 24 months if I admit that I'm the source of Probie. They want me to cooperate with law enforcement, including turning over names of people like you and your sales team. Then they're going to crucify all of you with mandatory sentencing."

"What did you tell them?" immediately leapt from Paul's mouth, although he didn't sound overly concerned. Ronnie wasn't offended by his slight fear; some people will give any name necessary to avoid jail.

Ronnie declared, "What do you think I said? I told them to go fuck themselves and maintained my silence."

With a sense of relief, Paul leaned in and gave Ronnie a brotherly hug. He was proud of his friend. Paul knew he could trust Ronnie, but he couldn't help having a little doubt. He was lucky to have Ronnie standing against the wall with him. Not everyone would have. As they pulled back, Paul said, "I knew you weren't a snitch. You may be a college boy, but I know you've got some street in you."

Ronnie acknowledged that sentiment. "Yeah, you taught me a lot in that regards."

Paul was about to interrupt him, but Ronnie cut him off, "I'm not done. They wanted more from me. They wanted me to turn over all the cash and any financial records involved with Probie, plus any physical evidence. Lastly, they wanted me to issue a public statement denouncing the university's marijuana research as a complete failure and a waste of the taxpayer's money."

"Really?" Paul didn't know what emotion lead the response. They had worked hard to make Probie a popular brand on the streets and Ronnie had spent years researching how beneficial his medical strain, St. Billy, would be to the world. They weren't street thugs; they weren't selling hard drugs. Probie and St. Billy could change the world and now these pricks wanted to take that all away.

As his lips tightened and his forehead tensed, Ronnie said, "And that last part pissed me off the most. They totally shut down my laboratory and confiscated my entire crop. Our research is set back years over this and political grand-standing seems to be the motivation behind all of the bullshit - that and money."

"You even made cable news." Paul went on, "You and your lab were on the World Cable News Channel. I couldn't believe it. They put your mug shot up and they showed your whole research facility. I have to say it was more than impressive. Your research plants were off the chart. I'd never seen anything like it, even with Probie. You look like the weed-king."

Ronnie's face turned melancholy as his eyes turned down toward the concrete. He just nodded.

Paul just continued as he asked, "Do you know what pissed me off the most about that broadcast?"

Turning his gaze back to his friend, Ronnie inquired, "No what?"

"Right in the middle of that broadcast, they called Michigan A&M the grow school." Paul explained, "I couldn't believe it! I almost wanted to get a lawyer and sue them in court for stealing my trademark."

A small grin appeared on Ronnie's face, he knew Paul was trying to make him feel better.

Paul was pleased with himself as he continued, "I'll tell you though, it was almost a blessing you got busted at your university lab instead of Probie's grow room. If you were busted at Probie's grow house, it would have been over for you. I guess you got out of the game just in time." He paused a moment. "Well, maybe just a little bit late."

Again, Ronnie rolled with the humor, but this time he had to ask, "Whatever happened to Probie?"

Paul's face lit up as his eyes widen. "Man, Dem Creek Boyz are pros. They brought in a real crew and four semi trucks. They loaded everything very neatly and well organized, including all the equipment, in the middle of the night. Everything is gone. Probie has moved on without us."

Ronnie asked, "What about the money?"

"We're paid in full," explained Paul, "They dropped the cash in duffle bags, dollar for dollar. I think the reason they paid us up without any problems is because that Baby Hutch dude really liked you."

A slight expression of pride appeared on Ronnie's face.

Paul informed him, "I can have your cut over to you anytime you want."

Ronnie just shook his head. "No. Just hang on to it. It's probably not a good idea for me to be in possession of a large volume of cash. We'll deal with that later."

"I've got you, bro." Paul still appreciated the trust that Ronnie showed in him.

With his emotions swirling again, Ronnie's face went blank as he started thinking about the bigger legal picture in front of him, growing overwhelmed.

Noticing, Paul refocused his friend, "Hey!" With a slight shake to his head, Ronnie snapped out of it. Paul added, "You know you only have one way out of this." His manner was serious.

Bringing his attention back to his friend's face, Ronnie was listening.

"You can never take a plea bargain, no matter what they offer." Paul explained, "You know too many serious people in this game now and if you take any deal, that's like yelling out to the world that you're a snitch. That will be probably detrimental to your health."

That is a nice way of putting it, thought Ronnie. He would be dead within minutes of signing a plea bargain. It wouldn't surprise him if one of the guards turned out to be the executioner.

Ronnie nodded, acknowledging his friend's street lesson. It's not very often that Paul had something to teach Ronnie, but when he did, Ronnie paid attention.

Paul's stare pierced into his friend's eyes. "Ronnie, I want you to understand that at first, they're going to think you're weak. You're an honors graduate student and they're going to assume you'll wet your pants with thoughts of your degrees and your future corporate job going down the toilet. So, they're going to play tough with you. They'll try to scare you with talk of trumped up charges and long term prison sentences - all the other shit that frightens the hell out of suburbanites." His eyes narrowed as Paul added, "You have to stonewall 'em. You have to turn down every deal."

With an acknowledging nod, Ronnie listened intently as Paul continued his coaching lesson. "When that fails, they're going to change up their tactics. They're going to try to be your friend. They're going to offer soft deals with little prison time. They're going to offer the option of expunging your criminal record down the line so you can hide it from your future corporate employers. They'll say that as long as you cooperate with them and give up the names of the people you know until they're satisfied, but none of it will be true. They'll try to own you and use you for all they can, because what's your recourse if they renege on your deal? Nothing."

Ronnie stared back coldly. "So, my best option is to take everything to trial and gamble with 10 years of my life."

"Yeah," Paul explained, "but they have a shitty case. They unknowingly busted you at your university research lab, probably thinking it was Probie's grow house. All evidence of Probie is gone. The only thing they have on you is your university work. They were so eager to nab all the publicity that they threw everything out to the media, calling it their Probie-bust. They were bragging all about it in their press conference, saying that they took the latest menacing drug off the streets. When they find out that there isn't a single Probie plant in their bust, then they'll realize they have yolk on their face. They're on the hook, not you."

Paul paused for a moment as a few students walked past them to get to the library. He resumed his lecture, "You can let them off the hook, if you take a plea bargain and issue a statement undermining the public confidence in the university's medical marijuana research. You caving in is their saving grace."

Ronnie was impressed by how well thought out Paul's theories seemed. As his confidence increased, he nodded his approval.

Understanding that they were both now on the same page, Paul continued. "When they find out they don't have any physical evidence of Probie and you're not taking a plea bargain; they'll have only one recourse: to trash your university research in the courtroom. They're going to claim that growing marijuana, regardless if for research or not, is breaking the law. While they're at it, they're going to try discrediting your research as some leftist hippie subversive bullshit that's going to undermine America. With the right jury, that can go south on you. You got that?"

Ronnie agreed, wondering if Paul should be his attorney.

Looking directly into Ronnie's eyes, Paul said, "I know you believe in your research, but you're going to have to explain the benefits of it to the public. They're going to have to understand it if you want their support. Can you handle that?"

With his confidence growing, Ronnie answered, "Yeah, I can handle that."

"Good. The media is already interested in your court case." Paul explained, "If you can explain how you're helping people with your research, then in a sense, you're going to put the benefits of weed on trial for the nation to see. If you can pull that off, then I think you can get your freedom."

Ronnie could feel his face warm as he felt the astonishment.

Paul added, "If you're acquitted, the Probie case will be closed. Everyone's warrants, including mine, will be torn up. We'll all get our freedom back." A smile spread across Paul's lips as he asked, "Can you handle that?

Nodding, Ronnie agreed. It was a crazy plan. Ronnie from two weeks ago would have tried to figure something else out to avoid this radical Timothy Leary movement. But there was no other choice, and frankly, Ronnie didn't want one. This was the moment he never knew he'd been waiting for; this was the moment when the world would finally learn about his research and medical marijuana strain, St. Billy. People were going to find out the truth about the benefits of his marijuana.

Shaking his head slowly with a little disbelief, Paul looked at his friend and said, "Dude, you're going to put weed on trial in front of the whole country."

23

KRISTY HARDING

Sitting in the back of his father's Ford Expedition, Ronnie Harding rode with his family on his way to the Masonic County Courthouse, which was located in downtown Capital City, across the street from the Capitol dome. It was the most important car ride of his life so far, because it was the opening day of his trial. Ronnie believed he had the most loyal family members in the world.

Wearing an off-the-rack, dark blue business suit, Ronnie felt he'd never be able to accurately express his gratitude to his parents or to his older brother for standing by his side as they had for the last two months. Ronnie and his family were steadfast during the entire investigation and judicial routine as he turned down every plea bargain he was offered. The family was committed with Ronnie to have his day in trail.

Ronnie's belief in family commitment was only enhanced by the warmth he felt on his skin as his girlfriend, Molly, sat next to him in the SUV, holding his hand. Molly proved beyond a shadow of a doubt that she was standing with him too. She never wavered, not once, during any of his pretrial activities. Ronnie knew that this type of loyalty was something you couldn't buy at the store. He also knew that Molly was a perfect fit with his family, especially with his mother, Sue. The two women had clicked almost instantly when Ronnie had brought Molly home and introduced her to his family.

The matriarch of the Harding family was a strong willed woman who had bonded quickly with Molly over the last couple months. Molly had a fear base about her, an insecurity that stemmed from her grief of losing her sole parent, her beloved father. Molly's fears would have had her shying away from any form of adversity or confrontation. That wasn't the Harding way. The loving matriarch offered her wisdom of looking life's challenge in the eye. Respect wasn't found in the results of the battle, but rather, in the fight. There was no self-respect in running from a conflict. Molly learned how to put steel in her resolve, especially when it came to issues of rallying around the family. Ronnie's legal matter was a prime example of this creed.

As the car ride continued, Ronnie thought about his regrets. His life's choices were rooted in mischief and a catch-me-if-you-can arrogance. Now caught up in his legal matters, Ronnie witnessed how his family endured everything right next to him. He was sure that everyone in the SUV had lost some sleep over his dumb decisions. That fact was rehabilitating more than any prison bar. The thought of dragging the people who loved him into his legal bullshit was enough to straighten him out as he entered into the third stage of grief: bargaining. Ronnie pledged to himself that once this was resolved, no matter how it worked out, he was never going do this to his family ever again. From here on out, the boring, straight and narrow path was perfectly okay with him.

The thoughts of remorse continued until Ronnie heard his brother, Kenny, who was sitting in the front passenger seat, yell, "Hey look, protesters!"

Ronnie lifted his head to see out the window and saw about a dozen anti-drug protesters carrying signs outside the courthouse. He read the first one that was held by heavyset white man. His sign read, "NO TAX $ FOR DRUGS!" The sign had a cartoonish green pot leaf in a red circle with slash through it. Ronnie shook his head in disbelief, before reading the next sign, held by an elderly woman, which read, "Shame on you A&M!" However, the sign that bothered Ronnie the most was held by a 12-year-old freckled boy and it said, "Drugs ruined my Daddy's life." Ronnie's tongue immediately clicked as he let out an uneasy chuckle.

Reading each sign, Ronnie thought, *everyone is entitled to their opinion, even if they're protesting me*. Regardless of his opinion on civil liberties, Ronnie didn't feel like he was worth any protest. He pondered that some more as his family's SUV pulled into the courthouse parking lot.

When Ronnie and his family, including Molly, made their way into the courthouse lobby, they were greeted by Kristy Harding. The diminutive green-eyed blonde was married to Ronnie's brother, Kenny. As in-laws, Ronnie and Kristy tolerated each other, but Kristy had a lot of deep-seated issues with Ronnie. She considered Ronnie a first class fuck up and a waste of potential. His current legal ordeal was a perfect example of why his sister in-law felt the way she did.

Ronnie felt had a mutual resentment toward his sister-in-law, although he did his best to keep these feelings to himself. He felt that she was too judgmental of others, while thinking her world was way too perfect, a textbook example of a suburbanite stone thrower. Ronnie buried his resentment because he absolutely adored his niece, Kimber. Ronnie also thought pissing off his brother, who was currently his attorney, would be counterproductive to his trial. His desire for freedom kept him from running his mouth. Ronnie grinned, remaining on his best behavior, as he watched Kristy walk up to his brother and greet him like a hero with a lovable hug and a kiss.

Feeling a slight gag reflex in the back of his throat, Ronnie excused himself from his family for some fresh air as he walked back out to the stone steps in front of the courthouse. He took a seat on one of the steps, off to the right, and stared at the protesters standing at the sidewalk in front of the courthouse. Ronnie turned his gaze up to the beautiful white Capitol Dome across the street. Passing time, Ronnie studied the Dome's ornate architecture, and he could have sworn he heard a train whistle in the distance.

"Hey Ronnie Lee, can I join you?" Kristy Harding asked, interrupting his daydream.

Courteously, Ronnie patted the stone step beside him, offering her a seat. "Take a seat."

Wearing a dark top and gray slacks, Ronnie's sister-in-law took the seat next to him. They both stared at the protesters quietly for a few moments until, Kristy broke the silence, "Ronnie, you know how I feel about you. I also understand what you think of me, but I want you to know that I love you very much, regardless of our differences. You're the best uncle I could wish for my daughter to have. We're family." Her words were word encouraging.

"Thanks Kristy." Ronnie offered a tight lipped grin, appreciating the olive branch his sister-in-law had offered.

"Ronnie, I want to tell you something." Kristy confessed, "Your brother quit his job with the law firm."

Ronnie reacted, "What?! He was about to make partner."

A look of concern emerged on Kristy's face. "Well, he asked the senior partners for a leave of absence so he could work on your defense. They told him to settle your case as quickly as possible with a plea bargain and get back to work. That didn't sit well with Kenny." Her eyebrows raised as her face lit up. "And in the Harding way, he basically told them to go fuck themselves."

Ronnie reacted again as he was about to stand up, "I can't let him do that! He's not throwing away his career over me."

Kristy placed her hand firmly on Ronnie's thigh to keep him from standing up. She exclaimed, "You can't talk to him about it!" Ronnie halted as he listened to his sister-in-law explain the rest of her story in a calm manner. "Ronnie, your brother has always been a hard worker, but he has always played it safe and followed the rules. Life, for Kenny, like your father, always had to have a map, a rule book, or instructions - something for him to follow. But, it's always been his dream to start his own law firm and to be his own boss. He never knew how to break free from those societal rules of climbing corporate ladders. That type of risk taking is not natural for him, but it is so easy for you. It's the one thing that your brother always envied in you."

Hearing that, Ronnie's eyes turned toward the downward stone steps in front of him as the realization took hold of him. He pondered her words for a moment, before returning his attention to his sister-in-law. She continued, "That's why there's so much resentment between you two. Kenny was brought up to believe in that things have to be done in a certain way. In your brother's world there always had to be rules in place and they always had to be followed. To you, those rules are merely suggestions, because you just do what you want to do. You always have. You enjoy a freedom of spirit that your brother is just now starting to learn."

A little overwhelmed by the epiphany, Ronnie could only muster, "I didn't know he felt that way."

Kristy smiled and asked, "You know what he said to me last night?"

Ronnie shook his head.

His sister-in-law explained, "Kenny said to me that quitting his job and starting his own law firm was the best decision of his life. He felt the liberation of going on his own, but it's scary because he has no safety net anymore. Your brother went on to say this is how Ronnie must feel every day. So you've been teaching him something every day of your life."

Ronnie's soul was filled by warm feelings with Kristy's words. He conceded, "I have a lot to learn from him too."

His sister-in-law nodded with an impish grin before she said, "Somewhere between the two brothers is the perfect man."

Whatever doubt Ronnie had in his head about his legal circumstances, they dissipated with her statement. He was made whole again and found a new resolve.

Seeing the new confidence on Ronnie's face, Kristy said, "Well, you are the very first client of our new law firm. I want to know - are you ready?" She finished her pep talk.

Ronnie stood up and waited for his sister-in-law to do the same. When she did, Ronnie leaned in and hugged her. There was new found feeling of solidarity as Ronnie knew that his legal crisis was uniting his family in a way he'd never seen before. He answered her, "Yeah, I'm ready."

"Good." Kristy added, "Let's do this." Her smile was warm and encouraging.

The two walked back inside the courthouse lobby where the rest of family greeted them. Ronnie walked up to Kenny and asked, "You got me, brother?"

The taller Kenny looked directly in Ronnie's eyes with a steely determination and answered, "I've got you, brother." Kenny held out his hand.

Ronnie locked his grip with Kenny's palm and the two pulled each other in for a hug. The brothers held each other for a long moment and when they pulled back, they noticed that every other family member had tears in their eyes. Kenny's and Ronnie's eyes remained dry, as they were now focused and ready for the battle.

The rallying around the family was now set as Kenny took the lead, saying, "Come on, Ronnie. We've got work to do." The two brothers walked into the courtroom with heroic confidence and they took their respective seats at the defense table. The rest of the family took their seats with the other spectators, and the trial was ready to begin. Ronnie turned around to look at Molly, who was sitting next to his mother. Molly smiled and offered a comforting wink. Just then he felt warmth and returned a subtle nod before putting his game face on.

Sitting at the defense table, Ronnie glanced around and took note of how plain the large courtroom looked. The appearance of the room reflected an efficient and cost effective design, lacking in any sense of ornate decorum. The tables, desks and rails, including the judge's bench and the jury box, were made of hardwood, unimpressively stained a light blonde tone. A rich green carpet provided some sense of contrast. A four foot cast of polished copper that resembled the Great Seal of Michigan was hanging on the wall immediately behind the judge's bench.

The judge who presided over the trail was the Honorable Nicole Wildman, a middle-aged Caucasian woman with dark wavy hair, who had a reputation of being fair during her proceedings, but harsh during her sentencing. The jury was made up of nine people, including three women and six men, and it appeared to be an ethnically diverse group. The foreman of the jury was Dale R. Gentry, a 56-year-old white male, who had served on four previous juries over the years, each one having led to a conviction. The prosecutor was Raymond Knox, who had a simple nickname: Hard. It was a nickname earned from his reputation. When you drew Hard as your prosecuting attorney, you ended up going against the toughest lawyer they had in their office.

Upon looking around the room, Ronnie returned his attention to his brother, who sat next to him. Ronnie found the back of this throat completely dry, so he swallowed whatever spit he could muster.

Noticing, Kenny asked, "Do you want some water?"

"Yeah," answered Ronnie.

Kenny reached out to the clear plastic water pitcher and filled both glasses on the table. "Here," Kenny offered.

Ronnie grabbed the glass and took a sip before his brother asked, "Are you ready?"

"Yeah," was the only word Ronnie could get out.

With a confident smirk, Kenny said, "Good, because here we go."

At that moment, the bailiff asked for the courtroom to stand as Judge Wildman took over the trial proceedings for the People of the State of Michigan vs. Ronnie Lee Harding. Ronnie was mesmerized as the opening statements set the tone for his trail. He watched as the prosecution claimed that they were going to prove, beyond the shadow of doubt, that Ronnie was the expert and mastermind who had started a new illegal marijuana trade on the streets of Capital City. Ronnie was the suspected kingpin for sale of Probie. The prosecutor also declared that the research that Ronnie was doing, growing large volumes of marijuana at Michigan A&M University constituted a violation of the law and should be dealt with accordingly.

In the past, Ronnie would have described his older brother's legal skills in bland terms such as efficient, steady and reliable, but today he watched Kenny's performance as a man full of passion and charisma. From his opening statement, the new Kenny was trying to convince the jury that Ronnie was a just researcher, that he followed the rules, that his goal was to help society, and that the prosecution had it all wrong. Kenny talked about a political agenda, according to which Ronnie was to be a sacrificial lamb. Ronnie couldn't have been prouder of his older brother's efforts.

Watching the trial proceed, Ronnie also developed a great respect for the prosecution and their investigators as they worked and constructed the truth. Ronnie was the only person in the room who knew the facts, and the prosecution was putting them together right in front of him. However, there were some obvious holes in their theories.

The prosecutor, Raymond Knox, retained an expert witness in the area of cannabis research from the University of Mississippi. This paid expert theorized in accordance to their extensive database at his university that Capital City, Michigan had a unique strain of marijuana floating on their streets. He theorized that this illegal strain of marijuana, called Probie, which was uniquely high in both THC and CBD, was actually a genetic offshoot of a medical research strain high in CBD, which was registered under the name 'St. Billy'. This medicinal marijuana was cultivated in the shadow of Capital City on the campus of Michigan A&M University. The expert witness declared that the registered cultivator of the St. Billy strain was the graduate student, Ronnie Lee Harding. Ronnie had assisted in Professor Rittenburg's research. The expert declared that in his opinion, Ronnie Lee Harding was most likely the cultivator of the illegal form of marijuana, Probie. It was his expert opinion that Ronnie would be one of the few people in the country with the expertise and knowledge to develop this unique strain of marijuana.

Again, Ronnie's throat went dry as he watched the proceedings continue while Kenny cross-examined the expert witness through rounds of verbal sparring. Ronnie's brother got the expert to admit under oath that his testimony was only a theory based on conjecture. The expert had no proof. The defense raised level of doubt.

The prosecution then took its turn trying to link Ronnie to Paul Mollett in order to name the pair as the main suppliers of Probie in the city. The prosecutor called Gerald Duffy to the witness stand. Even though Ronnie had never seen Gerald before, he knew that Gerald was a part of the Probie sales team set up by Paul. This was confirmed as Gerald admitted, under oath, that he was a part of the network that sold and distributed Probie in the REO Town neighborhood of the city. The prosecutor then asked Gerald, "Can you identify the parties that provided you with your supply of marijuana?"

Gerald answered, "Yes. It was Paul Mollett and Ronnie Harding."

The prosecutor used a remote and the digital projector mounted on the ceiling to display a digital image on the movie screen hanging on the far wall. An image of Paul Mollett's mug shot with his trademark long black hair appeared on the screen. The prosecutor asked the witness, "Can you identify this man?"

Gerald confirmed, "That's Paul Mollett."

"Can you identify the other man who was charge of providing you a wholesale supply of marijuana?" The prosecutor's face was determined.

Gerald answered, "Yes." He then pointed directly at Ronnie at the defense table and said, "That's him. Ronnie Harding. He's the brains behind everything."

Ronnie's mouth sprang open in shock, because he had never seen Gerald before in his life. His ears began to ring, as his blood pressure spiked. Unbeknownst to Ronnie, Gerald had cut a plea bargain deal to sell out whoever the prosecutors wanted in exchange for an extremely light sentence. In this case, Gerald's damning finger pointed directly at Ronnie. This was planted evidence to fill in the gaps in their investigation. The witness had no idea who Ronnie actually was, but Gerald did what he had been coached to do.

Upon hearing that, Kenny leaned over to Ronnie and whispered in his ear, "Who is this guy?"

Ronnie turned his head and quietly said, "I don't know. I've never seen him before."

A smirk appeared on Kenny's face as he leaned in to his brother. "That's all I need to know."

When it was Kenny's turn to cross examine the witness, he initially asked, "So, how do you do know the defendant?"

Gerald smugly answered, "He's been my main weed supplier for the last couple of years. I know him pretty well."

Kenny immediately followed up, "Can you tell me if Ronnie Harding has a high voice or a low one?"

The witness paused and stared Ronnie for a moment.

"Remember, you're under oath," Kenny reminded Gerald.

An obviously flustered witness answered, "I don't know."

With that reply, the levy broke, as Kenny pounded the witness with a series of personal questions. All Gerald could say was a repetitive, "I don't know."

Seeing his witness crumbling on the stand, the prosecutor, Raymond Knox, objected to protect Gerald from completely caving.

Judge Wildman overruled and allowed the series of question to continue.

Kenny continued to ask these personal questions about his brother until it became apparent that Gerald knew little to nothing about Ronnie. Doubt in Gerald's story spread through the jury.

The day went on as the prosecution called more witnesses and presented more exhibits of evidence, including video of Ronnie bailing out Paul Mollett, the other suspected drug dealer, at the police station, linking the two together.

The prosecutor also provided ample video evidence of Ronnie's university research facility, showing the largest cannabis plants that anyone in the room had ever seen. The prosecution was trying to make two important theories stick. One, that Ronnie was an outright illegal drug dealer. The other was that Michigan A&M's medical cannabis research was illegal as defined by the law and Ronnie was a participant.

Ronnie's brother counterpunched, as a good defense lawyer should, by undermining the confidence in the prosecutor's case. He identified every flaw and gap in their investigation. The one thing that stuck out from the defense was that the investigators had never found any Probie in connection with Ronnie. There was no physical evidence, only conjecture. There were numerous objections on both sides throughout the proceedings, but Judge Wildman mostly over-ruled. She allowed a lot of leeway for the lawyers to simply fight it out. Even with numerous recesses, the day felt long before the judge declared the court adjourned.

Proud was the only way to describe Ronnie's feelings toward his brother right now. Kenny had fought the good fight in the court-room today, full of charm and zeal. As much as he was bursting with pride over his brother's performance, Ronnie was also full of appre-hension, because he knew that the prosecution and their investiga-tors had built a hell of case against him. Ronnie also knew that their case wasn't far from the truth. The angst was all over Ronnie's face as he sat alone at the defense table. He knew he was gambling with 10 years of his life.

After talking things over with his family, Kenny returned to his brother, and said, "Hey Ronnie, there are a lot more protesters out-side - like a couple hundred more."

"Great. More people who want to burn me at the stake," mumbled Ronnie.

"No," Kenny added, "There are a couple hundred people outside the courthouse that are pro-Ronnie protesters and they are severely outnumbering the anti-protesters from this morning."

"Really?" Ronnie's face lit up.

A smirk smeared across Kenny's lips while he said, "Yeah. I talked to Kristy too and you're trending on all the social networks. '#FreeRonnie' is everywhere - people are telling your story. You're going viral. There are a lot of people taking up your cause."

Inside Ronnie's head, there was a little ego monster peeking out of the closet. His impulses wanted him to run outside and join the

Pro-Ronnie protesters, but his current fears kept him in check. The excitement was only momentary, as the look of concern returned to his face.

Kenny saw the worry in his expression and asked, "You alright, brother?"

"Yeah," answered Ronnie, but his face couldn't hide his trepidation.

Kenny was a seasoned defense lawyer, so he understood Ronnie's concern. The older brother offered, "Day one is usually the roughest day; the prosecution just kicks your ass all over the place. But now is when I need you to put your faith in me. Tomorrow it will be the defense's turn up at the plate and my turn to take a swing. I want you to know I'm going to fight like hell for you and I can't wait for you see what I'm bringing to the courthouse tomorrow."

24

THE FOREMAN

Those two lawyers really brought it yesterday, thought Dale Gentry as he resumed his seat in the jury box. It was day two of the trial known as the People of the State of Michigan vs. Ronnie Lee Harding. It was his fifth time serving on a jury, and the 56-year-old had been named foreman of the jury. The previous four times he'd served had led to boring convictions.

As Dale looked around the courtroom, he thought about his previous trials as a juror and came to the conclusion that taking the court-appointed lawyer was a sucker's move. During each of the cases he'd sat, Dale had watched the pathetic effort those court-appointed defense attorneys had put up. Dale felt when a person in legal trouble takes the court-appointed attorney, he's just made a serious mistake, thinking that he's getting legal representation while saving some money.

In Dale's past trials as a juror, he'd watched how the court-appointed attorneys simply rolled over and allowed their clients to be steamrolled by the prosecution. Those trails had been a little boring and pathetic to watch, but this case seemed different. Both the prosecution and defense had brought their A-games to the court. Yesterday, the courtroom had been filled with fireworks as there were consistently passionate objections, although strong cases were made by both sides. It was like a heavyweight boxing with both sides delivering solid blows. To the foreman, this case was a spectacle in comparison to his past trial experiences. The television coverage and the growing number of protesters only added to Dale's excitement.

The foreman was hoping the second day of this trial would be just interesting, as it was now the defense's turn to present its case. It didn't take long; Professor William Rittenburg was called up first. The jury foreman thought that the professor was well spoken as he explained the nature of his research. During Rittenburg's testimony and cross examination, Dale Gentry thought the professor's information was concise, but at times, a little hard to follow. The expert's evidence about certain chemicals in the marijuana plant being used as a treatment with certain ailments sounded promising, but his explanation was sometimes difficult for the average Joe to understand. The professor also presented documentation that showed how his research was in sync with Federal regulations that were administered by the U.S. Food and Drug Administration and the Department of Justice. It seemed that all the rules had been followed, at least according the Federal Government. Now, it was a question of state law. Dale watched intently as the defense called the next witness to the stand.

Standing proudly in the center of the courtroom, the defense attorney, Ken Harding looked over the gallery and called out, "The defense would like to call Faith Nicholson to the stand."

The eyes of the jury foreman followed, as a woman with dark hair and fair skin made her way to the witness stand. She was wearing a dark blue pant suit as if she were on her way to her office job. When the 30-something woman made her way to the stand, she raised her right hand and the bailiff administered her oath.

Faith was sworn to give her testimony, stating "I do." She then took her seat.

Ken Harding noticed that the witness was a bit nervous as he approached her. Walking calmly, Ken offered a comforting nod to her before he asked, "For the record, will you please state your name and city of residence."

The witness cleared her throat and spoke clearly into the microphone, "My name Faith Nicholson. I currently reside in East Meridian, Michigan." Faith paused for a moment, before she added, "I'm formerly from Madison, Wisconsin."

"When did you move to Michigan?" Ken Harding asked.

Faith replied, "I moved here a year and a half ago."

Ken noticed how Faith's nervous energy subsided as she steadied herself. He asked her, "Why did you relocate?"

"For my son, Benjamin," Faith explained, "A little after my son was three months old, he started having severe convulsions. Each day the seizures grew in quantity and intensity. The doctors diagnosed my son with Myoclonic Epilepsy."

Ken held up his left hand to pause Faith's testimony. He raised a hand held remote control in his right hand and pressed a button. The ceiling mounted digital projector came to life and displayed a video on the movie screen that hung on the far wall. The video on the screen displayed an infant boy lying on his back with a medical tube in the base of his throat. The boy's arms were held out in front of him, moving slightly back and forth, twitching. After a few moments, Ken pressed pause on the video display and asked Faith, "Can you explain what's happening here?"

Faith bit down on her bottom lip before she explained, "That's my son, Ben, at five months old. His physical seizures were becoming so intense that he stopped breathing. He was actually turning blue, so on this day, we rushed him to the emergency room and the doctor put a tube in his trachea to help him breathe."

"Is this normal?" Ken asked.

With a simple nod, Faith replied, "Yeah. Ever since this day, Benjamin has had periodic episodes of grand mal seizures that so extreme that he stops breathing. At one point, he was having 15 or 20 seizures a day. The worst part was when his doctors told us that there was nothing the medical community could do to help my son. The doctors told me that my son had Dravet syndrome, which is a genetic condition. There was no medication, no therapy and no treatment for him. He was stuck with this condition as a prisoner in his own body."

Ken gently looked directly at Faith, and asked her, "Is this what brought you to East Meridian, Michigan?"

"Yes." Faith elaborated, "I came here in hope of participating in Professor Rittenburg's research at Michigan A&M University. He was granted human clinical trials by the FDA and was looking for candidates. When my son was selected and approved, Professor Rittenburg was the only person who was offering my son a chance at a normal life, so I decided to leave Wisconsin for Michigan."

"And how is your son doing today?" Ken inquired.

Faith offered small grin expressing a sense of relief. "Today, Ben is just over two years old and thanks to the professor's medication, developed from his strain of marijuana, my son is only having about one seizure a week. The professor is also collecting data and refining his dosages and his method, hoping to eliminate all of Ben's convulsions. The professor and his staff are dedicated to solving this crisis for parents like us."

Ken faced the jury as he asked the witness, "Would you consider Professor Rittenburg's research a success?"

"Oh yes," Faith responded, "without a doubt it has worked for my son. He is right there in the gallery."

The foreman of jury turned his head and saw a young toddler playing next to his father, showing no signs of seizure.

Walking toward the jury box, Ken spoke out, "Ladies and gentlemen of the jury, I would like to enter this video as Exhibit-B." The defense lawyer pressed play on his remote control.

The foremen watched as the video displayed on the movie screen showed the same little boy, Benjamin, running and playing like a normal child. He also glanced at the boy's mother, Faith, sitting in the witness chair. Even though she held her composure, the mother's eyes watered as she watched her son on the screen. The foreman took note of the mother's gratitude and relief.

Ken pushed pause on the remote and the video stopped. He approached the witness stand. "Mrs. Nicholson, you understand that Professor Rittenburg's medical marijuana research is at the heart of this criminal proceeding. The defendant, Ronnie Harding, is being charged with a variety of drug charges for his work with the professor. He was the actual marijuana grower who cultivated the marijuana that became the medicine that helped your son. Would you consider the defendant's work to be criminal?"

"You know; I'm taking this witness stand at great personal risk to my family." Faith clarified, "I'm telling the public that I'm giving my infant child marijuana extract. I run the risk that some ignorant bureaucrat at Child Protective Services may now come to my house to take my child away, thinking that I'm trying to get my own son high. That's not the case. What's being developed here is not a narcotic, its a medicine, something to give my son a shot at a normal life." Faith turned her head toward Ronnie Harding, sitting at the defense table. She looked directly at him and added, "The defendant obviously took an academic risk at his personal expense to help families like mine. I feel it's my duty to stand with him and declare in this public forum that his work is no way criminal, regardless of the law. What the defendant is doing is actually developing a medicine to help children, like my son." Faith returned her attention to the lawyer standing in front of her.

With an appreciative glance, Ken said, "Thank you Mrs. Nicholson." He walked away and took a seat at the defense table.

As the defense lawyer sat down, Ray Knox, the prosecuting attorney, stood up and approached the witness stand, where Faith was still seated. It was the prosecution's turn to cross examine the witness. Mr. Knox asked in a boisterous tone, "Mrs. Nicholson, was there ever a time that you thought giving marijuana extract to your infant son made you a bad mother?"

The witness' face soured slightly upon hearing the question. "No. But I do know there was a time during this ordeal when I knew for a fact I was a bad mom."

Feeling he'd found his opportunity, the prosecutor asked, "Can you elaborate?"

"Yes." Faith explained, "When my child was initially suffering from his condition, I felt stuck in a constant state of fear. I was watching my child suffer every single day. The medical community had told me there was nothing they could do for my son." Faith's eyes began to water as she continued, "Maybe it was the constant worrying and the exhaustion, but I remember one night, lying in my bed, I actually hoped that my child would have a seizure and die peacefully in his sleep." Bringing a tissue to her eyes, Faith pursed her lips for a moment in an attempt to maintain composure. She added, "That's when I knew, in that moment, that I was a bad mother. I was stuck in despair. That's when Professor Rittenburg's research team became my beacon of hope."

At that instant, uncontrollable tears flowed from Faith's eyes as a testimony of her sincerity. It became a powerful moment. Faith turned her gaze toward the defendant's table and stared directly at Ronnie Harding. She added, "I understand that I take a personal risk by testifying here, but I also appreciate that defendant took a risk in assisting with Professor Rittenburg's research. He did it to help families like mine and that's why I have no problem offering my testimony. I want the truth to come out."

Feeling that he was running the risk of damaging his case, the prosecutor paused for moment and tactically declared, "I have no further questions." The witness left the stand and the prosecutor took his seat back at his table.

The foreman of the jury watched as the defense attorney took over the proceedings by calling up one of the investigative police officers, Michael Finch, and Ming Zhāng, the Capital City Police Department Chief Forensic Scientist. Through an aggressive series of questions and a thorough cross examination, both sides performed excellently. To the foreman, one fact came clear. There was no Probie found during the arrest of Ronnie Harding. It was confirmed during the testimonies that all the marijuana plants seized were of the medical variety and had almost no THC content, making them worthless as a street drug. The only real purpose of this confiscated crop was to cultivate an experimental medicine for research.

The attention of the jury foreman was drawn to the stand when the defense called up the actual defendant to testify. When a defendant takes the stand in his own defense, it's typically considered a high risk maneuver. Most defense attorneys would strongly advocate against it. The foreman watched intently as Ronnie Harding stood up and walked to the witness stand, where he was sworn in to give his testimony. Once he took his seat, the foreman was impressed with Ronnie's ability to sincerely articulate his passion for his research. Ronnie was clear in explaining that he enjoyed cultivating his plants, which was serving a medical benefit, especially because his work helped children. He felt that the research had been done with the utmost transparency and had consistently met every demand of law enforcement.

When the defense stepped down, the prosecution stood up and immediately came after Ronnie. The prosecutor immediately cross-examined Ronnie. "Mr. Harding, what is your relationship with the well-known Probie dealer, Paul Mollett?"

Ronnie could feel his heart race inside his chest, but with a long exhale, he remained calm. "I barely know the guy," he answered. He was perjuring himself in order to protect his family, his life, and his girlfriend.

The prosecutor held up the remote control and large black and white photograph appeared on the screen. It was the image of Ronnie and Paul hugging when Paul was bailed out of the Capital City jail by Ronnie. The prosecutor asked, "Well, can you explain this photograph of you two together?"

"Yeah," Ronnie answered, "I can explain. Paul is a friend of a friend."

The prosecutor interjected, "How so?"

Looking directly back at the prosecuting attorney, Ronnie said, "Well, at the beginning of the summer, these two girls moved into the apartment across the hall in my building. The property management company could verify when they actually moved in. Anyways, after getting to know these two girls, I started to have feelings for one of them, Molly. Her roommate, Francesca, was dating Paul at the time. The night before that photo was taken, Francesca and Paul were arrested. I just bailed them out."

"Why did you bail them out?" The prosecutor inquired.

Ronnie thought about the question for a moment before he answered, stating, "Because I wanted to look heroic and noble to the girl I was crushing on." He turned a slight glance at Molly sitting in the gallery.

The prosecutor walked over to the movie screen where the photo of Paul and Ronnie in an embrace was displayed. The lawyer asked, "Can you explain why in this photo you look like long term friends?"

Again, thinking about the question for moment. Ronnie answered, "I guess anyone would be appreciative if someone had just bailed them out of jail."

The prosecuting attorney heard some snickering in the courtroom, and immediately started firing off a series of questions aimed to trip up the defendant. Ronnie was too well coached, and he kept his nerves under control while he listened to each of the prosecutor's questions. Ronnie pondered each question for a moment as he steadied himself, before delivering his answers.

The foreman of the jury watched as Ronnie's boyish charm took over with each reply. From his past experiences, the foreman would watch the nerves of defendants get the best of them. Usually, defendants react quickly by answering questions before they were completely asked. They would sometimes ramble on, saying too much or coming off as arrogant. In either situation, the defendant was likely to hurt his or her own case with the testimony.

The prosecutor relented and allowed Ronnie to return to his seat next to his brother, his lawyer. After both the prosecution and defense went through their rebuttals and made their closing statements. The case came to a close and judge instructed the jury on how to deliberate. The members of the jury were now the upholders of the law.

When the court had adjourned, Ronnie leaned into his brother's ear and whispered, "Thank you, Kenny. You were spectacular."

"Why thank you Ronnie." Kenny replied, "And you were pretty awesome yourself."

Ronnie asked the natural question, "What do you think the jury is going to do?"

Kenny turned himself in his chair so he was looking his brother directly into his face. "Ronnie, you know I'll always tell you the truth. It all depends on the jury. This whole Probie thing fell by the wayside because their case fell apart. The question is now whether growing marijuana, even for medical research is a violation of the law. The quantities that you grew during your research put you in violation of the state law, even if the federal government gave you their blessing. With this jury, I think it could go either way."

Accepting the terms his brother had laid out for him, Ronnie closed his eyes and nodded his head. When he reopened his eyes, Ronnie said, "Thanks again, brother." The two brothers stood up and hugged it out.

At that moment, the rest of the Harding family, including Molly and Kristy, joined Kenny and Ronnie at their table. Both girls hugged and kissed their respective brothers as if they were heroes. There was excitement in both of their eyes. Kristy broke the news, "You guys will not believe this."

"What?" Ronnie's voice jumped a couple octaves.

"There are almost 10,000 people protesting outside the court-house and the protest has spilled over onto the Capitol lawn." Kristy explained, "And I would say that 90 percent or more are pro-Ronnie supporters. There's a bunch of pro-marijuana people out there. There are pro-research advocates. There are civil libertarians. There are all sorts of demographics out there. According to internet chatter, even the Ann Arbor students are out there supporting you."

Kenny interjected himself into the conversation, "My people are here?"

Kristy confirmed, "Yeah, the Ann Arbor University students are here. The Hash Bash organizers have mobilized and they're here to make a statement to law makers."

Shaking his head, Kenny said, "Leave it to Ronnie to unite the Michigan A&M kids and the Ann Arborites. Two student bodies, who usually hate each other, coming together over the antics of my little brother."

Ronnie gazed over at his family. There were smiles on every Harding family member's face. Ronnie asked, "Hey, you guys want to take a look?"

With a smile, Kenny answered, "Yeah, let's go check it out."

25

WORLD-CABLE NEWS CHANNEL

B rittany Wise had a case of histrionic personality disorder during the process of social maturation from a little girl into a young woman. Since elementary school, she had needed to be the center of attention and in her mind, if she wasn't, there was something wrong with the universe. Brittany's physical appearance played a role in her personality disorder; she was a natural redhead with a pretty face and attractive athletic figure. However, it was her persona that made her the most eye-catching. Brittany had an optimism about her that had a magical, fairy-like energy, which created her allure. Her smile won over many people, and Brittany knew that once she had your attention, she had you captivated.

As for Brittany's choice of career, she had only one prerequisite: she had to be seen by as many people as possible. Her desire to be the center of attention had led her to her current job: Brittany worked as a field reporter for World-Cable News Channel, The W-CNC. She had ambitions to move up to newsroom anchor and eventually to host her own national television show. It was that all-eyes-on-me desire that drove her forward in her industry.

Initially, when Brittany's editor had assigned her to Capital City, Michigan to cover a medical marijuana trial, she'd felt disappointed. There were so many high profile stories on the docket! However, her unbreakable optimism pushed her to make the best of it. The

Michigan medical marijuana trial turned out to be blessing in disguise. It began with only about a dozen protesters at the beginning of the trial, then swelled to over 15,000 people and continued to grow. The court case seemed to have its finger on the pulse of an underlying issue. The country wanted to know what was going on with the trial and Brittany was ecstatic to deliver the story.

The editor-in-chief of World-Cable News Channel ordered Brittany and her crew to video tape as many varying opinions from the protesters as possible. The post production staff would go through and edit the footage they gathered for the story, and it would be broadcast during the evening's news. Brittany knew her job was to find the story and put it on camera. She also understood that on-air conflict would boost ratings.

Scanning the crowd, Brittany could identify which people were bursting to share their opinions of the trial. She looked at her cameraman, who held up five fingers, before he said, "Brittany, we're taping in five, four, three..." He dropped one finger with each number, counting silently before pointing at her.

The news reporter's eyes came to life as she turned on the charm, aiming to attract every potential viewer. Brittany gazed into the camera and spoke, "We're here in Capital City, Michigan, where the trial against a university graduate student, Ronnie Harding, has been turned over to the jury. Ronnie Harding was allegedly growing a large quantity of marijuana for medical research on Michigan A&M University's campus. Although the research program had obtained approval from the federal and state law enforcement agency, the local police department from Capital City multi-jurisdictional taskforce arrested the graduate student and charged him with narcotic manufacturing with idea that growing marijuana, regardless of the motivation behind it, is a violation of the law. This is the heart of the controversy."

Gracefully swinging her arm, she directed the cameraman to pan the camera to the right to show the boisterous crowd standing behind her. It was a carnival-like environment. Brittany narrated, "As you can see, the number of people out here voicing their opinions on this subject has grown immensely as the trail continues. It is estimated that there are more than 15,000 people out here demonstrating, and the atmosphere has been, let's say...festive."

In the background, the sound of loud, repetitive chants of "Free Ronnie! Free Ronnie!" could be heard. Social media networks were also being put to use as photos and videos of the protest were posted constantly.

The cameraman turned his lens back to Brittany as she said, "Out here we have a multitude of people with various opinions on this trial. How about you, sir?" She turned to a large bearded white man wearing a fall jacket and held her microphone out toward him.

As the man stepped toward the microphone, Brittany asked, "What is your name and where do come from?"

The large man said, "My name is Bran McGowan and I come from Howell, Michigan."

"Hello Mr. McGowan, what brought you out here today?" asked Brittany.

Rubbing his beard, the man said, "I'm here to voice my opinion. I'm sick of the government taking my tax money and spending it on things I find morally reprehensible, like paid abortions for the poor. My tax dollars shouldn't be used for that! I'm against it and I'll be damned if my tax dollars will be used for it. I also find it offensive that my tax dollars are used to grow pot. The government shouldn't be in the drug business. That's why I'm here - to voice my opinion."

"Thank you Mr. McGowan." The reporter beamed and turned to a younger, brown skinned man in a blue baseball cap to her left. "What about you? What do you think about the issue?"

The 20-something brought his fist to his mouth and cleared his throat, before he said, "First of all I would like to respond to what this man said. I respect his first amendment right to speak his mind freely and that's why we're all here - to debate the issue at hand. That's what this country is founded on, setting a man free to speak his mind. With that said, I understand how a person could be morally offended by the actions of the government. This gentleman is offended that abortion is offered as an option for Medicaid recipients. Well, I'm offended by nuclear weapons, but my country has them. I had to learn to accept it. I just have to live with the reality that another part of democracy is compromise. We talk things over and decide what direction to go. Not one person will be entirely happy with the choices, but we all have to deal with it in one way or another. In a nation with nearly 320 million people, we have to come to an understanding that we don't get everything we want, but we can find some space where we all can live - common ground."

The bearded man who had previously shared his opinion yelled out angrily, "There's no common ground on abortion, pal!"

This was the conflict the reporter had been looking for. Feeling out the situation, Brittany encouraged the young man to continue, "What's your opinion of the medical marijuana case?"

"Well, I'm a graduate student and researcher at Ann Arbor University," the young African American man said, "and I don't smoke pot, but I'm here making statement for academic freedom. Proper choices are based on solid information. Researchers are out there to gather that information so society can weigh the options, regardless of the day's politics."

Brittany then probed another question, "Well, what if he broke the law?"

"I guess that's for the jury to decide," answered the graduate student.

Offering an enticing expression, the reporter said to the graduate student, "Thank you for your opinion." She turned her attention to an older woman and asked, "Well what about you? Why are you here?"

The pudgy gray haired woman stepped up to the microphone and answered, "I'm against drugs in any form. My daughter got caught up in them. She started when her friends introduced her to Vicodin as a recreational drug. That became her gateway, and those so-called friends introduced her to something even cheaper and more effective: heroin. We've been struggling with her addiction ever since. I believe legalization and social acceptance of marijuana will create an even larger gateway drug to harder ones, like crack and heroin. As a concerned parent, I'm here to voice my fears about this issue, hoping that other parents and children won't have to go through what I did."

As the older woman completed her statement, another middle aged man from the side forcefully stepped toward the microphone. The man looked into the camera and said, "I would like to add to what this woman just said." Brittany saw herself slowly losing control of the situation. She watched as the man's eyes widened with a crazed look before he added, "This heroin problem is all the CIA's fault. They're trying to financially prop up this government in Afghanistan by dumping opium on the streets of our country in mass quantity of heroin. It's all the government and Illuminati!"

As the man tried to continue with his conspiracy theory, Brittany took back her microphone. She brought her fingers to her right ear, listing to her producer's instructions through her earpiece. The crowd behind her was growing overexcited. Nodding her head, the reporter looked into the camera and said, "After a day of deliberation, the jury has reached its verdict. They're about to announce it now."

Inside the courthouse, the Harding family had gathered in the lobby. Inside their circle there were a lot of lighthearted conversations. Even though jokes and laughter were common, nervousness and anxiety were just below the surface as they waited for the bailiff to give them their instructions. It was Kenny Harding who walked up to the family circle and broke the news, "Okay folks, the jury is ready to announce their verdict. We have to go inside."

Hugs were exchanged as the family steadied each other for what was about to happen. As the family walked in, Kenny called out to his brother, "Ronnie, can I talk to you?"

Stopping, Ronnie walked over to his brother. "Yeah?"

Every other family member entered the courtroom.

Pulling Ronnie aside, Kenny waited a moment before he started talking. "I want you to understand something. I say this to all my clients. No matter how the verdict turns out, I want you to understand the importance of being stoic. I want you to keep your emotions under control, even if the jury convicts you. I want you to act like a man. Do you understand me?"

Nodding his understanding, Ronnie answered, "Yeah, I got it."

Kenny added, "Remember there are three charges: possession with intent, manufacturing, intrastate trafficking. We have to beat all three for it to be a good day. We lose on one, it all turns bad. You got me, brother?"

"I got it." Ronnie nodded his head.

"Now," Kenny explained, "remember what I told you about holding your shit together. Don't you dare give them the satisfaction of showing emotions during the verdict, especially if it goes badly. Take it like a champ - chin up."

Initially Ronnie nodded his understanding, before asking, "What do you think the jury will do?"

Raising his eyebrows, Kenny said, "I don't know. The prosecution was really happy about this jury selection. I can see it going either way on any of the charges."

Ronnie remained mute as his eyes turned to the floor. That train whistle was going off in his head.

Kenny waited a moment before interrupting his brother's contemplation. "Come on, man. Let's do this."

Just then, Ronnie snapped out of it and looked at Kenny. "Okay, I'm here."

With that said, the two brothers walked into the courtroom and took their seats at the defendant's table. Ronnie watched the jury walk in and take their seats. He tried to get a read on what they were thinking, but there was just no way to tell. It didn't take long before the bailiff announced, "All rise for the Honorable Judge Wildman!" Everyone in the courtroom stood up.

The dark haired woman took her seat at the judge bench and immediately said, "Thank you, ladies and gentleman, please have a seat." Every person in the courtroom sat. Judge Wildman spoke clearly into her microphone, "The court has been notified that the jury has reached a verdict on all charges of this case. Please have the foreperson of the jury hand the verdict to the bailiff."

Ronnie's ears popped and began to ring as his blood pressure spiked and his nerves kicked into high gear. Shaking his head slightly, Ronnie watched the bailiff walk over to the foreman and take a folded piece of paper. The court officer took the verdict and handed it to the judge, who unfolded and read it for a long moment. Judge Wildman refolded the piece of paper and returned it to the bailiff, who took it back to the foreman of jury. The judge then announced her instructions, "Will the foreperson of the jury please stand and read the verdict."

The bailiff handed the paper to the foreman, Dale Gentry, who stood up. Dale cleared her throat and spoke loud and clear, "On count number one, possession with intent to distribute, we, the jury, find the defendant not guilty."

The small ruckus broke out in the gallery, which was quickly quieted, as the foreman continued, "On count number two, intrastate trafficking, we the jury find the defendant not guilty."

The ringing sound returned to Ronnie's ears as the verdict of the charge he feared the most was about to be read.

"On count number three, drug manufacturing, we the jury find the defendant..." The foreman paused before stating, "Not guilty."

Instinctively, Ronnie raised both of his hands to cover his nose and mouth, as the roar of pride rose from behind him when the gallery erupted. People in the courtroom began to post the verdicts on their social networks. Still breathing into his palms, Ronnie felt his brother enthusiastically patting him on the back. Lost in thoughts of relief, Ronnie turned to Kenny and hugged him. They then turned toward the gallery and saw their parents hugging one another. Ronnie also saw Molly and Kristy beaming at them with tears in their eyes.

A pounding sound echoed in the courtroom, as Judge Wildman used her gavel to settle the room. She instructed, "Bailiff, please the take the verdict to the clerk for proper recording. Ladies and gentleman of the jury we would like to thank you for your service, you may now consider yourselves dismissed. This court is now adjourned." There was one final tap as the judge used her gavel one last time.

Ronnie watched as the judge stood up and left the courtroom for her chamber. He then turned to his brother standing next to him and said, "I don't think I can ever repay you."

Just then Kenny's wife, Kristy walked up and said, "You don't have to. Your people already have."

"What do you mean?" asked Ronnie.

"Well," Kristy explained, "I set up Kickstarter campaign to see if we could build you a legal fund, and as of right now, we've raised over $35,000 and it's still coming in. I imagine there are a lot fans of marijuana and those seeking a cure for epilepsy out there looking to support your cause. Also our voice mail and emails are jammed full of marijuana growers who want to retain our legal services. Actually, our new fledgling law firm owes you Ronnie, for the publicity you've afforded us. We're going to have a lot of business coming up, all because of you."

The thought warmed Ronnie's heart.

Kenny, with all his cockiness, said, "See, remember when I told you there's a reason why lawyers make more money than farmers."

Ronnie thought about all the money that he had stashed away in gemstones hidden all around town. He knew his brother's comment was oh-so wrong. Ronnie just shrugged his shoulders and relented.

Molly was finally able to break away from Ronnie's parents and she ran up to her boyfriend. Ronnie greeted her with a hug and kiss. He looked at her face and said, "I'm so sorry for dragging you into this."

"It's behind us now," consoled Molly.

Still feeling indebted, Ronnie simply said, "Thanks."

Molly tilted her head slightly and asked, "Ronnie, do you think we can get out of town for a little bit?"

"Yeah," answered Ronnie, "that's a great idea. Let's give it some time and let this storm blow over."

Feeling happy about his comment, Molly's expression turned slightly serious. She asked, "Can I talk to you alone for a second?"

Ronnie answer, "Sure."

The couple walked over to an open space near the corner of the courtroom for some privacy. Molly turned and faced her boyfriend. Ronnie looked at her as her eyes turned to floor. She was looking like she had to get something off her chest.

"Go ahead, Molly," encouraged Ronnie.

Her eyes still focused on the floor, Molly bit down on her lip for a moment and said, "Ronnie, I want you to know I've been staying loyally at your side through this whole thing." Molly lifted her gaze and looked directly into his eyes. "From this moment on, if you want to be in a relationship with me, I have some terms."

Understanding the seriousness of the matter, Ronnie said, "Okay, go ahead."

Molly eyes narrowed as she said, "First of all I believe everyone deserves to have things in their past kept private, but as of right now, Ronnie I need you to promise me that you will never lie to me for any reason. From now on, lying to me is a deal breaker. Do you understand me?"

Ronnie understood that Molly had pieced together the truth of his double life. He also understood that his future life would have nothing to do with his past life. Ronnie answered her, "Molly, you have my word."

A stern expression appeared on her lips and Molly's eyes narrowed even more. "Also, from here on out, you will never be associated with anything illegal. My heart can't take it. I will not sit through another trial watching you twist in turn in the wind. Am I clear on this?"

Ronnie could feel heat from her stare. "Yeah, I promise. I never want to put you through this again."

As soon as he said it, Ronnie watched Molly close her eyes as all the tension left her face. Her left over angelic expression displayed nothing but relief as she let go months of frustration. Seeing that, Ronnie took her hand and leaned in. He kissed her lips to seal his promise.

Spending time with Ronnie's mother, Molly had learned not to shy away from conflict and to stand up for herself. Feeling proud, she opened her eyes and as the two looked at each with a mutual understanding. Ronnie instinctively leaned in to kiss his girl again, but was interrupted by his brother's loud voice, "Hey Ronnie! They're organizing a press conference in the lobby of the courthouse. They want you to make a statement."

Ronnie saw the child-like excitement in Kenny's actions. Ronnie knew Kenny was enjoying the limelight and free publicity. Ronnie was more than happy to help out his brother's fledging law firm. He answered, "Yeah, I'll be there."

Ronnie then turned to Molly and asked, "You want to come with me?"

She just shook her head, "Nah, you two go ahead."

With a head nod, Kenny called Ronnie to walk with him to the lobby. As the two brothers started walking, Kenny turned his head and said, "Try not to saying anything stupid."

A smirk appeared on Ronnie's face as he listened to brother's put-down. It was the first sign that Ronnie's life was returning back to normal.

26

THE HUTCHINSON FAMILY PICNIC

Looking down on his iPhone, Niles Hawthorne saw it was 9:37 on Sunday morning, nearing the end of August. Sunday was always an important day because it was the day the cash receipts were counted for the weekend's business endeavors at the night club, Quiche Lorraine. Niles was a dark skinned and intimidating figure who typically wore a black t-shirt. On top of his normal job of club security, it was Niles' responsibility to personally protect the club owner, Brian Tatum, while he added and recorded the weekend's cash.

Brian was more than a business owner; he was the main attraction in his own very successful stage show, The C.C. Divas. Brian was a cross dressing star and when he put on his glamorous woman's clothing, wig and make up, he became his alter ego, Cocoa Lavender. His paying customers loved his alternate persona, and the cash that his night club brought in made it the perfect money laundering operation for his illegal marijuana business. That business had grown 10-fold over the last five years since Detroiter, Baby Hutch, had taken over the Probie production from Paul and Ronnie.

Niles patiently stood inside the night club's main office in the basement while he watched his boss, who was in his male persona, count the large sum of cash at his desk. To Niles, something seemed off. "Hey boss, are you alright?"

Brian looked up as the automatic bill counter whirred and answered, "Yeah. Why?" His forehead crinkled.

With his deep rich voice, the bodyguard said, "You seem a little fidgety today."

Closing his eyes and pressing his lips together, Brian relented, "It's that obvious?"

"Well, yeah," Niles' eyes rolled before he asked, "What's up?"

With a long exhale, the club owner answered, "I'm returning to my hometown this afternoon. The Creek neighborhood of Detroit." His words were exhausted and labored.

Niles' lips curled into a smile. "What's so bad about going back to your hometown?"

Brian's face couldn't hide his childhood trauma as all of his deepest issues came rushing to the surface. "I just hated it there. They could never accept a person like me. They were consumed with beating the gay out of me, instead of getting to know the type of person I was. I couldn't wait to get the hell out of there."

"So, why are you going back?" asked the bodyguard.

Placing another stack of bills in the automatic money counter, Brian answered, "It has to do with our business associates. Over the last five years, Baby Hutch and Dem Creek Boyz have taken over the Probie production and we've been prospering ever since." The bill counter spun and whirled again, before Brian jotted down the total in his ledger and said, "I respect the way Baby Hutch and his brother have been dealing with us. They have been growing and producing a lot of that special weed while we've been moving their product. It's a good match, plus they want to talk about some other business opportunities. That's why when Baby Hutch invited me to his family picnic, I felt obligated to go, even though it's an area I vowed to never return to."

Niles' lips curled into a tight grin, before he said, "Man, there's nothing I love more than a black family picnic."

"I wouldn't know." Brian's eyes had tinge of sadness.

"What do you mean, you don't know?" Niles blurted, "You still black, aren't you?"

The expression on the club owner's face immediately lightened up as he answered, "Yeah, on the surface I'm black skinned, but I always felt that the black community had no room for a fabulous drag queen like me. They always made me feel like an outcast." Brian's eyes narrowed, "To tell you the truth, I never really needed their acceptance or approval. I built my own community and family from my band of misfit toys."

Niles immediately asked, "Then why all the angst?" Doubt was in his voice.

Brian tilted his head so his eyes turned toward the ceiling. "Well, that devil may care attitude works best when you don't have to see those people who were throwing stones at you before. Now, I have to go meet with them face to face, I'm back in their realm of their judgments again. It's got me defensive and uptight."

Niles understood that Brian was in a new environment. The bodyguard knew his boss was normally arrogant and couldn't give a fuck about what other people thought of him. Niles saw the insecurities, so he offered some of his wisdom, "Boss, you always wanted people to be open minded toward you and your community. You preach it all the time, but how about offering that same open mind to the possibility that people can grow and change, because no one ever remains the same. Everyone deserves a chance at redemption."

Brian offered a humph in response, and returned to work, but that little pearl of wisdom resonated in his head for the rest of the day as he finished counting and recorded his week's legal and illegal earnings.

Later that day, as he drove about an hour from Capital City, Brian was still thinking about Niles' words and starting to feel a little anxious, before he pulled in Emanuel Steward Park, on Detroit's Southwest side, just downriver from the Ambassador Bridge. The park was huge, so Brian picked up his phone and dialed Wayne

Hutchinson, otherwise known as Baby Hutch. "Hey man, I'm here," Brian spoke into the phone.

Baby Hutch answered through the phone, "Keep driving. We're on the far side. Park right next to the playground equipment and I'll meet you."

"You bet." Brian answered, "Can't wait to meet your family."

Driving on the winding paved road through the large urban park, Brian looked out his window and appreciated the late summer day. The sunny midday sky was picturesque blue with a few wispy white clouds above. Brian gazed at the kids running around, enjoying themselves on the playground equipment. He parallel parked his new black Cadillac CTS and got out of the car wearing white cargo shorts and a light purple v-neck t-shirt.

"Hey! Over here," Baby Hutch yelled out, waving his arm in the air.

Brian smiled as he walked to his friend. They locked their hands together while pulling each other close for a welcoming hug.

Baby Hutch offered his greeting, "Glad you made it." The gracious host was wearing a Nike sports outfit composed of bright red silky gym shorts and a matching red polo shirt. Over his polo shirt, Baby Hutch wore a yellow short-sleeve t-shirt with black print along to the chest that read, "It's a Hutchinson thing, you wouldn't understand".

Reading the yellow t-shirt, Brian offered a crooked grin before he replied, "Thanks for inviting me." He also looked at the large gathering of people, who all wore matching yellow t-shirts, and then he said, "It's been a long time since I've been to a family picnic."

Baby Hutch offered a smile and encouraged Brian to join them, "Well, come on then. Let's go meet my family."

As they walked over, Brian looked closer at the large gathering of people in the corner section of the park. Brian's fears of being judged for being fabulously gay were rising to the surface. He was stage performer, so being nervous in front of a crowd was new to him. His mind was starting to fill with doubt and insecurities. With a deep breath, Brian steadied himself as he walked with his friend toward the large picnic area.

As Brian walked by the food table, he noticed the stack of barbecued pork ribs glazed with a dark red sauce sitting next to dripping hamburger patties and crispy grilled hotdogs. There were also large bowls of buttery mashed potatoes and corn and a wide array of pasta salads and prepared greens. The dessert table was covered in a variety of pies, frosted cakes, doughnuts, and an assortment of cupcakes and brownies. Of course there was that dreaded orange ambrosia salad that someone always seemed to bring to these kinds of gatherings.

Wafer thin Brian was a healthy eater and was very particular about what foods he would put in his mouth. He sarcastically thought, *I think I already have heart disease and diabetes just looking at this table.*

"The food looks good, doesn't it?" asked Baby Hutch.

Brian answered disingenuously, "Yeah, it looks great. Can't wait to dig in." He also took a look around at the large gathering of people, who all seemed to be enjoying themselves, eating, laughing and telling stories. The young kids were running around and playing on the playground equipment, while the teenagers were on their phones checking out the latest social media updates.

As Brian enjoyed his surroundings, a large man and a substantially smaller woman approached him, both wearing the same yellow t-shirt. Brian was awestruck by the sizeable bronze-skinned bald man.

Baby Hutch spoke up, "Hey Brian, I want to introduce you to my big brother Bill Hutchinson and his wife, Francis. They run our business operations."

Brian extended his hand. When Bill shook it, Brian was amazed how small the man's hands were in comparison to his own. Brian also looked into Bill's face, and the large man's one crooked eye that darted off to the side. With a momentary lapse of awkwardness, Brian immediately recomposed himself until he remembered his manners, "It's a pleasure to meet to you and I appreciate the invitation to your family picnic."

Shaking his hand, Bill returned the greeting, "Yes, it's a pleasure meeting you, Brian. We've heard so much about you over the last five years. It's great that we finally get to meet face to face." The two men unlocked their hands and Bill introduced the woman next to him, "This is my wife, Francis."

Offering a lighter hand shake, Brian said in charming way, "It's also a pleasure to meet you and I have to say that your hair is absolutely stunning."

The woman, with jet black corkscrew curls of hair, replied, "Why thank you, Brian. It's a good thing that the weather is sunny, it always seems to rain whenever I get my hair done. And you know how black women feel about their hair getting wet." Her essence was charming.

Brian closed his eyes for a moment and offered an agreeable nod.

Francis's expression turned a little somber, before she said, "Brian, I want you to know that your mother and I were good friends before you two moved away. I'm sorry about her passing. It was really hard on me when I heard."

Brian saw the sincerity in Francis's eyes. "Thank you for saying that. My mom was my best friend and my biggest supporter. I miss her every day." The two offered each other comforting expression.

At that moment, Bill Hutchinson interjected, "Brian, we invited you here to talk about some business, so if you want to grab a plate, we can sit down and talk about some opportunities."

Waving her hand briskly, Francis interrupted profoundly, "Before we get into that, I want to give Brian one of our t-shirts." She handed over the gift. Brian's mouth opened in astonishment. He immediately took the yellow shirt and pulled it over his own t-shirt.

Francis read aloud the words printed across the front of the shirt. "It's a Hutchinson thing, you wouldn't understand." Francis offered an adorable smile. "Brian, I want you to consider us family. It would be an honor for me to watch out for Lorraine Tatum's boy." Francis hugged Brian.

Brian maintained his composure while hugging Francis, but on the inside he was completely blown away. All his fears of judgments of his gay lifestyle were completely unfounded -- the Hutchinson family was nothing but welcoming to him. As Francis pulled back from her hug, Brian slightly shook his head and blew a puff of air through his puckered lips as he adjusted his mental state. Francis's face was completely warm and gracious.

"Okay, okay, okay." Bill interrupted and then asked, "Can we talk about a little business?"

Francis giggled, "Sure baby, but let Brian get himself some food."

Brian waved his hand back and forth. "No. I'll eat later. Let's take a seat and talks some things over."

With a sweeping hand motion, Bill guided the four of them to take a seat at a nearby picnic table. Bill and Francis sat on one side, while Brian and Baby Hutch sat on the other. With his fingers interlocked and elbows resting on the tabletop, Bill unknowingly showed off his rather large, muscular arms as he started the meeting, "Brian, you're by far one of our best business associates. Over the last five years, you've been our best mover and most importantly, you've been timely and ethical with the money. We've had zero problems with you."

Appreciating the compliment, Brian replied, "Well, it's easy to move product when it's the quality of Probie."

In that moment, Baby Hutch cleared his throat as he interjected himself in the conversation, "We're going to start with changing the name. We've always hated the name Probie, so we're going to begin a process of rebranding it for the future."

"What are you going to call it?" asked Brian.

Baby Hutch answered, "Night Train. We're renaming it after another Detroit sports legend."

"Night Train?" Brian thought about it for a moment. "I like it," he added.

Francis cleared her throat as she took control of the meeting. "Brian, we've brought you here to talk about some other issues in addition to our current business arrangements."

"Like what?" asked Brian.

With a couple taps of her finger on the top of the picnic table, Francis explained, "You know we've made substantial investments in the real estate of the Creek section of Detroit. We've been buying all the property in our neighborhood for next to nothing, because it's been so crime-ridden in the past, no one would touch it with 10-foot pole."

Bill entered the conversation, "Yeah, the crack and boy epidemic hit our community pretty hard. Addicts weren't able to clock in and go to work anymore, but they desperately needed their fix, so it all became about robbing, stealing or tricking in order to make that money. The whole neighborhood was nothing but derelicts, thieves and hookers." Bill glanced over to his brother, before returning his attention to Brian. "So, we had to take some steps to chase out those dope dealers, and when the area went dry of cocaine and heroin, the crack heads and junkies had to go somewhere else. That's how the neighborhood cleaning process got started."

Lifting his perfect eyebrows, Brian asked, "How did you chase the dealers out?"

A grin appeared on Bill's lips, before he made clear, "It was simple negotiation followed by some steps to show we were serious. I explained to each and every one of those dealers individually that this is our neighborhood, the place where we live and where we are raising our families. I also let them know that they have cash and we have cash. They've got guns and we've got guns. But I fully clarified that there are a couple more things we can get that they can't. That's earth moving equipment and shipping containers. Burying a mother fucker alive or duct tapping his ass up in a cargo hold on a slow boat China is not a good way to die. We only needed a couple of demonstrations and news spread that the Creek neighborhood was now off limits for that type of dealing." The tone of the conversation was chilling.

Brian's eyes widened; he couldn't hold back his concerned expression.

Noticing it, Bill added, "Fuck 'em! Any dealer that pushes crack and heroin is creating the next generation of slaves. I'm not really fond of slave traders. They destroy individual lives and families in order to make a buck, and I don't want them in my neighborhood."

"So, weed money chased out crack and smack money?" inquired Brian.

"To be accurate," Bill clarified, "our weed and other operations gave us the funds to go toe-to-toe with evil. Then it became a battle of wills and as of now our will has won out, because we're fighting to save our community. Our actions drove up the cost of doing business in the Creek, so those folks had to look elsewhere to do their bullshit. It's just simple economics and self preservation."

Hearing that, Francis lifted her hand, and moving her fingers like she was casting a spell, as she inserted herself back into the conversation. "As our neighborhood was being cleaned up, we took steps and acquired all the available real estate. Since no one wanted it, because of the stigma attached to the Creek, we've been obtaining almost all the available properties for next to nothing. We've been knocking down the dilapidated structures that have been blighting our community. Those eyesores have been a haven for criminal activity and vermin for far too long and they've been killing property values. We've also been renovating a lot of structures that were salvageable, flipping those houses along the way."

With a slight head tilt, Brian inquired, "Well, where do I fit in?"

Francis rubbed her hands together, before she said, "We're on the next step, which is engineering our own demand for these properties that we're holding. We're not leaving it to chance; we have way too much money invested here."

"And?" pressed Brian.

With her kind dark brown eyes, Francis drew in Brian deeper into the conversation. "We would like to partner up with you to open a night club, like yours, in the Creek."

Brian's face contorted, like he'd tasted into something bitter. He paused for a moment before asking, "You do realize that I'm gay and that my club is gay rave club that puts on drag queen shows?"

Taking in a deep breath, Francis explained, "Yes Brian, I do know you are gay; you are also a successful business man. That's why we're talking. I would like to offer part ownership of the Maple Leaf Theater in our commercial district along with the needed working capital. You would have what you need to create yourself another successful club. We would be partners. I think that this business will be the first of many businesses from the gay community to open in our commercial district."

As his expression lifted, Brian asked, "I always thought black people love themselves some Jesus. Then they used that reason to hate faggot people, like me."

Francis smiled and said, "I know you're referring to Pastor Rick. Well, you don't have to worry about him anymore. He was recently convicted on charges of arson and insurance fraud. Ricky Darnell and his friends were setting fire to his church while spray painting racial slurs on the church's wall, trying to make it look like the KKK was doing it. He was caught on video doing it by a passerby on his phone. The judicial process didn't go well; the insurance company pressed full charges against the pastor."

Reaching out, Francis placed her hand placed it on her husband's shoulder before she continued, "As for me, I do love Jesus, but I view it this way. When I'm in the bedroom with my husband; what happens is between him and I and no one else. So Brian, whatever you're doing in your bedroom is none of my business. Judgment is reserved for God only. This conversation is purely about a business opportunity for both of us."

Intrigued, Brian asked, "Then why involve the Gay Community?"

Francis then raised her eyebrows. "Because I've done my homework. The Gay Community has a strong record of urban redevelopment. As a community, Gays will buy into an area that's cracked out, but that has potential, because they can get it cheap. They plant their rainbow flag down in that section of town, claiming it. They open up dance bars, night clubs, coffee shops, and hair salons. They also patronize their own businesses, keeping the money in the community.

Most gay couples have two incomes and no kids, which means they have more discretionary dollars. As the economy progresses, the previously cracked-out neighborhood is cleaned up and real estate values drastically improve. The area is now considered urban chic; it's a hip place to hang out. Then it gets patronized by everyone: black, white, brown, gay and straight. But the most important color in this equation is green, as in money."

Brian didn't say a word, but he had a hard time concealing his tight lipped crooked grin.

Still on a roll, Francis continued, "You see Brian; we pre-bought all the property in the Creek. We cleaned up the neighborhood. We chased out the bad criminals. Now we're looking to fill our buildings with good tenants and paying customers. This is where we are hoping that our two communities can work together. I would like you to become our ambassador."

Brian had started off this morning fearing he was going to be judged and discriminated against by the people from his old hometown for being Gay. Astonished, he hadn't considered that he might be welcomed back in this manner. Brian listened as Francis continued to speak, "I would like to work with you in building an annual art and music festival, so we can show other communities how we breathed life into a once dead section of Detroit. We can show everyone how we've broken the trap. There's a chance to make a lot of money here. I just want you to work with me, Brian."

Brian's eyes turned toward the picnic table as he pondered their conversation for a bit before returning his attention to Francis. He said, "I would love to work with you, but I would need to see all the details. So, give me a little time to think about it."

"Sure," Francis replied, "take all the time you want. I've said everything I needed to say. So, how about now, we go get some food and you let me introduce you to the rest of the family."

Brian couldn't contain his smile as he said, "That sounds great."

Walking through the crowd, Francis introduced Brian to everyone attending her family picnic. Each and every person warmly greeted

Brian, especially the nicely dressed women with stories of his mother. After an hour and a half, Brian had caught up with some old friends and made some new ones along the way, but it was time for him to go.

Baby Hutch walked Brian back to his car. As the two approached Brian's vehicle, Baby Hutch said, "Man, thanks for coming by. It was great having you here."

With a grin, Brian looked down at his new yellow t-shirt, before he replied, "Thanks for having me. You really do have an extraordinary family."

"I really appreciate that," returned Baby Hutch.

Standing next to Brian's car, the two shook hands and brought each other close for a hug.

As they both pulled back, Brian said, "Hey, I've got to get going. There's another business venture I'm checking on."

"Hmmm," Baby Hutch inquired, "another business venture?" A smile appeared on his face. "You tell Ronnie I said hi."

27

THE LAVENDER FARM

Leaving the Hutchison family picnic and driving an hour and half west from Detroit, Brian Tatum ended up in the Irish Hills section of Michigan in a township called Brooklyn. Brian didn't get out of Capital City much, so as he drove through over winding roads and rolling hills, he was compelled to stop on the roadside a few times to take in the scenery. Getting out of his car, Brian realized how much splendor was in nature. His favorite stop was one at an Arabian horse farm where he watched the white steeds gallivanting in their paddock.

With his mind suspended in wonder, he realized that he wasn't in a hurry anymore. Brian thought about the concept of time; he knew he was missing out on a lot by being so busy, too busy, with his business endeavors. Realizing that making money was all consuming, Brian knew he deserved a time out and pulled over to enjoy the views, which was something new to him. While enjoying the surroundings, Brian's mind slowed as he took in all the sensations. A new feeling was taking ahold of him - a feeling of complete tranquility. He exhaled deeply and all tension left his body.

After half an hour of doing nothing but watching white horses feeding on grass, Brian reached into his pocket and pulled out his iPhone. He pushed the phone's button. "Be-beep," the phone toned.

Brian spoke into the speaker, "Siri, call Ron Harding."

The phone spoke in an elegant female voice, "Calling Ron Harding."

Brian's phone rang three times before Ronnie answered it, "Hey partner, you almost here?"

"I'm about 20 or 30 minutes away from you. I had to stop and watch these beautiful white horses," answered Brian.

Ronnie nodded his agreement, "Yeah, they are pretty, aren't they?" Ronnie abruptly added, "Oh hey! I forgot. When you arrive, as you approach the house, park to the left toward the pole barn, away from the gazebo. Okay?"

"No problem." Brian replied, "I guess it's time for me to get back to work. I'll see you in a little while, partner." His voice was relaxed and subtle.

Brian stared at the horses for the last time. He waved and said, "See ya, guys," before walking back to his car.

Getting back to his journey, Brian started up his engine and looked at his GPS; he figured he had 20 more minutes of highway driving south before he would arrive at his destination. After a while, following the arrows and voice instructions of his phone's Google Maps application, Brian pulled into a driveway with a large black metal arch. The sign on the curved arch read, "Molly Farms" in big white block letters. Driving in, Brian noticed a smaller handwritten sign with balloons attached to it planted in the grass, in front of the arch, before the long driveway. The smaller sign read, "Watts-Jackson Wedding". Brian checked the time on his phone -- it was 6:07 in the evening.

As Brian drove closer to the white farm house and gazebo, he noticed the 40-some cars parked to the right. Brian also noticed an outdoor wedding taking place at the gazebo. The nicely dressed wedding guests were seated in neat rows on white wooden folding chairs just before the gazebo, where the wedding couple stood exchanging their vows. Beyond the gazebo was the most beautiful sight that Brian had ever laid eyes on. There were numerous large, neatly manicured domes of purplish-blue flowers in rows heading off to the horizon.

The stunning scenic view was emotionally overwhelming to Brian as he shook his head slightly.

Remembering his instructions, Brian drove his Cadillac to the left, away from the wedding guests, and parked his car between the pole barn and the farm house. As soon as Brian got out of his car, a lovely floral fragrance hit his nose. Instinctively, he closed his eyes and took in a deep breath through his nostrils. The sensation was utter delight as he pulled back his head with his eyes still shut. When Brian opened his eyes, he saw Ronnie Harding walk toward him wearing jeans and a dark green Michigan A&M t-shirt.

Ronnie asked warmly, "Is it that good?"

With his left hand holding his elbow, Brian brought up his right hand to his eyes. "I can't believe it. I just want to cry. When you asked me to invest into a farm, I was thinking corn, cows and chickens. I had no idea that a farm could be so beautiful." Brian paused a moment before he closed his eyes and lifted his nose in the air. "And the smell is so intoxicating. I've never smelled anything so pleasant before."

A confident grin appeared on Ronnie's lips when he directed his friend's attention back toward the wedding procession at the gazebo. "Brian, you are part owner of every plant that's grown on this farm. Every lavender flower growing there, behind that gazebo, blossoms partly because of you. Three years ago, when I asked you to invest in me, I didn't know what you would say, but because you said yes, I was able to pull this off."

With an astonished expression, Brian said, "Cocoa Lavender is part owner of a lavender farm." His voice was full of amazement.

"Yeah," Ronnie said as his grin grew into a smile. "But it's more than just a lavender farm. There's something unique growing out there in front of you."

Brian's eyes lit up when he asked, "What's that?"

Ronnie explained, "After I stepped down from Professor Rittenburg's medical marijuana research project, I wanted to see if I could rev up chemical production of other plants, so I started crossbreeding lavender plants. What you see in front of you is something that no other farm has. It's a successful new strain of lavender plant. I crossed the Grosso variety with the Buena Vista and our genetic shake out is a truly remarkable plant."

Interjecting, Brain asked, "How so?"

"Well, we ended up with a hulked out version of both plants." Ronnie explained, "A normal lavender farm produces 1,800 to 2,000 pounds of dried flowers per acre, which will yield between 15 and 20 pounds of lavender oil, which will give about two to three gallons. Our plants are workhorses - they deliver six to seven times that, so we get 90 to 140 pounds of oil, which gives us 10 to 16 gallons for that same acre. There's more."

Brian's shock made him react, he asked, "What?"

Ronnie answered with confidence, "There's a test for how lavender smells, whether it's sweet, like citrus, or pungent, like garlic. Our oils resulted in the highest degree for pleasantness of floral fragrances. We have a plant here that is the most productive in highest quality of lavender oils in the world. And you know what the best part is?"

With his eyes wide, Brian exclaimed, "Ronnie, you're killing me here. Just tell me!"

A huge toothy smile appeared on Ronnie's face, "We just got our plant patent from the U.S. Patent and Trademark Office. I named it Loraine's Lavender."

Brian's eyes welled up. "You named it after my mom."

Ronnie nodded. He knew the devastation Brian had suffered when he'd lost his mother to cancer.

Immediately, tears rolled down Brian's cheeks as he brought his fingers up to cover his nose and mouth. Emotionally overwhelmed, Brian whispered through his hands, "Thank you."

Feeling amazing about making his friend's day, Ronnie patted his friend on his back before he said, "Come on in the house. I'll show you the numbers. That'll cheer you up."

Still emotionally overwhelmed, Brian nodded and followed Ronnie up the front steps of the large wraparound porch before they both entered the large farm house. Brian was expecting a rustic home, but when he looked around he was a little surprised to see a more contemporary décor with modern style living room set and walls that were painted with swirls of artistic flair in tones of almond and cream.

Waving his hand, Ronnie instructed, "This way, my office is over here,"

Brian followed. When he stepped into Ronnie's office, Brian saw an L-shaped desk, cluttered with stacked papers and full file boxes.

"Have a seat," invited Ronnie.

When Brian took a seat, Ronnie handed over a clip board. Brian asked, "What's this?"

Leaning against his desk, Ronnie explained, "It's our contract with an Ohio soap manufacturer. They're starting a line of high end soaps and they placed an order for our lavender essential oil."

"How much?" asked Brian

With smirk, Ronnie answered, "All of it. We have 60 acres producing an average of 15 gallons. That yields us 900 gallons of oil which converts into just over 115,000 ounces. The contract will pay $9.50 per ounce which will give a gross receivable of just under $1.1 million upon delivery, and they're offering us a multiple year deal."

Brian's eyes widened, he asked, "Are you kidding me?"

"Nope," replied Ronnie, "You're holding a signed contract right there."

His body filled with astonishment and Brian reacted with a question, "How did you do all of this in just a couple years?"

Ronnie raised his eyebrows and offered a slight head roll, before he explained, "Well, after my Probie adventure, I took some time and tried to be a normal graduate student again. That didn't go so well, but I had to let some time pass for let things to die down. I had all my cash converted into gemstones so I could stash it around town easier. When the time was right, me and my friend, who's a gem specialist from Bloomington, Indiana, drove out to New York City to convert those stones into the highest amount of cash that we could get. We're in Midtown Manhattan on 47th Street and we met with some Orthodox Jews to work out a deal. We did some backdoor dealings with some Sri Lankans and Indians from Mumbai. To tell you the truth, I was just relieved to get back to Michigan with my cash in hand and my skin on my back. I'd converted the stones into just over $550,000 in cash by selling off all the stones except for one, a flawless, emerald cut diamond, about one carat. I used it to propose to Molly."

Brian was entertained by the story, but followed up with, "$550,000...that's a good sum, but that can't be enough to pull all this off."

"It wasn't." Ronnie clarified, "Right after my trial I was approached by a publishing company to write my story. They gave me an advance of $15,000 and sent over a writer to interview me and write my book. I thought she did a good job, but I didn't think too much about it until a year later, when the royalty checks started to come in. The publisher found a niche market in the medical marijuana dispensaries and book started to sell. Each month, a check came in at different amounts. I picked up another $200K. It was a good sum, but I needed more. That's when I asked you to invest. Once you said yes and gave me that $250,000, I was able to put this plan in motion. It's been five years since my trial, but now we're here."

Brian chuckled a little before asking, "Well, was it tough financially while you were building this?"

Ronnie crossed his arms and blew a puff of air past his puckered lips. He made his struggle clear. "Hell yeah, it was. Me and Molly got married a year after my trial. She had just graduated college and decided to forego Architectural school in order to help out with the business. We used every penny in land acquisition and getting those flowers to take root and bloom into what you see now. The royalty checks from the book were still coming in, but they were inconsistent and definitely tapering off. Money was getting really tight. After the second year, the hedge rows of flowers were really starting to take shape and that's when Molly came up with the idea of using our farm for weddings and special events."

"I saw that outside. It looked great. How's that been working out?" asked Brian.

Lifting his eyebrows, Ronnie said, "It basically saved our asses. As the flowers bloomed, Molly was taken by the scenery. She took a bunch of photos of the farm and created some brochures and a marketing video. She posted the video on YouTube and sent the link to all the wedding planners she could find. Several of those event planners made the drive out here and when they saw what we had to offer, it was a done deal. They started selling our farm for us, and we started hosting weddings. From the months of June to August, when the flowers are in bloom, we're booked solid for every Friday, Saturday and Sunday. We have a wedding on each of those days and we charge $8,000 for each service. That brings in a quarter of a million dollars per summer and allows us to stay afloat until the farm could sustain itself."

Brian got up from his chair and walked over to the bay window. He stared at the on-going wedding ceremony. He also thought about the spectacular view and delightful fragrance in the air. Brian turned toward Ronnie and said, "That reception would definitely be unforgettable. So, Molly did all that?"

"Yep." Ronnie answered proudly, "She basically held us together during the tough times. She covered all the bills and got us the working capital to get us here. She also..."

Brian interrupted Ronnie with a shout of excitement, "Speak of the devil! How are you doing, girlfriend?"

Turning, Ronnie saw Molly enter the room wearing black maternity pants and a powder blue button down shirt to conceal her baby belly.

With a pleasantly surprised look on her face, Molly exclaimed, "Brian! When did you get here?"

"Just a bit ago," answered Brian as he walked over and hugged Molly. She kissed him on the cheek.

Looking down at her protruding belly, Brian jokingly said, "Girl, you got fat!"

Molly giggled as she rubbed her tummy. She played along with the joke. "No I didn't. I'm going to have a baby." She then smacked Brian gently across the shoulder. He flinched as they both laughed.

Brian asked, "So, how far along are you?"

With her eyes turning toward the ceiling, thinking, Molly returned her attention to Brian, before she answered, "I'm between seven and eight months. We're estimating the birth at the end of September or the beginning of October."

"Libra," Brian replied, "Holiday baby."

Molly's forehead crinkled. "There's no holiday at the end of September."

Smiling, Brian clarified, "All Libras are holiday babies, because they were conceived around the holidays of the previous December. So, it looks like you and Ronnie got a little too merry between last Christmas and New Year's."

Her expression lightened up and Molly acknowledged the idea with a simple hum. Then she gave Ronnie a harsh glare. He responded by holding up both hands and offering a boyish grin.

Brian then asked, "Do you know if it's a boy or a girl?"

Rubbing her stomach, Molly answered proudly, "It's a boy. We just picked a name for him."

"What's that?" Brian inquired.

Molly revealed, "We're going to name him Paul Kenneth Harding."

Not saying a word, Brian lips pressed together and raised his eyebrows as his eyes darted toward Ronnie.

Just then Molly said, "Well, Brian I have to get back to the wedding, but we'll catch up later."

"You bet, girl. I'll see you later." He leaned in and kissed Molly's cheek.

As soon Molly waved and left the room, Brian turned and faced Ronnie. "Pauley?" asked Brian.

Ronnie just nodded.

"Well, how's my little Indian boy doing?" Brian's face was full of curiosity.

Leaning back on his desk, Ronnie began to explain, "During my trial, Paul disappeared. I never saw him. He never sent a text or called. Roughly six months after my trial, I got a letter in the mail with nothing but a 310 phone number written on it. I called it and it was Pauley. After my arrest, he boogied out of Michigan. He took his money and drove to Venice, California."

Sitting back in his chair, Brian asked, "What's he doing out there?"

"He told me he was trying to break into the acting world." Ronnie elaborated, "But I don't think he understood that the concept of the 'casting couch', and how it applied to men too. When he learned that if he wanted to break in that Hollywood game, he may have to sleep with certain powerful men in order get some of those jobs that were out there, and he wasn't down with that."

"So, what he do?" Brian reacted.

Clearing his throat, Ronnie clarified, "Well, he headed off to the San Fernando Valley and enrolled into a couple talent agencies for the adult film industry. Considering his lack of impulse control and revved up libido, it seemed like a good move for him. He basically said that real Hollywood was sleazier than the porn business."

In a high pitched voice, Brian blurted out, "Wait, wait, wait. Pauley is a porn star?"

"Well, kind of." Ronnie explained, "Like in every business, sometimes you have to start off on the bottom rung. So, in the beginning, he had to take some jobs that not a lot of people wanted to take. He started off in making fringe pornography."

Consumed by curiosity, Brian asked, "Like what?"

With his eyes turning to the floor, Ronnie said, "Like sex with older women."

"You mean MILFs," interjected Brian.

Ronnie looked directly at Brian and said, "No, more like grandmas."

Busting out laughing, Brian could contain his joy. "Oh that's too good. Pauley is having granny sex! Can we go online and watch him later?" The merriment in the room continued.

"Whoa, I'm not done." Ronnie explained, "He's also had sex with women with lots of facial hair. I'm not talking a little facial hair either. I'm talking about full beards, like the ones on a typical Amish fella."

Hearing that, Brian laughed uncontrollably as he leaned back and almost fell out of his chair. Tears were starting to flow from his eyes as he cried out, "Pauley is having sex with the bearded ladies too! There's gay, straight and bi, but Pauley is most definitely tri-sexual. He'll try anything!"

The laughter in the room roared, and Ronnie spoke up again, "Paul found in his niche making niche porn. In Paul's defense, he's been doing really well in these markets. He just broke his way into mainstream porn, so he's been doing a lot of scenes with some very beautiful women. But he's been pretty pissed off lately."

"Over what?" Brian was drying his tears from laughing.

Shaking his head, Ronnie elaborated, "He was pissed off about the difference in pay between men and women in the adult film industry. You see, the gals in mainstream porn can make up to $2,000 per scene while the men are only making $200 for the same work. He thinks he's doing most of the physical laboring during his scenes and its outright gender discrimination. He was thinking about filing a complaint with Equal Employment Opportunity Commission under the Lilly Ledbetter Fair Pay Act. He actually Googled it up."

Giggling, Brian sarcastically said, "Well, equal pay for equal work."

The two were having a great time at Paul's expense, but Ronnie refocused the conversation, "Actually, on the good news, Paul met a new girl and he claims he's in love. She's works in the adult film industry too. She goes by the name Champaign something. Paul told me she's from Bentonville, Arkansas and made her way out to Los Angeles looking to become a movie star, but ended up in the adult film industry too." Ronnie picked up his Galaxy phone and scrolled through his photos with his thumb. "Here is a picture of them." He handed his phone to Brian.

Looking at the photo, Brian said, "Oh my God, they are a cute couple." He handed the phone back to Ronnie.

With a gleam in his eye, Ronnie acknowledged, "Pauley definitely looks better with his hair black and grown out again. He also told me that he's happy. That's all I could ever wish for a person, is that they find their bliss."

Brian nodded his agreement.

"Well come on," invited Ronnie, "let's go stand on the porch and we'll watch the rest the wedding ceremony."

Again, Brian nodded in agreement and the two men walked out of the office, through the house, on to the large wooden wraparound porch. The shadows of the trees were starting to get long, as the sun was starting to set. Engrossed in the view, Brian still appreciated looking at the large lavender farm in full bloom. The smell was still intoxicating. He looked at Ronnie standing next to him. "Hey partner, I want you to know that this is so impressive. You building this from scratch says a lot about you. You're a man of many talents."

Ronnie watched the wedding guests enjoying themselves with the newly married couple. Hearing Brian's words, Ronnie was proud of what he accomplished. He turned his attention to his friend and said, "Thanks Brian, but wait until you see what I'm going to do next."

Fin